Natalie Anderson adores a happy ending. So you can be sure you've got a happy ending in your hands right now—because she promises nothing less. Along with happy endings she loves peppermint-filled dark chocolate, pineapple juice and extremely long showers. Not to mention spending hours teasing her imaginary friends with dating dilemmas. She tends to torment them before eventually relenting and offering—you guessed it—a happy ending. She lives in Christchurch, New Zealand, with her gorgeous husband and four fabulous children. If, like her, you love a happy ending, be sure to come and say hi on facebook.com/authornataliea, follow @authornataliea on Twitter, or visit her website/blog: natalie-anderson.com.

Pippa Roscoe lives in Norfolk near her family and makes daily promises to herself that *this* is the day she'll leave the computer to take a long walk in the countryside. She can't remember a time when she wasn't dreaming about handsome heroes and innocent heroines. Totally her mother's fault, of course—she gave Pippa her first romance to read at the age of seven! She is inconceivably happy that she gets to share those daydreams with you. Follow her on Twitter @PippaRoscoe.

THE KING'S CAPTIVE VIRGIN

NATALIE ANDERSON

A RING TO TAKE HIS REVENGE

PIPPA ROSCOE

MILLS & BOON

First Published in Great Britain 2018
by Mills & Boon, an imprint of HarperCollins*Publishers*
1 London Bridge Street, London, SE1 9GF

The King's Captive Virgin © 2018 by Natalie Anderson

A Ring to Take His Revenge © 2018 by Pippa Roscoe

ISBN: 978-0-263-93549-3

MIX
Paper from
responsible sources
FSC® C007454

This book is produced from independently certified FSC™ paper
to ensure responsible forest management.
For more information visit www.harpercollins.co.uk/green.

Printed and bound in Spain
by CPI, Barcelona

THE KING'S CAPTIVE VIRGIN

NATALIE ANDERSON

For Dave and the kids—
here's to a long, hot, happy summer,
playing cards in the campervan,
and thank you for showing such patience with me
for 'just doing another twenty-minute burst'…

CHAPTER ONE

'WHAT DO YOU MEAN, you don't know where she is?' King Giorgos Nicolaides glared at his security chief.

The uniformed man shifted and took two attempts before answering audibly. 'I have the entire team on it now, Your Majesty.'

'Now?' Giorgos, ordinarily so cool that people genuinely believed he had ice in his veins, was lethally close to losing his temper. 'You're telling me that Princess Eleni hasn't been seen since late this morning, yet I am only hearing about it *"now"*?'

It was *hours* after she'd last been seen. It was now evening—dangerously close to darkness.

'She went into the hospital but never made it to the usual ward that she visits.'

Every muscle in Giorgos's body strained as he fought to control his innate instinct to sprint from the palace and start combing the streets for his sister.

Breathe. Think. Assess. 'So where did she go?'

The man before him paled at Giorgos's soft query. 'We're working on that, Your Highness.'

'I assume you've checked all available security footage?'

He fisted his hands in a fierce attempt to hold back the rage threatening to overwhelm him. Why had his supposedly elite security soldiers waited so long before informing him? *Unacceptable.*

'Her guard is to be fired,' he snapped, unable to resist the need to take *some* kind of action. 'As soon as she is found I want him gone.'

'Yes, sir.' The man all but fled from the room.

Giorgos took no satisfaction in knowing that other heads

would also roll once the situation was under control, because for now he needed every one of those 'elite' soldiers to be out there trying to find her. Trying to *rescue* her.

Because she'd been taken—Eleni never would have left the hospital willingly. And when he got his hands on the foul bastards who'd stolen her with the intention of doing heaven knew *what*—

He halted his horrendous thoughts and stalked the perimeter of the large room. *Find her.* They just had to find her. *Fast.*

'Sir—'

Giorgos whirled back as the soldier re-entered the room. As he registered the expression in the man's eyes he felt his blood chill. This was a man who'd faced horrors before—not only in war, but in natural disaster rescue and recovery operations. He'd experienced the gamut of human devastation. And right now he looked wary. *Why?*

'What?' he rapped. His brain couldn't compute complete sentences.

'One of the street cameras shows—'

'What?' He stalked forward and gestured at the laptop the man held. 'Show me.'

Impatiently Giorgos stared at the screen. The footage was grainy, but the identity of the woman on the screen was unmistakable. Giorgos watched his younger sister walk alongside a tall man—away from the hospital—to a car parked not far along the quiet side street. He watched as she got into the car and allowed the man to drive her away.

The man who'd held no gun or knife or any kind of discernible weapon. The man who'd almost been smiling. There'd been no apparent coercion, no apparent threat. Giorgos's blood ran so cold he actually shivered.

His sister had *chosen* to leave.

The very night her royal fiancé was flying in to see her she'd run away with another man. And it had taken Giorgos only that one look at the man to know Eleni was in big trouble. That slimeball held his head high and had an arrogance to his long stride. He wasn't afraid to be seen and he clearly knew what he wanted—Princess Eleni Nicolaides. And now it seemed he had her.

The question was why—what was he going to use her *for*? But that answer was also blindingly obvious. The man was a predator, an experienced seducer Giorgos recognised it instantly because once upon a time he, Giorgos, had been a using bastard like that too.

He clenched his fists, seething with impotent fury. He didn't blame his sister, only himself. She was naive and innocent and young and she'd been duped—no doubt about that. Bitter bile burned the back of his throat. This was entirely his fault He should have protected her more, should have kept her safer... But heaven knew he'd tried. Right now he couldn't understand *how* this man had got access to her.

'Who is he?' He breathed the question slowly.

Before his security chief could answer Giorgos's mobile rang. He froze, his gaze locked on that of his soldier. They both knew very few people had his personal number. He forced out a breath as he snatched the phone from his pocket and swiped the screen.

'Giorgos, it's me.'

His sister scrambled to speak before he had the chance to.

'Eleni. Where are you?' He was so relieved to hear from her he barked his words like bullets. 'Come back to the palace *now*. Do you have any idea of the trouble you've caused?'

But she didn't answer immediately—and her pause put Giorgos back on high alert.

'I'm not coming back yet, Giorgos. I need time to think.'

'Think? About what?' Giorgos didn't think at all before

berating her. 'Your fiancé is already here. Or had you for-gotten that you're about to go on tour with him?'

The image of her calmly walking away with that other man replayed in his mind—walking away from her duty, from her country. How could she? He'd never have believed her capable. She'd always embraced her role and been ac-cepting of her future. Everything was perfectly prepared and the plans had been in place for over two years. This was an excellent match for her—she well knew that, as royals, their lives could never entirely be their own.

'I can't do it, Giorgos.'

'Can't do what?' His impatience almost got the better of him.

There was another moment. Giorgos listened closely to the unnatural silence, sensing a new level of danger.

'I'm pregnant,' she said softly.

He closed his eyes, gritting his teeth. He couldn't speak. Couldn't bear to think.

Pregnant.

With one word he was transported back to another time—to another woman. The split-second recollection of the devastation that had ensued slammed into him as if it had been yesterday.

'Prince Xander isn't the father,' she added.

It was his worst nightmare—he'd longed to protect her from exactly this kind of mistake.

'Who?' he finally whispered. *'Who?'* That ferocious anger was unleashed.

'It doesn't matter—'

'I'll kill him. I'll bloody— Tell me his name.'

'No.'

His rage ran unrestrained and he shouted into the phone. 'Tell me his name, Eleni. I'll have him—'

'Call off the hounds, Giorgos. Or I swear I'll never re-turn. I will disappear.'

His jaw dropped and he was stunned into silence by her interruption. Eleni *never* interrupted him. Never swore or answered back. And she sure as hell never made *threats*. What had happened to his sister?

Again a reprise echoed in his head—of his *own* head-strong argument with his father, his own defiance that had led to such destruction. Recklessness and impulsive action like this led to chaos and calamity. The last thing he wanted was for her to suffer a lifetime of guilt and regret. He knew too well how heavy that burden was.

'It doesn't matter who it was,' she followed up firmly. 'He didn't seduce me. I was a fully willing participant. *I* made the mistake, Giorgos. And I need to fix it. Tell Prince Xander I'm sick. Tell him I ran away. Tell him anything you like. But I'm not marrying him. I'm not coming back. Not yet. Not till I've sorted it out.'

Shock at her rebellion almost made him stagger. 'Are you with him now?'

'I'm not marrying *him* either,' Eleni said.

Giorgos muttered a series of swearwords through gritted teeth. She was so damn naive.

'This child is mine. Pure Nicolaides,' she said. But then her tone softened to include the gentle plea he'd rarely been able to resist. 'And please don't blame Tony for losing track of me. It wasn't his fault.'

'Your protection officer has no idea where you've gone. He's clearly incompetent. He has been dismissed.'

'But it's not his *fault*.' Eleni's voice rose, returning to that uncharacteristic tone of opposition. 'I told him—'

'Lies,' Giorgos snapped. 'But it *is* his fault that he lost track of you. His employment is not your concern.'

'But—'

'You should have thought through the consequences of your actions, Eleni. There are ramifications for *all* the people of Palisades.'

He closed his eyes again. This hurt so much. He needed to make her see sense and stop this foolishness before even more damage was done.

'How do I stop a scandal here, Eleni?' he asked as gently as he was able, making himself focus on her and not his own tortured past.

The past he could not change. But the future? That he *could* help to forge. He would care for his sister however he could. He owed her that, given it was his fault she had no father.

'I'm so sorry,' she said dully. 'I take full responsibility. I'll be in touch when I can.'

Giorgos kept his back to the man in the room long after she'd ended the call, realising how close he was to losing her. That simply was *not* an option. His sister was all that remained of his family and he'd vowed to protect her—and their family name.

'His name is Damon Gale...' his head of security ventured quietly.

Giorgos drew in a deep breath before turning to take on the battle.

'Everything,' he said firmly. 'I need to know every last thing about him. I want all records of him entering and exiting the country. I want to know who he is and what he does—down to what he has for breakfast and what detergent he uses. I want *everything*. Nothing is too small or too trivial to know.'

'We're already putting together a dossier.'

'I want it in less than an hour.' He wanted it *now*.

'Yes, sir.'

Alone once more, Giorgos paced the room as he waited for the vital information to arrive. How had this man got to Eleni? When had he had the chance to seduce her? He'd arranged a perfectly suitable engagement. She would be going from this palace to another nearby. And she'd been pleased—hadn't she? She'd always understood the expectations of her.

He turned as his security chief finally re-entered the room fifteen minutes later.

'We've been running all palace footage through facial recognition software,' he started.

'And?' Giorgos prompted him curtly.

'It seems Mr Gale was a guest at last month's hospital ball.'

'The hospital ball?'

Giorgos was so surprised he dumbly repeated the man's statement. But then he looked at the open laptop the man had carried in. There, frozen on the screen, was proof that this Damon Gale had breached the gates of Giorgos's own damn palace.

A series of four images had been captured from the security footage. The ball—a masquerade—was an annual fundraiser for the hospital, and yet Damon Gale hadn't bothered with a mask even then. He'd walked in with one woman, but had then been caught on camera promenading in the ballroom with another. A tall, slender woman in blue—and even with the mask and the wig she wore Giorgos knew it was his sister.

So the arrogant jerk had seduced Eleni in her own home, under Giorgos's very nose. He'd had the gall to ditch his date while he went princess-hunting.

Giorgos looked back at the first image and could hardly focus for the fury rising through him at the sight of Damon's date. She too wore no mask, and she was stunning. There was pretty and then there was beautiful, and Giorgos had met plenty of both—models, actresses, heiresses—enough to be jaded…spoilt, even. But this was a woman in another league altogether.

Both serene and haughty, while subtly flaunting her sexy curves, her brunette hair was long and thick and hung in a seductive swathe to the narrow waist that was the cinch between her bountiful breasts and curvaceous hips. But even though she had the ultimate hourglass figure, it was her face that was utterly arresting—the pure symmetrical beauty of her wide eyes, upturned nose and pillowy pouting lips.

She was indisputably, classically perfect. Every inch of her spoke of femininity and sensuality. Her undeniably exquisite features meant she'd be a woman who understood her power and her worth. The dress she'd chosen emphasised that fact—it covered, yet clung, and he knew she'd deliberately chosen it to emphasise every killer curve.

A hot rage brewed deep in Giorgos's belly—he was familiar with beautiful women who toyed with men. Who betrayed them. But *why* had Damon Gale left her side to target Eleni?

'Get me a print-out of this picture,' he snapped.

'Of Mr Gale?'

'Of them both. Who is *she*?'

Why had this man gone to seduce Giorgos's innocent younger sister when he'd walked in with *this* woman? What part did this…this *vixen*…have to play in it?

'Her name is Kassiani Marron. She's known as Kassie and she works at the hospital.'

'*My* hospital?' Giorgos tensed as his fury burned hotter. 'So *she* brought him to the palace?'

'Actually, Mr Gale held the invitation. She accompanied him.'

Giorgos drew in a sharp breath. She was Damon Gale's date—he'd asked her to attend with him yet set his sights on Eleni? Giorgos was stunned. This woman held such sexual allure…

'Ms Marron is Mr Gale's half-sister,' the officer added. 'She is the illegitimate daughter of John Gale, Damon's father, an American diplomat.'

So she was Damon's half-sister—*family*. Of course. It

made sense. She was the feminine feline equivalent of her predatory brother. Scalding hot satisfaction rushed through Giorgos's system, flooding his rage and turning into another emotion altogether. An emotion he had no inclination—and no time—to define.

He narrowed his gaze on her image and tried to process the revelation rationally. The vixen would have information. The vixen would have answers. The vixen would *pay*. Adrenalin charged his system like a lightning bolt of electricity, empowering his drive and focus.

He whipped his head up to glare at the security chief. 'Where is she now?'

'At the hospital. Would you like me to bring her to you?'

'No.' Giorgos turned away from the screen with speed. 'I will go to the hospital.'

'Sir?' The officer looked startled.

Giorgos shook his head. As if he could trust *any* of his security team to deal with this situation, given they'd lost Eleni and not even told him for the better part of the day? No.

No.

This needed urgency, delicacy and above all *control*— the one thing Giorgos had in abundance. He needed to do the interrogation himself. And he'd extract every ounce of information he could from her. By whatever method was necessary.

'Bring my car,' he ordered. 'Immediately.'

'You shouldn't be working late on a Friday night.' The junior doctor leaned over Kassie—too close—with a winning smile. 'You should be coming to dinner with me.'

Kassie took a breath, then answered with well-practised firm but dismissive politeness and eased back from his breach of her personal space. 'I still have half an hour on my shift.'

And she'd be on the ward for at least another hour afterwards. She had too much paperwork to catch up on. Never mind that it was Friday night.

'I have a booking at a very nice restaurant.'

'And of course you don't want that booking going to waste.' Kassie maintained her slight smile, despite the disappointment edging into her.

The guy was probably nice enough, but already her temperature had dropped at the thought. And he was only suggesting dinner—totally tame—anything more intimate would have had her freezing in a nanosecond. Sadly, it was going to be another no from her.

'Fortunately there are plenty of others about to end their shift,' she said.

'But I don't want to go out with any of them. Only you.'

And *there* was a line she'd heard before. 'You don't even know me,' she pointed out gently.

But he'd *heard* about her—she knew that.

'You know Kassie doesn't date anyone in the hospital,' Zoe, one of the nurses, piped up with a smile, quickly shooting Kassie a glance of pure sisterhood solidarity. 'Why don't you ask Terese? She's super-fun and a great dancer.'

Super-fun and a great dancer. Two things Kassie wasn't.

The doctor looked at Kassie, but she avoided his gaze by studying the chart she was carrying, happy to let Zoe rescue her.

He finally turned. 'What about you?' he asked Zoe. 'What are *your* plans tonight?'

Zoe shrugged and her smile turned coquettish. 'You tell me.'

He smiled back. 'Half an hour at the main entrance. I'll be waiting.' He sent Kassie a smug glance and strode down the corridor.

The nurse giggled before he was entirely out of earshot

and turned to Kassie. 'Are you sure you didn't want to go out with him, Kassie?' she asked. 'He's totally hot.'

'Dr Hot is all yours.' Kassie sighed deeply. 'And thank you.'

'Oh, no—thank *you*! I'm delighted to take him off your hands.' Reassured, Zoe giggled again. 'I just don't understand why you don't date any of them. If I were you I'd—'

'Be getting back to my work—which is what I'm going to do,' Kassie interrupted swiftly with a firm smile.

But she appreciated Zoe's assistance. It wasn't worth the embarrassment of trying to date any more. She just didn't feel things the way normal people did. But that was fine. She'd long since accepted it and chosen to focus on building her career.

Zoe had turned away and Kassie became conscious of the nurse's sudden silence. In fact the entire ward was abnormally silent. The gentle bubbling hum of soft conversation had ceased. A prickle rasped down her spine and she turned around to see what the issue was.

'Good evening.'

A man stood right in front of her. As she stared up into his face her lips parted but she remained wordless—silenced by the hard glow of his striking green eyes and the furiously cold glare he was directing her way. Dazedly she recognised that this tall, imposing figure wasn't just anyone. She was used to the King's sister, Princess Eleni, visiting the hospital, but not King Giorgos himself.

How long had he been standing there? Had he heard all that conversation? To be caught out talking dating by anyone was mortifying—but by the *King*? Why was he here at all? Why hadn't they been notified? Why hadn't there been the usual security sweep before anyone royal arrived?

A billion thoughts flooded her feeble brain, but the one that her mind locked on to was the most banal and the most unbelievable—*so handsome*. King Giorgos was so incredibly handsome.

She'd lived here all her life but never seen the King up close before—and had certainly never imagined he'd be as good-looking in reality as he was in print. Impossibly, he was more so. As he towered over her she was conscious of his physicality—of the broad shoulders and muscled body that his perfectly tailored suit hinted at. It struck her that the immaculate stitching and fabric was nothing more than a fragile veneer, masking his raw masculinity. His dangerousness.

And where had that *idiot thought come from?*

She mentally slapped herself. So he was tall, dark and handsome? She knew that. Everyone knew that. So what? More importantly, where *was* everyone? Where was her ward manager? She tore her gaze from his to see Zoe a short distance away, walking with a uniformed soldier who must have accompanied the King.

'Don't you know who I am?' he asked.

Her attention snapped back to the column of masculinity blocking her path. Of course she knew who he was.

'Yes, I do,' she muttered breathlessly, instantly mortified by the brevity of her answer. 'Sir,' she added. 'I mean, Your Highness.'

Oh, hell, was she *flustered*? Kassie was *never* flustered.

He was still staring at her. His piercing green gaze narrowed, deepening his frown to appear even more disapproving than before. Another prickle rippled down her spine—and it was not only awareness, it was edged with something *else*. A foreign kind of anger kindled. What was he waiting for? Was he expecting her to curtsey? Bend her knees and scrape the floor? Roll over before him?

But then a sudden image sprang to her mind—of herself on her back and him arching over her—sensual, inappropriate and so unexpected and *shocking* she gasped softly.

His gaze sharpened. 'Will you show me around the ward?' he asked with stinging sarcasm, as if he shouldn't have had to.

The last thing she wanted to do was spend another second in his company when her dormant sensuality had decided to spark up—*and malfunction*.

She cleared her throat, panicking. 'Is there anything in particular you would like to see?'

Why on earth would he want a tour, last thing on a Friday? And, crucially, how quickly could she get this over with so she could step outside and examine the fact that she'd just had a flash of an X-rated fantasy for the first time in her life—*ever*? A totally alien heat flooded her body.

'I'd like to understand what my sister likes to see when she visits.'

Kassie tried to pull on a sympathetic smile and get her mind back on track. 'We missed the Princess today.'

'You usually see her.' He was coldly confirming a fact more than asking a question.

'Every week.' Kassie nodded, happy for the distraction. 'Is she well?'

The icy expression in his eyes instantly slid into steely hostility. She stared back at him, stunned by the animosity so apparent in him. Had the question been rude? Should she not have asked? Why not show concern for the poor woman?

The temperature plummeted as the silence stretched, tearing at her equanimity and customary conciliatory manner.

'The Princess likes to spend time with the younger patients,' she said crisply, deciding to end this as quickly and as politely as possible. Fortunately she was experienced at building barriers to distance herself and end conversations early. 'Most of them are having their dinner and will then be prepared for sleep.'

'Are you saying this is an inconvenient time?' His query would have been perfectly polite if it hadn't been for that slight edge in his voice.

'It's outside of customary visiting hours,' she replied, with as much diplomacy as she could summon.

'Then let's not disturb them.'

Relief bloomed in Kassie's chest and she managed an actual small smile as she waited for *His Arrogance* to depart. But he too waited, watching her far too closely. His lashes lowered and he lazily looked her up and down. She stiffened. Was he *really* looking at her body? The *King*?

Men had been looking at her body since she was a young teenager and had first developed the curves that so many guys seemed instantly to equate with sexual appetite. They looked, they made assumptions, they made passes. And then they made slurs, because she didn't respond the way they wanted. So, as always, she froze at this visual inspection—but stared hard back at him, glaring to convey her anger at his audacity.

He ended his trailing inspection of her and met her gaze directly, his green eyes imprisoning her attention. She couldn't have torn it away if she'd tried. And, deep within her, an unexpected kernel of energy popped—a spark that set her nerves to smoulder. And then another. Suddenly every muscle tightened, coiling with kinetic energy. Her body *simmered*.

Ordinarily Kassie had no flight-or-fight mode—she simply froze. But now? Now she felt primed to *act*.

He wasn't anything like his serene sister—a sweet woman who liked to laugh and draw pictures for the patients. There was no laughter in him—only leashed energy. She could almost *feel* waves of emotion rolling off him—impatience barely concealed. It didn't seem right for such a big man to stand so still. He was like a predator about to attack. His fiery gaze trained on hers.

She was clearly going crazy. She didn't get flustered in the presence of royals or other supposedly important people. She didn't get overwhelmed. She didn't get struck speechless. And she certainly didn't start thinking about sex. Always she remained cool. More than cool. Outright frosty.

She knew very well that in the doctors' ranks she was famed for her frigidity. That was the only reason why that guy had come to try his luck with her just before. And she'd rejected him—just as she'd rejected every one of the others who'd heard about her and who'd come to ask her on a date. It was no longer about her as a person, but her as a challenge. Rejection from her was a rite of passage for new recruits.

'How else may I help you?' she asked, her throat dry.

'I require your assistance,' he said curtly.

'You need a physiotherapist?'

Insanely, the thought of touching him was…*not what she'd expected*. No, the thought of touching him made the skin beneath her uniform sizzle rather than chill.

Startled by her own stunning inconsistency, Kassie quickly denied him. 'I'm sure there's someone with more experience who can assist—'

'It's you I want,' he snapped.

She flinched. *Want?* What did he mean by 'want'?

She stared up at him, transfixed by the total derailment of her thoughts. By what she thought she could read in the banked heat of his green eyes. Was this some kind of weird pick-up? Because if it was this was worse than any of the attempts she'd been subjected to in the past.

Mortified, she felt as if acid was burning a hole right through her pride.

'Want for what?' She couldn't even speak properly—her voice was reduced to a whisper—but her words were rude.

Because it wasn't quite her pride that was burning—it

was something deeper than that. Something more complicated. Had he heard the rumours about her? Was he here to try his luck?

Impossibly, he looked even more remote. 'It is a delicate matter.'

Somehow her brain conflated 'delicate' with *intimate*. Another whisper of a vision—of being close to him—scattered her remaining rationality to the four winds.

Was she *blushing*? She never blushed. Never responded to any suggestion of closeness with anything other than revulsion.

'In what…?' She paused and cleared her throat to force herself to continue, repeating her question. 'In what way do you want me?'

He had not lifted his unyielding stare from her face and she knew he was watching the heated colour mottling her skin. Too late she realised that he *knew*. He saw right thought her and knew the appalling direction her thoughts had taken. And too late she realised the innuendo so blatantly obvious in the question she'd so innocently asked.

'I'm not about to act inappropriately with you,' he said, very slowly and softly. 'I do have a modicum of self-control.'

He had self-control? Did that mean he *wanted* to act inappropriately with her? She was so shocked she simply couldn't speak.

He took a step closer, his voice lowering further still. 'You need to come to the palace. My assistant will bring you there immediately.'

No. Every instinct warned her against being alone with him. Because even being with him here in public like this was causing a reaction within her that wasn't normal. Not for her.

Emotion surged—fury coalesced with fear and summoned rebellion. She didn't care who he was. She wasn't going to blindly do as she was told.

'I don't get into cars with strangers,' she said as calmly as she could. 'I don't go anywhere without knowing why.'

He regarded her steadily, that arrogant tilt curling his lips. 'Are you defying the express orders of your King?'

She sucked in a breath and replied before thinking clearly. 'Are you abusing your position of power to *control* me?'

His mouth opened and then closed. His nostrils flared as he exhaled. 'Yes,' he said with carefully controlled quietness. 'In this situation I will do whatever it takes to get what I need from you.'

This time *her* jaw dropped. 'I don't see that there's anything I can do—'

'But you don't see everything, do you?' he said sharply. 'You don't *know*.'

'Then tell me.'

'We haven't the time to waste—'

'Then put me in chains,' she snapped. 'That's the only way you'll get me to leave with you.'

Her defiance shocked her. She'd never stood up to anyone so overtly. She worked hard and did as she was told— kept out of trouble and tried to stay invisible to men. But the arrogance of this man was bringing out a side she'd not known she had. Not a good one.

Determinedly she held his stare—and something flickered in his green eyes. She realised he was imagining it— her in chains—and he was enjoying the vision. The heat swamping her now was intolerable, and she dragged in a searing breath as wayward nerves deep within her body fizzed into life.

But suddenly he straightened, and in a blink that cold hostility returned to his expression.

'I need your help with a personal matter,' he said irritably. 'That is all I am prepared to discuss while we are in a public place. Does that satisfy your safety concerns?'

She was lost for words. How could *she* possibly help him with a personal matter?

His gaze narrowed. 'Have I given you reason not to trust me?'

'I don't trust anyone,' she answered honestly.

Not intimately. And she certainly didn't trust *him*. King Giorgos had a good reputation—he was serious, intense, and it was known that he worked hard and long hours—but that edginess he carried, and the unexpected, unexplained demand he was making...

Her body was sending out all kinds of chaos signals—the shivers down her spine, the speed of her pulse, the breathlessness, the *heat*. Maybe she was coming down with something. But, no, in her gut she didn't trust anyone—not him, and now she was beginning not to trust herself.

His smile was slow and not very reassuring. 'No doubt you have your reasons.'

Of course she did. 'Several,' she replied coldly.

He offered nothing more than a dismissive shrug. 'Regardless of your hesitation, we need to leave.'

She shook her head. 'I have to finish my shift.'

'Leaving a few minutes early will make little difference. Your manager has already been informed.'

Shocked, she stared up at him, registering his planning. He hadn't come to the hospital to visit patients and to spread cheer.

'I came here for you.' He quietly confirmed her thinking. 'And I'm not leaving without you. If I have to get my security team to forcibly remove you, then that's what I will do.'

'No, you won't,' she challenged him—because this she *did* know. 'You care too much about what people think.'

King Giorgos was remote and dignified and there'd never been a breath of scandal about him. He was *Giorgos the Perfect*, while his sister was *Eleni the Pure*.

He blinked rapidly. 'I beg your pardon?'

'You're the hard-working, serious King who can do no wrong.'

'You *do* realise you're insulting that "hard-working, serious King" to his face?'

'Because he *is* doing wrong. You can't *make* me go with you.'

'I can—because this is too important. We are leaving,' he ordered. 'Walk with me now.'

'You're serious?'

He took another step closer—a shade too far into her personal space. 'Are you going to make me get the chains? Because if that's really what you want, then of course I wouldn't dream of disappointing a lady.'

His sneer was mortifying. That humiliating blush burned again. She hadn't meant it about the chains, yet here he was implying that she was doing this only to...to *flirt*? She *never* flirted.

What was wrong with her? This man made all the rules—he owned the nation...his face was on the currency—and she was snapping at him like some schoolgirl with an immature crush.

'Of course not.' She avoided his eyes and muttered contritely, 'I'll just get my bag and then we can leave.'

She was startled when he kept pace with her as she went into the small office.

'Why are you following me?'

'I'm not giving you a chance to hide anything or any time alone to contact him.'

Contact who? She stared at him uncomprehendingly.

'Just get your things,' he muttered.

It finally dawned on her that this had to be a case of mistaken identity—he'd confused her with someone else and there was nothing *she* could help him with. *She* was nobody. She did nothing but work at the hospital and then go home to read up about more work. But she'd go with his assistant now and they'd soon realise she wasn't the person the King sought. Then they'd bring her back here and all would be forgotten.

Reassured by this reasoning, Kassie grabbed her satchel and slung the strap over her shoulder.

She almost had to run to keep pace with him moving through the hospital. He'd lost patience and wasn't slow. She stepped into the sleek black car idling right outside the back entrance. To her surprise King Giorgos walked around and got into the seat on the other side.

'I thought I was going with your assistant?' she said. She'd been looking forward to a quick resolution.

He directed a quelling look at her as the car glided off, taking them away. 'Do you *ever* stop questioning?'

'Not when there's this much to be questioned. Where are you taking me? And why?'

'*I'm* the one who has the questions, Ms Marron.'

The edge in his tone forced her to regard him directly. Something lurked in the back of his eyes—a streak of wildness that surprised her.

But it wasn't entirely a surprise. From what she'd seen of him at a distance—in the news and on the television—King Giorgos had always appeared to her like a wild man forced into refined clothes. It wasn't that he wasn't civilised—of course he was—but it was as if he might break free from the polished uniform at any moment. He was too elemental to be contained.

Idiot.

She scoffed at her wayward thinking. She was just unused to a man his size. He was taller than average, with a powerful set to his extremely broad shoulders. Lean and muscled, his physique and demeanour were imposing. And this close she could see his hair was a little bit too long, and a faint edge of stubble showed on his jaw, adding to the impression of edginess—of a man chafing at his constraints. And right now he was clearly inwardly struggling to contain a fierce emotion.

But the thought that King Giorgos might be struggling with latent rebelliousness was pure imagination. This was *King Giorgos*. The man had been King since his late teens—earnest and capable beyond his years. Yet suddenly all she could do was think about that streak of wildness and the size of his muscular thighs and the promise of physical power…

What was *wrong* with her? She swallowed, but it didn't ease the dryness in her throat.

She realised that he was silently scrutinising her as much as she was him. But he had that hostility in his eyes again, and a moody set to his jaw. His whole positioning was tense. Something was off. Something was wrong. And she had no idea how she was supposed to help.

'Is it Princess Eleni?' she asked softly.

He sat very still. 'What makes you say that?'

'She missed her visit today. She never misses her visits.'

He watched her…waiting. Something swirled in the atmosphere between them. The luxurious car suddenly felt cramped—as if she were too close to him, as if he could see into her mind. She felt compelled to fill the silence—anything to deflect this pull she felt, pushing her nearer to him.

'She was unwell last week,' she added, licking her dry lips.

'Unwell in what way?'

Foreboding slithered down her spine at the ice in his voice.

'She was dizzy. She said she'd had a bug recently.' She frowned as she swallowed again. 'Is she okay?'

If she wasn't then the King ought to be summoning a doctor, not a physiotherapist.

'Did anyone else notice that she was unwell?' he asked. 'Did anyone ask about her?'

Kassie shook her head—then froze. Damon, her half-brother, had appeared just after the Princess had walked away. He'd asked her who she'd been talking to. Now she thought about it, Damon had been *too* curious—and stunned when he'd learned the Princess's identity. Why had he been so surprised?

'Ms Marron?' the King prompted.

Chills whipped across her skin, chafing where heat had burned only moments ago. Perhaps this *wasn't* a case of mistaken identity. Perhaps there was something *very* wrong. She barely knew her half-brother, Damon, but she wasn't about to throw him under a bus. Not until she understood exactly what was going on.

King Giorgos's expression hardened as she remained silent. He knew she was holding something back. How did he *know* that?

'You attended a ball at the palace a few weeks ago,' he said coldly.

'Yes.' There was no point in lying—but she didn't need to offer any more information than necessary, right?

'Why?'

Her heart thumped. 'It was for charity. For the hospital.'

'But you didn't go with the hospital staff. You attended as the guest of someone else.'

She hadn't been one of the lucky staff to win a lottery invitation, but Damon had taken her—the only thing she'd let herself take from the half-brother she'd met only a few months before. Damon had seemed preoccupied when they'd left the ball, but she'd been too deep in thought herself to notice much; she didn't really know him well enough to ask if he was okay. She should have asked.

But then Damon had asked that random question—more than once. *'Did you see that woman in the blue wig and black mask? Do you know who she is?'*

Kassie hadn't even seen who he'd meant—there'd been

plenty of women in wigs…it had been a masquerade ball, after all. It could have been anyone, right? But not Princess Eleni. Everyone knew that the Princess hadn't attended the ball that night because she'd been unwell with a migraine.

But once more Kassie remembered the look of utter astonishment on Damon's face when he'd learned that Princess Eleni was the visitor he'd overheard at the hospital that day a few weeks later.

'You see my sister every week. I hear she likes to talk to you?'

She hadn't answered King Giorgos's earlier question. She realised now he hadn't needed her to because he already knew. Just as he already knew the answer to this question too.

'I take her on her tour of the ward, yes.'

'And when she was unwell last week…?'

'She didn't stay. No one else was aware she was unwell.' None of the other staff, nor the other patients.

'No one?' he pressed, astute and seeking. 'What aren't you telling me?'

She panicked, desperate to deflect his questioning. 'Your sister might put up with your bullying, but I'm not going to.'

He stiffened. 'That's what she told you? That I bully her?'

She couldn't hold his scorching gaze, and was unable to lie. 'No. I never spoke with her about anything personal. She never mentioned you.'

Her foolish eyes had minds of their own and they couldn't resist looking into his again. He kept watching her, and suddenly nothing else seemed to register or matter. Nothing but this moment in which the world tilted, shifting something within her. Something deep and profound and *frightening*.

She forced herself to glance away, but he reached out and touched her chin, drawing her gaze back to his. There was no veil over his expression now. He was lethally, icily angry.

'Tell me everything you know,' he ordered.

'Or what?' That deep curl of fear forced the defiance from her—a primitive instinct to hold him at bay even though she knew it was rude, perhaps wrong. 'You're going to torture me?'

'It's a tempting thought,' he muttered. 'And you seem to like the idea of chains. But I can think of a *better* way to extract the information I need.' His eyes narrowed. 'A more fitting way.'

She couldn't breathe. His words—his promise—sucked all the air from her lungs.

The opening of the car door startled her. Only then did she realise that they were inside the palace grounds. The large iron gates had automatically closed behind them. Locking her in.

'Come into my palace,' he demanded, curtly exiting the car to stalk ahead of her.

'Said the spider to the fly…' she muttered beneath her breath in annoyance at his peremptory tone and total lack of manners.

He stopped walking and spun so quickly she almost bumped into him from behind. *Damn*, it seemed the man had supersonic hearing.

'You think I'm going to make you my prisoner?' he asked, so softly that all illusions of her personal safety were shattered.

King Giorgos was pure predator and she'd never felt in so much danger. Nor had she ever felt such primitive exhilaration.

Suddenly she wanted to sprint from him. Instead, as always, she froze.

'You think I'm going to eat you?' he added with the slightest huskiness.

It wasn't the sexual innuendo that shocked her but her

sudden sensual response to it. Another of those incredible flushes burned her at the blatant carnality of his taunt.

'I think I'm right to be wary.' She pushed the words past the croak in her throat.

'Because you're guilty as sin?'

Kassie squared her shoulders and made herself look directly into his shadowed, judging eyes. 'What exactly is it you think I'm guilty of?'

CHAPTER TWO

RIGHT NOW GIORGOS could believe her guilty of nothing. And everything.

Kassiani Marron wasn't what he'd expected—she was much, much more. More beautiful than the pictures from the ball—impossible as he'd thought that could be, especially considering she was wearing the most horrendous uniform he'd had the misfortune to clap his eyes on. And in his decade as King he'd seen a million uniforms.

This was a drab, shapeless tunic with a high collar that revealed no skin whatsoever, paired with black trousers and utilitarian shoes. Her stunning hair was swept back into a neat braid and she'd not applied any make-up to accentuate those thick curling eyelashes framing her enchanting deep brown eyes. Nor had she bothered to rub any gloss on her full, kissable pout.

Because she didn't need to.

Because despite this apparent lack of artifice, and despite the dullness of her attire, she'd easily capture the attention of any red-blooded man in her vicinity.

Frustration bit hard, forcing him to grit his teeth. He was hardly about to demand that she strip. Because wasn't that what she wanted? Wasn't she playing her part in a honey trap? Wasn't the sexual undertone to every word spoken between them part of her plan?

He'd watched her shoot down that doctor who'd asked her on a date with the coolness of an ice queen. The poor guy had been so transfixed by her he hadn't even noticed his King standing at a little distance just behind her. He could understand the man's focus. She made it impossible to pay attention to anything else when she was in the room, with the dazed sensuality of her wide-eyed gaze and parted-lips pout. It was a wonder there hadn't been any medical malpractice cases at the hospital.

So he'd keep the lights on low and not let himself be blinded by her exquisite features. He needed information from her—that was all. He refused to be taken in by her manipulative flirtation or her challenges.

He led her down the darkened corridors, not taking her to the formal meeting room as he'd planned. He needed more privacy than that, and he needed the control he felt in his personal quarters. He had years of self-imposed re-straint behind him—this meeting with her would be en-tirely manageable.

'Are you taking me to the dungeons?'

And there it was—another sultry challenge to his con-trol. Her breathy voice prodded his simmering anger. She had no reason to defy him if she wasn't guilty. Her attempt wasn't going to work the way she wanted it to.

'As I have already said,' he answered softly, 'I'll use whatever methods are required to extract all information.'

He felt her slight misstep, as if she were shocked. As if she were afraid he really *was* going to take her to a torture chamber. Another ripple of awareness swept over him and he gritted his teeth harder. Oh, she was so very skilled, with those sensual words and those eyes, while somehow sending a blush of innocence and naivety sweeping over every inch of her luminous skin.

He stepped aside for her to enter his suite ahead of him. He watched her glance about the dimly lit room, her mouth held firm, her shoulders tense as she looked everywhere but at him.

Irritated that he ached for her attention, he snapped his first question. 'You went with Damon Gale to the ball. Why?'

She turned to stare at him briefly.

'Just answer,' he growled. He had no patience left for her games.

She glanced at the dark-toned painting hanging on the wall rather than addressing him directly. 'He introduced me to a couple of medical technology investors and a robotics researcher.'

Giorgos frowned. So it had been a business meeting? He didn't think so. 'And to return the favour that night you introduced him to Eleni?'

Wariness bloomed in her eyes. 'Princess Eleni wasn't there.'

'She was—and you introduced them.'

Kassiani shook her head. 'She wasn't there. I didn't see her.' She puffed out a breath. 'I heard that she was unwell— that's why she wasn't at the ball. And I never would have presumed to speak with her even if she had been. She's the *Princess*.'

Giorgos paused. Veracity rang clear in her voice like the echo of a pure bell.

Disconcerted, he chose another angle. 'But you told Damon when he could find Eleni at the hospital?'

Damon had returned to Palisades for a number of short visits since the ball. And he'd been to the hospital each time. She flushed and her gaze dropped. She couldn't deny that.

Rage gripped him and he tensed, holding himself back from shaking her. 'You told him. And then he took her.'

Her jaw dropped and she lifted her long lashes, turning a stunned look upon him. '*Took* her?'

'Where?' He stepped closer, no longer caring about protocol and personal space and not buying into her plan. 'Where did he take her?'

'Eleni's *missing*?'

'Don't act as if you don't know.' He grabbed her upper arms, unable to hold back a second longer. He needed her to realise how serious this was.

Needed to feel her skin.

It was soft and silky and instantly he wanted to touch more.

'What was the plan?' he asked harshly, restraining his wayward thoughts. 'We know they've gone on his boat. Where is it going? Where is he taking her?'

'What do you mean, they've gone on his boat?'

Kassiani's soulful eyes were wide and her kissable lips parted in surprise.

'Are you saying Eleni isn't here?'

'Tell me everything,' he growled, somehow pulling her closer still.

'I don't *know* anything.'

Frustration bubbled over. How did she dare to be so heartbreakingly beautiful as she looked up at him with those passionate eyes and lied to him? How could she have the face of an angel but the soul of a liar and a cheat? How could she manipulate her sensuality to ensnare her victims?

'Sleep with lots of the surgeons, do you?' he snarled at her.

She flinched, but kept her gaze trained on him. He stilled, watching anger supersede that other undefined emotion in her molten brown eyes.

'You have no right to question me about my personal life,' she said with cool dignity. 'That's harassment. Whatever your problem is, it has nothing to do with me.'

'*Doesn't* it?' He had the feeling it had everything to do with her.

But she was right. He shouldn't have asked her that. He wanted to cut out his tongue for that stupid lapse in control. Wasn't it exactly what she'd been pushing him to with her mention of chains and dungeons and torture? Wasn't this underlying sexual element to their conversation exactly what she'd planned?

He'd fallen into her trap.

He released her instantly. He shouldn't have crossed that boundary. He always kept his distance and discretion, never mixing women into his public life. At least not since he'd been crowned and had determined to prove himself to those disapproving courtiers who'd blamed him—rightly—for his father's premature death.

But he'd been off balance from the moment he'd seen her image on that screen. He was thunderingly furious—how could he have got so distracted? His sister was alone out there—*pregnant*—and yet he couldn't concentrate on finding her because all he could think about was how stunning this woman was. All he felt was this appalling urge to touch Kassiani more. To wreak his revenge—and bury his guilt—in the most pleasurable of ways. To have her surrender everything to him—her information and then her body.

He jerked back, releasing her to reassert his teetering self-control. Clearly it had been too long since his last affair.

'Tell me about the night of the ball.'

Her tongue touched her pillowy lips. Giorgos turned completely away, unable to bear looking at her a second longer. He ran his hand through his hair as a hot wave of anger engulfed him. Determined to dispel the claustrophobic feeling, he jerkily stripped out of his suit jacket and wrenched off his tie. He saw her gaze follow the ribbon of silk as he threw it across the room to a low chair.

'I barely know Damon. There's nothing I can tell you,' she answered, still watching as he unclasped his cufflinks and rolled his stiff shirtsleeves to three-quarters. Her eyes widened as he worked and her skin pinkened again.

'Eleni was in disguise at that ball.' He ground out the shocking fact he'd discovered. 'Deliberately. She went to meet him and *you* helped them.'

'No.' She shook her head. 'Damon only decided to go at the last minute, when he realised that it would help me. Because he could get me those introductions. He hadn't planned to meet with the Princess. There's no conspiracy there.'

'Wrong,' Giorgos argued obstinately. 'He planned this. He's taken advantage of her.'

'Perhaps she took advantage of *him*?'

Never. 'She's alone out there with that philandering jerk while her fiancé is *here*, waiting for her.'

'The fiancé *you* selected for her,' Kassiani needled. 'And perhaps Eleni seduced Damon? Mightn't that be possible?'

Because that was what *she* would do? She was a vixen— so certain of her sensual power. But Eleni had been raised in a world with vastly different expectations and duties.

'*You* might be a mistress of seduction, but my sister is not the kind of woman you are.'

She actually coloured more, and he heard another hitch in her breath. Why did he have such a visceral sexual response to this woman? Especially when he was certain she was toying with him.

Angrily he strode across the room to switch the lights on full, needing to shatter the thickened atmosphere with its sense of intimacy.

She blinked and then looked about the room again with undisguised disapproval. 'This is one of your meeting chambers?'

'Actually, this is part of my private suite.'

She turned those stunningly soulful eyes on him, they were now widened with something akin to horror. 'You *choose* to live like this?'

Like what? He rested his hands on his hips and stared at her, daring her to voice her sultry criticism.

'It's like a mausoleum in here.' She waved a graceful hand in the air. 'Impersonal dry paintings, uncomfortable antique furniture…' She turned a sharp gaze on him. 'And a cold, controlled atmosphere.'

She was trying to bait him, but it wasn't going to work.

'This palace has been impeccably maintained,' he said shortly.

'I can see that. There's not a speck of dust. Not a painting out of place. The whole palace *appears* perfect. Just like you.'

'What does that mean?'

'It's all a gilt facade—there is nothing beneath. No story. No soul.'

'After five minutes alone with your King you have come to such a flattering snap judgement?' He growled caustically. 'What makes you so certain I'm cold?'

Who did she think she was to insult him? Her daring smacked of manipulation once again. And the worst thing was that it was working. Sensual heat had turned his bones to cinders. All he wanted was to slam her against him so he could assuage the ache of his hard body against her lush softness. God, he wanted her surrender. For the first time in a decade he didn't have complete control of a situation and he wanted to claim *some* part of it back.

'Your plans for your sister...' she said, too calmly. 'You're not really worried about her—you're worried about how this all looks.'

He stilled. He didn't care about her insulting his decor, but she didn't get to opine on his relationship with Eleni. She didn't get to question his loyalty. 'I'm *not* worried about my sister?'

'Clearly not,' she said, dropping the mocking smile. 'When you're insisting on marrying her off. You're using her for royal publicity. This is all about the Nicolaides machine.'

'This marriage is for her protection,' he said coldly.

The scepticism in her eyes was like an acid peel on his heart. 'Protection from *what*?' She glanced about the room again. 'When she lives in a prison like this?'

She made it sound as if it were horrible. 'You have no

idea of the pressure she faces. The relentless public scrutiny. They circle her like sharks.'

The pressures on Eleni were untenable. It was bad enough for *him* to have to bear, but worse for the women of the family. The judgement was intolerable. The expectations too high.

'So your answer is to send her from one prison to another?'

'Royals marry royals,' he said icily. 'It is best that way.' Only those reared within the system had the tolerance and the acceptance.

'But not you,' she pointed out. 'You're almost a decade older than she is, yet you're still not married. What about *your* well-being and protection?'

Oh, he was well aware of his duty, and he had a plan for when the time was right. But he felt Eleni needed security sooner. And he was right.

'Is it so wrong to want my sister to be happy and well cared for?'

He was incensed by her judgement. She knew nothing of what life in this palace was like. She knew nothing about his sister. Eleni was an innocent, naive young woman who'd been sheltered her entire life while at the same time juggling immense pressure. Whereas the woman before him now was more than worldly, more than aware of her sensual power. She knew exactly how to wield it. She'd brought a whole hospital full of doctors to their knees—and the horrendous uniform only served to expedite their stripping fantasies.

'By marrying a playboy jerk who was never going to be faithful to her?'

Yeah, she knew *nothing*. 'You shouldn't read the tabloids,' he mocked, unconsciously stepping closer. 'Nothing of what they print is true.'

'So nothing of what they say about you is true either?'

she fired back, stepping up to face him square-on. 'You're *not* honourable or kind or devoted to your duty?' She laughed bitterly. 'Are you saying that behind your perfect reputation there's a monster?'

'I don't mind being a monster if by that you mean I'm doing the right thing. Your brother has stolen the most precious thing in my life. He has hurt her. He will pay.' He was beyond angry—he was hurt.

'The most precious *"thing"*? That's what she is to you? A commodity to be bartered? A possession?'

'It is a figure of speech,' he snapped. 'Nothing and no one is more important to me than Eleni. She is my responsibility. She is—' He broke off.

He didn't want to admit such personal truths to this shallow Siren. Didn't want to confess that he didn't want Eleni to make a mistake that could have the same consequences.

He glowered at Kassiani, somehow right in front of her now, as he tried to stay in control. 'You do not get to judge my family. You do not get to judge *me*.'

'I do when you're punishing me for something you think my half-brother has done. Something I don't even know. Where's the fairness in that?'

Her anger was unwarranted. 'In what way am I "punishing" you?'

'By bringing me here against my will.'

'Just give me the information I need. It's simple.'

'There's nothing I can tell you. I barely know him.'

'There's plenty you can tell me. You're choosing not to.'

Her jaw dropped. 'No wonder Eleni ran away from here. From *you*.'

He braced himself against the flinch her words caused. 'Because…?'

'Because of your inability to *listen*. You say I don't get to judge? But that's *all* you do. You don't need me here— you've already worked out everything on your own and you only want me to confirm your theories. You're not actually willing to consider an alternative, let alone the *truth*. I bet you haven't even considered Eleni's own wishes. Do you even know what they are?'

Her accusations had hit a nerve. Rage and regret clouded his reason, making the last of his self-control splinter.

'When did you last talk to her about her marriage?' Kassiani pressed, clearly aware that she'd struck a raw spot. 'Did you talk to her at *all*?'

'Be quiet!' he snapped, reaching out to grab her hips and *make* her listen. 'You say I'm not willing to consider an alternative?' he jeered. 'What alternative are *you* suggesting—with your delays, your attempts not just to distract but to provoke me? Is *this* what you want me to do? Retaliate?'

He hauled her that last inch closer, until she was pressed against him. Until there was no denying the reaction he had to her.

'Fine,' he snarled. 'Win what you want. But I want to know *why*?'

Kassie couldn't speak. She had no idea why. This could have been settled so simply in a five-minute quiet conversation, but the second he'd appeared before her she'd reacted to him with such intensity.

The need to push back against his arrogant orders had been visceral. She'd operated not on thought, but on instinct. And the terrible thing was that her instincts were telling her to push in another way now. To push closer still. It was terrifying, but her physical awareness of him was so acute it almost hurt. His thighs were pressed against hers, and his rock-hard abs and his masculine arousal were evident between them.

Shocking. But it was more than that. It was thrilling.

His green eyes gleamed as he towered over her. Having shed the jacket and tie he looked less civilised—more like the man she'd somehow known him to be. With that wildness uncaged, with the constraints of polite society vanished, he was all ferocity. All power. She'd suspected that he was *built*, but this was ridiculous.

A feeling deep inside her began to unfurl—one that had been so tightly bound that its snaking, unfettered release was too good. *Irresistible.* Her pulse pounded loud in her ears as her blood raced like quicksilver.

'Is this what you want?' His voice was hoarse as he asked again, his muscles straining.

'No…' But her voice was so constricted only a whisper emerged.

She'd never wanted a man close like this. Holding her. Caressing her whole body with just a breath. And yet deep within there was a softening, even as another tension coiled tightly. For once she wasn't cold—not frigid with distaste and stiffly rejecting the contact. No, right now she was burning with a fever such as she'd never known. And the only way to ease it even slightly was to rub against the press of his body. He was both the source and the cure for this contagion. His arms were tight bands about her—the welcome bars of a prison she'd never have believed she'd ever wish for.

His hand cupped the side of her face, holding her so she couldn't turn her gaze from his. Powerful, searching, his eyes held not just hostility now, but arousal too. Anger laced with lust. She was transfixed, but not frozen. She'd gone from feeling nothing to feeling everything. To yearning for something she'd never before wanted or even understood.

'Me neither,' he gritted. 'I don't want to stand here. I don't want to hold you. I don't want to want you.'

And all the while his gaze saw right through her. All the while his head lowered, bringing his mouth nearer to hers.

'You're a liar,' she whispered shakily.

'So are you.'

She could have said no again. She could have turned her

head away. But she did neither of those things. If anything she tilted her chin at him, meeting him in the moment he put his mouth to hers.

For a split-second old instincts surfaced and she stiffened, her body screaming its rejection. But the pressure of his mouth changed immediately. He softened, eased, and ultimately coaxed until her eyes closed. In the velvety blackness it was as if she'd been drugged and was now drowning in a warmth of sensation and bliss. His hands drifted delightfully, sweeping up her back—*holding* her but not forcing her against him. No, *she* was the one who pressed closer.

Muscles... Yes, she'd known he had muscles. But never in her life had she wanted to rub against a man the way she did now. Without thinking, almost without realising, she opened her mouth. His tongue slid between her parted lips, stroking lightly, teasing, before pulling back to trace the full pout of her lower lip. She felt the gentle throb of her pulse there, so highly sensitised she almost moaned. His lips covered hers again and his tongue strayed deeper—piercing, stroking the cavern of her mouth. She mewled as he caressed her more gently, more intimately than any man had. Licking. Sucking. Taking.

Her response was so sudden, so profound, that she began to tremble. Her fingers curled against the fine cotton of his shirt. She could feel the heat of him through the fabric. The heat that melded with her own. Something shifted deep inside her. Something irrevocable. And overwhelming.

It was a kiss unlike any other she'd experienced. Those other few had been sloppy or hard, and always quick, because they'd simply left her cold. This was anything but cold.

A great wave of sensation welled within her until she literally rose with it—reaching up onto her tiptoes, blindly stretching her arms over his shoulders, locking her hands about his neck, holding him as close as he held her. She flattened her breasts against his hard chest—her full, heavy breasts, with their achingly tight nipples—and the friction against his unyielding strength was devastating.

Something else swirled—a new kind of hunger that pushed her to rock her hips against his. She moaned as he immediately held her with stronger hands. Every cell in her body sang as he braced himself to absorb the strain of her body and she writhed with her need to get closer still to his hard strength. He sealed his mouth to hers again and he held her hips to grind against her.

For the first time in her life, Kassie had only one word in her mind, chanting over and over.

More.

More. More. More...

CHAPTER THREE

'YOUR HIGHNESS—'

The door opened and Giorgos released her so quickly Kassie almost fell. Instantly his hand shot out and gripped her arm to support her. His grip was hard. So were his eyes—like banked furnaces—and his gaze lasered through her. Assessing. *Judging.*

Dazed, she could see his thoughts racing. But she had no idea how the man could possibly *think* after experiencing that…that…

She recovered her balance in another moment and surreptitiously tugged her arm free, fighting to catch her breath quietly. Mortification flooded her. She'd just been caught in the King's arms like some shameless courtesan. But at the same time the interruption was welcome, because she had no idea where that might have gone if they hadn't been broken apart like that. She'd never done that or felt that—she'd been right to be wary of him. He was dangerous. And fascinating.

Sensation swirled around her body and embarrassment blushed over every inch of her skin. She realised the King was still staring at her, a thunderstruck expression on his face.

'I apologise, Your Highness, but we have found—'

'What?' He whirled away to bark at the man.

'These were hidden in the Princess's wardrobe.' The man held out some fabric and what looked like a knotted blue wig.

From the frown on his face it was clearly something Giorgos recognised. Kassie suspected the truth now—*the woman in the blue wig*—Eleni's disguise.

'Leave it on the table,' Giorgos snapped. 'And close the door behind you.'

The man's face was completely blank as he swiftly left the room.

'You're searching her private things?' Kassie whipped up her scorn, desperate to put space between them.

'My sister is missing,' he seethed. 'Of course I am searching her rooms for clues. I'll do whatever I have to do to find her.'

Her pulse thundered. 'And that's what that kiss was?' He'd thought he could seduce her into spilling all the secrets she didn't even hold?

'Sorry—was I too gentle? You wanted the chains?' He suddenly smiled—a wicked, dangerous smile, as if he knew something she didn't. '*You're* the one fixated on becoming my prisoner. You know what that tells me about you?'

She glared at him. She didn't want to know what he thought of her now. She just wanted to get out of here—immediately—so she could try to assess and control the incoherent emotions coursing through her body.

'You obviously know everything. Doubtless you've read some dossier…'

'Actually, there was a lot left out,' he drawled.

He *truly* had a file on her? For how long had he been prying into her life? 'What *have* you learned?'

'You're the only child of Petra Marron. Your father is John Gale—though he doesn't acknowledge you as his daughter. You grew up in a small village an hour north of Palisades city. You excelled at school, and studied for your physiotherapy degree part-time after your mother became unwell with cancer. Upon graduation you took a job at the hospital and have been there ever since. Your employment record is exemplary. Your patients speak highly of you. But your social media accounts don't show much in the way of relationships.'

She trembled, outraged by his physical and emotional invasion of her life and his ensuing obvious judgement. 'Perhaps I like my privacy and choose not to broadcast the details of my life to everyone.'

'Aren't you lucky to even have that choice?'

As if she were about to start feeling sorry for *him*! Her life had been reduced to a few sparse paragraphs, making it sound dull and unexciting, when in reality it had been rich and rewarding and heartbreaking.

'And what do you think you've learned from that collection of facts?'

'I already know you're not as perfect as that piece of paper makes you appear,' he said softly. 'I know you're not honest. I know you're deceptive, And I know you use your looks to—'

'To what? Seduce men into doing what I want?' She laughed, bitterly hurt by his unfounded accusations and assumptions.

She'd *never* used her looks—quite the opposite. She'd fought to be taken seriously—not to be tainted by preconceived opinions based on the shape of her body and the actions of her mother. And he was the worst of all—accusing her of hurting Eleni in some way.

But it was the blistering betrayal of her own body right now that appalled her. Scornful tears stung her eyes. 'Newsflash, Your Highness—here's some truth for you,' she snapped. *'I don't like to be touched.'*

She stilled at the look of shocked disbelief on his face, then shook her head, backing up as he stepped near her again. 'And that *wasn't* a challenge.'

But she'd read his frown of intent and the awful thing was that it wasn't honesty she wanted now, but his touch. That hidden part of her—dormant all her damn life—had been roused. But instead of being pleased about it, it terrified her.

'Not a challenge?' he questioned, and then he muttered grimly, 'Not the truth.'

She lashed out, trying the only way she could to push him away. 'I am *nobody's* precious thing. Certainly not to the half-brother I barely know. You will hurt no one but yourself. You'll get no revenge here. Only a stain on your soul. Sorry to disappoint you.'

'A stain on my soul?' Giorgos laughed equally bitterly. Did she think he'd kissed her out of some medieval quest for vengeance on her family? Have mercy! It had taken only one second for him to lose his head completely when he'd got his hands on her heaven-sent curves.

'When you take advantage,' she clarified. 'When you exercise power over another just to make yourself feel good.'

Her bitterness made his skin shrivel with shame. Because for a moment there that was exactly what he'd wanted to do. Slake his anger and his frustration by satisfying himself with her beautiful body beneath his. Even now raw, desperate lust racked him in a shiver he could hardly contain—and he was furious with himself.

'Eleni is pregnant,' he gritted, goaded by guilt into revealing the terrible truth to her.

'What?' She paled. 'And you think Damon has taken her?'

He watched her. 'I don't believe she left willingly.'

But even as he said it, his sister's words echoed in his mind. *'I'm not coming back... Not till I've sorted it out.'*

'What does he want to do?'

'Apparently he's prepared to marry her.'

Relief bloomed in her face.

It only sharpened his anger. 'You think this is a *good* thing?'

'Maybe she cares about him. Maybe they're actually in love.'

'Maybe this is a fairy tale,' he growled derisively. 'Eleni

is naive. If she does think she's in love with him it's because he's seduced her. He's conned her into believing it.'

'You're not going to give her any credit, are you?' Kassiani said, almost sadly. 'In your world she's just too innocent and too sweet and *too stupid* to make a decision on her own.' She suddenly flared up at him. 'Could you be *any* more insulting? No wonder she ran away. Either way, you're not going to believe her. Either he kidnapped her against her will or she went willingly because he bamboozled her. Because you think she's a brainless idiot. I bet you *totally* bully her.'

Giorgos blinked at her sudden snap. He didn't bully Eleni—she'd been happy with the arrangements he'd made...hadn't she? His stomach bottomed out. If she was happy, why wasn't she safe at home here in the palace? Was this woman right? Had he underestimated Eleni's ability to make her own decisions? He needed to talk to her. But how could he?

He hadn't had a proper conversation with her in years.

The truth whispered, tormenting him. Guilt at his ineptitude curled, squeezing the air from his lungs. He'd thought he was doing the right thing. Maybe he'd been wrong all along. *Again.*

'My sister is in trouble,' he said starkly. 'All I want to do is help her. Help me help her.'

He heard her raggedly drawn in breath and saw the trembling of her mouth as she finally realised how desperate he was feeling.

'There's nothing I can say,' she said dully. 'Truthfully, I only met Damon a few years ago. He offered to help me.'

'Why?'

She hesitated before answering. 'He's a more genuine man than our father is. He's more caring. He'll want to do what he thinks is *right*.' She looked at him. 'He will want to protect both her and his unborn child.' A sad, twisted little smile curved her lush mouth. 'In a way, I feel sorry for the Princess. Between the two of you she's going to have quite a tough time.'

Giorgos stilled. Damon Gale was *protective*? He was not going to repeat the mistakes of his father? Kassiani was an illegitimate love-child. The abandoned daughter of an abandoned lover. Damon wasn't going to do that to his own child.

Perhaps his meeting with Eleni *hadn't* been contrived. Certainly on paper it seemed Damon Gale didn't need money or fame. In fact he actively sought privacy, as did his half-sister. So if his seduction of Eleni was by fate rather than some Machiavellian manipulation then Damon was only doing what he felt he had to. And if Giorgos was in the same position he had to admit he'd have done the same thing. Hell, a decade before he'd tried to.

He breathed out a long sigh, accepting that he was going to have to break the news to Eleni's fiancé that the planned wedding was off. He was going to have to back his sister. He was going to have to trust her.

He glanced up and saw Kassiani looking at him directly. Such sweet torment, standing only an arm's length away, watching him with a concerned look in her eyes. A concern that he hadn't earned.

His gut tightened as desire rose again.

No, neither concern nor pity was what he wanted from this woman. And that was wrong too.

'I want to go home,' she said softly.

Giorgos instinctively shook his head, instantly rejecting the idea of her departure. 'You can't. You know too much.'

'I won't breathe a word to anyone. Not to protect you but for your sister, who is kind and intelligent and funny and perfectly capable of making her own decisions.' She paused, her pout becoming pronounced. 'How you two can be related is beyond me.'

'You're not going home tonight,' he muttered as need speared through his body.

He wanted her to remain locked in the palace with him—to have her within his control. The remnants of his desire to punish her had now morphed into the fantasy of pleasuring her. Of seeing her aroused and begging for release. He could do it—he could please her. And in doing so please himself.

It had definitely been too long. And she... She *didn't like to be touched...*

He gritted his teeth, holding back a growl. Maybe he *was* no better than some twelfth-century warlord, taking a pretty captive to suit his pleasure—every bit the bastard she'd painted him. But right now he didn't care. He just wanted to forget everything in hedonistic pleasure.

He knew he could. He knew she'd liked his kiss. She'd wanted more. It would take little to make her want more again. Her molten chocolate eyes were now almost entirely black and he was losing himself in their bottomless depths.

'I'm not staying here,' she uttered in the faintest whisper.

Because she knew it too—knew that acting on this electricity arcing between them was inevitable. That was why she wanted to run away.

'You say you don't like to be touched,' he challenged her. 'But you enjoyed my touch. Not at first, sure. I took you by surprise, and I apologise for that, but don't lie about what happened then.'

The thought that he might have disgusted her was appalling. That he might have subjected her to something she had felt repulsive. Her reaction initially had been stiff, but he'd dismissed it as surprise because suddenly the floodgates had opened and she'd been ardent in her response.

And as he watched her closely now, as he listened to her, he saw other signs—the brightness of her eyes, the frantic beat of the pulse at her neck, the way she kept licking those lips that were obviously dry and bothering her. He remembered the way she'd softened and opened up for him. That hadn't been a moment he'd forced—that had been a moment of her surrender. Not to his will, but to the emotion flooding her. The desire for deeper touch.

She'd been attracted to him. She still was. But she didn't want to be. And perhaps he could understand why.

'Someone hurt you,' he said. His anger lit again, but this time in a different way.

She frowned at him searchingly, then rolled her eyes. 'Not in the way you're thinking.'

'No one has touched you when you didn't want them to?' He didn't believe her.

'They have. But I stopped them.'

He lifted his brows.

'It wasn't about control or anything worse.' Her colour rose. 'I just mean a kiss at the end of a date…'

'How did you stop him?'

'Men don't like a lover who doesn't respond. No matter the attributes she might have.'

He shook his head. She knew her 'attributes' were like catnip to any red-blooded man. But he knew there'd be some men out there who wouldn't care about whether she responded to them or not. Those men would just take— in which case she'd been lucky. But her lack of response was…*interesting*.

'You didn't respond to them?' He felt very still inside.

'As I said, I don't like to be touched.' She folded her arms, looking like a spiky ball of defensiveness.

Did she mean she didn't feel anything at all? Or she just hadn't met a guy who could actually push her buttons? 'Are you saying you're frigid?'

That flush covered her skin and he watched her as she refused to answer. He realised now it was the truth—or at least she thought it was.

'You don't feel things that way?' He framed the question more gently.

For a second he didn't know whether to believe her or whether this was another game. But then, she hadn't been playing any game at all, had she? She hadn't known a thing about Eleni and Damon.

He thought about the doctor who'd asked her for a date this evening. Her refusal had been polite and firm and *practised*. That nurse had teased her, but she'd stepped in and helped her deflect the guy's attention as if she'd known it made Kassie uncomfortable. And there'd been a stiffness within her when she'd first met him. Now her lips were still clamped shut, but he could see the trembling of her body.

'It's *not* a challenge.'

Her voice was low and husky and he could feel the mortification emanating from her. She clearly wished like hell she'd not said anything.

'I don't take it as one,' he reassured her. But then he smiled. 'I don't need to prove something I already know.'

She looked confused.

'You felt "that way" when I kissed you.'

She shifted and her skin flooded again with deepened colour. Her gaze dropped from his. 'Please don't embarrass yourself.'

His laughter was husky and amused. 'Kassie...' He'd heard the nurse call her that—he liked it.

'Please.' She closed her eyes. 'I don't see why it's all that amusing.'

'It's not that it's funny. I'm relieved.' He leaned close. 'I didn't want to think I'd hurt you that way. Contrary to your earlier assumption, I *don't* get off on forcing my attentions on unwilling women.'

'I know that. I'm sure they're all very, *very* willing.'

She still wouldn't look at him. But he couldn't look away

from her. 'Right now I'm only interested in you. And I think you're willing.'

'No,' she denied.

'Be honest,' he dared her softly. 'Sometimes you can't help who you're attracted to. Even if you don't like the person, chemistry can be just chemistry.'

'But you *can* choose whether to act on that attraction or not,' she said crisply.

'So you admit there's attraction?' He smiled. She was thawing fractionally. 'You're used to choosing not to act. Maybe you're used to choosing to *avoid*. Not because you *can't* feel, but because you're afraid to.'

She shook her head vehemently. 'You're wrong.'

'I don't think so,' he said. 'Aren't you in the least bit curious?'

She rolled her eyes again, but it lost the desired effect because he could see how her fingers were trembling.

'It's not something I need,' she said.

Didn't *everyone* need touch sometimes? Even he did—in the strictly controlled liaisons he occasionally permitted himself. But if she was being honest then Kassiani Marron's confession had just eliminated her from contention for one of those brief, discreet dalliances.

'The conversation is only academic,' he assured her quietly. 'The last thing I would do is touch you now. Or hurt you.'

'If you don't want to hurt me, then let me leave.'

For another fleeting second he questioned whether she was truly as innocent as those wide eyes would lead him to believe. He'd been lied to by a beautiful woman before.

But then he remembered the shocked stillness of her body when he'd been foolish enough to touch her when he shouldn't have. The frankly inexpert answer of her kiss. And her reaction afterwards—the rapid rise and fall of her breasts as she'd worked to recover her breath, the trembling of her limbs. She'd been more than aroused. She'd been stunned. And she *was* being honest.

The realisation forced him to shut down all the burning want within his body. He was extremely cautious when selecting a lover and would never have an affair with a woman who was clearly fragile—no matter how beautiful she might be. Kassiani Marron was a risk he was unprepared to subject himself to. Duty forbade it. The past forbade it. And the past had already come back to haunt him.

His sister was now in a position he'd hoped to avoid for her. His interest in Kassie would have to be ignored. This night was nothing more than a moment that she would soon forget.

Kassie watched as his expression changed from intensely speculative to serious and then to blank. She felt his withdrawal of interest almost as a physical chill—and for once she felt regret at successfully putting a guy off.

'I'll ensure you get home safely,' he said as he stepped away from her.

'I'm sure your assistant will be very efficient.' She couldn't keep the coldness from her own tone.

He turned, catching her gaze with his. 'You know I'm escorting you myself.'

'You're just trying to find out more information.'

His sudden chuckle caught her by surprise.

'So suspicious,' he mocked. 'Are you this wary with everyone?'

'You're every bit as defensive as I am.'

'I think you already know you set me on edge, Ms Marron.'

And he didn't like it. That eased her own issues with his effect on *her*. 'It seems we're even.'

His laugh encircled her with a warm glow. The tension lifted for the briefest of moments and she couldn't hold back her answering smile. When he was like this he was the most incredibly attractive man. And now that she could relax a fraction she realised it was a *good* thing—to find a guy attractive? *Go her.*

Something flickered in his eyes before he mastered control of himself and became the serious monarch again. 'It really is time for you to leave.'

'Freedom. At last,' she muttered mock-demurely. 'Thank you, Your Highness.'

She heard a sharp intake of breath but he said nothing. He stalked ahead of her along the long dimly lit corridors, their gold detailing providing a muted gleam in the vast shadows. He was fascinating.

That unsettling feeling deep in her belly stirred again, spreading that strange ache. Once more she replayed that kiss—the shocking heat that had flooded her body surged again. *Desire.*

She almost stumbled as the need to feel his body against hers again made her stupid muscles weaken.

'Truly, you don't need to accompany me.' She tried to deflect him as they emerged into the night. She might as well have tried pushing a marble slab up an icy slope.

'It's my duty to ensure you get home safely.'

'You don't trust your own security people?'

'It's my responsibility.'

That rebellious feeling flared again. '*I'm* not your responsibility.'

'Right now, your welfare is.'

The guy had an overblown hero complex, thinking himself responsible for anyone he thought was weaker or less able. He was determined to be the protector.

'The way your sister is your responsibility?'

He checked his stride, then kept walking. 'No. Not like that at all.'

He made a small gesture with his hand and the waiting

security team by the car melted into the shadows. He held open the rear door and she got into the car. She watched as he walked around the vehicle to get in the other side, next to her.

The driver moved the car forward the moment he'd closed the door. The palace gates slid open and they swiftly glided through the dark, quiet streets. She stared ahead blindly, hyper-aware of his gaze on her.

The silence in the car thickened. The emotions swirling within her were too strong to contain—they leaked out, heating the atmosphere between her and the silent presence beside her. He was lethally powerful, yet she sensed that extreme protectiveness actually masked vulnerability. As arrogant and as privileged as he was, he was exposed because he loved his sister. He wanted what was best for her.

Kassie couldn't help but respect him for that. Because part of her wished *she'd* had someone who'd cared like that in her life. Someone who loved her and watched out for her. King Giorgos might be arrogant, but she understood that he wanted what was best for the ones he loved.

Fool, she mocked herself. One kiss and she was thinking herself half in love with the man already? The sooner she got away from him and back to her mundane, safe world the better.

But as the car pulled up to her small apartment she hesitated and turned to him. 'I won't say anything,' she promised in a low voice. 'You may not believe me, but I do want the best for Princess Eleni. And I understand that you do too.'

'I don't require your approval, Ms Marron. I will find Eleni and I will bring her home safely.'

He didn't like knowing she'd seen his vulnerability. She understood that too.

She licked her dry lips. 'I'm certain you will.'

He got out of the car at the same time she did. She veered

away from him as she walked to her door, quickly trying to find her keys and unlock it, but her fingers had become buttery and useless.

'Thank you for bringing me home,' she said with mechanical politeness. 'I'm sorry I couldn't be of more assistance.'

His lips curved and that gleam lit in his eye again. 'Never apologise when you are not actually sorry.'

'I'm sorry that you're worrying,' she pointed out coolly. 'I wish there was something more I could do.'

He looked at her but didn't answer. For a moment that thing swirled between them again. The memory of his body pressed against hers flashed into her mind. The foreign sensation of delight sizzled deep in her blood cells, beating heat into her cheeks again. Her throat clogged. She couldn't speak again if she tried. Nor could she move.

He took one step nearer. Night shadowed his eyes and she couldn't read his expression. But she could feel it—the sharp edge of desire. Only in her inexperience, her naivety, she couldn't truly be certain that it was shared, or if it was only her crazy, out-of-control body.

He took the key from her useless fingers and stretched past her to unlock the door. She'd never felt as frozen as she did in that moment. But it wasn't ice immobilising her muscles. It was heat and want and an appalling sense of anticipation.

He regarded her closely. 'You'd better get inside, Ms Marron. Now. Before…'

He trailed off and she stared up at him.

'Before what?' she breathed.

He gazed down at her in silence for a long, long moment. But this time he didn't act on the impulse that had shocked them both. He gave a clipped nod and then he turned and strode into the darkness.

Kassie slowly entered the safety of her tiny apartment.

As she locked the door she leaned back against it, accepting the reality that she would never see King Giorgos again.

And wasn't that good? He was arrogant and stubborn and saw only the worst in her. There was nothing in common between them.

But she pressed a hand against her ribs, willing away the ache. His departure from her life shouldn't bring any sense of loss. Yet it did. Which meant she was more broken than even she'd believed.

CHAPTER FOUR

I DON'T LIKE to be touched.

Her words haunted him. Not a challenge—no, Giorgos had no desire to overpower her. But he did have a duty to warn her, because she wouldn't like being hunted either. And she was about to be.

Keeping Eleni and Damon clear of the paparazzi's long-range lenses was easy enough, but Ms Marron had none of the palace's defences at her disposal. He was not having anyone else suffering because of the burden of the crowns that he and Eleni wore.

Half an hour before the announcement was due to be made he went to her apartment. It was less than two days since he'd met her. But he'd spent too many minutes thinking about her and he knew she wasn't going to welcome his reappearance.

There was no reply to his forceful knock on her door. It took his security man only a moment to pick the feeble lock.

'Wait for me out here,' he ordered as he stepped inside.

'Sir...?'

He glanced back to silence the man with a look.

Her apartment was small but cosy—there were books stacked on an old table, a pot plant on the windowsill was flowering, and the room had a sense of comfort. But one of the window fastenings was loose and in her bedroom the curtains were too thin. The sight of her neatly made narrow bed tightened his skin.

She wouldn't be safe here and it was his responsibility to ensure her safety. *He* was the one responsible for the mess they were now in. He clamped down on the searing satisfaction he felt at the thought of having her with him again.

This was for *her* benefit, not his. *Her* protection. And he'd prove to himself that his full control was restored.

'Pack her a bag for a few days,' he said to the waiting guard as he strode out of the small unit.

He swallowed his guilt about invading her personal space—hell, he was used to living with guilt. She'd be furious, but too bad. She was too vulnerable to remain there for the foreseeable future.

He quickly slid into the unmarked car idling at the kerb. 'The hospital,' he instructed his driver. 'As fast as you can without drawing attention.'

Kassie's pulse kept skipping beats in a maddeningly unpredictable rhythm. She'd barely slept these last two nights. When she was alone in her little apartment the memories teased and that sweltering heat returned. The recollections were too intense, too intimate. She'd curl up in a ball and squeeze her eyes tight shut to block them, but it didn't work. Cold showers hadn't worked either.

Why did fate have to be so fickle? Why was it that the one man who'd ever turned her on was the one she could never have? The one she'd never actually want?

The only way to stop those thoughts was by distracting herself with her patients and paperwork. She'd worked on her files all afternoon, stopping briefly to snack on a sandwich from the vending machine on the second floor.

Now, as she was on her way back through the ward to her office, she saw one of her patients in distress.

'It's sore?'

She felt for this youth who'd sustained a crush injury; they were trying to prevent an amputation. The boy was tearful, but she kept talking to him quietly as she carefully massaged the area above the damage, taking care not to inflame it.

'Thanks.'

She smiled at him gently. 'It's going to take time. Don't try to do too much too soon. It's easy to make that mistake.'

She stepped out from behind the curtain to go back to her office and her stressed heart stopped beating altogether. King Giorgos was standing right on the other side of the curtain, immaculate as always in another impeccable suit.

'You're eavesdropping?' she whispered furiously. 'Have you no respect for *anyone's* privacy?' She hurried to get out of earshot of the other patients. 'What are you *doing* here?'

'What are *you* doing here?' King Giorgos countered lazily, walking with her. 'You're not rostered on this weekend.'

She gaped at him. How did he *know* that? 'I needed to complete the paperwork I didn't finish the other night.'

'That wasn't paperwork.'

'He was in pain—you expect me to ignore him?' She shook her head and snapped at him tartly. 'I'm sorry—I'm not like you.'

His mouth flattened. 'You must come with me now.'

'I can't leave. I have to work.'

'It's cancelled for the week.'

The week? The ground shifted beneath her feet. 'Why?'

'Because your life is about to get crazy.' He glanced into her office. 'Get your bag. You're coming with me now.'

'This again?' She folded her arms and glared at him. 'Is your life incomplete without a captive? Must you always have a female in chains in the palace?'

A sharply amused gleam softened his stern expression. 'You really *do* have a fixation with me putting you in chains, don't you?'

A trickle of something delicious and dangerous seeped into her. Engaging with him like this gave her a thrill she'd never have believed she'd actively seek.

'I'm doing this for your protection, Ms Marron. Not for

your pleasure. Or mine,' he said pointedly. 'A helicopter is waiting on the roof.'

She stopped walking. 'You can't be serious.'

'And *you* can't be this naive. They're already on their way.'

'They?'

'Journalists, cameramen, paparazzi, vultures. Whatever you want to call them.'

'Why would they want to bother *me*?'

'They are going to touch you,' he warned her grimly. 'They are going to pry.'

'I don't care what they write about me.' She held herself stiffly. It couldn't be anything worse than she'd heard over the years.

He looked pityingly at her. 'It's not what they write—it is the way they follow you...stalk you, harass you, call out to you. They'll speak to anyone you've ever spoken to in your life... You need to get away—at least until the initial furore dies down.'

He walked to the door leading to the stairwell, expecting her to follow him.

The desire to flout his demand flared. 'You can't be—'

'Move,' he ordered curtly. 'Or I'll carry you up there myself.'

His threat merely sharpened her urge for insubordination.

'You just can't cope with someone who doesn't instantly submit to your demands, can you?' She defied him with an all-out assault. 'You expect everyone to bow and scrape and scuttle to do your bidding. Especially women. Do you kit out all your lovers with a set of knee-pads?'

He froze, but his eyes lit with such danger she thought she might have gone too far. Where had her aggression come from? The instinct to push back had been irresistible, but she'd never been *shrewish* before.

'What?' she asked, faking bravado. 'Did I strike too close to home?'

He tugged her into the stairwell and slammed the door behind them. 'You are *so* determined to provoke a reaction in me,' he whispered, hemming her in against the cool wall with his hands. 'So keen to make me lash out in a specific way.'

He leaned closer still.

'You want me to do what I did the other night so you can cast me as your villain. But the truth is you liked it. You're attracted to me. You want me. You just don't want to admit it.' His lips curved with arrogant satisfaction.

'I don't want you.'

Her heart thundered. She was shocked at his verbal attack. Shocked more by the unfurling betrayal of her body. He was right. She *did* want him.

His gaze swept down, lingering on her tightened breasts.

She gasped. 'You're the most arrogant creature who walked the planet.'

'Well, that's a step up from being a monster.' He laughed. 'And at least I'm honest.'

'You want honesty?'

'It'd be a good start.'

'You're the *last* man I'd be attracted to.'

He snorted. 'I think I'm the *only* man you have been attracted to.'

He was right—which was all the more annoying. Why did it have to be *him*, of all people?

'Everything comes too easily to you,' she grumbled. 'You think you can have any woman you want. Everything in your life is disposable.'

'*Nothing* in my life is disposable.' His smile gained a bitter edge. 'Everything I do has more consequences than for most people. Nothing is forgotten.' He stepped back but took her clenched fist in his hand. 'Did some power-ful, wealthy man hurt you, Kassiani?'

Of course. Starting with her louse of a father.

'What makes you think there was only one?'

'Poor little thing… But the pity card isn't going to work on me,' he muttered, unmoved. 'Your past isn't my prob-lem. I'm concerned only with now. And right now you need to come with me.'

'And if I refuse?'

'You just want me to toss you over my shoulder.' He laughed again at her expression. 'Do you think I wouldn't dare?'

She stared up at him. He would. But she couldn't give in this easily—especially considering he was the one man she found sexually attractive.

'I am trying to save you from a horror-fest,' he growled.

'I can take care of myself.'

He released her fist with a theatrical sigh and dug into his pocket.

'Take a look at the damn screen.' He flicked his phone around, almost shoving the screen in her face. 'This is the mob outside your apartment right now.'

There was a bunch of men standing around outside her apartment. Guys in jeans and tees on scooters, with cam-eras and lights and phones. One was repeatedly banging on her door.

'How can you see my apartment?' She frowned. 'Have you put cameras on me?'

'This is a live feed from my security team. I have some-one stationed in the building across the street to keep an eye on the place and the other is…' He swiped the screen again, fury flickering across his face as he checked the screen before showing her again. 'You can't go home. Not until I have this under control.'

Kassie stared at the grainy image on the screen. There

were two guys right in her back yard. 'They're going through my *rubbish*?' Appalled, she leaned back against the cool wall for support. 'That's sick.'

'*Now* do you understand? You don't want to be running that gauntlet. You don't want to hear their questions and have their cameras in your face. You need to leave with me. Now. They'll already be here at the hospital, trying to get through Security.'

'Why are they even here?' She was shocked—she didn't understand it at all.

'Because your half-brother has just married my sister.'

She gaped at him for a full five seconds.

'What?' she muttered breathlessly. 'He's what?'

'They returned. They married. This afternoon.'

She registered the grim tension in his eyes. 'Are they okay? Is Eleni okay?'

'I think so.' Uncertainty flickered across his face, but then he straightened. 'More okay than *you're* about to be if you don't come with me now.'

And was Giorgos okay? Because, to be honest, he didn't really look it. He looked pale and, frankly, right on the edge.

Wordlessly, she turned and walked up the stairs with him, so full of questions that she didn't know where to begin.

Less than two minutes later she was strapped in to take the first helicopter ride of her life. Giorgos handed her a headset and she put it on with fumbling fingers as the machine lifted into the sky.

'We have a secure channel.' His voice sounded too close, too intimate, even though he sat a foot apart from her in his own surprisingly spacious seat. 'Not even the pilot can hear us.'

Yeah? Well she wasn't about to have headset sex with him. She was too busy clutching on to the armrest and remembering to breathe, trying to get her head around the developments of the last ten minutes.

'Are you okay?' he asked, a reluctant smile breaking his frown.

'I'm fine. You?'

'I will be.' He shot her a look. 'I'm sorry.'

So was she. Because there was scandal here. Her mother had been a mistress—the 'other woman'. And she was a child born of lust. The exact sort of juicy scandal that royals ought never to be tainted with...

'How do you cope with it?' She gestured to the phone he still held. 'How do you live with that level of intrusion?'

'I don't have to. They don't scrutinise me the way they would you or any woman.' He frowned. 'I know it's not right. That's why...'

'You never have a girlfriend? You'd never subject any woman to this.'

'I can't protect anyone from it.' He sighed. 'Someone born into the craziness understands it, and at least has built the defences to cope with it. But the women get it far worse than the men.'

'This is why you're so protective of Eleni?' It made sense to her now.

'I've seen what it does to other women in public positions. I've seen their skeletal figures and the strain on their made-up faces at the stress of having their dress choices stupidly picked apart.' He shoved his phone back into his pocket. 'I didn't want that for her. *Ever.* I wanted her out of the spotlight as much as possible. To go from the safety of one palace to another.'

'But you can't hide her away from life.'

'Obviously not,' he said grimly. 'She was too vulnerable and naive.'

'Because she hadn't been out there—living life like a normal young woman, making mistakes—'

'That was impossible,' he argued strongly. But then he sighed. 'And now she's made the oldest mistake in the world...'

'So you've made Damon marry her?'

'I don't think I could make him do anything he didn't want to—he's *your* half-brother after all.' He shot her a look. 'He all but abducted Eleni to prevent her marrying Prince Xander. *He's* the one who pushed for this. Eleni thought she could go it alone.'

'And you don't think she could?' Kassie felt her fighting spirit stir. 'My mother went it alone.'

'And was it easy?'

'Of course not, but—'

'Then you know exactly why I didn't want that for Eleni,' he interjected. 'But it was Damon, not me, who convinced Eleni that marriage was the best answer. I wasn't the bully this time—it had already happened.'

His gaze narrowed on her thoughtfully.

'And how was it for you?' he asked quietly.

'How was what?'

'Your mother's decision to go it alone?'

'She didn't really have a choice, given my father was already married,' she muttered through gritted teeth. 'She avoided other men.'

'And she taught you too well. You avoid *all* men.'

'Do you blame me?' she flared. 'I watched my mother wait and wait and wait for her lover to deliver what he promised. She settled for second-best for so long, taking someone else's crumbs her entire life. And for what? Lies and rejection and heartache and sickness.'

'She wasn't ever interested in anyone else?'

'Because getting another man is all that matters?' Kassie was incensed.

'I imagine there were many men interested in your mother.'

'Because all a man wants is a beautiful woman?'

'*Must* you interpret my questions so simply? I'm quite certain your mother had multiple attractive qualities. Intelligence. Spirit. Determination. Compassion—'

'And you're certain of this—?'

'Because her daughter shows the same things, of course.'

She didn't know quite how to respond to that. He was mercurial. Shockingly honest. Suave. Dangerous.

'But you're determined not to be the same as her,' he said.

Kassie stiffened. 'I loved my mother...' And she was loyal to her, even though she'd frustrated Kassie so much. And hurt her.

'Of course.'

'They're really married?' She couldn't believe it.

He pulled out his phone again, turning it so she could see the picture he'd opened. Her heart softened at the sight of her half-brother and the Princess. Laughing, close. Their connection would be obvious to anyone who looked. Perhaps it was going to work out.

'They look happy.'

'Appearances can be deceptive—'

'No.' Kassie pointed at the sparkle in Eleni's eyes and her glowing smile. 'You can't fake that.'

He didn't answer as he studied the photo again.

'I don't know Damon well,' she admitted with full disclosure. 'But I *do* know he's a far better man than our father has ever been. Damon's a *good* man.'

'Only time will tell,' Giorgos answered quietly.

He didn't trust people. She supposed he must have reason—just as she had reason.

'Where are you taking me?' she asked.

'The Summer House.'

The royal holiday retreat? She shifted on her seat, her gaze sliding from his.

'Eleni and Damon need space alone at the palace,' he said calmly. 'You need to get away from the intrusiveness of the paparazzi. And I can continue to work there.'

'So it's convenient for you?'

'When did you last have a holiday?' he cajoled with a glint in his eye. 'When did you last spoil yourself? You've spent all your adult life either caring for your mother or studying so you can care for others. You deserve a break.'

'Are you implying that I ought to *thank* you? As if you're doing me a *favour*? This isn't my dream holiday.' She suddenly choked on a laugh. 'And you think you're not arrogant!'

He grinned smugly. 'Look out of the window now. I think you'll find it's not so bad.'

She finally braved a glance down to the coastline. It was a stunning island—fertile gardens, impressive rock formations and aquamarine waters. She saw a low building, growing larger as they neared it. Set into the cliff, it almost formed part of the rocks itself.

She gazed at it as they circled to the rear of the building, where there was a helipad. The windows gleamed but the silence of the place astonished her. There were no crowds of attendants. No other buildings nearby.

She walked with him—initially wary—but the Summer House was nothing like the palatial monstrosity in the city.

It was large, but not vast or ostentatious. Where there were overly ornate gold decorations in the palace, there was white simplicity here. There were no paintings smothering every wall, or chandeliers hanging from the ceilings, or sculptures and furniture crammed into every corner. No, here there was pale, honey-coloured flooring, and white walls, and luxurious space and a sense of serenity so profound that the power of speech was stolen from her.

It truly was beautiful. And private. More than that, it was *intimate*.

'It's built into an existing cave network. Above us there's a garden—not large, but private. And there's a pool that's partially inside a cave, partially in the sun.'

'It's…' She wasn't too proud to be honest. 'It's not what I expected. It's much simpler.'

Warm and restful and so beautifully light and fresh she just knew all those soft furnishings were the most luxuriant one could get.

'I knew you'd like it.' His smile flashed—but it wasn't that arrogantly satisfied one, there was genuine pleasure in his eyes. 'Not as formal as the palace.'

'No.'

Kassie's heart thudded as something darkly sweet slipped beneath her guard. He'd *wanted* her to like it. He'd wanted to please her.

That sense of cosy intimacy grew. The night was closing in, the brilliant blue sky swiftly darkening with each passing second, and Kassie's awareness deepened. She was now alone with him—effectively trapped here with him for who knew how long.

A shiver ran along her spine.

Not a thrill of anticipation. It couldn't possibly be that.

She ought to be outraged by him taking her, but somehow his revelations on the helicopter ride had taken that particular wind from her sails.

'Are you hungry?' he asked.

She shook her head. 'I had a snack at the hospital.'

'Then I'll show you to your room so you can get comfortable.'

He led the way down a wide corridor. Where was his room? She didn't dare ask.

He waited for her to enter ahead of him. It was simply and sparsely decorated, with white walls, white furnishings and white linen on the wide, wide bed. Yet somehow it wasn't cold and impersonal—it was warm and inviting and too intimate for her to be in it alone with him. That intense feeling fluttered—and with it came that curl of fear.

'Is that my bag?' She stared poisonously at the small carry-all that had been placed on the hand-carved wooden rack at the end of that magnificent bed.

She whirled to face him, turning her back on the searing intimacy of the beautiful bedroom. He stood impassively, not answering, his gaze not leaving her face.

'Did you go into my apartment? Did you pack my clothes?' She whipped her anger to ice.

He shook his head. 'One of my men packed.'

'So some random guy I've never met has raided my underwear drawer?'

He cleared his throat. 'I thought you would prefer to have your own things rather than accept an entirely new wardrobe paid for by me. Especially not underwear.'

He was right about that, of course. But he was still wrong. The outrageously high-handed behaviour was shocking, and she was seized by the desire to better him.

'Whatever made you think that?' she asked brazenly. 'What woman *wouldn't* love a selection of new dresses and shoes and, yes, underwear to waft about a place like this in? Especially if she didn't have to pay for it.'

He blinked, but then a slow smile spread across his face. 'Don't worry,' he soothed. 'If you're that upset about me not seeing your underwear you can show it to me yourself later.'

There was a pregnant pause as she read the searing challenge in his eyes. The ripple of banter brewed into brooding resistance. She couldn't tear her gaze from his—was locked in a moment of intensity. His magnetism was overwhelming. She almost needed to glue her feet to the floor to stop herself walking towards him.

'I'm not sleeping with you,' she muttered low.

'Did I offer?' he replied, his gaze still not leaving her.

She flushed, but continued with her deflection because

she *had* to solidify her position. 'We're practically related. You're—what? My brother-in-law now?'

'I'm not *any* kind of brother to you,' he said softly. 'Not even close.'

'You're standing close.'

Somehow he was. Somehow in the past few minutes he'd got close enough to block out everything else in the world. Close enough for her to feel his heat.

He reached out, carefully brushing back a lock of hair that had escaped her braid. '*Not* brotherly,' he muttered huskily.

'I... I get that.' She swallowed, suddenly sweltering.

'Then I'll leave you to unpack.' He stepped back. 'Rest. Swim if you like. If you need anything just ask one of the staff. The few that are here are my most trusted employees and they'll get whatever you need. Please feel at home here.'

He *had* to be kidding. This place was small to him, but larger and more luxurious than any home *she'd* lived in. But she couldn't help exploring her room. There were two other rooms attached—a gorgeous sitting room, with a sofa and a comfy armchair and a wide set of windows leading to a balcony overlooking the water. And then there was the bathroom.

She caught sight of her reflection in the gleaming mirrors and almost died. But she turned her back on the large bath—she couldn't quite relax enough for that. She'd freshen up in that magnificent shower.

The jets of water were sublime. The soaps and shampoos deliciously scented. The towels soft and fluffy and, yes, she was lost to decadence for a good half-hour. But as she dressed in the jeans and tee shirt that had been folded with annoying perfection into her bag she wondered what he expected her to do—if anything.

She quickly re-tied her braid and decided. She refused

to hide in her suite and wait to be summoned into his presence…

But, despite the simplicity of the house, it proved to be larger than she'd initially thought. The curving corridors confused her—it really *was* built into a cave network and it really *was* utterly divine.

On her way back from another dead-end corridor that had led to that incredible pool he'd mentioned, a sleekly attired man met her.

'May I help you, miss?'

'I'm just looking for the King.'

The man's eyes widened slightly as he glanced down and noticed her bare feet. 'If you'd like to wait, I can tell him you're looking for him.'

She saw she'd missed a corridor off to the left, and from there she could hear soft music playing. 'There's no need—I can tell him myself. He's down there?'

The man didn't deny it, and didn't stop her, but he did look alarmed.

'Don't worry.' She smiled at him.

She didn't bother knocking—just opened the door and walked in.

'You've been prowling around?'

Giorgos was sprawled back on a large sofa, his tie askew, his shirtsleeves rolled up and a dangerous gleam in his eyes. A silver platter of delicacies sat on a low table in front of him—olives, meats, breads—all untouched as far as she could tell. The bottle of whisky next to the platter, however, had definitely been touched, and the amber liquid more than half filled the crustal tumbler he was holding.

'Looking for your private lair.' She nodded. 'It seems I've finally found it.'

'I like the door shut.' His hot gaze lingered on the dampened ends of her braid and he took a long sip of his drink.

Kassie held her breath as she closed the door and turned

back to face him. Playing with fire was for fools, and she was afraid she might be the biggest fool of them all. And yet she couldn't quite walk away.

'Is your room to your satisfaction?' he asked in a mockery of civility.

'I suppose it will do,' she mused slowly as she perched on the distant arm of the sofa he was sitting on.

'Maintaining your reputation of being difficult to please?' He quirked an eyebrow at her. But his hint of a smile faded the longer he gazed at her. 'I'm tired, Kassie,' he suddenly blurted out roughly. 'I don't want to do the right thing. I want to do everything I shouldn't. If you don't want me to do that then you need to walk away right now. *Please.*'

She cocked her head and looked at him closely, realising that beneath that in-control demeanour there was a man who was tired and hurting. And alone.

'You're upset.'

'I'm hard,' he argued bluntly. 'I'm tired and I want to lose myself in sex. I want to kiss you until you sigh and spread your legs and let me plunge as deep as I can into you. And I'm not sorry if I'm shocking you. I'm being honest about why you need to leave the room. *Now.*'

She almost fell from her perch. His harshly expelled words *did* shock her. But she realised he'd intended them to. He wanted to scare her away because he didn't want to be seen like this. Because he was feeling vulnerable.

Too bad.

'As if you can't control yourself... I *know* you can.'

'But I don't want to,' he ground out. 'And that's when things get tricky. I'm ordering you to leave.'

'You were the one who dragged me here.' She smiled serenely at him and let herself slip down off the wide arm onto the seat of the sofa.

He growled again and took another sip of his whisky.

'What will you do if I leave the room?' she asked.

He studied the contents of his glass. 'Continue to get drunk.'

'Is that your secret vice? How boring.'

'Are you calling me *boring*?' He leaned forward and set the glass on the low table in front of him. 'You're right, I am. I haven't got drunk in a decade.'

'So it won't take much, then, will it? Perhaps I'll need to save the kingdom from a king with a hangover? We don't want your legendary impartiality to be impaired. Perhaps I should stay and talk to you for a while.'

'You're determined to torment me,' he groaned and pressed his hands to his eyes. 'What did I do to deserve this fate?' He winced and muttered beneath his breath. 'Don't answer that—I already know.'

'You're the one who brought me here.'

He opened his eyes. 'And I'm going to regret it.'

'You think?' She laughed. 'We all want things we can't have.'

'Of course. There are many things I can't have. Many things Eleni didn't have. And that was *my* fault.'

'Are you wallowing in guilt and self-pity?'

'Utterly.' He picked up his glass again. 'I failed her.'

She heard the serious thread beneath that mocking tone and couldn't help but respond honestly. 'She's an adult. She's made her own choices. You have to let her get on with it.'

'I'm trying.'

'I know.' She smiled shyly at him. 'I also know it isn't easy when you're used to being in complete control.'

He looked at her sombrely. 'You would know.' There was no irony in his tone, no sarcasm.

But she shook her head and laughed. '*So* not the same. I can't get the career track I want. I can't—'

'I mean complete control of your *emotions*,' he interrupted. 'Of your body. You don't want distractions.' He reached out and took her hand. 'Yet you respond to me,' he said quietly.

She curled her fingers into a fist, but she couldn't lie to him. 'Apparently so.'

'Why do you think that is?'

She turned her gaze on the glass. 'Perhaps it's the power. Perhaps in that way I'm as weak as my mother.'

'She was attracted to a powerful man?'

'The most powerful she'd met. John Gale was handsome, intelligent. He promised the world and delivered nothing.'

'What happened?'

'Nothing. That was the point.' Her chuckle was bitter. 'He lied. He was greedy. He kept her enamoured for years. She put her life on hold for him. She jumped when he called. She always jumped...' Kassie trailed off, embarrassed.

'She loved him,' Giorgos said.

'It wasn't *love*.' Kassie frowned. 'She didn't love herself. She accepted too little from him.'

'And now you don't accept anything from any man?'

She shot him a look, but he shrugged and continued.

'You live alone...you're fiercely independent. And you don't date...'

'You've changed your view. You thought I'd slept with all the doctors,' she said pointedly.

'I'm sorry about that. I was worried about Eleni and I wasn't thinking clearly.'

'But you took one look at me and made up your mind.' She shook her head. 'Don't worry—you're not the first guy to do that.'

He sighed and reached forward to put his glass on the table again. He turned to face her. 'I'm sorry for that too. Is that part of why you don't want any kind of relationship?'

His apologies mollified her—and his honesty encouraged her own. 'It's not that I don't want a relationship—

doesn't everyone want that special person? To be in love and be loved? It's that I don't *feel* any attraction. There's a difference.'

'Yet you feel attraction to me?'

She nodded. 'Isn't fate cruel?'

'Because I'm powerful?' He watched her. 'What if I had no power?' he asked softly. 'What if there was no crown, no palace, no Summer House…just an average man in a tee shirt and jeans. Would you still respond to me?'

Of course. Because his power wasn't to do with all those external things, it was an intrinsic part of him. And she responded on an equally intrinsic level.

'There is no point wondering "what if?" The fact is you *are* the King, you *have* a crown and palaces and all the power.'

'So there can be nothing?'

'Exactly.'

'There could be this moment,' he tempted.

'Don't…' she whispered.

'There's no reason why we can't we enjoy each other's company.'

'There's *every* reason.'

She should have left when he'd told her to, but she'd thought she could remain immune to him and keep herself at a distance.

No, you didn't.

'There's every reason to steal a moment, Kassie,' he said softly, his expression revealing his awareness of her wavering contrary thoughts. 'Don't you deserve just a moment?'

'As if it would be *good* for me?' She rolled her eyes.

But that little voice of truth whispered, mocking. It *would* be good for her. And the heat unfurling in her depths was the real reason for staying when he had told her to go.

'I'd make it good.' He chuckled at the look she shot him.

'You know it's true. Why don't you let me try and we'll see how you like it?'

'As if I haven't heard that line before!'

'You already liked it a little. I think you might like it a lot.'

He scooted along the sofa until he sat the merest inch from her. Her skin sizzled and her pulse raced. Every cell yearned for him to come closer still. She refused to look at him.

'I could make you feel so good. You know that's true. I already make you feel.'

She swallowed hard. 'You're not being fair.'

'No.' He smiled at her. 'But life isn't fair.'

She looked into his eyes and the second she did so temptation screamed along her bones. 'Your H—'

'Call me Giorgos,' he gritted. 'I'm not your King. Not here.'

'You can't—'

'That's a command,' he snapped. 'When we're alone I'm not your King, and you're not my subject. You're my equal. You may always speak freely—even when I don't like what you're saying.'

'You're *commanding* me to speak freely?' she teased.

'Yes.' He glared at her. 'I want to understand what you're thinking.'

'I already speak my mind—you know you can't stop me. And you already know what I'm thinking. You know you confuse me.'

'Then let me make it simple. All I want, right this second, is to kiss you,' he said plainly. 'Are you willing to let me do that?'

The desire—so new, so rare, promising so much—was irresistible. How could she not explore this—just once—now she finally felt it? It would doubtless be a mistake, but only a little one. And it was one that might be worth the price she would have to pay.

'One kiss,' she breathed. *'One.'*

With slow deliberation he brought his hands to her face and gently tilted her head towards him. She caught the light that kindled in his green gaze as he angled and lowered his head so he could brush his lips against hers in the softest, gentlest sweep.

That wasn't fair. That wasn't a real kiss. And suddenly she realised that she wanted a real kiss—one like that passionate encounter of the other night.

And then he was back, his mouth roving over hers and his tongue teasing her sensitive lips apart. She gasped and he was there, and all that giddy warmth flooded her. She closed her eyes and for the first time truly sank into it. He was so powerful. So commanding. And as he took his time and his care something shifted within her. Then shifted again.

Then he slowly eased the pressure, until he finally lifted his lips but kept his hands framing her face. She kept her eyes firmly closed.

'Was it so awful?' he prompted softly.

She didn't want to look at him and admit the truth. She didn't want to break the magic. She didn't want to go back, or go forward in time, she just wanted to remain suspended in this moment of utter bliss.

'Have I kissed you into a catatonic state?'

She laughed, an irrepressible bubble of delight bursting within her even as tears stung. She blinked them back, opening her eyes to see him—too close, too tender.

'Oh, she breathes, she smiles. She lives.' He was smiling at her, but there was that glint in his eyes. 'Was it so terrible?'

She realised that under that arrogantly teasing question

there was concern. Slowly she shook her head. 'Why did you stop? You know you could have done...more.'

'Because I wanted you to *want* more,' he answered with an arrogant shrug. 'I wanted to leave you wanting.'

His honesty was both shocking and thrilling. 'Well that's not fair.'

'Actually, it is. You've left *me* wanting for days now.'

'Unintentionally,' she said indignantly. 'I wasn't even aware.'

'You *were* aware.'

She looked down. She had been aware of the electricity between them. She just hadn't been certain he felt it to the same degree as her. And she hadn't known how to handle it.

She heard him give a muffled groan beneath his breath and he bent closer again.

'I'm going to kiss you again, Kassie. And I'm going to touch you.'

Heat flooded her. 'Where are you going to touch me?'

His smile flashed—wicked and approving—and it made her want to wriggle closer.

'I'm going to kiss you. I'm going to cup and stroke your breasts until they're tight and aching. And then I am going to slide my hand into your panties and touch you where you're hottest. Where you're already wet.'

Her jaw dropped. She was shocked at his explicitness.

'Just my words make you wet.' He took advantage of her parted mouth and kissed her again. Hot and fierce. 'Just my words make you want it.'

She trembled and knew he felt it.

'I think your body knows what it wants,' he muttered. 'I think it knows just what to do.' He pulled her so she was lifted into his lap. 'Are you going to let it?' He kissed her throat. 'Are you going to let *me*?'

Oh, there was no choice at all any more.

'Kiss me...' she breathed.

He didn't hesitate—delivering the long, slow kisses that served to torment her. She wrapped her arms around his neck, holding him close. Never had she known kissing could be so good. So different. So playful. So intense.

He nibbled her lips with a tug of his teeth and then licked the small sting, caressing it with his lips. His hands held her close as he teased her, playfully alternating between soft and shallow kisses and deep lush sweeps of his tongue right inside her mouth. Dizzying, drugging...*delightful*.

Her blood ran hot and hotter still, and she began to wonder if he'd meant what he'd said—if he was ever going to do what he'd promised: touch as well as kiss. She ached for him to go lower, to touch where he'd threatened so wickedly. She was tight and aching all over—not just her breasts but in that hot, secret part of herself.

She moaned—unable to verbalise it. She didn't want to fight it any more, nor to wait. She wanted him to make this ache end.

Slowly, with infinite patience, he kissed down the column of her neck, nipping at the sensitive skin. As he went he gently slid his hand beneath the hem of her tee shirt and up to cup her breast. She gasped as his thumb stroked across the taut tip of her nipple.

'Giorgos...' she moaned.

He returned to kiss her mouth—the gentle teasing replaced with a fierce passion that she instinctively met. An innate urge drove her to suck on his tongue as he plunged it deep into her mouth. His groan of response only made her hungrier.

Readier.

His hand swept down across her stomach firmly. *Finally*. And she was on fire. She moaned again and writhed— twisting to try to get his touch where she wanted it. But he was strong, holding her still while he kissed her and stroked lower, and lower still, slipping his hand beneath the waist of her jeans, beneath the cotton of her panties.

In reflex she pressed her legs together, but all that did was trap his hand—*there*. Right there. His fingers teased. Skilful, knowing fingers. She squirmed as she fought to accept the overwhelming pleasure of his intimate touch.

And acceptance—indeed the need for more—won. Her legs parted and she recklessly pushed her throbbing source of desire against his hand. Because it felt so good. *He* felt so, so good.

And he answered—giving her more, and then more still. That primal pulse thrummed between them. Her hips circled as he drew breathless moans from her until she arched, taut, every muscle screaming with tension as he held her suspended in that long moment of searing, aching need.

She convulsed as pleasure shattered her. Her cry was caught in his rapacious, hard kiss until he released her mouth, allowing her to gasp as she rode the waves he'd summoned within her. In a half delirium she glimpsed him gazing down at her with glittering satisfaction as she came apart in his arms.

She buried her face in his chest so she wouldn't have to meet his searching gaze and he let her, as if he knew she was feeling too exposed, too vulnerable. His fingers stroked through her hair, holding her close, and she could feel the fast beat of his heart and the rapid rise and fall of his chest as he cradled her.

A slow spread of sweetness relaxed every cell, and then more than sweetness…euphoria. It was a joy so sharp she couldn't contain it. She lifted her chin and smiled at him, even as her eyes welled with gratitude, and she felt the fizzing feeling of total goodness.

'That was amazing,' she whispered with unrestrained astonishment. 'Just…amazing. I never… *Gosh.*' She couldn't think of the words to express it.

'That was your first orgasm?'

Something flickered in his eyes as she nodded.

'Thank you.' She pointed her toes as another last spasm of delight rippled through her and puffed out a breath of amazement.

'The pleasure was mine,' he said gruffly. He stood, tossing her a little in his arms to hold her more easily. 'It's late, Kassie. It's been a big day.'

And it wasn't over yet.

Desire and anticipation hummed throughout her body as he carried her down the corridor to her room and placed her on that big white bed. She sat up, biting her sensitive lip as she wondered what he'd do now. She wanted him to stay close to her and do that again. All caution had burned away in the heat of her attraction to him.

But he pushed her back down on the mattress and then stepped back. 'This time I think we really do need to walk away. I'm not ordering you. I'm asking you.'

'Giorgos…' she breathed.

He shook his head and backed away quickly. 'Have mercy on me.'

Her heart lurched as he closed the door, leaving her alone in that beautiful bedroom. And she finally understood just what a wicked devil he was. He'd done exactly what he'd set out to do. He'd left her wanting.

More.

CHAPTER FIVE

KASSIE WOKE IN a rush, instinctively realising she'd slept late. Given the events of last night, the fact she'd had such a deep, dreamless sleep was incredible. But the big bed was decadently comfortable and the room temperature had been deliciously cool on her hot skin.

She quickly showered and dressed, adrenalin rippling through her veins as she darted along the labyrinthine corridor to his 'lair'. She guessed he'd be there, at work already.

He was sitting at the large table, rather than on the sofa, clad in another of his suits. His frown didn't lighten in the least as he glanced up from his open laptop to watch her walk into the room.

She closed the door and avoided looking at him by focusing on the papers in front of him. One sheet held an incredibly long list of engagements— dates, places, times, people who would be in attendance—but it was the newspapers next to it that claimed her attention.

Kassic's thudding heart sank as she read the bold headlines. The media had gone after Giorgos in their coverage of the astounding news.

King Denied Romance!
Forced into Unhappy Engagement!
True love wins!

The photos they'd included of Giorgos were not kind—his expression was stern in every one—while each picture of Eleni showed her smiling and beautiful. In one she was looking up at her brother as if he were chiding her, but even Kassie understood now that he'd only wanted to do what was best.

'Poor Eleni, bullied by her big brother.' Giorgos's smile didn't reach his eyes. 'Big, bad me.'

'Oh, I don't know.' Kassie smiled. 'It might be nice to have a protective brother...'

She almost wished she'd had one, to stand alongside her and stare down the jerks who'd harassed her.

She glanced at him. 'Why have you gone all frowny face again?'

He was glaring at her. 'I've already told you there is nothing brotherly about what I've done for you. Nor is there anything *nice*.'

He rose from the table and moved around to stand in front of her. That was all he did—just stood that little bit too close, studying her far too intensely with those gleaming eyes. And she reacted—aching for him to take those few inches closer to her.

'Not brotherly,' she choked. 'I got that already.'

He fascinated her, and right now the shadows beneath his eyes were all too human, revealing hurt and worry. Had he got any sleep?

In embarrassment she realised far, *far* too late that while she'd had that 'release', *he* hadn't. She'd gone to bed like the cat who'd got the cream and promptly fallen asleep, while he'd... He'd *what*?

She cringed as she realised she didn't even know if he'd been aroused by what had happened. He'd made it all about *her*—her acquiescence, her pleasure—and taken nothing himself. He'd put her ahead of him. Just as he'd put Eleni ahead of himself now.

'You've taken the blame instead of her,' she said quietly. 'Pinned yourself as the villain to protect her.'

'The speculation will die down quickest that way,' he said dismissively.

'Eventually,' she acknowledged. 'But the commentary isn't kind to you.'

He was being slammed in the press in a way he'd never been slammed before.

'I can handle it.'

He shouldn't have to. He'd only been trying to support his sister.

She skimmed the first paragraphs of the report. 'So they're saying you blocked her romance and that you don't approve of her marriage.'

'And they're be right.'

'You don't *really* think that. I know you want her to be happy.'

'Suddenly you think so much better of me?' A smile quirked the corner of his mouth. 'I'm thinking you must have slept peacefully last night.'

'You'd never have let the marriage go ahead if you hadn't decided to trust her.' Kassie ignored his reference. He'd impressed her and, yes, that was quite a change from only a day ago. But it wasn't because of the way he'd kissed her last night.

'It was in the best interests of the country to get Eleni's situation sorted quickly.' He walked back behind the table.

'It was in *her* best interests. *She* was your priority. Don't deny that.'

'She's *always* been my first priority,' he said dryly. 'You just chose not to see it. But now it seems I'm not quite the monster you first thought.'

He frowned as he turned his laptop to face her. A news service was streaming on the screen.

'It's not just me they've latched on to. They're still outside your apartment. And they've interviewed one of your co-workers. One who met Damon when he visited you. They put you and the hospital as the link between them.'

'Just as you did.' She shrugged.

She chose not to care what they thought of her. She'd heard it all when she was growing up.

'But it wasn't your fault.' He turned to stare at the laptop screen again. 'It was Eleni.' He rubbed his hand over his forehead. 'Nevertheless, it is better for them to think worse of me than her.'

'You think they'd judge her if they knew the truth?'

'Of course they would—you know that.'

'There shouldn't be anything wrong with a woman acting on her desires.'

He suddenly laughed. 'Says *you*, the expert.'

She quietened, embarrassed and a bit hurt. He had no idea…

His expression turned regretful, and then surprisingly tender. 'But it's not like you don't have any desires, is it, Kassie?'

She looked away from him. 'Foolish ones. Ones that shouldn't be acted on.'

'Because you don't want to be judged?' He angled his head so he could keep looking into her eyes. 'The way your mother was judged?'

'I've already been judged. I was judged for years simply for being her daughter—the illegitimate child of the other woman,' she said scornfully. 'That fact made me an instant sex object in my home village when I was a teen and developed curves.' Her gaze narrowed. 'And boys and men don't like it if you say no to them when they've cast you as the village floozy. Then they judge more. And then your reputation is sealed.'

He frowned. 'Did no one defend you?'

'Who *was* there?'

Her mother had kept to herself. Her schoolfriends had become jealous of the attention she attracted. She'd become isolated. And then her mother had got sick and she'd retreated completely.

'That must have been tough on you,' Giorgos said grimly.

'It wasn't so bad. I survived. And I no longer care what anyone says or thinks of me.' She shrugged off his sympathy because she was stronger for her experience. 'I just want to live my life the way *I* want to.'

'That would be fair enough if you actually did. But you don't. You don't let yourself have that element to your life at all. And you're right—a woman shouldn't be judged at all differently from a man for having sexual desire.'

He glanced again at the screen.

'You shouldn't watch it,' she said, because she did know how it hurt, even when you told yourself not to care.

'I need to know what they're saying so I can figure out my response.'

'What's your usual response?'

'To say nothing. We never comment on personal issues within the royal family.'

'Have there been many?'

'Not in recent years,' he growled.

'So why watch it if you're not going to say anything?' She smiled and shook her head. 'Why let yourself care at all? It isn't worth it.'

'Because I am the King and I am in the public realm. I have a responsibility to my people. What they think is of vital importance.'

'But you're still *human*. Not perfect. You're allowed to make mistakes.'

'I don't want them hurting Eleni,' he said softly.

Kassie looked at the screen. Incessant questions and negative commentary blared from it. 'Perhaps you can show your support for her *and* shut your haters down.'

'How do I do that?' He arched a sceptical eyebrow.

'Why not prove to the world that you're happy to welcome Damon into the family by inviting his parents to dine with you? Show that you're trying to make amends and accept the situation. Open up a bit.'

'Open…? Invite his *parents*?' Giorgos laughed harshly. 'You *know* he's not close to them.'

'That doesn't matter—no one else knows that. They'll come. They love nothing more than sucking up to powerful people,' she said bitterly.

He looked at the screen through narrowed eyes and then looked at her. 'Perhaps I don't need to invite his parents,' he said slowly. 'Not when I already have *you* right here.'

'I'm the *scandal* of the family.' She recoiled. 'You can't use *me* to regain your approval ratings.'

'Actually, that's all the more reason to use you,' he mused thoughtfully. 'If I'm willing to accept his illegitimate half-sister, then I'm showing just how open-minded and progressive my monarchy is becoming.'

For a moment she was thrilled at the thought of him accepting her publicly—of him spending time with her as if he were proud to. Her pulse quickened. 'Are you going to let me drag you into the modern world, King Giorgos?'

He kept studying her, an odd light in his eye. But then he sighed. 'I'm not. No.'

Disappointment hit and it was strong. 'Why not?'

'What was the point of my bringing you here to escape the press hounds if I now set you right amongst them?' He walked over to put his hands on her shoulders and smiled at her. 'But it wasn't a bad idea.'

'*Must* you be so patronising?' she grumbled. 'It's obviously a fantastic idea. You can control media access to me. Isn't that what you've always done anyway, for both you and Eleni?'

The more she thought about it, the better it seemed. She could help him. And she wanted to.

'I won't let you down. Believe it or not, I *can* stay silent when I need to.'

'Believe it or not, I don't *want* you to stay silent.' He drew her close.

'Giorgos…be serious.' She couldn't hold back her smile at him. 'I can *help* you here.'

'Do I need help?'

'Perhaps it's okay to protect yourself as much as it is to protect your sister. And to protect your sister's husband's half-sister—who is in no way any kind of sister to *you*.'

His sudden amusement was good to see and her pulse skipped.

But then he sobered. 'You don't want people to judge you,' he said. 'I cannot put you in such a public position. I won't use you like that.'

'You haven't been listening to me,' she muttered. 'I don't give a damn what they say about me. You're the only one who cares about that. And, let's face it, the media are already on me—literally digging in my garbage, for goodness' sake. All because I'm Damon's distant relative. Hiding from them isn't going to work long-term. But you presenting me to them might assuage that initial interest. And they won't give a damn about me once they discover how boring I am. I can take advantage of your authority over the media.'

He regarded her closely, clearly thinking hard but revealing little. 'Why would you want to do this for me?'

He shook her gently, but she felt the tension in his body as he angled closer to her, as if he couldn't help himself.

She lowered her lashes demurely. 'You're my King.'

She heard his sharp intake of breath.

'Is there nothing you want from me in return?' he asked silkily, bending closer. 'No way in which I can help you?'

Oh, he was a devil. His words invoked a temptation within her and the possibilities of this situation swiftly crystallised—clearly. She wanted to feel what she'd felt with him before. She could take advantage of his obvious expertise in that area too. Just *once*. Just for herself.

'Maybe I'll stay here for a few more days,' she said breathlessly. 'I'll be seen with you, just as a distant family member, to show your acceptance of Eleni's marriage.' Her heart pounded.

'And in return...' He watched her solemnly, looking every bit the powerful plunderer. 'How may I help you, Ms Marron?'

He only called her that when he was feeling edgy...when he was exerting inner control.

'You know already,' she said, very low.

'You want me.'

'Yes.' She swallowed and pushed through her nerves. 'Teach me. Everything. I know there's nothing afterwards. I don't want any claim on you. Or any relationship. I just want the moment. Now.'

'Why?'

'Why do you think?' She tossed her head and glared up at him, angry with him for making her confess *everything*. 'I've never wanted this with anyone before. I thought I wasn't...*normal*. I want to be normal. Perhaps if I've done it once and liked it then I can like it again...with someone else.'

He suddenly stilled. 'Done what once? I only helped you to orgasm last night.'

'I'm not talking about orgasms.'

His jaw dropped. 'Are you telling me you've never done this...at *all*?'

'I'm a virgin, Giorgos.' She was suddenly burning.

'How...?' he breathed.

'What do you mean, how?'

'You're twenty-three. You're...'

'What?'

His gaze skittered across her body and he hesitated a second. 'Beautiful.'

'You mean buxom. But, you know, the size of my erogenous zones doesn't equate with their ability to actually work.' She felt herself blushing all over. 'I already told you—I don't like to be touched. At least I didn't,' she corrected with a mumble. 'But I liked what *you* did.'

And she wanted to know that she could get everything within her working properly. He could help her with that.

He released her shoulders and stepped back, shoving his hands into his pockets.

'My virginity doesn't matter,' she added quickly, when she saw his expression shut down as he turned away. 'It's just circumstance. Don't make it into something it isn't.'

He whirled back to face her. 'How can you say it doesn't matter?'

'Did *your* first time matter?' She blushed furiously as she asked.

He huffed out a harsh breath. 'My first time was with a woman who was a little older than me and a whole lot more experienced.'

Despite herself, she was diverted. 'How old *were* you?'

A rueful smile quirked his lips. 'You don't want to know. It was scandalous.'

'Oh, I want to know,' she muttered. 'You can't shock me.'

'I think I can,' he laughed. 'I was fifteen—she was twenty-six.'

Kassie didn't know whether to be awed or appalled. 'Were you in love with her?'

'I was incredibly grateful. She was a generous teacher.'

Jealousy smarted. 'You were with her for a while?'

He looked somewhat uncomfortable. 'I was young, brash and hungry. I was with many young women in my late teens.'

Kassie's eyes widened in surprise. 'You were a man whore?'

'I...' He looked startled, but then laughed. 'I guess you could say that.'

'But you never have a girlfriend.'

She frowned. There'd never been a whisper of romance regarding the King in the press. According to the media he just worked hard all the time. But was he still a secret man whore? Well, *duh*. Given his skill, of course he must be. But how could he have a string of lovers and no one know anything about it?

'Occasionally I do. Discreetly.'

'Discreetly?' She stared at him with blatant disbelief. 'You can't help but tease me that way… Every other utterance between us is inappropriate.'

He suddenly laughed. 'Only with you. And only because it bothers you so much.'

So he didn't flirt shamelessly with every woman he met? An odd twinge of relief softened her. 'Do they last long? Do you care for them?'

Could she be one of his girlfriends for just a little while?

'I trust them as far as I'm able to trust anyone.'

She swallowed hard. 'In my experience, that's not very far.' And trust was a different thing from *caring*.

But he didn't reply.

'Why is that?' she prompted him. 'What woman betrayed you?'

He was Europe's most eligible bachelor, but he wasn't known as any kind of 'Playboy Prince'. He was too hardworking, too serious.

'There's no way I can casually date, or meet someone new without the world watching. And I think it takes time and space to build trust,' he said, failing to answer her actual question.

Well, that was fair enough, but he wasn't exactly trying with anyone, was he? And then she understood why. He was all about duty.

'Caring doesn't matter, does it?' she realised. 'Because

you'll settle for some sort of arranged marriage with a princess of some remote European country some time.'

He paused and looked her directly in the eyes. 'Yes.'

She was quiet, processing this flat acceptance of a future so unloving.

He kept looking into her eyes, and suddenly intensity stormed into him. 'Won't it make it awkward in the future if we have an affair now?'

Was he going to agree to her terms?

She tried to suck in some much-needed oxygen. 'Awkward in what way?'

'At family events?'

'*What* family events?' She suddenly giggled. 'I'm barely *family*. I'm not going to come to the palace for Christmas.'

'What *do* you do for Christmas?' He cocked his head.

'I work on the ward.'

'Of course you do.'

'I'm not an angel.'

'No?'

'Of course not. I'm as human as you are.'

'But we both know I'm better than most,' he teased. 'Why else would you be asking me to teach you the delights of carnal desire?'

'Don't tease.'

'Then tell me *why*,' he suddenly snapped. 'Honestly. How do you think this can possibly work? How, in any way, do you not get hurt in this?'

Oh, so he assumed that *she'd* get hurt but not him?

'I know you're not going to hurt me because you *can't* hurt me,' she answered vehemently. 'This is just for now—while I'm staying. Then it ends. You can't keep me strung along for months or years because no one can know. It can't even last weeks because of the risk of being found out—I know that's a risk you won't take. You can't marry me. You can't love me. You're no threat to me long-term. I'm safe from hurt simply because of the truth of our circumstances.'

She already knew this would lead nowhere—other than to a hopefully awesome experience for herself. One she really didn't want to miss out on. Not now she'd had a *glimpse*.

'And you're not going to fall in love with me?'

She refused to rise to his arrogant baiting. 'I'm not going to be with you long enough for that to be possible.'

'You think falling in love is dependent on time? Is there no such thing as love at first sight?'

'Of course not,' she snapped. 'Lust, yes. Love? That takes longer to develop. You just said yourself—it takes time to build trust and caring and all that stuff.'

'I'm *so* glad you're such an expert on this. You've satisfactorily allayed *all* my concerns.'

She flushed. 'Don't be facetious.'

She wasn't going to fall for him. She just wanted to be 'cured'—to feel normal sexual arousal, to have sex. *Good* sex. If she could do it with him, then she could do it with someone else in the future…

But her innards curled with distaste at that thought. And there was the truth: she couldn't regret this happening because if she didn't get that with any other guy then she would at least have experienced it once with *him*. She wouldn't have missed out on that sensation in her life. Because up till now, she'd been sure she would never feel it.

'Don't tell me you didn't try to tempt me into this,' she said softly. 'Don't act like this isn't exactly what you want.' The colour flamed in her cheeks as she called him on it.

If he denied her, when she'd felt his passion, she'd be angry. She wanted to be able to trust her instincts as she discovered her sensuality.

'Okay. I won't lie. I want you. Our chemistry is off the charts. Maybe it's because it's so damn inappropriate.

Mostly it's because you're so bloody beautiful and you set my teeth on edge every time you open your mouth. And, yes, I wanted you to come to me like this. I wanted to provoke you.'

A wave of satisfaction swept over her. 'Then what are you waiting for?'

He stared at her for a second and his eyes widened. 'You think I'm going to tumble you into bed this second?'

'Why not?'

Hadn't she waited all her life already? She'd never wanted a man like this. She'd always run from any possible encounter. Every barrier she could raise, she'd erected. But now? This was her one chance to be normal. To feel again what she'd felt last night.

He laughed delightedly, but then groaned. 'Kassie, you're enough to tempt a man into total madness.'

'Don't laugh at me.'

'I'm not laughing *at* you.' He cupped her face and looked into her eyes. 'All your life you've missed out on the build-up, the anticipation.'

'I don't need to anticipate this any more than I already do.' He didn't get it. 'This is a first for me. I want it to become *normal* for me, the way it is for everyone else.'

He dragged in a breath. 'If you trust me to do this, then trust me enough to do it my way.'

She paused, a curl of anticipation flickering through her. 'Are you being bossy again?'

He lifted a shoulder. 'What did you expect? Leopards can't change their spots, and I've been the boss almost all my life. Give me some leeway. I won't let you down.' He sighed. 'And the very least you can do is have some breakfast. You must be hungry...' His eyes lit with laughter. 'For *food*. Come on.'

He led her out into a small private patio. Her mouth watered as she saw a silver tray laden with pastries and fruit.

'Let's start with this, okay?' he said.

'With what?'

He lifted a finger. 'Touch your finger to mine.'

She pressed the tip of her finger lightly against his.

'Look at me.'

How was it possible for her to sizzle with just this tiny, most innocuous of touches? But it wasn't tiny, and somehow she couldn't tear her gaze from his. The connection, just from touching fingertip to fingertip and looking right into his eyes, was insanely strong.

Desire shook like a quake deep within her. She shivered with longing. 'This is—'

'Intimate,' he said softly. 'This is going to be *very* intimate, Kassie, don't try to tell yourself it isn't.'

She had to resist the sudden urge to pull back.

He saw it and he smiled. 'That's why we're going to take our time and start with the simple sweetness of holding hands.'

Warmth bloomed as his fingers laced through hers.

'I'm not twelve,' she grumbled beneath her breath, and grabbed a pastry with her free hand.

'Thank heavens for that.' He laughed. 'You know to ask for anything you'd like to eat? Swim. Read anything you can find in the library.' He glanced at his watch and frowned. 'Now I have to go—I can't be late to my meeting.' He looked at their entwined hands and then released her. 'We'll have dinner out here tonight.'

'You don't need to romance me. I've already said yes. In fact, I'm the one who asked.'

'I don't need to *romance* you…?' His shoulders shook. 'You just want wham, bam and it's all over?'

'I've never felt desire like normal people—' She broke off and glared at him. 'Why are you laughing *again*?'

'What makes you think this level of desire is *normal*?'

She didn't want to think this was anything more or less than normal. 'This isn't anything special.'

He looked at her seriously. 'One thing I learned from my debauched youth is that perhaps it *should* be special. Especially the first time.'

She shook her head.

'In this moment, Kassie,' he explained with seemingly infinite patience. 'I'm not talking for ever. I'm talking in this moment. We let this be special in this moment. Okay?'

'At least I know you're not going to kiss and tell,' she said with a wry smile. 'I know I can trust you to keep this discreet.'

Giorgos requested his driver go slow, so he could prepare properly for his meeting, but he couldn't get his mind off Kassie. He'd trusted no woman this way in years, never bringing one into his home. He relied on clandestine rendezvous in the private house he kept in the city for that express purpose.

He had no desire to take Kassie there. But Kassie wasn't like other women. Kassie was just... Kassie. And she looked at him with such innocently questioning hunger that he nearly lost his head completely. Rationally, he knew he shouldn't touch her. He should send her away. He could keep her safe far away from his side. But he couldn't resist keeping her close. He was tired of the guilt and obligation he would have for the rest of his life. He wanted to feel better. Helping Kassie made him feel better.

Liar.

He grimaced. She made him feel like a god. Or, more accurately, a selfish, greedy devil. He wanted more than he deserved. But couldn't he have it just this once? For over a decade now he'd been the perfectly behaved Prince, dutifully fulfilling his destiny, maintaining everything as it ought to be maintained... He'd not set a foot across the line of being discreet and controlled.

Until Kassie. Within two minutes of meeting her he'd crossed the line to inappropriate and then full-on outrageous. But it went both ways. Whatever chemistry was between them, it was strong. He shouldn't have agreed to her request, but it felt right to get rid of the attraction between them. And the only way to do that was by sleeping together. Ignoring it would only make it worsen and he'd always wonder *what if?*

He had enough regrets to live with already. And he truly did want to help her—she thought she was damaged, that she wasn't normal, and she wanted to feel things. He wanted that for her too—he wanted nothing more than to see her flushed and screaming with pleasure. And sated. Her honesty and her courage in what she'd asked had floored him.

He tried again to focus on the meeting preparation. He had wanted to prove he could resist his desperate urge to tumble her into bed there and then. Hell, he'd wanted to. But he had to be able to take it or leave it as he chose. And, more importantly, he needed to give her the space and time to change her mind.

If she didn't, then they'd have their moment. He'd take her slowly and savour every second, make sure she was right there with him every step of the way. He was determined to make it the best for her. He almost couldn't cope with the prospect of burying himself deep in her lush, tight body—of showing her just what she was built for. His mouth dried and his muscles bunched.

Ignoring the meeting notes, he sent a message to his secretary, requesting dressing assistance for Kassie—because the bargain had been struck and she'd want to maintain her end of the deal. She had pride—he understood that about her. And he respected her for it.

He didn't return until nightfall, semi-pleased with the

way his day had gone—with his ability to concentrate on the meeting. He *could* keep everything under control with Kassie.

But within two minutes of him getting back to the house trouble hit. She was there. She was beautiful. And she had that teasing, disarming smile on her face as she looked up from where she lounged on his sofa. The sofa where he'd made her scream her release last night.

'How'd it go?' she asked.

For a moment Giorgos didn't know what she meant as she looked at him with warmth and expectation in her gorgeous eyes. Was she asking him about his meeting?

'Fine,' he answered awkwardly.

'They didn't give you a hard time?'

She really wanted to know. No one *ever* asked him how his day had gone. Because usually no one was waiting for him to return home. His sister had always been at the classes he'd arranged for her, and his assistants had been busy fulfilling his requests. He'd always turned his focus to the next meeting, the next event, the next decision.

He rubbed his hair as he realised she was still sitting there, waiting for a reply, her eyebrows slowly lifting.

'A hard time?' He shook his head. 'Not to my face. They wouldn't dare.' He sighed. 'Most of those at the meeting today know to hold their tongue.'

No one had ever loitered, waiting for him to return, to ask him how his day had gone. That Kassie was dong so now touched him. He grimaced at his newfound neediness. If he told her that he liked it she'd probably call him out for being sexist or something—expecting to have a woman waiting for him at home. Truth was he didn't ever expect to have that. He couldn't ask someone for that. But all the same it was nice...just this once.

'Because they're afraid of you?' she asked.

'I hope not. I think they just know it's pointless. We

have work to be getting on with, we can't be wasting time on…that stuff.'

'So you just keep going with the "to do" list?'

'Because the "to do" list is important.'

'So is taking a break—you told me that yourself. Maybe this is a good time to take a break.'

He rather liked the contrary mix of subtle ribbing underpinned by gentle concern. It could be reciprocated.

'How was *your* day?' he asked, but he had to cough away the huskiness. Was he *this* unused to enquiring after someone? How socially inept *was* he in this level of simple intimacy?

'It was good.' Her smile was shy.

Well, that wasn't enough of an answer. 'What did you do?'

'I went for a swim. I raided your library. I watched a movie.' She listed them all off.

It still wasn't enough. He wanted to know whether she'd truly had a nice afternoon. He wished he'd been here to see for himself.

'A movie?' He sat on the sofa arm and tugged off his tie. 'What movies do you like?'

'Action.'

He glanced at her keenly. There'd been a distinct sensual purr to that reply. 'And now you want action of your own?'

'Don't you think you've kept me waiting long enough?' She leaned closer with a confidential whisper, even as that blush swept across her beautiful face. 'I'm ready to progress from the holding hands phase.'

He took her hand in his and felt the jolt of electricity. His entire body stiffened in anticipation. 'Are you, now? What if I'm not?'

'You're the experienced one here—why do you need to prolong this? We don't have all that much time.'

'And you want to make the most of it?'

'Do you blame me?'

She was going to kill him. She was so sweet, so eager, and so damn inexperienced. He released her hand to slide off the elastic tie securing her braid and slowly began to release the sleek twists of her hair.

'Well, then, I should prepare you. We're not going all the way tonight, Kassie.'

Her pout appeared. 'Why not?'

Because that was what he'd decided. For her benefit and to prove his own self-control.

'There are other things to take pleasure in first.' He skimmed his hands down her arms.

Those bewitching deep brown eyes widened farther still, until they dominated her beautiful face.

His gut tightened. 'Let me show you what I mean.'

He'd been longing to do this for days. To kiss every inch of her soft body. If she could put herself entirely into his hands now, then they'd find the ultimate pleasure when he finally claimed her completely.

He tried to take his time, to savour his first full taste of her, knowing that this was her initiation into this deliciously intimate delight. He tried to stay gentle. But the scent and sweet warmth of her, the unguarded, untutored response of her, made it impossible. As he finally peeled her panties to the side he glanced up, catching wariness and embarrassment, but also determination. And trust.

He vowed again, deep within himself, to help her conquer the instinctive resistance that she sought to overcome with soft kisses, firm hands and patience.

'I have you, Kassie,' he murmured as she shivered and squirmed beneath his touch. 'I won't hurt you.' He wanted only to bring her pleasure. Suddenly it seemed to be his most important mission in life. 'You can let me do anything.'

The softest sigh escaped her and those slender, long legs

parted. He tasted the heated acceptance of her body with its slick welcome for his tongue. He kissed her, sucking softly on that small, sensitive bud. She stiffened and he heard her catch back her cry.

'There's no one to hear you but me,' he muttered hungrily. 'Don't hold anything back.'

And then, to his intense satisfaction, she didn't.

'Kassie,' he said softly. 'Look at me.'

Panting, she obeyed, opening her eyes to look straight into his. That feeling was still spreading though her body, honeyed bliss seeping into every cell. Her smile blossomed and a laugh bubbled out of her. The exquisite feelings of lightness and happiness were uncontainable.

He brushed her hair back from her face and his expression softened. 'Not so bad?'

Little aftershocks ricocheted around her body and she knew he felt them. He was holding her loosely. Carefully. Talking gently and ensuring she was centred. For just this moment—just this once—she fully appreciated the strength of his protectiveness.

'What about you?' She paused, realising he hadn't had the same release she had. He was still aroused and unfulfilled. 'Your...partners...they reciprocate in the same way?'

'I don't expect you to.'

That jarred. She didn't want him treating her as anything less or anything more than his other 'companions'. She sat up, realising that the King was on his knees on the floor in front of her. 'What if I want to?'

Something flickered in his eyes and he slowly shook his head.

'Consider this part of the exploration of *my* needs. I'm curious.' She glanced down his body, still hidden in one of those damned perfect suits. 'I want to understand how this works for you too.' She wanted to know how he looked, how he felt, in that ultimately vulnerable moment. She didn't want him to hold that back from her. 'It's only fair.'

'You have a fixation with fairness.'

'I want to explore everything about this attraction. *All* senses.' Suddenly she was angry and embarrassed by his denial. 'I don't want you martyring yourself for me,' she said harshly. 'Making this all about my pleasure only—as if you getting me off somehow makes you a better person. Just because you've helped a poor frigid girl get to orgasm. I want you to *want* me. To have me the way you want to. To have the pleasure that I have. The way you want it.'

He stared at her, colour deepening in his face. 'Kassie…'

'I told you already,' she whispered fiercely. 'I haven't got anything to lose here. I want what I want and how I want it. If you don't want me the same way I want you, then walk away. I'm not going to be your charity case.'

He moved so quickly she sucked in a shocked breath. He savagely strained forward, pushing her back against the sofa, grinding his hips against hers.

'Does *this* feel like I don't want you?'

The rigid length of his erection dug into her stomach. Her toes curled. How was it that it took only this? Only a few words and a simple touch for her to be so aroused when she'd never been turned on before in all her life?

She trembled and gripped his hips as he lifted away from her. She wriggled beneath him, sliding lower until she slipped right off the sofa and was sitting on the floor, while he was up on his knees before her. She heard his muffled swearing and tilted her head so she could see up into his face.

'Teach me,' she said simply. 'What do you want me to do? How can I please you?'

'You only have to look at me like that and you're half-way there.' He looked into her eyes. 'Kiss me,' he muttered rapidly. 'Touch me. I ache for you to touch me.'

She fumbled, butter-fingered, with his belt and zipper. Half-laughing, half-cursing, he helped her until his manhood jutted free. Her jaw dropped at the sight of him—the size. She licked her dried lips.

He groaned harshly. 'Just touch me.'

His skin was flushed and she realised how near to the edge he was. And so she touched him. Gently at first, then with greater pressure as she felt him press against her. With one hand, then two. And then with her tongue.

Could she make such a strong and powerful man tremble? Power sluiced through her veins as she gained knowledge of him. She used her mouth, kissing him hard, sucking and stroking, taking him in as deeply as she possibly could.

'Stop, Kassie.' His fingers tightened painfully on her shoulders and he pulled her away. *'Stop.'*

'Why?' she demanded plaintively, desperately wanting to continue. Because that had felt good to her too. That had felt exciting. 'Did I do it wrong?'

'No.' He shook his head, his breath shuddering.

'But you didn't…'

'Not this first time.'

'I'm not scared. I want to—'

'Kassie.' He hauled her up to sit on the sofa, so he could stare into her eyes. 'I know what you want—and you'll have it. But I have wants too. And I don't want my release until I'm tight inside you. I want to lose myself in you. Right inside you.' He rested his forehead on hers. His gaze was close and searching. 'Kassie?'

'Okay.' Kassie's pulse slowly settled and a poignant longing trickled into the lingering warmth. She wanted that too. She wanted that more than she'd ever wanted anything. 'But why have you stopped?'

'Because I told you before we started that we weren't going all the way tonight. This is enough for now.'

'No, it isn't.' Why on earth would he possibly think that this was *enough*? 'I'm not going to regret this. I want you. I want *this*.'

'Not tonight, Kassie.'

She stood up, a streak of coldness entering her bloodstream. 'You think I'm going to change my mind.'

He too stood, and reached for her wrist, holding her close while keeping her away from him at the same time. 'I'm giving you a chance. One last chance.'

She looked at him seriously. 'I don't need you to protect me in this way.'

'Perhaps I'm protecting myself.'

She shook her head. He wasn't. He was being the King—the decision-maker, the protector. The dominator. But she would forgive him this once, because she wanted what she knew he would give her in the end.

It wasn't easy for him to walk away from her now. His chest rose and fell rapidly as she stepped away from him. His lips twisted, as if he were regretting her obedience. She wanted to tease him for that, in the same way that he'd teased her. The remnants of that languid feeling made her movements relaxed and assured. Confidence in her body soared. In their chemistry.

She suddenly turned back and strolled towards him. He didn't move as she reached up and kissed him the way she'd learned from him—with all her aggression and desire—until she felt his tension snap and he jerked back from her with an audible gasp. The fire in his eyes should have alarmed her. Instead she sent him a soft smile of pure satisfaction.

'Get to your room,' he ordered huskily. 'And lock the damn door.'

'If I don't?' she murmured back. 'Will you tie me to the bed?'

He stepped after her again, gripping her wrists and twisting her arms to pin them tight behind her back, pushing her body hard into his.

He retaliated just as she'd desired—kissing her with complete carnal dominance until she was breathing hard and begging. But he just stood there, his feet planted wide, his hands exerting such control—holding her fast even as he tormented her, reducing her to nothing more than a mass of need and pleasure just by using his mouth.

'Go to bed, Kassie,' he growled, and released her. He strode to the door, opening it and waiting for her to walk through it. 'Go *now*.'

'Why do you have to be so controlling?' she whispered in reproof as she stalked past him. 'You know I'm no threat to you.'

CHAPTER SIX

SHE WAS AN *absolute* threat. He needed to prove to himself that not all his control was gone. But in the smallest hours he lay wide awake. He was fooling himself. He had *zero* control left—and he was reduced to fantasising about how he'd make it the best for her, imagining all different scenarios and tying himself in knots.

What she'd asked of him was so personal, and it was a privilege that he refused to abuse. While it was a delight for him too, this was about *her*. Perhaps he could even think of it as one little redress in the balance of guilt he carried.

Conceited jerk.

He threw back the sheet and stalked to get a fresh glass of water. As if he were doing *her* a favour! This was all for *him*. He wanted her in every way and he'd manipulated her into being here. Into staying. Into asking him to take her virginity. He'd done everything he could to get her in his grasp. Hell, he'd effectively kidnapped her from the hospital. The 'pause' he'd insisted on tonight was nothing more than a lame attempt to ease his conscience over yet another moment of guilt...

But it was buying her some time to ensure she truly wanted this, right? He figured nothing would make that decision clearer for her than being presented with it in the cold light of day. So he'd suffer through the agony of lust through the long, slow night. That was the least penance he could do.

Kassie woke late again, but she didn't feel as rested; she felt hot and niggly. *Needy.* She wanted to confront him and provoke him into finishing what they'd started last night.

She just didn't quite know how. No doubt he'd be working already, anyway, and she'd have to wait through another whole torturous day.

He was high-handed. Arrogant. *Honourable.* Which was utterly annoying. Why did he have to be so protective? Why wouldn't he throw caution to the wind and take this risk? What *was* it that had caused him to have such little trust in people?

Bothered, she got out of bed and picked a strawberry from the breakfast tray that had been delivered to her private lounge. She bit into the fruit and felt her body eagerly absorb the fuel, but those edgy fires still smouldered within her.

She slipped on the simple white bikini she'd borrowed from the collection in the pool room the previous day. It was the only one decent enough to cover her curves. She walked down the cool corridor to the cave that had been incorporated into the building. There she discovered that Giorgos wasn't working. He was swimming lengths in the sheltered end of the crystalline pool. His movements were powerful and strong and, if her eyes weren't deceiving her, he was swimming *naked.*

She leaned back against the wall, her knees absurdly weakened as heat burnished her body. From the tips of her toes to the very top of her head she felt the driving urge to touch.

He slowed, then lifted his head to stare at her.

'You're not working.' She wanted him to swim nearer.

He stayed low in the water. 'I'm trying to keep my cool.'

'Are you angry?'

'Not angry, no.'

'Didn't you sleep well?' she asked innocently.

Intent flashed in his eyes. 'Come into the water with me.'

Anticipation slid over her skin—warm feather strokes

that caused shivers. Because no doubt he meant that literally. But she slowly shook her head, because the truth was she didn't think she could actually stand on her own two feet right now.

'Ah…' He swam to the edge of the pool nearest her. 'If the mountain won't go to Mohammed, then Mohammed must go to the mountain.'

'Are you calling me a mountain?'

'A snow-capped, ice-cold, beautiful mountain. One that hides a volcano two hundred feet down. One with a *very* molten core.'

'Oh, please.' She rolled her eyes.

But that core was already melting, and he chose that moment to lever himself out of the pool onto the edge in a single swift movement. As she'd suspected, he was utterly, gloriously naked. What she hadn't realised was that he was aroused. Hugely, undeniably aroused.

Kassie's jaw dropped as she struggled to breathe. She couldn't speak—couldn't tear her gaze from the pulsing vision of complete masculinity. She'd known he was big, but she hadn't factored in that he'd be as big…*everywhere*… Or that his muscles would be so honed, so deeply defined.

His hard erection jutted, straining high. She'd touched him there—kissed him there—last night. An intense need to do that again rocked her. Here. Now. The wave of sheer lust was so fierce she trembled like a flimsy blossom in a storm.

He stood unashamedly watching her reaction with heat and amusement in his eyes. 'Does the sight of me scare you?'

'I don't think "scare" is the right word,' she croaked.

Lazily he picked up a white towel from the folded stack on a nearby table. 'What *is* the right word?'

'Awe,' she mumbled. 'Shock and awe.'

She watched, leaning limply against the wall as he

wrapped the towel around himself, hiding him from her view.

'Spoilsport,' she whispered.

He didn't stop fastening the towel, but he stepped closer. 'You slept okay?'

She nodded and swallowed. 'And now we have the entire day before us.'

He cupped her cheek. 'No, we don't.'

At the touch of his fingers on her she felt that heat roll over her again. 'Why not?'

He didn't answer. He was too busy looking at her mouth. It was almost as if he wasn't aware of anything else any more. Her lashes lowered lazily—her eyes wanting to focus only on him. He was so magnificent.

And then he kissed her. That fire deep within her fizzed, launching those exquisite sensations into every limb— weakening, warming… She was so willing. And he *knew*.

Suddenly his mouth and his hands were everywhere. He pushed aside the cups of her bikini top so he could nuzzle her breasts. The way he worshipped them made fierce pride blossom. Never had she liked her body the way she did today—now she revelled in it. And as he kissed her breasts one hand delved lower still, skimming beneath her bikini bottoms. She liked this too—arching her hips away from the wall to press into his teasing hand.

He sent her a look of satisfaction before claiming her mouth. She liked that even more. And as he plundered her mouth with his tongue, in teasing, deep licks, he parted her intimately, stroking her slick seam before slowly sliding a finger inside. She gasped, tensing, but he kept rubbing back and forth across her sensitive nub with his thumb and she shivered as that delicious, foreign feeling strained her control.

'That's it,' he muttered in between those crushingly passionate kisses as she moaned and began to rock against him. 'You're so hot.'

He worked in and out, sliding faster and faster, deeper. Her hips bucked as she became accustomed to riding him. As she became enraptured. She was so hot, so spellbound by the sensations he stirred, she was almost rendered catatonic as he'd once teased her she would be.

Her eyes closed and she helplessly—brazenly—moaned every time he pressed closer, as the towel around him gently abraded the ultra-sensitive skin of her upper thighs. The pressure of his body was unbearably good. She wanted to slither to the floor and feel all of his weight above her, all of him within her. But it was too late. She was shuddering—screaming—as he shot her to the stars.

'How many times are you going to make me lose control like this before you give me what I want?' she groaned breathlessly, her eyes still closed.

'Dozens,' he admitted, pulling her so she rested against his broad chest. 'Dozens and dozens.' He gently rubbed circles on her back. 'It's something you should enjoy every day. You're getting used to feeling that hot need. You're not resisting the sensations any more—you're embracing them. You're less afraid.'

'I'm not afraid at all.' Not with him.

Her limbs tingled. That rush of pleasure had only made her more determined than ever.

'Then you're nearly ready.'

'I'm ready now.'

'Then the anticipation will make it even better.' He stepped back.

She hadn't realised that she could still feel frustration despite just having had the pleasure of orgasm. She was so close to experiencing it all and she wanted it now.

'But—'

'I have found a suitable event for you to accompany me to,' he interrupted.

'An event?' she muttered, aghast. 'Today?'

How could she *possibly* pull herself together enough to appear in public after that shattering experience?

Amusement warmed his expression. 'A personal grooming assistant is arriving shortly. She'll have a selection of outfits for you and she can style your hair and make-up. You'll get the Cinderella treatment you missed out on.'

Personal grooming? Rebellion rose. She hadn't meant it when she'd said she wanted a new wardrobe—she'd just wanted to disagree with him. And, from the teasing gleam in his eye now, he knew it.

'Of course you *could* wear your hospital uniform, or those worn jeans you had on yesterday.' He shrugged. 'But the world will be judging. There'll be an article in the press analysing every item you're wearing with designer and price details attached.'

'They won't be interested in what I'm wearing. I'm only Damon's half-sister.'

'They're interested in any woman within five feet of my vicinity,' he said, displaying his innate supreme arrogance.

She rolled her eyes. 'Because really they're mostly interested in you?'

'Truthfully? I think you'll find there is a strong fascination with you.'

She frowned and shook her head, but he cupped her cheek, stilling her.

'It's human nature to admire uncommonly beautiful things, Kassie. We can't help ourselves. You know you draw attention from both men and women, young and old alike. It doesn't matter whether you're wearing a sack or a G-string—they're still going to stare.'

He thought she was uncommonly beautiful? A tiny spark

glowed inside her—because from him that was nice. But *only* from him. Not from the rest of the world.

'They'll see me as a sex object,' she muttered. 'Because of my shape.' They'd done that to her mother.

'Everyone does that to you initially, don't they?' he muttered. 'That's why you work so hard to prove that there's more to you. Even when you shouldn't have to prove it. Even when they should just know.'

His astuteness surprised and pleased her—but then she realised he understood because he was the same.

'You do that too,' she said slowly. 'You work hard to prove yourself as King. All the time.'

But when he was alone, unhindered by all the world watching him, there was another element visible to her. He had something caged within him that he wouldn't let the rest of the world see.

'I have far more to prove—for far more nefarious reasons than being good-looking.' He waggled his brows at hers.

'*Ridiculously* good-looking,' she amended with a gurgling laugh as she realised that something of what he kept locked away in public was his sense of humour.

'They see me as a sex object because of my birth—my title, money, power.'

'They'd see you as a sex object *without* the title, money or power,' she corrected him dryly. 'It's your face and your physique. Muscles cause brain meltdowns, you understand.'

'Because we can't help but admire beautiful things,' he reiterated with a chuckle. 'I ignore it. You can ignore it too.'

'Yet you want me to dress up for them?'

'I want you to be comfortable. That doesn't have to mean a designer dress and layers of make-up if you don't want it to. Do what you wish,' he said dismissively.

For half a moment she felt like wearing something completely outrageous—just to shock him and the rest of the world.

'In the end it makes no difference to me,' he added wickedly. 'You'll still end up naked in my bed tonight.'

She stared at him—stunned. 'It makes a *huge* difference to you. You're *all* about appearances. You're the one who cares about that too much—not me.'

'You think?'

'I *know*. Everything is just so. Everything is perfect and proper and done the way it's been done for decades.'

'Not everything is proper. And everything is definitely *not* perfect.'

'No?' She dared him to explain. 'What *is* it you think you have to prove? What *are* those nefarious reasons?'

That roguish glint in his eyes sparked. 'Too terrible to talk about.'

'I don't believe you,' she said softly.

'Why not?' His amusement faded. 'When have I lied to you?'

She waited him out.

'Too terrible,' he repeated quietly, with no teasing in his eyes at all now. 'Don't ask again.'

'So you're going to leave me hanging just because you want your moment of mystery? You don't need to catch me on a hook and reel me in, or play some kind of obscure pity card. I'm already going to leap into your bed the second you finally crook your little finger.'

She shocked a low laugh out of him. 'You're saying I can *trust* you?'

'Why would you think you couldn't?' She was stupidly wounded by his laugh. 'I'm going to let you inside me.'

'I don't trust *anyone*,' he said quietly. 'Don't take it personally. I didn't even trust my own sister's judgement. Now she's left with Damon. I've pushed her away.'

'No, you haven't. She knows you love her. And she loves *you*—that's why she was worried about letting you down.

You've proved you're trying to trust her now by letting her go,' she said softly. 'So why can't you try with me too?'

'That isn't what it is between us.'

'So it's okay for you to help *me* with something, but you won't let me do the same for you?'

'What makes you think *you* can help?'

She flinched as his riposte dumped her right back into *her place*. Who did she think she was? 'Of course. Silly me. I can't.'

'Kassie.' He sighed. 'Doing this with you is a sign of trust for me. But just because we're physically intimate it doesn't mean I have to open up all my past agonies to you.'

So there *were* past agonies. She'd somehow known that. 'Sometimes just talking something through can help,' she said softly.

'There's no point.'

'You prefer to keep working through your never-ending "to do" list?'

'That's right.'

'And "Take Kassie's virginity" is just another item on that list?'

'Yes.' He squared his shoulders. 'You offered me a deal, Kassie. It's time to make good on it. You need to go and get dressed before we attend the unveiling of a local sculpture. You have two hours before your presentation to the world as the newest adjunct to the Palisades royal family.'

'The *pity* relation, you mean.'

He glanced at the watch on his wrist. 'I'll meet you in my library in ten minutes and introduce you to the stylist.'

She fled, desperate for a cold shower. Then she quickly tugged on jeans and a tee and prepared to swallow all her pride and embarrassment about using the services of a *personal grooming assistant*. She'd spent all her life dressing to disappear into the background, to avoid the eyes of men. But this time... She wanted *him* to notice.

The assistant was waiting with Giorgos when Kassie entered the room fifteen minutes after she'd left him at the pool.

'Meet Thea,' he said, his remoteness fully restored. 'She'll help with your hair, make-up, clothing—'

'I hope you're quite the magician.' Kassie forced a smile, battling her shock at the impassivity Giorgos could summon so effectively. 'I'd love you to help—especially with my hair. It's so thick I—'

'It doesn't need cutting,' Giorgos interrupted roughly.

'Okay, well…' Kassie bit the inside of her cheek, refusing to blush. 'Perhaps Thea and I should go and make our plans somewhere we won't be a bother to you.'

Giorgos glared at her. She met his hard gaze defiantly. As if she'd let him dictate about something so personal! Wordlessly, they clashed for two seconds too long. Then he nodded curtly and turned back to the papers on his desk.

Kassie gritted her teeth, barely restraining a growl at his mute dismissal. The guy was unbearably arrogant.

'I'll show you the way, Ms Marron,' Thea said smoothly.

Kassie jumped. She'd almost forgotten the woman was actually there. But if the stylist was at all curious about Kassie she hid it well. Her assessing gaze held nothing but professional interest as she led her to another guest suite, in which an assortment of luggage and garment bags were waiting.

'I've brought a selection of clothing in a variety of sizes. I wasn't sure… You're not as tall as the Princess.'

'No.' *Not as willowy. Not blonde.* 'Much shorter. Rounder in places.' Kassie couldn't stop mumbling.

'Yes.' The woman nodded. 'And I know exactly how we'll emphasise those assets.'

Panic hit. Kassie had deliberately never emphasised anything. But she remembered the teasing in Giorgos's eyes and her determination to surprise him roared back. Thoughtfully she studied the stylist herself—she was beautifully attired, completely professional… This woman wasn't going to let Kassie out in public looking anything less than 'perfectly appropriate'. Her career depended on it.

So she relaxed and surveyed the garment bags with interest. 'What do you suggest?'

Two hours later, feeling well versed in the art of smiling while saying little, Kassie strolled along the corridor to Giorgos's room.

Just outside the door she felt her heart begin to thump, but she pushed on and walked in anyway. He wasn't seated at the desk but was standing looking out of the window pensively.

'Giorgos?'

He turned. Her breathing stalled—not in anticipation of his reaction, but because of her own impossibly powerful response to the sight of him. He wore another suit, so sharp her eyes watered. Tall, lean and purely predatory, he regarded her silently. For a half-second she was tempted to turn and run. But the fire in his gaze froze her in place.

'Ms Marron.' Slowly he walked towards her. 'You look…'

She waited, but he didn't finish.

Heated amusement—*satisfaction*—trickled through her. 'I've rendered you speechless.'

'Mmm-hmm.'

He stopped right in front of her. Too close for her to remain cool or rational or breathing.

'You're not good at talking at the best of times,' she whispered.

'I talk.'

'Niceties and nothingness—with barriers up all the time that you don't let people past.'

'Are we on *this* again? What do you want to know everything for?' he answered equally softly. 'You're a physiotherapist, not a psychiatrist. And I am *not* one of your patients.'

Fair enough, she supposed. 'You want intimacy without intimacy?'

'I just want *you*,' he muttered bluntly.

Her heart beat heat throughout her body until she was melting. She breathed slowly, welcoming the delicious feeling he brought to life within her.

I just want you.

In the end, what did it matter if that was all there was? Because there was only *now*.

'Message received.' She smiled at him. 'And ditto.'

His face lit up. 'Twirl for me.'

'Pardon?' She paused, eyebrows raised.

'I've paid for the make-over—I want to appreciate the full result.'

The urge to defy him bit, but she kept her eyes on him. And kept her cool. Because a snap back was what he wanted. She didn't know why he'd decided to bait her, but the hunger in his eyes was unmistakable. So was the edgy awareness. Was he testing her? She realised that perhaps this might be more uncomfortable for him than for her. Perhaps she too could play with provocation.

So she forced back her embarrassment and bent her head oh-so-meekly. 'Certainly, King Giorgos,' she acquiesced breathily as she turned slowly. 'She buffed my skin,' she added in a soft whisper over her shoulder. 'All over. So I've not a hair out of place. I guess I'm polished enough for you to be seen with now.'

'Vixen,' he accused huskily. 'You enjoyed it.'

She shrugged and studied her highly polished fingernails. 'I've had harder mornings.'

'And you're enjoying my reaction to the result.' He cocked his head, a rueful light entering his eyes. 'Everyone will look—are you sure you want their eyes on you?'

'They'll look anyway eventually—when I come out of hiding. At least if I'm with you they'll keep their distance.'

'There might be speculation, but I believe I can offset that.'

Her pulse raced too quickly at his appraisal. 'Speculation about what?'

That smile returned—the rare, all too wicked one, full of carnal intent. The one that made all her senses dizzy.

'How do you offset it?' she asked unsteadily.

'I play up the protective angle. Apparently I'm good at that.'

'*Too* good,' she answered tartly. 'And *I* don't get to offset it at all?'

'I won't let them come after you,' he muttered, almost as if he were convincing himself.

'Of *course* they'll come after me—at least for a bit,' she scoffed. 'The dress doesn't matter. I'm not from the right side of the tracks or the right layer of society... They'll talk about my mother—'

'What will they say about her?'

She paused. 'That she was John Gale's mistress for twenty years. A shameless temptress who never truly succeeded in stealing the man she wanted.'

'Why did she wait for him for so long?'

'Because she was weak.' Kassie shrugged sadly. 'You should have seen her when he told her he was coming for one of his visits. She'd dance around, she'd dress up... And then he'd come, and he'd swing me around for a moment, and then they'd disappear to her room.' She frowned, remembering the loneliness that she'd felt then. 'There was no real relationship between them. No romance. There was him turning up to take her to bed and then her bottoming out when he left again.'

Her mother's mood swings had been wretched. But then

she'd rally and they'd go on happily together—until her father called again.

'She always waited, believing in him, never moving forward. She always welcomed him back despite that disappointment time and time again.' She'd never understood why.

'You're angry with her?'

'Because she didn't fight for what she wanted. Because when she got sick she didn't fight that either.' She had been so passive, accepting so little. Kassie was never going to do that.

'So are you going to fight for what *you* want?'

'Don't I already?' She lifted her head. 'Aren't I doing exactly that now? I know what I want—from my job, from you and from this one performance in front of the world now. This is on *my* terms, Giorgos.'

'Good for you,' he said, glancing away from her. 'Hopefully they won't delve all that deeply into your background. It's not uncommon to be illegitimate now. Or to have been raised by a solo parent. That stigma has eased.'

Maybe for normal people—but Eleni and Giorgos weren't anywhere near normal…they were royalty.

'Yet times haven't changed enough for our King to consort with a commoner?' She smiled at him sweetly. 'He still has to find himself a princess.'

'Some things just can't be changed.' He shrugged.

'And you don't *want* to change them,' she challenged softly. 'You've kept everything the same since your father died. So full of tradition you hardly consider your future.'

'Because it is important to honour our forefathers,' he said, stiffening.

She paused, realising she'd touched a wound. 'You must have loved him very much.'

'I only wish I had told him so when he was alive.'

'How old—?'

'Seventeen. I was seventeen when he died.' He pre-empted her question sharply. 'Seventeen and stupid.' He turned away from her. 'We need to leave.'

Giorgos hadn't made such a massive mistake in a long, long time. Allowing himself to get side-tracked by something personal… Allowing himself to think he could have a moment of fun alongside the execution of his duty… What had he been *thinking*?

He hadn't, of course.

Bringing her with him had been total madness, because he couldn't concentrate for looking at her. In that simple white dress, with its perfectly demure neck and hemline, she was the epitome of sensuality. No gilded artifice required. Her hair had been left loose—it hung in a glorious, glossy swathe down her back—and her make-up appeared minimal. Her lips were not coloured, but their natural rose-pink had been intensified somehow, and her skin was flawless and glowing.

All he wanted to do was kiss her. He shouldn't think about the traditional significance of the colour of her dress, but he was too sharply aware of her innocence and inexperience…her sweetly sultry desire for his touch. The primal pleasure he got from knowing it was only he who'd touched her—who had aroused that begging, writhing wanton—set his teeth on edge.

He ached to return to the Summer House so he could slowly strip her bare. He'd waited long enough. Teased her enough. She was ready and he was too far gone to care about the risk any more. He just wanted her. *Now.*

Thank heavens he'd retained enough nous to ensure that this public appearance would be a brief one—a quick stop to unveil a new sculpture in the garden of a nearby gallery. He'd say a few words, drop the curtain on the marble, smile and leave. She'd be on show for thirty minutes or less, if he could manage it. He just had to manage his own mind. His own emotions. His own damn body.

He was utterly, painfully conscious of her walking beside him into the gallery's garden. She was staggeringly beautiful. He saw eyes widening and jaws dropping as they passed the gathered guests. There were more people lining the street than usual. Of course there were—they wanted to see how things stood since Eleni's marriage announcement. The curiosity in the crowd flared—murmurs, questioning tones lifted as they stared in fascination at the exquisite woman accompanying him.

He shouldn't have brought her. He shouldn't have used her in this way. He should have kept her hidden. *His.*

She was silent as she walked. Shy. His hand itched. He longed to take her hand in his—to shield her from the intense interest of the invited dignitaries and members of the public. But he couldn't—he'd embarked on this selfish plan and it was too late to turn back. He was careful not to touch her, hardly to look at her. Not to give the wrong impression or let anyone suspect how desperately he wanted to declare his possession of her.

The urge to reach out for her was so intense it sent him off balance. Distracted, he could hardly focus on the short speech he'd prepared. He couldn't stall them the way he'd intended to. His mind blanked—because all he could think of was her. In the end he was forced to admit the discomfort of this situation as he introduced her to the waiting media and the world.

'Ms Marron needed some space away from the scrutiny of the press currently camped outside her home,' he announced through gritted teeth, making them aware of his displeasure at her treatment. 'That is why she is my guest for a couple of days. She's a private citizen and must not be hounded. Naturally she is delighted for her brother and Princess Eleni, but I insist that you respect her privacy.

We welcome *all* of Damon's relatives into our family. Any questions must be directed to me.'

'Where's Prince Xander?' a reporter queried.

'Prince Xander has returned home.' Giorgos fought to keep his message on track. 'He is a gentleman, and I must stress that all blame for Eleni's earlier heartache lies squarely at my feet. However, she has forgiven me, and we now move forward together as a family.'

Eleni hadn't wanted him to be labelled a bully. But he knew he deserved the discomfort of this grilling—and that he shouldn't have dragged Kassie into it. He was acutely aware of her standing beside him now, quiet and beautiful, and he just knew she was expecting him to deliver. He damn well would.

'Where is the Princess now?' another reporter asked. 'When will we meet Damon?'

'Princess Eleni and Mr Gale have gone away for the privacy they need at this special time. I may not always show it, but I do understand that they are in love.'

Something rough tickled his throat and it tightened, making speaking even harder. He glanced briefly at Kassie and caught her beautiful, genuine smile at him. He forced his eyes front again, an unnamed emotion firing through his blood.

'Rightly or wrongly, I have always tried to protect my sister and I am very pleased she has found happiness. It is...' He cleared his throat awkwardly, wishing like hell he'd cancelled this appearance, because this was one truth he was suddenly compelled to admit to the world and it was *hard*. 'It is all I have ever wanted for her.'

Kassie dragged her gaze from Giorgos and looked over the crowd in front of them. For a moment there was complete silence, and then a wave of audible support spread—culminating in a huge cheer. This close, Kassie could hear the individual murmurings of the shiny-eyed, smiling women.

'*He's so handsome...*'

'*He's so protective of Eleni...*'

'*What a brother...*'

For the first time that she could ever recall he'd come across as all 'Giorgos' and not pure 'King'—a hurt, caring man, not a dignified, remote figurehead. And she was just as touched as everyone else present.

She quickly glanced down, hoping to hide her burgeoning emotions and the deepening fascination she had in him.

A few moments later he unveiled the sculpture to more applause. The rest of the visit passed in a blur of smiling faces and respectful distance. But she was conscious of intense scrutiny. So many people were watching her, listening, *judging*. But she didn't care what they thought of her—she just wanted to ensure their support of their King.

She didn't want to let him down, so she quietly expressed her gratitude to both King Giorgos and Princess Eleni whenever she was asked for a comment. And then it was all over. One of Giorgos's assistants escorted her to the car. Then Giorgos himself settled in beside her. There was no word from him, no shared look or laugh, and certainly no touch. Fine by her. Their intimacy was her secret to treasure. Her choice.

But even as they drove away from the crowds his distance didn't lessen. If anything, he seemed to become more remote. He sat silent, unsmiling and stiff, staring out of the window away from her. She couldn't think why his frown had returned when everyone there had looked happy. She'd heard the bubbling chatter of approval after he'd spoken and the rising inflections of excitement and support. How could he not be pleased?

She didn't dare speak while the driver might hear them,

but she couldn't resist watching him, looking so *correct* and so regal in his fine suit. So on edge.

Only once they were safe inside the gates of the Summer House did he turn his head and catch her staring—but still he said nothing.

Her heart pounded—had he changed his mind? Didn't he want to do this with her any more?

Kassie walked ahead of him into the building, marching straight to the private lounge he liked. Once there, she turned to him, determined to breach the defences he'd put up. 'You won them over. Completely.'

He shrugged off his jacket and undid his tie with rough gestures that revealed his irritation. 'I talked too much.'

'No, you didn't.' She was surprised he'd think that—he hadn't said all that much at all. And what he *had* said had been lovely. 'You were honest with them.'

Her heart stopped as she realised how emotional he actually was at this moment.

'Do you feel vulnerable?' she ventured softly.

He stared at her moodily and didn't respond. That silence, that look, told her the answer.

'Everyone does sometimes,' she said. 'Feel vulnerable, that is.'

'I am the *King*.' He paced away from her with leashed strides. 'I'm not supposed to be…'

'You're still allowed to be human. What's wrong with coming into this century and showing some emotion? It makes you relatable.'

'I don't need to be *relatable*,' he snapped. 'I just need to do my duty.'

He truly thought that was all he was meant to do? That upholding the crown was all he *could* do?

'What happened to work-life balance?'

'There is no difference between the two. My work *is* my life.'

'Why be such a martyr, Giorgos? What sins are you paying for?' She now understood that he really did carry some terrible burden of guilt.

'Back off, Kassie.' He looked lethally angry as he suddenly stalked towards her. 'You don't get to pry.' He reached out and grabbed her. 'What you get is *this*.'

CHAPTER SEVEN

HIS KISS WAS a merciless exposition of unleashed passion. Forcefully he swept her into his arms. Thrills flickered along her veins as she braced herself to withstand his ruthless onslaught and tried to kiss him back. He pulled her closer, bending her back until she was on the very tips of her toes, utterly at his mercy. And she loved it. Electrified, energised, she moaned at this intoxicating bombardment of pure pleasure to her body—and her soul.

With a curse he suddenly pulled back, releasing her and rubbing his hand over his face as he visibly tried to recover his self-control. She didn't want him to—she'd adored the desperate way he'd devoured her, as if he couldn't kiss her enough to satisfy his need. Not ever enough. Which was exactly how she was feeling. The deepest longing had been unlocked within her and she couldn't stand to have it denied now.

'Why are you stopping?' Dazed, she clutched at his shirt so he couldn't stride away from her.

'I'm too rough…' he groaned, but his hands automatically shaped her hips again, as if he were losing his inner battle for control. 'I'm sorry I snapped.'

She liked his emotion—his passion. It meant he was feeling something—the same way she was. *Feeling*, she'd decided, was a good thing.

She shook her head. 'Not too rough.'

'You're not used to a man's touch,' he said huskily. 'There were moments last night and this morning when I might have… I don't want to hurt you.'

'I liked it. *All* of it. I want more,' she said with ferocity, every last inhibition burned away by that kiss. 'I know it might hurt a little...' She huffed out a heated breath. 'I'm certain it'll be worth it.'

His breath whistled through his clenched teeth and his eyes locked with hers. Satisfaction and anticipation drummed louder and louder within her as she read that desire—that decision—within his blazing gaze.

He extended his hand and she laced her fingers through his. Together they walked across the smooth wooden floor to her bedroom.

It was mid-afternoon, so there was no dark night to hide behind. The window overlooked the blue waters stretching to the far horizon. Nothing broke that blue view of sea and sky. The room was light and fresh and utterly dominated by the wide bed.

Heat burgeoned inside her. She ached to lie on it with him, to feel him entwined with her, to feel his weight...

He stopped in the centre of the room and she stood before him. Again their gazes met and melded, the wordless communication heralding the intense connection that she knew they both craved. Slowly he moved, finding the hidden zip of her pretty dress. She held still, held her breath as he released the zipper and pushed the soft linen from her body, leaving her clad in only her underwear.

He unbuttoned his shirt, swiftly discarding it. He reached into his trouser pocket and pulled out a handful of small foil packages and cast them across that ready bed. Then he scuffed off his shoes, removed his socks and trousers, and finally allowed her the satisfaction of seeing him the way he could now see her—almost bared. And so intimate.

Her mouth watered and her lips tingled with the need to kiss every inch of the skin she could now see. Her fingers trembled, itchy with the desire to coast over his body—to caress and test the muscles that were so sharply defined. She saw his abs ripple as he flinched at her involuntary mumble as she feasted on the sight of his strained black boxers. A hot feeling pooled at the apex of her thighs. She wanted everything. And she wanted it now. But she was too tense with anticipation even to move.

He stepped forward and kissed her and her paralysis ended. She skimmed her hands over him, suddenly bold and hungry. He walked her backwards until her knees hit the bed. Trusting him implicitly, she let herself fall and he came with her, their limbs tangling in a frantic mass of desire. Her need to touch and kiss and lave was uncontrollable.

Inexorably, however, he caught her close and stilled her with the most carnal kiss of her life. He released the catch of her bra, his expression hot as he peeled the silk and lace from her burning skin. She'd never felt as aroused, nor seen anything as erotic as the look on his face as he tugged her white panties down her hips and revealed her sex to his seeking tongue.

She arched up instinctively at the first sweep. He growled in primal satisfaction as he tasted her readiness and her heat. Gripping her undulating hips with one hand, he held her where he needed to so he could continue that intense torment. As she writhed in hunger he fed her—one finger, then two, pumping her, priming her for his full possession. Fastening his lips to her, he feasted, flicking his tongue until she screamed with incoherent bliss. And as the ripples of her orgasm ebbed he kept his fingers plumbed deep, looking down at her ravenously.

He wasn't satisfied yet. And nor was she.

He released his thoroughly intimate hold on her and reached for protection. In seconds he'd stripped off his underpants and rolled a sheath down over his straining, massive erection. Her heart thundered. He was so huge, so stiff. She wasn't sure she could take him...

But she *wanted* to. She couldn't hold still for the wanting. His eyes on hers, he gripped her restless hips with both hands. Then he bent his head low again. Another luscious lick of his tongue spiked her pulse even more. She knew he was preparing her, but she couldn't wait any more.

'Giorgos...' Her wanton craving was audible.

He stilled, then moved up her body to brace himself above her. So close. She stared up at him, so intensely longing. So trusting.

He held fast, rigid above her. 'There's no going back.'

She didn't answer—didn't want him to give her yet another chance to change her mind. She ran her hand through his silky hair and pressed, drawing him down so she could kiss him the way he'd taught her. Elation soared as he gave her his tongue. But he still held that most masculine part of him an inch away from where she was burning with heat and want.

So as she kissed him—as she welcomed the teasing plunge of his tongue into her hungry mouth—she arched up, rubbing that desperately aching part of her against him. She moaned as she moved, discovering just how much she liked rubbing against him like this. And at last he moved— only the slightest push of his hips to press the thick head of his manhood against her slick sex, sliding between her folds only an inch before slipping back.

Her breath stilled as she assimilated the sensations and again he pressed. And then again. Gentle, shallow pulses that started to drive her wild. Suddenly she was swamped in the hunger for more—for *all*.

'Giorgos...' she breathed in pure mindless desperation. 'Please. Oh, please. *Please*.'

His sudden fierce thrust breached that thin barrier, plunging him deep into her narrow channel. She cried out at the enormous pressure that gave her both physical fullness yet also intense relief. He was *there*.

'Kassie?' He gazed deeply into her eyes, searching, questioning, wanting.

It was so much more than she'd imagined it would be. *He* was so much more.

'You're hurting?' he asked hoarsely.

'No... Yes...' she whispered honestly, and drew in a shuddering breath. 'No... It's just...'

He kissed her—a sweet, hot kiss—so that for a moment she was too stunned to be able to answer. But then she softened, relaxing into him, her body gradually accepting the possession of his.

And it was so good. She moaned as he began to move, spectacularly slowly. Giving her time to adjust to more... and then more. And then she moved too—experimentally mimicking that delicious rocking of his, interleaving their most sensitive places...

His hands swept over her, skilfully seeking other spots to tease, to treasure. He made love to her mouth, then her neck, then arched above her to tug with divine torture at her breasts while ploughing deep into her womb.

She gasped. That initial shock had now faded, leaving rapture to rise in the driving exertion of his body over hers. He was around her, over her, in her, and he left no part of her untouched. She moaned again as the physical was transcended and white-hot emotions bubbled as he worked her harder. She swept her hands over his chest and then gripped his shoulders, instinctively curling her leg around him to hold him close, urging him.

He met the unspoken desire—the challenge—and took her harder, higher. She panted as the sensations began to spiral, her breathless groans stoking his speed and attention until she cried out in complete orgasmic agony. And then, as waves of ecstasy rained through her body, he released his own—thrusting with unrestrained, unrelenting might before powerfully straining as hard and as deep as he could, spilling his seed into her greedy, clenching heat.

Long moments later he levered himself up from where

he was slumped over her to kiss her—a lazy, intimate, generous kiss that somehow bolstered her. She'd been torn apart, and now his luscious, long kiss put her back together. She was reformed. Different. Better.

She sighed with utter contentment as he rolled to his side and then pulled her to rest against him. She felt as if she was floating. 'I had no idea,' she whispered in wonder. 'I just had no idea.'

His answering smile was the most beautiful thing she'd ever seen. She smiled back, wide-eyed, as the aftermath of such intensity fired adrenalin around her body. She couldn't believe what had happened. Couldn't believe how powerful the feeling had been. Couldn't believe her heart would ever settle again.

He suddenly moved, standing up from the bed to turn and scoop her into his arms. He carried her to the bathroom, flicking the lever so water flowed from the multiple jets in the shower. She trembled as he set her on her feet. She was so keyed up by what had taken place. By what she'd felt. By the need to feel it again—to make sure it hadn't been a dream or a fluke... She needed—

'Breathe,' he said softly, placing his hand on her chest and feeling the frantic beat of her heart. 'Just breathe.'

He carefully lathered her body, massaging her all over with annoying gentleness, but there was a wicked smile lurking in his eyes when he caught her gasps and he took extra time to wash her breasts and down her belly.

She put her hand on his wrist as he was about to step away. 'I want to do it again,' she whispered boldly, her heart still beating that frantic tattoo.

'I know.' He wrapped her in one of the luxurious bathrobes and picked her up again.

'I am capable of walking.' She felt embarrassed, but at the same time she loved the care he showed.

'I like holding you,' he answered bluntly. He paused for

a second in the room, and then placed her on the sofa instead of the bed. 'Wait here a minute.'

She wondered what the problem was, but then she saw the bloodstain on the sheet and felt her blush burn. But there was an odd sort of pleasure too—that there was a mark of what had happened. That it had been no dream. It had been earthy and raw and *real*.

'I'll take care of it.' His voice was a little hoarse.

He left the room for a few moments, before returning with a pile of folded linen in his arms. In two seconds he'd bundled the soiled sheets and wafted a fresh sheet over the big bed. She walked over to help him.

'Uh-uh.' He shook his head. 'You'll mess up my corners.'

So she stood back, her arms folded as she watched him work. 'I'm impressed.'

'You thought I was too spoiled to know how to make a bed, didn't you?' he jeered at her. 'I wasn't about to order my staff to come and freshen the place. I'm not *that* much of an ass. I'm—'

'Considerate. Tender. Tough—in a good way,' she interrupted with a smile. 'And you really *do* know how to make a bed.'

'When I was first crowned I realised I wasn't anywhere near ready to take it on and I needed some discipline and order to my day. So I trained with my soldiers. And I make my own bed. Every. Day.'

'Impressive.' She chuckled at his self-mocking smile.

'But I'm not disciplined at *all* now.' He tugged her back down to the bed.

It was true, he realised. He no longer gave a damn about anything in the world other than pleasing Kassie. Sex was always enjoyable, but what he'd just experienced with her had been something else again. The honesty of her response... The unfettered enjoyment... He'd worked so hard to pull that from her. Pleasuring her had mattered to him in a way it had never mattered before.

He was always a considerate lover, and liked to ensure his partner's satisfaction, but he'd wanted the next level for Kassie. She deserved that—so sweet, so lonely. She'd been trembling like a leaf in the shower just now, and a huge wave of tenderness had risen within him. And her flush when they'd returned to the bedroom and seen that rumpled bed...

The most appalling Neanderthal satisfaction rippled through him at being her first—her only—lover. And he was going to do it again. And again. And he was determined to make it even better for her every time. He cared deeply about her experience. And realising that made his muscles tense.

'You're the most disciplined person I've ever met.' Her mouth formed the tiniest, most feline smile.

Another feeling rushed in—all intensity as he registered her blossoming confidence. That smile—that mouth of hers—was going to be the death of him.

He grabbed her hips and hauled her close, wanting to drown in the sensations she aroused within him and not analyse them any more. He kissed her, drawing in her sweet enthusiasm as she wriggled beneath him. His heart thundered as he touched her—she was so warm, so generous, so gentle.

'I don't want to have to do it any more,' he confessed in the intense relief of holding her.

'Do what?'

Resentment—rebellion—burned within him. What he *wanted* would always come second to what was *required*. That was the price he would always pay. 'Pretend to be so bloody perfect.'

'You don't *pretend*.' She frowned up at him. 'In what way are you *not* perfect?' She mocked him with that bewitching smile. 'You're handsome. Intelligent. And you've introduced me to the most magical experience ever. I'm working very hard not to fall for you, my King.'

He stiffened at her admission—even though he knew she was teasing, just to make him smile. But she didn't know the truth of him. Not the raw, ugly facts. Suddenly he wanted her to—so she no longer saw him as a poster boy for the monarchy. He wanted her to understand the poison of his past. And then—selfish, greedy bastard that he was—he wanted her to still want him. He wanted her to look at him with those desire-drenched eyes even when she knew how false he really was.

It felt like a betrayal for her not to know the truth when she had been so honest—so genuine and generous—with him.

'Your original opinion of me was an accurate one, Kassie,' he said, his throat tightening as he rolled to his side to face her. 'You saw straight through me to the truth.'

She stilled at the solemnity in his tone. 'I was defensive and on the attack and I judged you without thinking it through,' she said softly. 'But your mother died in childbirth... No wonder you were worried about Eleni. And Damon's father abandoned his lover in her hour of need... I can understand why you're wary of him.'

'Those things are true—and relevant to a point. But they're not the reason I've wanted to protect her too much for too long.'

'No?' Her eyes deepened. 'Then what's the reason?'

He glowered at her. He didn't deserve her adoration. And the toxic baggage he'd been shouldering alone for years would wipe it out. She wouldn't like him anywhere near as much once she knew. And that could only be a *good* thing. She might have claimed from the outset that she wouldn't get hurt, but hormones would come into play. The gentle warmth in her eyes when she looked at him told him she was too soft towards him already. The truth would burn back any building tenderness she felt for him.

He could only hope the desire would still remain.

'In my teens, I was even more arrogant that I am now.' He laughed, mocking himself. 'Of *course* I was. I could have almost any woman I wanted. It went to my head. Young, sexually adventurous… I didn't think about the consequences. I was having too much fun, and I was arrogant enough to believe I could do anything. Have anything and anyone. I was totally spoilt and I thought I was invincible. Nothing bad could befall me.'

'And then your father died.'

Those eyes deepened again in sympathy. But his sweet lover wasn't as clever as she thought.

'My hedonism killed my father,' he said bluntly. 'His death was *my* fault.'

'It was a car accident.'

'Caused by me. I got into trouble. Serious trouble.'

She drew in a sharp breath. 'Gambling? Drugs?'

'One of my lovers fell pregnant.'

Kassie's mouth formed an 'O'. 'Did you love her?'

'I was almost eighteen. She was nineteen. I thought I'd been careful. I was voracious, but I wasn't stupid. But contraception isn't infallible.'

He hadn't answered her question.

'We weren't in a committed relationship. We weren't exclusive.'

Her expression shadowed. 'So what happened?'

'She was in a panic, and frankly so was I. Her parents were traditional and she was scared.'

'Was she a princess?'

'Aristocratic. It wouldn't have been the perfect match, but it could have been made acceptable.'

'So it wasn't a forbidden love story?' She looked away from him.

'Not for me, no.' He sighed. 'We slept together only a couple of times. For me it was only ever a couple of times with each woman.'

'Tick one off and then move on to the next?'

'Exactly.' He sighed again. 'She was in my party circle. I slept with most of the women in that group.'

'*How* did I not know you're really such a man whore?'

He looked ruefully at her. 'I might've still been a schoolboy, but I was really good at sneaking around. I was good at lying to my security handlers. And it was a very small, select circle I was in. Everyone had a reputation to lose. Everyone was discreet.'

And amoral. He'd taken up every offer—and there had been many. In those days he'd devoted himself to nothing but hedonistic pleasure. His father had been absent and busy, his sister a kid in the palace nursery, and he'd thought he was invincible and entitled. He'd been an out-of-control brat.

'So what happened when she got pregnant?'

He'd realised he'd screwed up and he had wanted to do the right thing. 'I was going to propose to her. I phoned my father...we had a big fight. He wanted me to pursue a paternity test first. I was angry that he thought he knew more than I did. I wouldn't listen to him. I wouldn't come home.'

He'd been so arrogant, so determined to do what he thought was best and damn his father's opinion.

Kassie's eyes deepened. 'So he came to see you?'

'He didn't usually drive himself, but in this instance... He was speeding...' He closed his eyes so he couldn't see the sympathy in hers. 'He was killed on impact. They said he wouldn't have felt a thing.'

He'd never got over the shock of the soldier knocking on his door.

'It was completely my fault. I killed him.' He was as guilty as if he'd pulled a damn trigger and shot him. 'She wanted to press ahead with the wedding, but I felt I had to do what my father had wanted. I hated it that our last words had been so vicious. Doing that was the least that I owed him.'

He'd been devastated by what he'd done in defying his father's wishes.

'And what was that?'

'A DNA test to determine paternity,' he said grimly. 'It turned out my father's concerns were correct. I was not the baby's father.'

Kassie paled. 'She lied to you.'

'She was scared,' he said dismissively. 'I guess she was going with the safest option.'

Kassie gazed at him, her expression softening. 'You still defend her? Even though she betrayed you?'

'It wasn't like any of us were faithful. And she was young and under pressure.'

'And you *weren't*?'

He paused. He hadn't told her this in order for her to *pity* him, but to push her away for her own good. But now there was a searching look in her eyes that he couldn't withstand.

'I was ripped apart,' he muttered harshly. 'I ruined everything and then I had to stand up for my coronation.'

He'd hated it. He'd known he didn't deserve to hold his head up, let alone wear the heavy gold crown.

'It was all hushed up, of course. No one was ever aware of the real reason why King Theodoros was out driving so fast along the coastal road that night.'

'Oh, Giorgos.' She cupped his face with a tender hand.

'I am *not* the goddamn perfect King.' He jerked free— he didn't deserve such gentle handling. 'Never was. Never will be. I am an arrogant, spoilt idiot who destroyed everything. I was out of control—a guy who was careless with other people's emotions. I was the kind of predatory male you hate—one who liked to score women and didn't give a damn about the mess he might leave behind.'

His skin was suddenly too tight for his body and his heartbeat too hard for his chest. But he saw what he'd wanted to see—the sensual light was still in her eyes.

He shook his head. 'I'm a selfish bastard, Kassie. I'm not worth your time.'

He was a selfish, unscrupulous tyrant who'd manipulated her. *Hell.* He hadn't even intended to. He'd thought his honesty would repel her. But now she was feeling sorry for him, when the last thing he deserved was anyone's pity. But even in this bitter confession he gladly took the comfort of her body because he was so damn selfish. So unworthy. And too damn weak to resist.

'Not true,' Kassie wrapped her arms tight around his chest, holding him to her even as she felt him stiffen as if to pull away.

What he'd just told her was one of the saddest things she'd ever heard. Yet he still defended that young woman. He was still that protective, caring guy. No wonder he'd beaten himself up. No wonder he was so wary for Eleni.

'You tried to do what you thought was right. And you're not that out-of-control kid any more.'

He was far *too* controlled. And it made such sense now. He must have been so hurt—losing his father and then finding out his lover had lied to him.

'What happened to her?'

'She lives in the south of France,' he answered mechanically. 'She's been married for the last six years. Two children now, I believe.'

'That's nice. For her, I mean.'

'It is.' He looked grim. 'You understand now?'

'That you're still beating yourself up for the mistakes of your youth? For things that might have happened anyway? Yes, I see that.'

He'd made allowances for that woman—she'd been young and under pressure—and yet he didn't give himself the same leeway.

'He wouldn't have been on that road—' he began, his hands automatically holding her close.

'But he might have had a crash at some other time. You can't blame yourself. Fate just works how it works.'

'You're wrong.'

'I see people every day who've suffered accidents. Who've lost limbs and lost the lives they used to lead. At some point we all have to accept that life is what it is. Things happen.' She leaned closer. 'Shit happens. But we move on. We accept it and we move on.'

'We can only *truly* move on,' he answered, 'if we alter our actions—ensure that we don't make the same mistakes.'

'But sometimes things are beyond our control.'

'Much is *within* our control,' he argued. 'We're defined by the choices we make. It is *my* duty to uphold the values and the vision of my father.'

This was why he'd changed nothing within the palace. Why he'd become so over-protective of Eleni. Why he'd changed nothing—preserving all tradition. And he'd shut himself down too—not taking any risks. Because he was punishing himself—walking a tightrope all the time, trying to be perfect. Which ultimately—inevitably—was impossible.

'I'm glad she's been able to move on with her life...' Kassie began carefully.

'But you don't think I have?'

'I think you do an amazing job.'

His laughter was not joyous—it was edged in bitterness and mockery. 'Me? The bully? The over-protective tyrant who kept his young sister locked up in the palace has apparently done "an amazing job"? Don't let *pity* blur your vision now, Kassie. Don't think me something I'm not.'

'I know you're loving and loyal, and that you'd do anything for your sister. I didn't understand everything when I first met you.'

'But you were right. I'm selfish and greedy and I like to think I can control everything.' He laughed again. 'Don't worry—I'm not destroyed by the truth.'

'What *are* you?'

He stared at her, considering. Finally he spoke. 'Determined,' he said. 'Determined to take advantage of the freedom that's now between us. You and me, Kassie. This is what it is. And it is *only* this. Only for now.'

He suddenly moved, pulling her beneath him.

'Let's not waste time dissecting things that can't be altered. My past is past. My future is set. There is only this moment to enjoy.' He growled. 'And I'm tired. I'm taking a holiday.'

CHAPTER EIGHT

THREE DAYS. HE'D cancelled all meetings and appearances, citing personal reasons. At the same time he'd released a small statement, informing the media that Ms Kassiani Marron had left the country to seek privacy in Paris for a few days. Their 'alibis' were in place and he was a liar again—a selfish man choosing private pleasure over public duty.

But he couldn't resist. Just this once.

Three days—that wasn't much to ask in return for a lifetime of service was it?

That first morning they'd slept in. He hadn't realised how tired he was, or how incredible it would feel to laze and let time escape as if he had all eternity to spend. They'd floated for hours in the pool, making out, enjoying the warmth and the quiet. Then he'd taken her back to bed.

For the first time in a decade he'd not done his morning training. She'd been sweetly sassy when she'd offered to help him out with another kind of work-out. He'd encouraged her to explore him. To take the lead and do anything and everything she wanted. She'd made the most of figuring out the limits of his strength and stamina. His satisfaction had thrummed as he'd watched her hidden passion blossom. She had a delightful appetite for teasing him.

That pleasure dampened the doubts. Maybe he shouldn't have told her the truth, but he couldn't regret taking the risk. Rather it was a relief, in an odd way, for someone else to know what had really happened back then. It felt like for ever ago. In fact, in this moment, it felt like someone else's life. He finally felt free—as if he'd escaped who he was. Who he had to be. Just by being with her. Just for now. And he wanted it.

So he ignored the caution that licked at his spine every so often. And, as another day slid by, far too quickly, he knew he didn't want to waste any of these moments. There was more to explore with her than sensual gratification. He had other secrets—places to share. And he wanted her to have more from him than just those delicious hours in the bedroom.

She deserved so much more. She was generous and sweet and smart, and he had the pressing need to give her more than that, even if it was only for these few days. After what she'd told him of her parents' relationship, he knew it had been imbalanced. He couldn't offer her a 'normal' dating experience, but he could give her all his time right now—not just in bed. And he wanted hers.

'Why do I need walking shoes?' She raised an eyebrow early on their third morning together.

'So you can walk.'

'Walk where?'

'It's a surprise.'

The small helicopter was ready on the helipad, as he'd requested.

He held the door for her to climb into the front. 'Trust me?'

'Just this once,' she teased, but promptly hopped in.

He took the pilot's seat and looked at her as she strapped up her safety belt. He drew in a steadying breath. 'You really suit that colour.'

'Because I'm a scarlet woman?' she teased as she glanced down at the ruby-red tee that hugged her glorious curves.

'No, you just suit that colour. It brings out the depth of your hair and your eyes—and you're not scarlet. You're passionate and vibrant and the sexiest woman I've ever met.'

'Um... Wow.' Her mouth shut and she swallowed. 'I

don't normally wear it—for obvious reasons,' she confessed with a sudden smile. 'But it's my favourite.'

'You should always wear it—but I am not looking at you again for the next half-hour.' He huffed out a sigh and focused, beginning his flight checks. 'I won't get distracted. I've had a lot of training.'

He wanted to reassure her that he wasn't an occasional pilot whose rustiness might put them at risk.

'I'm sure you have.'

Her tone made him glance across at her, despite his vow not to. Her smile was a little sad. 'What?'

'I know how dedicated you are to all that you do,' she replied. 'You never give less than your absolute best, no matter what the situation.'

He didn't reply. He couldn't take that small compliment.

It was only a thirty-minute flight to a mountainous region in the north, where forest-covered peaks rose to touch the sky. He navigated the foothills, steering them through a narrow valley, where he landed on a small flat clearing about halfway up a large mountain that was otherwise inaccessible. Hidden here was a barely visible track, leading up beyond the tree line to the sun-kissed, craggy summit.

'What's the point of the helicopter if we're not going to use it to get all the way to the top?' she asked with a laugh as he pulled on the daypack he'd prepared.

'It's the *challenge*, Ms Marron.'

'Oh, of course.' She rolled her eyes. 'You do like a challenge.'

'As do you.'

He saw her smile in acknowledgement and felt a kick of contentment. He liked reading her, pleasing her. He liked her wit and her teasing. And—red-blooded man that he was—he liked the view as she scrambled up the narrow overgrown track ahead of him.

It staggered him that no other man had taken the time

to push past her immediate beauty to the stunning soul beneath. Why had she built those defences so strongly when it was evident—as he'd found as he'd got to know her—that she craved contact and thrived on companionship?

None had been the right companion.

'Why did you really want to go to the hospital ball?' he asked, tension pulling inside him. 'It obviously wasn't because you wanted to meet a man.'

'Actually, I *did* want to meet a man. I had a target.'

'I'm jealous,' he muttered with grim honesty. 'What did he have that made him so special?'

'A research facility.' That teasing note rang in her voice as she answered. 'One of the guests was a researcher. A couple of investors were there as well.'

He remembered she'd told him that now, back on the first night. And to his shame he'd not believed her.

'What research? What did you want to talk to him about?'

'Robotics. They're working on a new prosthetics prototype and I had an idea...' She tailed off.

'And you wanted to share it?'

She nodded.

'Did he like it?'

She turned back to face him, her smile radiant. 'He did. They've been in touch to talk about it more, and they've asked if I want to be involved at the testing phase, with one of my patients.'

'That's wonderful.' But then he frowned. 'Why couldn't you talk to him before?'

'I've never had the chance to meet him at the hospital.'

'Why not? You've worked there for years—you're highly regarded.'

'As a physiotherapist, yes. Not as a doctor. And this guy was only on Palisades for a few days. So Damon got me in to the ball to introduce me.'

'That was why Damon went to the ball?'

She nodded. 'He usually avoids those things.'

Giorgos suppressed a grim laugh—Damon wouldn't be able to avoid all those palace balls now he'd married a princess. 'And he had the invitation and the contacts because of his technology companies?'

'He offered to fund me, but I…' She glanced up at the steep track and puffed out a breath. 'I didn't want that.'

'Why not?'

'I don't want his money. Or anyone else's. I don't have the qualifications to work in that area at that level—I just want to share my ideas with the people who are working on it in case it might be useful.'

So she had the ideas, but not the paperwork. And she was too proud to accept assistance. Irritation prickled the base of his spine.

'I saw a picture of you at that ball,' he confessed. 'If I'd been that man I wouldn't have been able to focus on a word you said because you looked so damned sexy.'

'Well, *he* was polite and *he* did listen,' she said archly. 'And I borrowed that dress from one of the nurses.'

So what she'd said must have been good. 'You should be in on that project.'

She laughed. 'It's not my place.'

'But it's your thinking.'

'Other people are thinking the same. They're the ones who can drive it.'

'While your intellect is wasted and you don't get the credit and challenge you deserve?'

'Not wasted. I do good work with my patients,' she said, defensive pride rippling from her as she straightened to her full height.

'I know. That's clear. But if you have more to offer, then can't you do both? Couldn't you work part-time on the research and part-time as a practitioner? Have you asked if you could?'

'You make it sound so easy.' She shook her head.

'It should be. You ought to be able to maximise all your skills. You should tell the hospital that.'

'It's obvious you're used to making decisions.'

'It's my job.' He paused on the track beside her. 'You initially wanted to study medicine rather than physiotherapy?'

She wasn't as quick with her reply this time. 'Yes, but the training was long and expensive and my mother had got sick. I could complete the physiotherapy course sooner and be a help to her. As it was I studied part-time in my final two years, so it took me longer to finish.'

Part-time because of her mother's terminal illness. She'd been her sole carer. He knew that from the information his team had found. She put her patients—and her mother first. She was determined and proud. But he was determined too, and somehow he'd help her.

That tightness in his chest eased. 'We're nearly there.' He took her hand and led her up the last few steps of the narrow, rocky track until it opened out onto the small summit.

The wind grazed his skin. He liked the hit of oxygen— he was always able to think clearly up here.

'This is beautiful.' Radiant, she gazed across the view.

'Worth the effort?'

'Beautiful moments are *always* worth the effort.'

Something settled inside him in that moment. Peace. She understood. That was what she did—helped create beautiful moments. With him. Probably with her patients too. She looked like a goddess, with her eyes sparkling and her skin luminescent.

Touched, he turned and looked to the horizon, but he kept her hand clasped his. From here they could see right down over the island. The kingdom he'd give his life for.

'I haven't been up here in so long.'

'Why not?'

'Busy.' He gazed across the beautiful landscape and nodded in the direction of the capital. 'Being there.'

'It means everything to you,' she said softly.

'It's what I am.'

'It's *part* of what you are,' she replied. 'But not *all* that you are.'

She was wrong, but he no longer had the desire to argue. He turned and kissed her, reverently drawing from her the response that revitalised his own cold system. Another moment. But that was all.

He made himself move. 'I want to show you something.'

'More than this?'

With a smile he led her to a tussock at the farthest edge of the summit and showed her a small stone cairn that had withstood the wind and now gleamed in the sun.

'Oh…' She crouched down, her smile blossoming. 'You built this?'

He held out a water bottle to her. She took it and sipped while he took a stone he'd brought with him from his pack. With a permanent marker, he drew the date and his initial as she studied the stones already stacked into the mound.

'They all have your initial on them,' she said. 'Doesn't anyone come here aside from you?'

He shook his head. *Not now.*

'Is it forbidden to the public?'

'No!' He laughed. 'I just don't think many people know about it. It's hard to get to unless you have a helicopter and are confident about flying low through the mountain range…' He glanced at the cairn. 'My parents brought me here.'

Kassie knelt to examine the cairn more closely. 'You always bring a stone? Only one each trip?'

He nodded.

'That's a lot of trips.'

It was. 'Right from when I was small.' He should have come more. It always revitalised him. Or maybe it was the woman alongside him who was injecting the energy into his veins.

'A man of tradition.' She smiled up at him, a teasing light in her eyes.

'Is that such a bad thing?'

'Not at all. Not if the traditions don't stand in the way of progress.'

'Most traditions don't. I think they're symbols—connecting us to both past and future.'

He watched as she turned back to study the oldest stones on the bottom of the cairn. Coarse grass had grown, obscuring some, but a couple were large foundation stones. The initials could still be read.

She traced an 'A'. 'Your mother?'

'Antonia,' he confirmed quietly. 'It was her idea.'

'She came here often?'

'It was her favourite place.'

Kassie looked back at the stone. 'Was she lovely?'

'Yes.' Giorgos hunched down beside her. 'My father built the Summer House for her and she decorated it. It was her escape. She'd spend her holidays walking in these hills.' He tossed the stone in his hand and caught it again.

'Her escape?'

Kassie was looking at him with those deep brown eyes. Soft, bottomless, havens of emotion, revealing the caring nature that would be too easy to take advantage of.

'Because she didn't like the palace?'

'No, she did like it, but there isn't much privacy in public life.'

Her gaze skittered from his. 'So your father built the holiday home for her?'

'She spent a lot of time here when I was very young and he was working.'

'It was an arranged marriage?'

'Of course. But it worked well.' His chest hurt. 'They seemed happy to me.'

But his memories were few. He'd only been ten when she'd died.

'You must miss her,' Kassie said. 'It must have been such a shock. No wonder you worry about Eleni's pregnancy.'

He shook his head jerkily. 'With my mother the complications were unforeseeable and unpreventable,' he said roughly. 'Just unlucky. It's not a hereditary condition. Eleni should be as healthy as any other pregnant woman. She should deliver her child just fine.'

He'd already checked with the doctor.

'That's good.'

It was, but he didn't want to talk about his mother any more—or his father, or his sister, or any of them. He wanted to suspend time and savour this moment with Kassie.

He rubbed his fingers on the rough stone in his hand. 'You should place one to mark your visit,' he said huskily.

Her colour rose and she glanced about, but there were no loose stones on the ground. He'd remembered to bring one from the cave at the back of the Summer House. As always.

'You'll have to share mine.' He uncapped the marker again and with a deft stroke added a 'K' to the 'G'. 'It's tradition.'

He put the rock into position at the top of the pile, carefully wedging one edge of it into a gap between two others, so it would become part of the puzzle. Fixed and stable. It didn't mean anything other than being a record of this moment. It couldn't. But for a long while there was nothing but silence between them.

'We'd better go. The wind here gets cold if you stay too long.' He made himself walk away at last.

She didn't reply as he led the way back down the track. His heart thundered as an empty ache deepened in his bones. He needed to hold her, but he didn't. Because he couldn't let himself *need* to. Instead he forced himself to breathe and focus properly—and not look at her—before beginning his flight checks.

He'd sent his staff away for the day, wanting to be alone with her for every last moment they had left. Wanting one day of a normal, quiet life such as he'd never had.

'Here's the truth,' he confessed as he looked around the kitchen, hoping he could find the things he needed. 'I'm not a good cook. I'm inexperienced.'

'Inexperienced doesn't always equal not good,' she purred.

He chuckled, warmth trickling through him at her sassy confidence—the confidence she'd developed because of *him*. 'We'll have to see.'

'I'm not going to help you.' She leaned against the bench and sipped the champagne he'd poured for her. 'You'll have to fend for yourself.'

'What do you do at night?' he asked, locating some steak and fresh vegetables. 'You live alone. You don't go out? Have parties?' He sent her a sly look. 'You don't go dancing?'

'You know that already.' She frowned at him. 'Don't tell me *you* dance.'

'Not often. But I know how to.'

'Good for you.'

'Come on.' He laughed at her defensiveness and led her out to the private courtyard. 'You'll never have to dance in public,' he promised. 'Just here with me.'

He seared the steak and the vegetables on the outside grill and they ate simply, but well. Then he put some music on and held out his arms.

Reluctantly she stepped into them, her eyes promising

retribution. He didn't care—he just wanted to hold her. He hadn't danced in years. She, clearly, hadn't danced at all.

He was patient, taking the time to show her, to encourage her. It made for moments of laughter—and then she got it. And as the late-afternoon sun faded into night they danced on—little more than swaying together, really—talking of nothing significant and everything important. Silly tales of childhood holidays here that he'd not thought about in years. Anecdotes from his travels and meetings abroad. She countered with stories about her patients.

It saddened him that her life had all been work. She should have had holidays as a child too. But tonight they shared gentle laughter. And then it wasn't so gentle. He wrapped her in his arms and drew her closer still, choosing to forget how transient this had to be—how forbidden it truly was.

But the next morning he woke early, his ability to sleep stolen by guilt and the return of outside pressures. He couldn't avoid his duty for ever. There was no eternity for him.

He tried to ward off the grim feeling, but for the first time the weight of responsibility on him rankled. He wanted more of what he couldn't have. What he didn't deserve. And what she didn't want.

He left her sleeping and swam, but powering through a million lengths didn't work the bitterness from his body.

He stalked inside to discover she'd dressed and eaten breakfast already. She'd chosen a pretty dress, with only her bikini beneath it, and hadn't bothered with shoes. Her long hair was loose and gorgeous, and her kissable mouth was curved into a tempting smile. She was the picture of a summer sweetheart—a holiday fling. But in only a few hours his holiday had to end. His meeting this afternoon was one he couldn't reschedule. And she was due to return to Palisades tomorrow.

The disappointment cut so deep he had to turn away from her. He forced himself to think about work, but he was blocked by an internal shift. Something had changed within him and he couldn't focus properly...

Too bad. He had to. The escape was over.

Kassie noticed him grow quieter and quieter still as the morning progressed. He was withdrawing from her already. He had a meeting this afternoon that was too important to postpone and already he was back behind his large desk, attired in one of those exquisitely stitched suits.

Real life had returned. Their affair was all but over and they were due to return to Palisades tomorrow. So she was determinedly bright. She wasn't going to get melancholic just because time was ticking. She was not going to make any kind of scene.

But the unfairness of it ate at her. She grew angry at the softening inside her. The way she melted at nothing more than the *sight* of him. And she'd seen another side to him in these last days. The serious, uptight King actually *laughed*. He told stories using silly voices. He was open and frank and funny and interested and supportive and tender and a teasing rogue. And that moment on his mountain yesterday... The intimacy she'd felt watching him entwine her initial with his... That had been so unfair of him.

'What is it?' he prompted, looking across at her from the papers he was studying.

Of course he saw everything—as if she was a damn window through which he could see her soul. She hated it that she couldn't see *him* with the same emotional X-ray vision. She hated it that he was the one who could do this—why did it have to be *him*?

'It wasn't just the predatory men I didn't respond to,' she said without preamble, voicing her thoughts without really thinking. 'It was the nice guys too.'

'You mean you've actually encountered nice guys? Not just jerks who lust after your body?' he teased.

'Don't…' She half-laughed. 'I've met a bunch. Some of them were actually okay.'

Probably more than okay. It was just that none of them had spun her wheels.

'I don't know that I'd be as generous,' he muttered darkly. 'Are you saying you've actually had a boyfriend?'

'Almost. I guess…'

'You *guess*?' His gaze sharpened. 'What happened?'

'It was years ago—my first year at college. He was really nice.'

Giorgos put the papers down and looked at her. '"Nice" is an interesting word. But there's not a lot of passion in it.'

'He tried. He was patient. He was caring enough to understand that he needed to go slow…'

'But you felt—?'

'Cold,' she said sadly. And then her 'boyfriend' had got frustrated. 'We never got past kissing. And he was a *nice* guy.'

'I'm sorry.' He stood and walked to the sofa, where she was ignoring the book open on her knee. 'You don't think *I'm* a nice guy?'

She laughed—also sadly. 'I will pander to your ego and make this about you for just this one last moment. You know I think you're more than nice. I think you're amazing. But…'

'But you have buyer's remorse?' His eyes narrowed.

'I just don't understand why it has to be *you* who turns me on.' Her anger got the better of her and the neediness that had been creeping up on her leaked out. 'I don't want it to only be you that can do this to me. It *can't* be only you.'

The one guy she *couldn't* have. Not for good.

His gaze hardened. 'So what are you planning? You're

going to go browsing online for a boyfriend? Swipe your screen and match with a bunch of prospects?'

'Really?' She stared at him. Was he *jealous*? How could he get angry with her when *he* was the one who was out of bounds? 'I'm going to go home. Go back to work. And so are you.'

'Just like that?' He snaked out a hand and tugged her to her feet, putting his hands on her hips and pulling her against him. 'You think you're just going to turn this *off*?'

'I've lived without this side to my life for a long time,' she said, bravely squaring up to him. 'I can do without it now.'

The tension between them thickened, revealing the danger in the room— the festering malcontent that she realised he felt every bit as keenly as she did.

'You want to return to your nun-like existence?'

'Why not?' she flared as she felt his steeliness—and his arousal—grow. 'This is just sex.'

Somehow she'd angered him. She paused, anticipating she knew not what. Knowing only that something within him had been unleashed.

'Yeah. It is, isn't it?' He inhaled deeply. 'Turn around,' he ordered.

'What?'

'You heard me,' he snapped coolly, his hands pressing on her. 'Turn around.'

Excitement thrummed low in her belly as she glared at him, their eyes clashing in a battle of wills. In pure challenge. She lifted her chin and then pivoted on the spot.

She heard his hissing breath and his hands shifted. Rough. Fast.

'What are you doing?' she muttered as he walked her forward, his big body insistent at her back.

'Just helping you figure a few things out,' he muttered.

He pushed her forward until her palms hit the wall in self-preservation.

'What things?' she squeaked as he nipped at her neck and then licked the sensitive skin.

'If it's just sex,' he said roughly, pressing behind her, 'there's no need to take our time. No need to get naked. No need to stare into each other's eyes. We can just do it like feral animals. Fast and dirty. Right here. Right now. Get the goddamn release and go.'

His words shocked her. Thrilled her. Because this *was* just sex—that was all it could be. And she was unbearably aroused.

She instinctively used the wall as leverage to push herself back against him. *'Yes,'* she growled, angrily provocative. 'Exactly that.'

She was flattened, rendered immobile, by a hot, furiously hard man. *The* man. Sensual shivers ran down her spine as he flipped up her skirt and yanked her bikini bottoms down to her thighs. Then he grabbed her wrists, lifting her arms above her head and pinning them there with one hand. Delicious pleasure hummed through her body as she registered his passion. His other hand moved back to her hip, holding her hard. Then he thrust, growling as she took him with a gasp of pleasure.

'This is what you want?' he asked furiously. 'Me inside you? Me riding you until you come?'

'Yes…' She moaned again, lost to the demands of his body and his words. He thrust hard and fast and relentless, his hot mouth at her neck, his hands holding her fast, his possession total. And suddenly, shockingly quickly, she was right there, her body locked in the rigid paralysis that struck just before convulsions of pleasure.

'You want it from me,' he muttered. 'Any time, anywhere, anyhow. You can't get enough. You like it when I—'

Her scream drowned the rest of his words. She shuddered, her orgasm blinding her. Swift and violent, the waves of ecstasy screwed up every one of her muscles then released her, leaving her limp against the wall. He was still thrust deep inside her, basically holding her up. His breathing was hot on her neck and hard in her ear.

But then he withdrew. She shivered, her legs suddenly weak. He pulled her backwards, into his arms, and carried her to the sofa.

Dazed, she stared up at him as he joined her on the narrow cushions. 'You didn't finish?'

'No,' he answered grimly, gazing into her eyes as he locked back into position inside her. 'Not yet. I want to see you.'

He thrust just as deeply, but more slowly than before. He framed her face with his hands, looking into her eyes, not letting her turn away as sensations began to pile onto each other again.

'I want to look into your eyes. I want to see when you finally *understand*.'

That connection—chest-to-breast, eye-to-eye—their bodies not just sealed together but interlocked. He kissed her. Working not only to seduce, but to disarm...to overwhelm her.

She shook with the intensity binding them. The ecstasy she'd felt only seconds ago was nothing to the all-encompassing emotion she was drowning in now. It was such a heavenly way to die.

'Giorgos...' She was desperate to breathe.

'You still think this is just sex?'

He was angry with her. She trembled, shocked at the rawness of his question. Angered.

'It's all it can be.' She arched, tormented, arguing even as her body denied her words in its need for him.

'Too late,' he growled. 'This isn't *just* anything. It never was.'

He swept her into the maelstrom of their passion—right into the heart of the storm that brewed beneath the surface whenever they were near each other. She arched again, her body convulsing as it culminated in this—always this— pure, complete bliss.

But this time was different. This time something had been ripped away from them both, revealing stark need and the impossible, hopeless depths of their hunger.

She opened her eyes in time to see him driving hard in that final moment when all his muscles locked and his expression strained in the agony of ecstasy. His eyes were fixed on hers, with deep, wild emotion churning in the fiery green.

He whispered one last word at the moment of release— desperate anger in his demand. *'You.'*

He couldn't bring himself to lift his head and look at her. He couldn't bring himself to return to reality and face what he'd just done. But he couldn't stay crushing her like this on the soft sofa either.

He pulled away from her, quickly standing and adjusting his clothing. He was still completely dressed—his shirt untucked, his skin sweaty. Finally he braved a glance at her. She looked shattered. Her eyes were wide and vulnerable as she silently watched him. Her lips were more swollen than usual. A purplish love-bite stood out angrily against the creamy skin of her neck.

God, he'd been an animal. He had lost all control—just taken what he wanted, held her closer and tighter as he'd driven as deep as he could into her body. He'd lost himself entirely in the pleasure he found only with her.

But she'd been ready—wet and willing—and she'd pushed back on him just as hard as he'd thrust into her. It had been wild and reckless and it had turned him inside out. His orgasm had been the most prolonged and intense of his life.

But wrong. *So* wrong.

Cold, acidic guilt roiled in his stomach. He had just had unprotected sex with her. The one mistake he'd never, *ever* made. But she was the absolute temptation of his life and he'd retaliated insanely at the thought of her leaving. At the thought of her being intimate with some other guy. At her insistence that she would return to her home and this would end.

He'd rejected the notion in an irrational, explicitly physical way. He'd lost utter control—of his emotions, his mind, his body. All he'd wanted was to gorge on the succulent delight of her soft embrace. He'd forgotten his duty— to his crown, to his country, to his father, to himself. And to her.

He froze as the ramifications flashed through his mind.

'That never should have happened,' he croaked formally, struggling to clear the words past his clogged throat. 'I apologise.'

She blinked and slowly sat up, clearly confused as she tugged down the crumpled skirt of her pretty dress.

'I didn't stop to protect you,' he explained shortly.

Her gaze narrowed. 'You mean contraception?'

'I'll send for my physician immediately, to get an emergency contraceptive. There's no need for you to be concerned.'

He couldn't look at her. He couldn't cope with the image in his mind's eye of her pregnant. *Vulnerable.* The risk rendered his lungs useless. He walked away before he threw himself on his knees at her feet to beg her forgiveness. To beg her to...*what*?

'I'll make that call now,' he growled.

Kassie stared as Giorgos retreated behind the grim, forbidding demeanour he'd perfected over the last decade. She felt flayed. He'd just told her this wasn't 'just' sex and then in the next breath proved that that was *exactly* all it was. When cold reality hit—when the possible impact of their affair on the future was raised—he'd wanted nothing more than to reject her and run. The last thing he wanted was a long-term complication.

Well, she could put him out of his misery—even though he'd just thrust her into heartbreak.

'I'm not going to get pregnant, Giorgos,' she said, coldly quiet.

'We just had unprotected sex. Pregnancy happens,' he snapped.

'It wasn't unprotected.'

'What do you mean?'

'I'm on the pill.'

'Pardon?'

'The contraceptive pill. I won't get pregnant.'

He stared at her, clearly shocked. 'Why didn't you tell me sooner?'

'You didn't give me a chance,' she said scathingly. 'You were too busy planning for your doctor to come and save you from possible scandal.'

The truth? She'd wanted to see his reaction to the initial prospect—like the masochist she was. His horror had been unmistakable. Of course it had. He'd actually paled at the thought of her pregnancy. That had told her everything.

'Why are you on the pill when you don't have sex?' He frowned, his tone hostile.

'Don't you believe me?'

'You don't strike me as the type to pump yourself full of medication unnecessarily.'

And yet he'd just directed her to do exactly that—without even *discussing* it with her. He had no consideration of her wishes or her feelings. Had he really thought he could just order her to do as he wanted?

'How do you know it's unnecessary?' She bristled. 'There's more than the obvious reason for taking the pill. If you must know, my cycle is problematic and the pill makes it easier for me to manage.'

'But you've been staying here for the last few days. Did my men pack your pills?'

'When they went through all my personal things?' She was incensed. 'No, they did *not*. Because I keep them with me.' She marched to her bag and emptied it out on the table, snatching up the pack of tablets and thrusting it in his face. 'Here's your proof.'

She watched him. He just couldn't help himself. He had to check, his eye quickly seeing the empty spots in the blister pack. They proved she'd been taking the medication regularly. *He* proved he didn't trust her word.

'You think I'd lie?' she asked softly. 'You think I'd try to take advantage of you?'

He hesitated.

She sucked in a breath. 'I'm not her. You should know that.'

'I just…'

'No. No "just", Giorgos. I've *never* lied to you. I've never tried to trick you. But you still can't trust me.'

It hurt so much more than it should. Because she'd trusted him—utterly. And he'd treated her with such tenderness and respect. Her body, that was. But this was more than physical intimacy now. This was a threat to his future and now his true feelings were on display. He didn't want her—not the same way she wanted him.

Suddenly she realised just how much trouble she was in. How much hurt she was seconds away from suffering.

'I told you *everything*,' he gritted. 'How can you say I don't trust you?'

'You just proved it,' she said quietly.

Would it have been so awful if she'd got pregnant? Obviously to him, *yes*. He'd wanted to get rid of that potential problem as quickly as possible because he didn't care about her. But she...? She felt...

She paced, hiding her face as she realised just how deeply she'd fallen for him. How had she thought she could remain in control and *safe*? Because he was ultimately unattainable? That didn't matter a jot—he'd still got to her. She'd become entranced. Even though he was bossy and decisive and so...so damn strong.

It's just a crush.

He was her first—that was why she felt such a connection, right? But she knew just what a lie that was. It was like being hit by a bus—realising just how hard she'd fallen for him.

'I do trust you,' he said in a clipped voice. 'But I should have stopped,' he said quietly. 'I should have used protection. My anger was misplaced. I was angry with myself.'

'I should have stopped as well,' she snapped back. 'You don't get to assume total responsibility for what happened. It was as much my fault as yours. I knew there was something different. I *felt* it.'

The darkness in his eyes deepened. 'Did you like how it felt?' he asked, ever so softly.

Somehow he'd crowded her. Somehow she was back against the wall and he was right there in front of her.

Her breathing quickened. 'Yes...'

So close. He was so dear to her. And quickly they were back to this all-consuming intensity and desire. But now she knew there was nothing beneath that for him. She couldn't let him close again. Not when he hadn't even apologised for the real hurt—he didn't even know what it was.

'Stop, Giorgos.'

His jaw hardened. 'Why?'

She glanced away from him. 'I have to get back to work. So do you.'

'I will see you in Palisades?'

She stopped breathing. He offered such temptation. But goosebumps lifted. 'No.'

'I'll send for you,' he said urgently. 'No one will see the car under cover of darkness.'

She chilled at his plan. 'And will I leave again a couple of hours later?'

'Yes.'

A booty call?

'No one will know,' he added with arrogant assurance. 'I'm sure we can manage it. I'd build a goddamn private tunnel from your place to the palace if I could.'

It was *that* important that no one knew he was sleeping with her?

'Because I'm that much of a liability?'

He stiffened. 'That wasn't what I meant.'

She made herself breathe. Made herself remain strong for her own future—her own freedom. His acceptance of her in public had been only in her role as the black sheep of his new brother-in-law's family. Not anything else. She wasn't good enough for him to be seen with in a *relationship*. Clearly there was nothing worse than that idea for him.

Initially she'd been fine with their affair being conducted in secret—that had made total sense for them both. But that had been when it was a short-term fling—her lessons in sensuality. But for an ongoing arrangement? *No.*

'I should go now,' she said shakily. 'I want to go *now*.'

'Kassie—'

'We're over,' she interrupted furiously. 'It was only ever going to be these few days.'

That had been her decision. Her terms.

He didn't move. 'I don't want this to be over.'

'It has to be.' She gritted her teeth.

He placed his hands on her shoulders. 'Just a little longer.'

She quaked inside at his touch. 'Just a little longer?' She half-laughed, half-sobbed. 'You can't be serious. What do you want us to do—carry on an affair in secret? Or do I get to become your consort? Your concubine? Do I get to sit around and wait for you for ever and ever?'

'You're putting an overlay on this that doesn't need to be there. You're not your mother—'

'That's right. I'm *not*. I'll never be a kept woman. I'll never wait and wait…'

'I'm not asking you to. I'm not offering false hope—'

'You're asking me to stall my future.'

He dragged in a harsh breath. 'I'm asking you to stay in the present. To let this thing between us run its natural course.'

'Its "natural course"?' She laughed bitterly. 'You mean run until you get sick of me.'

He paled. 'Kassie—'

'So I suspend everything and wait to meet you in secret?'

She knew marriage—love—was never going to happen. Not for her—not from him. He didn't think she was worth public acceptance—not really.

'Secrecy is to protect you. For your safety.'

'So I don't get judged in the press for being your mistress?' she said scathingly. 'More like so you don't get judged for *having* a mistress,' she snarled, so, so hurt. 'What if I meet someone else?'

She saw the arrogant tilt of his chin at her suggestion.

'What happens when you finally decide to step up to your burdensome royal duty and propose to the perfect Princess?' she asked rawly. 'What happens when you finally choose your wife? What happens to me then?'

He froze. 'That's not—'

'You're happy to waste my time until then?'

'You don't want this to be over any more than I do,' he argued angrily, his fingers tightening on her skin.

'I want what's best for me. And that *isn't* you.'

'You said this was just sex,' he taunted her, that wildness flashing in his eyes. 'You said you had nothing to lose by being with me.'

'You really do want it all from me, don't you?' She was horrified. 'I might not have had boyfriends, but I've had other relationships—*real* friendships. With patients, with friends at work. I care about people.'

'And I don't?'

'You devote your life to your people, to your duty. But, no, you don't *care* about anyone. I pity you.'

'You don't need to feel sorry for me. I'm not one of your patients with some piece missing.'

'There's a *big* piece missing. In your chest.'

He laughed mirthlessly. 'So now I'm heartless as well?'

'Yes.' Because if he had any kind of heart—any kind of conscience—he wouldn't be asking this of her. He would understand why this was so abhorrent.

'Is it so awful to want to protect you? To care for you?' He cupped her cheek with tenderness, despite the frustration in his voice. 'The secrecy I'm proposing is because I care about you.'

How dared he make it seem that he was offering this for *her*?

'But you don't *want* to care about me—that's the point.' Her anger lit. 'This isn't about me at all. This is about you controlling everything in your life.'

'I *can't* control this,' he growled.

She closed her eyes. 'I refuse to be my mother. I'm not *settling*.' She couldn't wait for a man who was never going to give her what she needed. 'We don't want the same things. We don't *feel* the same things.'

'What *is* it you feel? Desire? For the first time in your life? And you're going to go and feel it with the rest of the world now? *No* man can give you what I can give you.'

'But I don't *want* the little you're willing to give me.'

'Not this?' He hauled her close against his furiously hard body. 'You're going to lie to my face and tell me you don't want *this*?'

Oh, she wanted it. She wanted it almost more than she wanted to breathe. But she would slowly suffocate and starve, because it wasn't enough to sustain her. She'd become bitter and lonely and poisoned by disappointment and emptiness. She'd become sick. Just as her mother had.

'Stop, Giorgos,' she breathed, begging him for reprieve.

He too was breathing hard. In his eyes she saw it—intention. She knew what he longed to do, the way he would touch her. The way she would touch him back. One blink, one word, and it would happen. She couldn't let it happen.

And he saw.

He blinked something away and stepped back, but not before a parting trail of feather-light fingers down her arms. Torturous...uniquely devious. And then his hands dropped. The farther he stepped away, the more she wanted him to come back.

'This is what you want?' His disbelief was audible. 'To go back to feeling nothing?'

She stayed silent because she couldn't lie.

Never could she accept the little he was offering. He didn't even understand just how little it was. Their affair hadn't helped her embrace her sensuality—it had served only to form an addiction that worsened every time he came near.

'I only want to protect you,' he said.

'That's a lie.' She lashed out. 'This is about protecting *yourself.*'

'You know I don't want you to suffer the way—'

'You could change,' she snapped. 'You could do things differently. You could raise expectations and the public would go with you. You lead—they follow. But you're too busy punishing yourself for things that happened long ago. And you don't want me enough to fight your need to maintain tradition. To fight for *me*. Not even to try to support me through it. You don't trust me. And you don't love me, Giorgos. And, no, I know you never said you would. But unless things change you'll never love *anyone*.'

'And you *will*?' His anger rattled. 'You think you've got it together more than I do? You've shut yourself off from finding any chance of love. You won't even go out on a date.'

'You're right—I won't. But now I know I need to change. And I need to change *this*—right here. If I'm too busy with you I can never have the chance to meet someone else. To meet the man who *is* right for me. Because it's not you, Giorgos. It'll never be you.'

She dragged in painful breaths and kept pushing.

'And that wasn't a challenge to your arrogant ego—that's just the truth. Because you were right—this wasn't just sex for me. I could have loved you. But you won't *let* yourself be loved. Not by me, or your sister, or anyone. You're not protective—you're arrogant and superior. You don't think anyone can handle things the way you can. But you handle *nothing* of true value. You use your guilt to hide from having an actual life, with real relationships. You have so much more to offer your people. So much more to give of yourself if you'd only set yourself free... But you're too much of a control freak and you're a coward. The truth is you have no intention of loving anyone—least of all *yourself*.'

She broke off, staring at him. She'd gone too far. He was deathly pale, but the wildness in his eyes burned. His breathing was loud and ragged. Slowly the ice returned to his expression. And slowly, with excoriating pain, she realised he wasn't going to argue with her. He wasn't going to fight. This had to be over. She had to leave. *Now*.

'I'm going,' she muttered, with as much dignity as she could muster, and walked out of the room.

He didn't answer. Certainly didn't follow her.

She showered and dressed again, in plain jeans and a tee, only to discover when she emerged from her suite that he'd left for his appointment early. Of course he had.

It was almost another two hours before he returned. Two hours in which she'd had time to plan. And pack.

He didn't come and find her when he returned. She waited for almost half an hour and then ventured to his lair. He was behind his desk, looking as remote as he'd looked that very first day. He watched silently as she approached him.

'I'd like to return to the city,' she said quietly.

'I've said I'm sorry,' he said stiffly.

'I know you are. But we both know this is over. We got carried away.' She lifted her chin proudly, but couldn't look at him directly. 'I've handled all those cameras on me. They've got the only story they're going to get. The interest is only going to die down from here—especially when Eleni and Damon return. I'll be perfectly safe.'

'I insist upon security for you.' He glanced at a sheet of paper on the pile before him. 'I'll make the arrangements.'

Kassie walked out of the room. *Just a crush.* Self-delusion was the only way to maintain sanity through this.

Less than an hour later she locked her hands tightly together in her lap and stared hard at them. She refused to look out of the window as the helicopter flew high, taking her far from him. She refused to cry.

Just a crush. She'd be over it in no time.

CHAPTER NINE

SHE WAS NEVER going to get over it. Three days had passed since she'd left him at the Summer Palace. Three days of no contact. No respite from her bleeding, smashed-up heart. The only way she'd coped was by going to work and pouring everything into her future there. But she could hold it together only so long.

When she returned home it hit all over again. He'd struck where it hurt most, by asking her to be his secret mistress. She'd been terrified of being wanted but not loved—as her mother had been all her life: *wanted* but left waiting, hoping, believing…and it never happening.

Her father hadn't given her mother what she'd deserved. Her mother had loved him wholly, unconditionally, giving him all the best of herself and accepting so little in return. And then, when she'd needed him most, he'd spurned her.

All her life Kassie had been so angry with her mother for that weakness. But now she understood just how much courage it took to love someone—how much bravery was required to put yourself on the line. Now she understood how deeply her mother had loved, however misplaced that love and trust had been, and she could take some pride in her ability to be able to love so deeply and so completely. Kassie could do that.

But her mother had refused to believe she could love that way again. Refused to end it with John Gale and try to start again. And *there* was the mistake Kassie wasn't going to repeat.

Inadvertently, it was exactly what she had been doing before, by not even trying, not even dating. But if she'd learned how to love once, surely she might again? She had to overcome this heartbreak, choose to live. And eventually choose to love again.

It would take even more courage to risk her heart and try again. But the next guy who asked her out... She was going to say *yes*.

Furious, Giorgos stalked the length of the palace and back again. And again. That last argument replayed round and round in his head. His anger didn't diminish—it just grew.

He'd asked her to be with him in a way he'd never asked another woman to be. But she had pride, didn't she? So much pride. And she had a career. She had a life.

He could give her a better one.

His arrogance mocked him. So too did the newspapers that littered the desk in his private suite.

'The physiotherapist'—the press referred to her that way. They'd investigated her, all right—honing in on the shy, natural way she'd talked to those guests at the sculpture unveiling. Then they'd dug out tales of her rapport with her patients—puff pieces that filled the gossip rags. They'd taken the illegitimate half-sister of the Princess's new husband to their hearts. 'Kassiani the Caring' had replaced 'Eleni the Pure' on the covers of the magazines.

Why did they insist upon putting the women in his life on damn pedestals for worshipping? Making them out to be more than human while at the same time treating them as *less* than human—as only two-dimensional.

Yet wasn't he every bit as guilty of that? Of thinking that neither Eleni nor Kassie could handle all that he thought *he* had to handle?

He studied a clipping about Kassie talking to the guests at that sculpture unveiling. So natural and poised, able to talk to anyone. She'd chosen not to let herself get physically involved with anyone before, but *he'd* been the one battling emotional frigidity. Where she was warm and giving he was ice, refusing to open up. And in doing that he had denied her too. When she deserved so much more.

And she was right. He *was* a coward. Hiding behind his supposed protective instincts to protect *himself.* He was terrified of making mistakes. Of not being good enough. Of not living up to the name he'd been burdened with at birth. Of letting everyone down. *Again.*

Of being hurt.

But *this* hurt so much. And he was so confused.

Her rejection enraged him. As for the thought of her finding another man who could satisfy her needs... That thought just about sent him insane. And that had been the problem. That had been when he'd lost control completely.

Yet when she'd asked him about his future wife he'd gone cold. Marriage was the last thing on his mind. All he wanted was Kassie at his side—in the secrecy of his home. He wanted her to be his alone. His secret. His treasure. He didn't want to share her with anyone. He didn't want her to be at risk or have to perform.

She made him feel so vulnerable. And why was that?

He closed his eyes as the painful truth hit him.

He'd thought he was so controlled. That he'd always done what was best for everyone—as if he was so damn all-knowing. But the only person who'd benefited had been *him. He* was the one kept safe.

He'd thought he was playing his role perfectly. Instead he was just a pompous ass. Emotionally lazy and never putting himself at risk. Not in any real sense. Maybe it was time to be the ordinary guy he truly was. The ordinary guy who'd made massive mistakes in the past and who'd just made another one. He'd pushed Kassie away because she threatened everything—his whole ordered world. But the truth was she *was* everything. She *was* his world.

Her words haunted him. *'You can't give me what I want...'*

He'd been too caught up in his own petulant outrage to ask the obvious question—*what* did she want? Initially she'd wanted an affair, but not any more. He knew what she *didn't* want—to be hidden away as his mistress, unacknowledged and having her value belittled…to be second-best to nothing. But he'd done exactly that to her.

He hadn't meant to. He'd been so thrown by his explosive loss of control, so afraid he'd ruined it, he'd wanted to buy some time to explore where this was going in private. He'd felt as if he was on a damn runaway train, and he'd wanted to pull the emergency brake for a moment to catch his breath. But he was a coward—because he'd already *known* where it was going.

She was right. It was time to make some changes. Not just within himself, but within the palace. He would put up a damn painting that *he* liked—one that hadn't already been there for centuries. One of his sister's. How had he been so obtuse as not to even let Eleni put up her beautiful paintings? He'd offered nothing but a total lack of support.

Kassie had put up Eleni's pictures in her office. Kassie had instinctively seen her depths and her value. Kassie saw the good in people—in her patients. She believed in them. She was kind and supportive and caring. All she'd wanted was the same in return. And he'd failed her.

But now he knew how much he needed her—wanted her. *Loved her.* She was the one—the only one for him. But he'd hurt her. She'd gone into orbit at the thought of being his 'kept' lover, long-term. Of being his secret. He'd retaliated emotionally—irrationally—and she'd wounded him with deadly accuracy.

But how did he become the man she needed him to be? How did he convince her to believe in him now?

He needed time, and a place where they wouldn't be interrupted. And, as much as he wanted to, he couldn't kidnap her a third time.

CHAPTER TEN

KASSIE HURRIED UP the path to her apartment. The security guard that she couldn't get rid of and was secretly grateful for had kept the photographers at bay, but she could barely contain her emotions until she got safely inside. Once in, she dumped her heavy bag, unable to attempt reading the report the senior researcher had sent across that afternoon. Not yet. Not now she was finally alone.

Hurt. She was still so hurt.

Hot tears streaked down her face. She'd been holding it together all day and now she could curl into a ball on the floor and howl her heart out. Again. For the fourth day in a row. When was she going to start feeling better?

A loud knocking on her door made her jump. She froze. She didn't want anyone to see her like this.

'Open up, Kassie, I know you're in there.'

Giorgos? No, no, no.

'Kassie?' He thumped the door again. 'Open up.'

He wasn't being quiet either. Furious, she wiped her eyes with her hands and unlocked then opened the door.

He took up almost all the space. He'd dressed down in jeans and a tee, with a cap tugged low on his forehead, but he was all King. The clothes made no difference. And he was gazing at her with such intensity—none of that regal remoteness in his hot expression.

His mouth flattened as he took in the signs of her distress. 'May I come in?' he muttered roughly.

She wanted to say no. To scream it.

'Of course.' She stepped back politely.

'I've learned not to invade your privacy without permission.' He looked pained momentarily. 'I'm not incapable of learning, Kassie.'

She closed the door but remained in the small hallway, determined not to let him get past the fragile defences she'd whipped into place. 'What do you want?'

He cleared his throat but kept his green gaze right on her. 'I wondered if you had plans for dinner tonight?'

She stared at him blankly. 'Are you asking me…?'

'On a date, yes.' He rolled his shoulders, looking awkward. 'I've never really asked a woman on a date before. You've been asked lots of times, and I know you tend to say no, but I was hoping you might go gently with me.'

She lifted her chin. 'Because this is all about *you*?'

The twisted smile faded. 'This is all about me *and you*. About us.'

'There is no us.'

'There is—there will be. There can't not be,' he said tightly. 'We just need to go gently with each other. I want the time and the space to get to know you. To court you. To do the things normal people do when they're starting a relationship. But unless we date in secret everyone is going to watch. I just—' He broke off. 'I'm just asking for one dinner. One date.'

Kassie stared at him, her pulse drumming. What did he mean by 'starting a relationship'?

'It's not that I don't want people to know we're involved,' he added suddenly. 'I just want us to have the chance to take this further without the burden and pressure of public interest.'

To take *what* further?

'It's not just sex, Kassie. We both—'

'You don't have to do this. I know you don't want to.'

She turned away. She couldn't cope with what she was reading in his eyes. She couldn't trust—

'If you'd let me actually finish, you might find out what it is that I *do* want.'

She glanced back at him.

'I told myself I was wary of scaring you off and coming on too strong,' he said softly. 'Really, *I* was the one who was scared. And you, like me, need certainty and security.'

She couldn't interrupt him now. The lump in her throat was too huge.

'I said some things I didn't mean the other day, and I didn't say the things I should have. My emotions got the better of me and I stupidly thought I could...' He drew in another breath. 'I thought that if we could talk over dinner then we might get somewhere.'

'Dinner?'

'Yes.'

'Where? When?'

'I took a chance and ordered pizza.'

'Pizza?' she echoed numbly.

'It should be here in about five minutes.'

She was lost for words.

'Say yes, Kassie,' he coaxed.

She had the feeling that if she did she'd be saying yes to so much more. And she wasn't ready to do that.

'I'll have some pizza,' she said guardedly. 'But that's all.'

'Great.'

His smile flashed, hitting her all the way to her toes.

'I've thought about this for days,' he said, slowly strolling towards her. 'What to say...how to say it.' His gaze didn't leave hers. 'May I ask you another question?'

'Already?'

She should have known he'd immediately want something more. He was too close. She backed up, but got blocked by the wall.

'Isn't this moving too quickly for a first date?'

He kept walking until he was only an inch away from

her. 'You know I can go from merely holding your hand to muffling your screams as you orgasm in less than a few moments.'

Heat flooded. 'You're—'

'Able to be myself around you. Able to take risks that I can't with anyone else. Because I know I can trust you. But you don't feel you can trust me because I let you down. And I'm so sorry about that. Give me another chance. Give *us* a chance.'

She shook her head and pressed her hand on his chest to stop him—but at the same time she was checking he was actually *there*. That this wasn't all in her head.

'Don't use our chemistry to convince me,' she begged him.

'You're already convinced. You know how good we are.'

'It's just—'

'No. It's *not* just sex. It never was.'

'Who's the one interrupting now?' She glared at him.

'I wondered about a public display. A moment of totally open vulnerability. Being that human guy, not the remote, bloodless King... But then that makes it all about me again, doesn't it?'

She stared at him silently, wondering what he was meaning now.

'And it limits your options,' he mused. 'How could you answer honestly if all the world is watching a public proposal?'

A *proposal*? Was *that* what this was? Kassie's legs trembled.

'How could you do anything other than say yes? Which would work in my favour, I guess—but then, this is you, and you don't tend to do things the conventional way. And besides, I don't want to manipulate you. You need to know exactly what you'd be walking into.'

'What *would* I be walking into?' she whispered.

'Madness. All those cameras. All that judgement. I always said I never wanted to put a woman through that. I watched my mother struggle with it. I wanted to protect my sister from it. I saw all those society women turn themselves inside out and change themselves to try to be someone else... I didn't want *you* to change. But I've realised I'm all too human, Kassie, and I'm completely selfish. I want you. Even though it's not in your best interests.'

'Are you still of the belief that it's up to *you* to decide what is in my best interests?' She stared at him. 'Seriously? You're *still* being over-protective?'

'It's a very hard habit to break.' He sighed, resting his hands on the wall on either side of her as he gazed into her eyes. 'I'm so sorry, Kassie. I'm sorry I let you think I was offering less than all of me. That you thought I wanted to keep you like some dirty little secret I was ashamed of. It wasn't like that at all. It's just that you are so precious to me that I feel scared. I want to lock you up and keep you safe.' He shrugged. 'I'm still working on that urge. The truth is I love you. I was just too stunned to realise it.'

She stared, still speechless, unsure she'd heard him correctly.

'I love you,' he repeated, and this time he smiled as he said it. A tender, wary, but fierce smile. 'I want to be with you and for you to be with me. And all that entails.'

'It's too soon,' she whispered. 'You barely know me.'

'I know you're honest and loyal and funny and serious. I know that you care about people, that you love to help people. And that you're lonely. I know that you deserve to be loved utterly...' He suddenly fell silent and a frown threatened. 'But if you think it's too soon for me to love you...then I guess you don't love me.'

He cleared his throat awkwardly and sucked in another deep breath.

'That's why I'm asking for time. It's what I meant the

other day, only I butchered it because I wasn't thinking clearly. I want you to get to know me properly. To trust me again. I can't tell you how sorry I am that I broke your faith in me.'

Deep distress welled up in her. She didn't want him to think that she didn't care. 'I was *scared*,' she whispered. 'I wanted so much more. I'd done exactly what I told myself I wouldn't do.'

'What was that?'

'Fell...' Her eyes filled with stupid tears and she shrugged her shoulders, because she couldn't put it all into words. 'For you...' she whispered.

His kiss was the gentlest thing, and it didn't last anywhere near long enough before he pulled back.

'Here's the thing...' He reached into the pocket of his jeans. 'Tradition dictates the King's bride wears the Cristallino Diamonds. This is the ring and this necklace is part of the set. There's also a tiara to match, but I couldn't fit it in my pocket.'

She blinked at the dazzling waterfall of sparkling stones cupped in his hand—polished, stunning, priceless. Her pulses roared as she shook her head. 'I can't... We can't.'

'Of course we can. I'm the King—I decide. I can marry who I want. And I want you.'

He tossed the necklace and the ring to the floor and framed her face with tender hands.

'You're not exactly disreputable, Kassie. Truth is, I don't deserve you and we both know it. But while the diamonds are beautiful and traditional, and full of meaning and importance, I want something just for you. *Not* traditional. Not because history says I have to. Just for you. Something that I chose in the hope that you would like it, because even though it hasn't been very long I hope I know you.'

He reached into his other pocket and drew out a small

box. He fumbled slightly as he lifted the lid so she could see the contents.

She gasped on seeing the ring resting on black velvet. The ruby was the richest red she'd ever seen—darkly passionate, it almost seemed to glow with an internal fire as it sat snug in its deep gold setting.

'You like it?'

A tear trickled down her cheek as she nodded. 'It's beautiful.'

'Like you.' He took the ring and tossed the box, and gently slid it down her finger. 'Beautiful *inside* as well as out. Hidden fires.'

His hands shook ever so slightly and he wouldn't let her fingers go.

'You don't have to choose,' he muttered. 'I hope you'll accept both. The public will expect to see the diamonds… without them they'll be sceptical, superstitious…but between us… I want this just for you. I want to *be* just for you. I *need* to be just for you. That's what I wanted when I made that stupid offer. For you to be mine. I was being greedy and I didn't realise it. I wanted to have you and protect you at the same time.'

'How many times do I tell you that you don't have to protect me?' Her voice cracked.

'Like you can't help yourself from caring?' He shook his head. 'I can't be something I'm not. You can't ask me to stop caring if I show it in wanting to protect you from a level of public scrutiny that only someone in my position can truly understand. You might as well ask me to cut off my arm. I can't do it.'

She gazed at him. 'We could do it together,' she suggested shyly. 'If you can trust me, I'll tell you when I need you to take me away and we can escape just the two of us to the Summer House.'

He stood very still. 'You'll tell me?'

'You know I will,' she teased, but her eyes filled.

He laughed suddenly. 'Yes. I love you, and I'm quite prepared to spend the rest of my life proving it to you.'

But then he frowned, his grip on her tightening.

'I couldn't admit even to myself the truth about how I was feeling. That afternoon with you when I... I've never taken that risk with anyone, Kassie. Not even all those years ago, when I was an arrogant, dumb youth, determined to score every woman he could—high on exhilaration and the power I had. I never once went without protection. But with you? I lost all control of myself, and that scared me. And then the thought of you pregnant with my child... It wasn't terrifying—it was thrilling. Which in turn was appalling. Was I suddenly some Neanderthal beast who wanted nothing more than to impregnate you and keep you locked in my cave for ever? *So* manipulative. And I denied the truth of that subconscious action and pushed you away.'

He drew in a ragged breath.

'I need to *earn* the right to have you by my side. Become the man you to *want* to be with.'

'You wanted me so badly you didn't bother to stop and think. I was exactly the same. I felt it too. And I wanted it. I was every bit as complicit.'

'But you knew pregnancy wouldn't happen. I didn't. And I took the risk anyway. It was the most selfish moment of my life. And the most telling.'

'I was hurt that you didn't even discuss it with me. You were just going to get your doctor to come and make me take that medicine. I thought you were horrified at the thought of any kind of future with me.'

'I couldn't bear the thought of manipulating you into a situation that you didn't want to be in. Of imprisoning you with me.' He closed his eyes. 'But at the same time I wanted it so much. *Too* much.'

'So you made yourself give it up?' She understood now. 'You really don't think you deserve happiness.'

'Then I realised that in pushing you away I might be hurting you. I was denying you. And in the end I couldn't do it even to myself. I don't want to let you go.' He drew in a breath. 'But you need to know what you'd be signing up for. Mine isn't a normal life. I have to let you choose.'

'How can you think there is *any* choice?' She gazed at him. 'Don't you *get* how much I love you? I'd do anything for you. I'll put up with anything I have to in order to be with you. I'm not afraid of the media or public interest. I don't care what they think or how they judge me. People have judged me all my life—it wasn't them I hid from. I learned to ignore them and carry on regardless. I'll just put my head down and do what I need to do. And what I *need* to do is love you.' Her eyes filled. 'All I want is to be able to love you the only way I know how.'

'And how is that?'

'Totally. Uncontrollably. With every part of me.'

'And I love you back like that and more. *More*, Kassie, you understand? So much more.'

He swept her into his arms and there was nothing between them but love and joy. In between breathless, urgent kisses they stumbled to her little bedroom and the narrow bed. He eyed it cautiously.

'Too small?' she teased.

'Perfect,' he argued. 'You'll have to cling to me.'

He drew her down on top of him, stripping her as he went.

'I like it when you cling to me. When you sigh…' He kissed her again. 'When you can't stop yourself from wanting me.'

'I never could…' she promised. 'From the moment we met.'

'I ache to give you everything,' he muttered, desperately, tenderly grinding into her. 'To love you.'

The completion she felt at that moment was so profound that more tears spilled even as she smiled at him. Entwined, they knew the magic they made together was too good to be restrained for long...

He cradled her close afterwards, his voice low. 'I came to the hospital this morning because I couldn't wait any longer. I saw you before you saw me and you looked so happy that I left before speaking with you.'

She heard the remnants of his hurt, understood his vulnerability was still real, and her heart warmed at knowing how deeply he felt about her.

'I'd been to see the head of the prosthetics department to get support for participating in that research project.'

'Oh, that's great.' He sat up and looked down into her face. 'Did you get it?'

'Yes—and they're really keen for me to work on other projects with them too. I should have spoken up sooner.'

'It's never too late.' He drew her closer with a happy sigh. 'That's wonderful.' He stroked her arms. 'You'll keep working there after we're married...?'

She smiled. 'I'd like to...'

'Of course. I'm proud of what you do.'

'But sometimes I'd like to travel with you...to do some of the things you do...'

'We'll work it out,' he promised. 'We'll find some kind of balance.'

'Do you suppose that poor pizza delivery guy is still waiting at the door?' She suddenly sat up.

He laughed and stood, grabbing a towel to wrap around his waist. 'I'll go get it.'

'Like *that*?' she shrieked, appalled. 'There might be photographers out there.'

'I'll be sure to show my best side.' He kissed her swiftly, with an arrogant laugh at her expression. 'I'm with you now—now and always—and I don't give a damn *who* knows.'

EPILOGUE

Six months later

'SHE'S BEAUTIFUL.' KASSIE looked down at the tiny baby nestled in her sister-in-law's arms. 'Just so beautiful.'

'She's tiny.' Giorgos leaned over her shoulder and put on his resting frowny face. '*Too* tiny. She looks like she could break easily. How long until she gets bigger?'

'Giorgos...' Kassie smiled and injected a warning tone into her voice.

'My brother is a marshmallow.' Princess Eleni, currently suffused in a maternal glow, wasn't hearing a bad word about anyone.

'Rest easy.' Damon patted his brother-in-law on the shoulder. 'I've got this.'

Giorgos sighed. 'I know...' He looked again at the petite baby and smiled. 'She's adorable.'

Damon and Eleni had decided their baby should be born in Palisades, so they'd returned to the palace for the last few months before she was due. In a couple of days they'd fly to Damon's private island, to spend time alone and bond together, but they'd just had a personal photo taken, to share with the public, with sweet Princess Antonia only a few hours old.

'You have to admit she is tiny,' Giorgos muttered as he walked with Kassie down the corridor towards their own apartments.

'And that scares you?'

'I'm not afraid to admit that she makes me feel vulnerable. I want to take care of her.'

'Hmm...' Kassie walked ahead of him into the suite. 'You might need to get used to that.'

'Get used to what?' Giorgos shut the door with a definite click.

Kassie turned to face him. She knew not to underestimate the blandness of his query. 'Being around tiny little people who take a few years to grow to their full size.'

He walked towards her slowly, his eyes intent on her. 'What are you telling me?'

'You're a smart man—you *know* what I'm telling you.' She backed up against the wall.

His eyes flickered. *Dangerous.*

'I thought you wanted to wait a while,' he said in a soft voice. 'We've only been married three months.'

Three months since that insanely massive wedding, with most of the world watching.

While they had created their own traditions, there were some things Giorgos had wanted to do in keeping with his position. Not because it was what had *always* been done, but because he'd wanted the world to know how proud he was to take her as his wife. That had meant an enormous state ceremony, with all the trimmings.

Eleni and Damon had supported her in those terrifying few minutes before she'd had to walk into the country's cathedral, packed with aristocracy, people and news cameras, and not trip her way up that endless aisle with everyone watching.

But she'd locked eyes with Giorgos and her nerves had evaporated. He'd grinned at her, and the whisper of a wink had been a giveaway flash of roguishness. And then his eyes had filled with pure emotion.

The video of that moment had gone viral—made into romantic memes shared millions of times. Suddenly the world had realised that the supposedly 'serious' King not only had a sense of humour, he had a soul, and their love story endlessly dominated the global media.

Fortunately they'd been able to escape to the Summer House for a blissfully private honeymoon.

'And I thought you were on board with that.' She chuckled happily. 'But, no, you've just had to go ahead and be dictatorial and bossy and decide everything for everyone, like the arrogant autocrat that you are.'

'It takes two to tango,' he noted. 'So it can't all be *my* fault.'

'No.' She nodded in agreement. 'And apparently two can become three.'

He inhaled deeply. 'Are you telling me you're pregnant?' His words were little above a whisper.

'Are you telling me you're finally listening?' she teased back breathily.

'Are you telling me you don't think I've already noticed?'

'Oh, *please*.' She paused, frowning as his smug look grew. 'Are you telling me you knew already?'

'Your breasts are fuller…you've been a little more tired than usual. And your period is late.'

He was *that* observant?

She pouted. 'You think you know everything about me.'

'No. I think I don't know you nearly well enough. I can't wait to watch you become a mother. I can't wait to watch you do everything.' He shivered. 'It's been hell, holding off on summoning the doctor to check you over.'

'The doctor already has checked me over,' she reassured him. 'I knew you'd instantly worry, but you don't need to. I'm in perfect health.' She leaned towards him provocatively. 'Apparently I'm in top physical condition.'

'I knew that too,' he growled. 'You tease me too much.'

'You love me for it.' She batted her lashes.

'You do it because *you* love the way I retaliate.'

He suddenly reached for her.

'And look where *that's* got me.' She yelped as he pulled her close. 'Happy,' she assured him, meeting the hunger in his kiss. 'So unbelievably happy. And terrified. And excited. I can't believe it!' She laughed with pure, unadulterated delight.

But his smile had gone as tension and intention gripped his muscles. 'I need you. Right now.'

'Yes.' She wound her arms around his neck, eager to offer the security she knew he sought—of knowing that she was strong and well and happy.

He tugged up her red skirt, knowing just how to draw that desperate response from her. 'Need to feel you,' he groaned as he drove home. 'I'm weak over you.'

She shook her head. Weak was the last thing this man was.

'I never knew I could be this happy.' She cupped his face as she met him, their passion coalescing. 'This fulfilled.'

Their connection blew her away—so constant, so complete.

'Me neither,' he confessed. 'I love you.'

And he didn't just tell her—he showed her. Over and over again. And in the end Kassie couldn't smile for kissing her King, her lover, her *everything*.

* * * * *

A RING TO TAKE HIS REVENGE

PIPPA ROSCOE

For my editor Sareeta.
Thank you for whipping this into shape
and helping me to see the way to a better book.
May it be the first of many!

PROLOGUE

London...

ANTONIO ARCURI GESTURED for the petite brunette to slide into the limousine ahead of him. He might be accustomed to ushering women he'd only just met into his chauffeur-driven town car, but not when it was business. Never when it was business.

Yet there had been no other option. His morning meeting had run unacceptably late, and now he could neither cancel this last interview for a new PA nor be late for his meeting with the other two members of the Winners' Circle—the racing syndicate he co-owned.

Antonio had been waiting almost a year to see his closest friends Dimitri and Danyl, his brothers in more ways than blood could ever account for. So he had been forced to multi-task. And Antonio hated nothing more than having his hand forced.

So far, the brunette—Ms Guilham—had yet even to raise an eyebrow at the somewhat unusual relocation of their meeting, which boded well. The way that she struggled with the wayward hemline of her skirt as it rose up over toned, creamy thighs the moment she sat back on the plush leather seat did not. The hemline that when she was standing bordered on the overly conservative was now a sincerely unwanted distraction.

Settling into the seat beside her, Antonio studied Emma Guilham from the corner of his eye. She was petite. Beautiful, he conceded, then filed and discarded the fact. Whether a future PA of his was attractive or not was irrelevant. At least she had finally stopped fidgeting with her skirt.

The limousine pulled away from the dark underground parking area of his London office, emerged into pale wintry sunlight…and into busy central London traffic. He cursed silently and resisted the urge to glance at his watch. He knew what time it was and he was cutting it fine.

'Your driver should take St James's and then Pall Mall. Christmas and Regent Street don't mix well.'

She locked her hazel eyes on his and Antonio felt a sudden start in his chest. Her gaze held no desperate eagerness to please, no fevered excitement, nor the sensual assessment he often felt when women looked at him. He knew he was attractive and took full advantage of the fact—though never with his employees.

But, most importantly, there was no pretence in her eyes. And that was both unusual and—to him—invaluable.

Compared to the three other interviewees he'd met, she was, on paper, the least impressive. At barely twenty-two, Emma Guilham was young. But while the other candidates had varied in age from late twenties to early fifties, she currently seemed the least flappable. He didn't need to look at her CV. His quick mind recalled all the pertinent information and he proceeded with the interview for the position of his new PA.

'You graduated with your International Business

Studies degree from SOAS after attaining four A levels. You can type one hundred and twenty words per minute, you like travelling and reading,' he stated, somewhat disconcerted to see the hazel flecks in her eyes transition into sea-green foam. 'You are hardworking— a fact repeatedly attested to by the CFO of my London office, where you have been working full-time for the past few months, and part-time for the year before that. At the same time finishing your degree—another thing my CFO repeatedly emphasised.'

A quick nod of the head was Emma's only reaction, which drew a frown to his forehead. Usually candidates like to expound on their virtues when he raised the opportunity to do so. He left a second, a breath of space for her to speak, but she remained silent.

'The position is in New York. I deal in high-stakes, highly confidential business acquisition and I expect long hours, absolute focus and complete discretion. Both in business matters and personal. I am not always present in the New York office, but your presence will be required there full-time.'

'Of course.'

He continued to watch for the smallest change in expression. She had yet to display the excitement or even the badly supressed shock and awe that he had so irritatingly witnessed through the previous interviews.

'You don't seem to be engaging with this interview, Ms Guilham.' He had no patience for time-wasters. And he had no need for a 'yes' woman, but still. This was... unique.

'You have yet to ask me a question, Mr Arcuri,' she said, with no trace of accusation or offence in her tone. 'May I speak plainly?' she asked, and he gestured for her to do so with a swift swipe of his hand.

'Mr Arcuri, I have attended three preliminary interviews for this position—one with UK HR, one with North American HR, and one with your previous PA. I am under no illusions as to my limited experience in comparison to more seasoned applicants, and can only conclude that your willingness to squeeze me in to your "commute" is a gracious courtesy. It is one that I appreciate.'

At this, the brunette rapped on the window to talk to the driver.

'Left here, then second right,' she said, before turning her gaze back to him. 'I believe at this point your choice comes down to personality. And as far as you're concerned, as my future boss, I don't have one. You want someone to live and breathe Arcuri Enterprises? That I can do. You want someone to handle an international diary? I can do it with my eyes closed. You want someone to bar the way and dissolve anything that might prevent your valuable time from being spent as you wish? I'm the one you want. Anything else your background checks can uncover or you don't need to know. I want to work for you because you're the best. It's that simple.'

The limousine glided to a stop outside the grand building of the Asquith Club in London just as Antonio was digesting the rather impressive and somewhat surprising speech that had filled the car.

Ms Guilham smiled, not unkindly.

Antonio felt a small smile pull at the edges of his lips in response.

'I have one question, Ms Guilham.'

'Yes?'

'If you were stranded on a desert island and you were allowed one item, what would it be?'

Antonio had heard many different answers to the question over the years. Mozart's music, the complete works of Shakespeare, a piano. But he'd only ever heard *her* answer once before. It was the one he had given himself.

'A satellite phone.'

He nodded, betraying nothing.

'Mr Arcuri, thank you for the opportunity to speak with you. I shall look forward to hearing from HR and hope that you have an enjoyable lunch. I'll see myself back to the office.'

With that Emma Guilham left Antonio sitting in the car, feeling stunned for the first time in some while. And he wasn't the only one, considering the way his driver was currently watching Emma's departure with something like awe.

As Antonio exited the limousine and made his way to the private room at the Asquith where Dimitri Kyriakou and Danyl Nejem Al Arain waited, he forced his mind away from the way Ms Guilham's hips had swayed as she'd walked towards Piccadilly Circus tube station.

With ruthless efficiency he refocused his mind on the Winners' Circle.

The three men had met as students, and their friendship had been forged in the depths of their darkest moments. Through it all they had supported, commiserated and celebrated with each other. And when, after university, Antonio had needed capital to start his business, Dimitri, Danyl and his maternal grandfather had been his first investors. He had, of course, paid them back with interest, and in half the promised time. But he had never forgotten the debt he owed his friends.

Antonio knew in his heart, in his blood, that he wouldn't be here today without them. And they would say the same of him. And now, after a year, all three men—each of whom regularly featured in the newspapers as some of the greatest living business figures—would finally be together in the same room again.

As he made his way towards the table in the private dining area a small blonde was hastily leaving, casting him with a frowning glance as she passed.

'What did I miss?' Antonio asked, taking in the appearance of his friends.

Wrongful imprisonment had taken its toll on Dimitri, yet his powerful Greek features still turned the heads of any nearby female. And Danyl didn't need to rely on his royal status as Sheikh in line to the Terhren throne. Brooding intensity radiated from him—as Antonio's last assistant had remarked.

Only the might of the American legal system had put a halt to their quarterly meetings—the one immovable feature in Antonio's increasingly full diary. But within the year Dimitri's innocence had been realised and proclaimed, and now they were finally back together again.

'A proposition,' Dimitri replied in response to Antonio's question.

'In public? During the day? Gentlemen, you're putting my scandalous reputation to shame,' Antonio asserted.

'A *professional* proposition,' growled Danyl through gritted teeth.

'She—' nodding to the exit made by the blonde woman '—wants to race for the syndicate in the Hanley Cup,' Dimitri clarified.

'We have a jockey,' interjected Danyl.

'She says she can win all three races.'

Antonio was mildly intrigued. 'That's not been done since…'

'Since her father trained the horse and rider twenty years ago,' supplied Dimitri.

Antonio's mind raced through the implications. '*That* was Mason McAulty?'

A rather undignified grunt emerged from Danyl's direction.

Antonio considered the possibilities...the amount of the winning purse, the attention from the global press. News of their racing syndicate had ebbed and flowed over the years, but no one could argue with the level of their success. Founded shortly after their university days, it had been the perfect venture for three men who loved the high-stakes world of gambling, horseflesh and adrenaline.

Antonio had once been a serious contender for international-level polo, but that had been before Michael Steele's actions had all but destroyed his family. Biting back the familiar anger that was never far away from his thoughts of the man, Antonio forced his attention back to the proposition.

'Can she do it?' he asked.

Dimitri shrugged, but Danyl seemed to be giving it some thought.

'Most likely,' he eventually said.

'I'm in,' Antonio stated with an innately Italian shrug of his shoulders. If Mason McAulty managed it, the win would be incredible. If she failed... Well, was there any such thing as bad press? Antonio liked the edge that it would place them on. Hell, he practically *lived* on it.

'Why not?' Dimitri said, throwing his hat into the ring.

Danyl nodded almost reluctantly, his lips a grim line of determination. Antonio might not know the source of the furious look Danyl cast towards the exit Mason

Mcaulty had left through, but he very much hoped she knew that she was playing with fire.

'Whisky?' Dimitri queried as Antonio finally took his seat.

'Absolutely,' Antonio replied, relaxing back and drinking in the sight of his friends. 'It's good to have you back.'

'Say that again and I'll *know* you've gone soft,' came Dimitri's terse reply.

'If I wanted to listen to a bunch of women gossip, I could have stayed at home and visited the harem,' Danyl concluded.

Antonio scoffed. 'You don't have a harem. If you did we'd never see you.'

But instead of relishing the familiar bond he had with his two closest friends, Antonio found his mind returning to the woman he had just decided to make his new PA.

Emma Guilham...

CHAPTER ONE

Eighteen months later...

EMMA SWEPT THE long tendrils of dark hair back from her face and into a discreet neat bun with swift efficiency. Even had she not seen Antonio Arcuri's occasional frown when a few strands would escape the hold these pins had on her hair, she instinctively knew that this was what her ruthless boss wanted from her. Discretion, speed and efficiency.

As she checked her appearance in the ladies' bathroom at the New York office of Arcuri Enterprises, the shadowed silver insignia of the letters *A* and *E* conjoined in the corner of each large mirror snagged her attention and sent a thrill of satisfaction through her.

She had come so far from her mother's small but comfortable home on the fringes of Hampstead Heath. She thought back to the quite outrageous way she had been interviewed by Antonio in that limousine, inching its way through London's Christmas traffic. She had, in her mind, been brazen. But then Emma had honestly thought that she stood no chance of getting the job. With nothing to lose and everything to gain, she had simply spoken the truth.

She had meant every word she'd said, and had stuck

to each and every one of them in the last eighteen months. She had fought so hard to be here—to be in New York, to be Antonio Arcuri's PA. And she wouldn't let his wholly uncharacteristic, unscheduled and increasingly imminent arrival now put her off her stride.

Ever since the ping had sounded on her phone at one in the morning, alerting her to the fact that Antonio would be back from Italy and in the office in less than six hours, Emma had felt something akin to panic. Only she had assured herself she no longer *did* panic. Instead, Emma had launched herself out of bed, scanned his appointments and found nothing in his diary to warrant such an unexpected return. So, she had no idea what to expect from her brooding Italian boss.

She had begun to look forward to the times when Antonio was away from the office. Whether it was for his immovable meetings with the other members of the Winners' Circle syndicate, or his visits to his offices in London, Hong Kong and Italy, she relished the time when she only had to deal with him through the separation of email and the occasional video conference. She welcomed these reprieves from his presence. Because in reality, in the flesh, Antonio was simply... overwhelming.

It was more than his classic good-looks. His bitter-chocolate-coloured eyes, set against defined cheekbones and a determined jaw would be devastating enough on any man. Along with the smooth Italian tan that contrasted with the deep rich wine colour of lips that were almost cruelly sensual. Every inch of him was honed, powerful and predatory. But she knew that even all those attributes combined didn't matter. It was the vitality—the authority that resonated from his very being—that really called to her.

But she had learned to temper her attraction. Refused to allow it to interfere with her work. She was here to do a job—not to lust after her attractive boss. She refused to fall into the trap so many other women had fallen into. Besides, she had goals—places she wanted to see, things she desperately wanted to do—none of which included Antonio Arcuri.

The door to the large office bathroom slammed open and a string of women rushed in, each armed to the hilt with make-up bags. Emma watched them for a moment, producing the tools of femininity that were used to enhance and seduce, delicately applying a million products as she once had, at the age of seventeen, using them with a heavy hand to mask the ravages of chemotherapy.

But she forced the memory aside. It wasn't as if Antonio cared at all about her appearance. Just her ability. Emma smiled ruefully at the row of Arcuri's female staff. Antonio had that effect on women. But not her. She might find her boss devastatingly attractive, but she wasn't going to be distracted by him.

She wasn't going to be distracted by any man.

Settled behind her computer in the outer room of Antonio's top-floor office, she let a feeling of control and calm wash over her. This was her domain and she loved it.

The clean chrome lines made the CEO's office on the twenty-fourth floor of the Manhattan skyscraper more than she could ever have imagined. The glass-fronted building afforded a highly sought-after vista of Central Park, allowing incredible views of the famous skyline to be her daily backdrop. The decor screamed money and wealth. Even if she only borrowed it during the day, before returning to her tiny apartment in Brooklyn each night.

Coming to New York had been the first thing Emma had been truly able to check off her Living List, after five years of remission had finally signalled the end of the terrible illness that had taken so much from her. And even if she had stayed in her role as Antonio's personal assistant for a little longer than she had originally intended, failing to tick off some of the other things on her Living List since coming here...she chose to ignore it. She was happy. And there was always time in the future—in *her* future.

'Do you know why he's here?'

Emma looked up from her desk to find James, a very nervous low-level exec, almost twitching with panic. He swept his glasses off his face, revealing bleary eyes, and cast her a look as other staff, equally nervous, watched from the corridor.

Word of Antonio's impending arrival must have spread like wildfire for, while it wasn't unusual to see *some* of the Arcuri staff beavering away at this ungodly hour of the morning, it was unusual to see *all* of them. But that was the effect of Antonio Arcuri. He didn't ask—he expected. He didn't demand—he simply didn't have to.

'Is he here yet?' James asked now, not waiting for an answer to his first question.

'Mr Arcuri has business to attend to, nothing more,' she said reassuringly, not really knowing if that was true or not.

'It's just that... Well, given the current climate...'

'Arcuri Enterprises is strong enough to survive *any* climate—current or otherwise,' Antonio's Italian-accented voice cut in harshly.

Emma hated the way he did that. Crept into rooms like a silent-footed panther. And she felt pity for poor James, who had turned from nervously pale to humiliated red with just one sentence from their boss, before fleeing the room.

Antonio turned on Emma. 'Why does everyone look as if they're about to get fired?' he demanded angrily.

Emma resisted the urge to sigh. He was clearly in *that* mood. A mood which made it easier for her to resist eating up the sight of his six-foot-plus powerful and lean frame.

'It is a little unusual for you to break your trip to Italy.'

'I need Danyl and Dimitri on a conference call immediately. And I need you to start a research file on Benjamin Bartlett. Everything and anything you can find on him and his company,' he said, throwing the last over his shoulder as he moved towards his office.

'I'll get the research team on it right away.'

'No,' Antonio said, pausing mid-stride. 'No one else is to know. I want you to handle it personally.'

With that, he stalked into his office, slamming the door behind him, and Emma sighed again. She closed the open folder on her desk concerning the Arcuri Foundation's charity gala—a project she had already invested much of her spare time in—knowing that she would have to take it home that evening. And as she dialled the numbers she knew by heart to get Dimitri and Danyl, she wondered just who Benjamin Bartlett was and why he was so important.

Antonio Arcuri willed the adrenaline coursing through his veins to subside. He discarded his suit jacket on the sofa and instead of taking a seat at his desk stalked towards the floor-to-ceiling windows fronting his office and flexed his hands.

He had decided to give the task of researching Benjamin Bartlett to Emma on the flight back here from his mother's house in Sorrento. He had been impressed with his calm, unflappable PA over the past eighteen months. Eighteen months in which he'd ruthlessly tamped down his initial and very much unwanted sensual interest in her from the moment she had stepped into the limousine on his way to the Asquith club in London.

Of course it helped that she dressed like the founding member of some religious organisation, and showed absolutely no interest in him whatsoever outside of their business interaction. He'd had PAs before who had raised their eyebrows and been uncomfortable handling some of his more indiscreet requests, such as fending off ex-lovers or acquiring suitable parting gifts. Despite what her conservative appearance suggested, Emma had handled each and every one without judgement or comment. The only thing she asked for was financial approval.

In short, Emma Guilham was *very* good at her job.

Which was exactly why he trusted her implicitly to handle the research on Bartlett. He couldn't risk news of his interest in the man leaking out before he'd had a chance to arrange a meeting with him. But it wasn't Bartlett himself that he was after. He could have taken or left his famous heritage brand, having no need to add it to his investment portfolio. No. It was the *other* potential investor that Antonio had in his sights. The investor that Antonio wanted to crush beneath his heel until no trace of him remained.

As he stood before the windows he didn't see a millimetre of the lush green sanctuary in the middle of New York's bustle. Antonio saw victory within his grasp.

Finally Antonio had the chance to bring Michael Steele to his knees. To cripple him completely, once and for all.

For so long he'd been nibbling away at the outskirts of Steele's business dealings. And each time Antonio took one more bite from the man's holdings he thought of his mother and sister. Of the shock and devastation Steele had wrought against his family with efficient ruthlessness. The subsequent pain that had nearly destroyed his mother, and the emotional scars that his young sister had turned against her own body until there had been almost nothing of her left.

Antonio had spent years clawing his way up the financial ladder...for this. The chance to destroy Michael Steele once and for all.

The buzz of the intercom cut through his thoughts and Emma's voice announced that she had Danyl and Dimitri on the line for him.

'What's wrong?' demanded Danyl.

Many would have been forgiven for thinking they heard anger in his voice, but Antonio knew better and identified concern.

'Nothing's wrong. In fact it's the exact opposite.'

'It must be...what?...six in the morning in New York?' queried Dimitri. 'Even *you* don't usually start until a bit later.'

'It's seven.'

'I feel sorry for your PA,' remarked Danyl. 'She just went into battle with my assistant to get me in on this call instead of calling the Terhren Secretary of State.'

'Don't feel sorry for her,' Antonio responded. 'Be impressed.'

'I am,' Danyl replied. 'Anyone who can put my assistant off state business is worth their weight in gold.'

'I have it. The way to take down Steele once and for all.'

Antonio didn't need to explain who he was talking about, nor why it was so important. Dimitri and Danyl knew what this meant to him—had meant ever since the age of sixteen.

'How?' asked Dimitri.

'I've been reliably informed that Benjamin Bartlett is looking for a healthy financial investment in his company. It would be Steele's last chance for financial security. He has the capital to invest, but not enough to survive without it.'

'And you plan to ensure that *you* win the investment,' stated Dimitri. 'Whatever you need—it's yours.'

Antonio smiled. 'That's not necessary. I can counter any investment offer he makes to Bartlett.'

'I've met Bartlett. I must say I'm surprised that he's looking for investment. He's always been financially stable.'

'You know him?' demanded Antonio. 'How?' he asked, his quick mind already working out how to use this to his advantage.

'He's a keen horseman. A regular feature on the international racing scene.'

Antonio frowned, scanning his usually perfect memory for any moment when he might have met the man amongst the numerous races they had attended as members of the Winners' Circle syndicate.

'He usually keeps to himself, though,' Danyl continued. 'Tends to stay away from the more *lively* areas that we enjoy. He'll probably be in Argentina for the first leg of the Hanley Cup. Do you know why he's looking for investment?'

'The why doesn't matter. I'll do anything to make sure that I win the investment and not Steele.'

Silence greeted his pronouncement. For a moment Antonio worried that the connection had been lost.

'Antonio, be careful. Desperation makes a man dangerous. I know this better than anyone,' Dimitri warned.

'I can handle the man.' Antonio practically growled down the phone.

'I wasn't talking about *him*.'

A knock on the door preceded Emma's appearance with the espresso he very much needed at that moment. Telling Dimitri and Danyl to hang on, he put the call on hold and waited for Emma to put the coffee on his desk and leave.

He was also buying time. Dimitri's warning hadn't fallen on deaf ears. But Antonio had spent years waiting for this day. He knew his mother would be saddened by his continued pursuit of revenge. She had pleaded with him over the years to move on. To put the hurt behind him—behind them all. But he couldn't.

As Emma retreated to her desk behind the door to his own office, he surprised himself by wondering if she would understand. There had been times when his usually conservative, cool-eyed assistant had shown a deeply hidden spark of defiance, something like the fight he felt at that moment. But as the door clicked closed he put that thought aside and resumed his call.

'That might not be the only problem that you face, Antonio,' said Danyl.

'Whatever it is, I can handle it.'

'I'm not so sure. Bartlett is notoriously moralistic. And your recent and very public exploits with a certain Swedish model might be a rather large putting off for him.'

An image of the blonde who had graced his bed for a number of months rushed into Antonio's mind. For the most part their encounter had run along the usual lines. Brief but sensually satisfying trysts whenever their diaries brought them together. Until she had started to ask for more. To ask for things he had told her wouldn't be part of their relationship. And when he had ended things she had quickly transitioned from a cool, poised and sophisticated companion into a raging, deeply resentful and incredibly publicly wounded lover.

'I can hardly be blamed for the fact she went to the press. I made her no promises—no lies were told. She knew the score and should have handled the end of our…interaction…with more finesse.'

'Whether or not she *should* have, she didn't. And Bartlett won't like it one bit. He has a strict morality clause for all his board members. And the last to break it two years ago is still looking for work, from what I hear.'

'What exactly are you saying, Danyl?'

'Well, you might need to take yourself off the market, so to speak.'

What? Shocked, Antonio didn't realise that the word had failed to escape his tightly clenched jaw.

'You've either shocked him into silence or you need to explain more clearly what you mean, Danyl,' Dimitri said, laughing.

'Marriage,' replied Danyl.

'Just because *you're* looking for a wife, it doesn't mean *I* have to.'

Everything within Antonio roared an absolute *no* at the idea. All the women he had encounters with knew the deal—even the Swedish model, though she'd seemed to forget it.

Short term, high hits of sensual pleasure were important to him. He was a virile male, after all, and not one to deny himself sexual satisfaction. But nothing more. He neither wanted nor needed the distraction of anything more permanent.

He washed away his distaste at the very idea of marriage with a hot, strong shot of espresso. He scanned his mind for any examples of a healthy, successful partnership and could not find one. Neither Dimitri nor Danyl had any particular fondness for the institution of marriage themselves, though for Danyl—being the future ruler of Terhren—it had become a considerably more pressing matter.

Their bachelor status was something that the press had latched on to more than once when covering the successes of their Winners' Circle racing syndicate. And it was certainly something that drew a wealth of beautiful women to their door. Was Antonio ready to consider closing that very door on the one thing aside from his business that he took *very* seriously?

'How bad is he really?' he asked his friends.

'That board member I mentioned…? He hadn't even had an affair. It was the rumour that Bartlett objected to.'

'Perhaps you don't have to…how do the Americans say it?…eat the whole hog—?'

'*Go*, Dimitri. It's *go* the whole hog,' interrupted Danyl.

'Please—we're talking about a wife, here. Can we leave out references to eating and hogs?'

'That's what I'm saying. Perhaps it doesn't have to be a wife.'

* * *

Emma had finished filing the quarterly reports, reassured countless staff members that, no, she didn't think Antonio's sudden appearance meant staffing cuts, and given consolatory smiles to a number of overly disappointed female employees who had failed to catch sight of Antonio before he'd locked himself in his office for most of the day. She had collated all the information she could on Benjamin Bartlett from initial online searches and saved it to Antonio's private drive, and finally settled down to eat the lunch she had missed three hours ago.

So, of course, as her mouth was full of avocado and bacon bagel, that was the precise moment Antonio Arcuri chose to appear before her desk. With a demand that took every ounce of her control not to choke on.

'Emma. I need you to find me a fiancée.'

Emma's usually focused and quick mind halted in its tracks. Of all the things she'd ever been asked by her notoriously difficult boss, this had to hit the top of the list.

'Do you have a particular person in mind? Or will anyone do?'

She had finally managed to swallow her mouthful around the shock that threatened to lock her throat in a seized position. And she was hopeful that her voice betrayed none of the sarcasm she felt so deeply, and instead projected only the smooth efficiency she knew Antonio prized so highly.

Emma loved being a personal assistant. She knew there were people who looked down on what they considered a lowly position. But, to Emma, the satisfaction of ensuring that her boss's day—his *life*—ran without stumbling blocks was important to her. She liked feeling indispensable. She liked knowing that she was part of something much bigger than she could ever achieve on her own.

And she liked fixing things.

If she was honest, it was because she knew how awful it was *not* to be able to fix something for herself. How scary and frustrating it could be. Whether it had been her breast cancer or the subsequent breakdown of her parents' marriage, she had been devastated by the sheer helplessness that she had felt at the time. And, whilst Emma might not have been able to fix the damage to her parents' marriage in the past, she could certainly help find Antonio a fiancée in the present.

Antonio pinned her with a gaze that would have removed a certain amount of testosterone from many of his male employees and likely increased the pheromones in the female ones.

'Was that sarcasm?'

'No,' Emma assured him, hoping the painful blush staining her cheeks wouldn't give her away. 'I simply wondered if you had your sights set on someone specific.'

'No,' he replied, frowning.

'So...' She battled on through the oddness of the situation. 'Do you have any parameters for this search? Wealth, previous marital status, level of attractiveness...?' She was desperately thinking of a polite way to say *bra size* when she registered with some surprise Antonio's confusion. He clearly hadn't thought this through.

'Reputation. She must be scandal-free.'

Emma fought to contain the rather un-ladylike snort that tickled her nose. It sounded as if he were looking to buy a prize heifer with an up-to-date vaccination history. Which made her wonder, horrified for a moment, whether the poor woman in question might in fact be required to present a full medical history.

'And I need her within two days.'

'Antonio, I'm not Amazon Prime. I can't just produce a...*a fiancée*,' she whispered harshly, fearing that she might be overheard, or even accused of some kind of highly salacious 'procurement' for her boss. 'Perhaps if you could explain the...the context, it might be slightly easier for me to...to understand what's needed.'

She knew she was stumbling over her words but, given his current mood, she clearly had to choose them wisely.

'I am about to set up a meeting with Benjamin Bartlett, who is touting for investment in his company. A company in which *I* must be the sole investor. And, being a notoriously moral man, Bartlett might be reluctant to involve himself with Arcuri Enterprises given...' He trailed off, circling his hands in a typically Italian gesture.

'Given your recent experience with Inga the Swedish—?'

'I know what she was, Ms Guilham,' Antonio cut in.

'Quite. So you need a beard?'

Antonio's hand went to the smooth planes of his chiselled jaw. 'A beard?'

'Not that kind of beard,' she said, suppressing the smile that toyed at the edges of her mouth. 'You need a fake fiancée to mask your previous indiscretions so that Bartlett will find you more palatable and therefore be more likely to welcome your investment.'

'In a nutshell, yes.'

'And am I to presume that all of this—' she said mirrored his Italian gesture '—needs to be kept under wraps? No one is to know about this, as well as the re-search into Bartlett?'

He nodded his dark-haired head once. 'There is an-other party interested in investing with Bartlett. My interest cannot get out to that person—or any other for that matter.'

The darkness of the warning in his voice was some-thing that Emma hadn't yet encountered in her boss. And that in itself was enough to inform her that this wasn't to be taken lightly.

Her quick mind filed the top-line notes of his re-quest. 'Okay. I'm going to need to clear your schedule tomorrow evening.'

This was why Emma was good, Antonio thought to himself. Apart from the slight slip-up of her earlier sarcasm, which he would happily put down to surprise, when she took on a task she was efficient, direct and held none of the self-doubt he had seen in staff twice her age.

He knew her announcement of his change of plan for tomorrow would be wholly and one hundred per cent in line with her new-found task. A task that she hadn't balked at, and had only posed pertinent ques-tions on. Mostly.

'Done.'

'I'll have your blue tuxedo sent to the dry cleaners and prepared for the gala.'

'What gala?' Antonio queried.

'The Arcuri Foundation's yearly charity gala. You are usually in Italy during these two weeks, which is why you are never sent an invitation.'

'We have a charity gala?'

For the first time in eighteen months Antonio was

surprised to see something like anger in Emma Guilham's eyes.

'Yes, we do.' She paused, once again masking her
obvious feelings on the matter with her legendarily cool
gaze. 'And it will be the perfect place for you to find
a fiancée.'

CHAPTER TWO

ANTONIO HAD SPENT the last twenty-four hours going over the research files Emma had put together on Bartlett—and the other research she had provided.

If he found anything distasteful about looking at the pictures and brief biographics Emma had collated of several of the single female attendees of that evening's event, he ruthlessly forced it aside. He had but one goal. And tonight would be the first step in achieving it.

Emma buzzed on the intercom, interrupting his thoughts to announce that the car was there to take them to The Langsford Hotel. Although it was only a fifteen-minute walk from the office, and he'd been inclined to make that walk, Emma had swiftly denounced the idea, saying that it wouldn't 'do' to have the CEO of Arcuri Enterprises *walking* up to the red carpet in front of the world's press. After all, she had said, she was apparently now in the business of safeguarding his reputation.

He'd repressed a smile. He was beginning to enjoy these brief glimpses of a dry English humour that she had hidden from him until now. Pulling at the sleeves of the tuxedo's jacket to fit them to the lines of his arms and torso, he opened the door to his office—and stopped.

Emma was perched on the end of her desk, leaning over towards the phone and looking quite unlike any way he'd seen look before.

She was still adorned in her usual monotone colours of black and white, and the wide panels of her loose dress covered all but the faintest glimpses of her figure. But her dark hair was piled up on her head in thick twirls, revealing strands of gold and deep reds that he had not seen before. It framed her heart-shaped face perfectly, and a light dusting of make-up served to accentuate the hazel and green of her eyes. A nude gloss lent a sheen to her lips that sent a punch to his gut more powerful than any brighter, richer colour could have achieved.

She looked natural and fresh—and so very different from the women he usually spent his time with.

'Yes, don't worry. The waiters know what to do. But because Ms Cherie was a last-minute addition to the invitation list we couldn't have known her dietary requirements before. The kitchen staff always make three extra portions of each main, so just reassure her that a vegan option will be made available to her.'

Antonio watched as Emma hung up the phone, catching the unusual sight of a long, shapely, creamy calf.

'Vegan?'

Emma turned, clearly surprised to find him standing there.

'Enough of a crime to scratch her off the fiancée list?' she asked.

'Not yet,' Antonio said, forcing his libido under control.

During the day—in her usual office attire—she wasn't so much of a problem. But even though Emma was covered from head to toe, that glimpse of smooth marble-like skin was enough to snare his attention. And he suddenly understood why Victorian England had deemed ankles the most threatening thing to society since smallpox.

Shaking his head to rid his mind of inappropriate thoughts about his PA, he led the way to the elevator that would take them down to the limousine waiting for them in the underground car park.

In the confines of the metal box, with Emma beside him, Antonio realised that it was going to be a long night.

Emma couldn't wait for this night to be over. They hadn't even arrived at the gala and she was already exhausted. It had taken every waking minute she'd had, not only to put together her research on Bartlett and compile the dossiers on Antonio's prospective fiancées—not that most of them *knew* they were prospective fiancées—but also to ensure that the foundation's gala wasn't single-handedly ruined by the very man in charge of organising it in the first place.

Marcus Greenfeld was a fusty old man, with fusty old ideas about how to run a charity. And it made her mad. She'd caught sight of his opening speech on the photocopier on the twenty-third floor and realised that something had to be done.

She'd hastily rewritten the thing, told a bold-faced lie to Greenfeld's assistant that Antonio had wanted to take a look at it, and sent it off to the teleprompter before Greenfeld had even been able to think of questioning it. Or question the three extra invitations she'd had issued to fiancée options four, five and six.

Antonio might have told her what he needed in a fiancée but, honestly, the man's taste in women was so varied she couldn't tell which way he would go. Though option two—the vegan Ella Cherie—was looking increasingly less likely.

As the limo pulled up to The Langsford she remembered she had yet to tell Antonio about the other last-minute invitation.

'Dimitri will be here tonight,' she said as they slowed to a stop. 'Danyl was…unable to attend.'

'Well, he *is* running a country.'

Emma wasn't so sure. She'd heard angry words in the background when she was on the phone to his assistant. There had been something behind the bitterly shouted phrase, *'I wouldn't go back to that hotel if you paid me!'* that had made Emma concerned that her suggested location for the gala might be a mistake.

But there was nothing online other than praise for this exquisite, world-renowned hotel. A hotel she'd heard of even back in London, when she'd scoured the press reports of its grand opening. She might never be able to afford to stay in the amazing hotel herself, but that didn't mean that she couldn't experience it vicariously through work.

'Why?' Antonio asked, and Emma wondered briefly if she'd missed something.

'Why, what?'

'Why did you invite them?'

'I thought that you might need some independent advice on your choice.'

Antonio looked at her, but she was unable to divine his thoughts.

'Wingmen—I thought you might need wingmen,' she clarified.

'Emma,' he said, with censure heavy on his tongue. 'I have *never* needed a wingman.'

And the answering shivers that rippled through her body told her just how right he was.

As she did at most events Antonio attended for work, Emma stayed discreetly behind him during the initial introductions, her quietly whispered words prompting him with the names of the gala's guests and their partners. There had been times in the past when the additional information she provided had saved him from embarrassment—especially once when Antonio had nearly mistaken a man's mistress for his wife.

He was surprised to see so many recognisable faces. He could honestly say that he had never given this gala a first thought, let alone a second. If it didn't contribute to bringing Michael Steele down, it didn't matter to him. Marcus Greenfeld—the man Antonio had inherited along with the foundation he had secured for Arcuri Enterprises all those years ago—had never demanded anything of him and he liked it that way. Antonio had never taken to the man.

'Natasha.'

Emma's voice cut through his thoughts. He turned to find her welcoming the statuesque and considerably beautiful black woman making her way towards him.

'How lovely to see you again,' Emma said, kissing the woman on both cheeks.

The answering smile spoke of a friendship between the two and he instantly recognised the woman as fiancée option number one.

'Natasha—allow me to introduce you to Antonio Arcuri. Antonio—Natasha Eddings,' she said, gently proffering the woman to him like a gift, before swiftly disappearing to leave him alone with her.

Within minutes Antonio didn't have to bring to mind

Emma's handwritten scrawl on her brief bio—*This is my favourite*—to see why Natasha was Emma's choice. Natasha was articulate and intelligent, beautiful and, in short, practically perfect. But while she might meet *his* requirements, he had the odd impression that he did not meet hers.

'It would seem that my usual and widely reported charm might be falling a little flat this evening,' he remarked, testing his theory.

Natasha smiled apologetically. 'I'm sorry, Mr Arcuri. Emma did explain to me the delicate nature of your…interest,' she said, clearly searching for suitable phrasing.

A shiver of alarm passed through him quickly, but she pressed on.

'I assure you that I don't know why—only that you are looking for a fiancée—and no one will hear about it from me. I know that Emma has not spoken to anyone else of it. But…'

'You are perhaps involved with someone?' he offered, giving Natasha a way out.

'I am. Whoever you choose will be a lucky woman. I am sure of it. But I'm afraid I am not she.' Natasha smiled gently, smoothing any potentially ruffled feathers.

'Rest assured, Natasha, whoever he is,' he said, referring to her involvement, '*he* is the lucky one.'

The smile that lit her features was bright and spectacular.

'Thank you. May I offer a suggestion, Mr Arcuri?'

When he nodded his assent, she continued.

'Perhaps you don't have to be looking so far afield.'

With that, she disappeared into the crowd, leaving Antonio with a thought that was matched only by a growing suspicion on his part. But the clinking of glass interrupted his partially formed idea, sounding out the fact that the opening speech from Marcus Greenfeld was about to begin.

Having prepared himself for the most boring fifteen minutes of his life, Antonio was faintly surprised at the warm, heartfelt introduction given by the man as he clearly outlined the charity's main functions. Though his voice was slightly stilted, the words were full of compassion and drive—and were, in a sense, a call to arms.

Looking across the audience, he saw them resonate, and a ripple of emotion shuddered through each of the attendees that he, himself, was not immune to. The only thing preventing the speech from being truly inspirational was the man delivering it.

From the corner of his eye Antonio saw his CFO, David Grant, approach quietly, and they greeted each other with a fond nod of welcome.

'I have to say,' Antonio said in hushed tones, 'Greenfeld's doing much better than I remember.'

His CFO frowned, then smiled. 'Ah... I heard that it was down to you, but now I'm beginning to think that your PA has been sprinkling her magic fairy dust over his speech—as well as over this gala.'

Antonio was confused. What had Emma to do with all this?

David let out a gruff laugh. 'For the last two months Emma has been running interference with Greenfeld and doing everything possible to ensure this night is an unusual success. You're always out of the country for this event, but it's been growing steadily more boring and more dull each year. It was Emma's decision to move the gala to The Langsford and provide gift packages for the guests. Not to mention rewriting the speech. She's done wonders.'

Wonders, indeed. Antonio was about to voice his frustration at the fact that his perfect PA had effectively been moonlighting, but David's next words stopped him short.

'I suppose it's only natural, given her personal experience. Cancer research is one of the main focuses of the Arcuri Foundation, and that clearly makes her the perfect support for the event.'

Antonio stared at his CFO. Cancer? Emma had experienced cancer?

A roar sounded in his ears and it took him a moment to realise that it was the sound of the guests applauding.

Emma had watched Greenfeld's speech from the sidelines of the large entertainment suite at the top of The Langsford. She had pretended to be checking the gala's gift bags, ensuring that the male and female packages were all present and contained the small bottles of champagne a local winery had been happy to supply. Other companies had also lent their support, through handmade bracelets and perfume for the women, aftershave and cufflinks for the men.

She knew she'd thrown Antonio's name around as if it was currency, but it had been worth it. And if her boss took issue with it, then she would set him straight. Tonight the gala was predicted to raise more money in donations than the last two events put together.

Once again she was pushing something bigger than herself out into the world, and this time she could do some actual good. Funding would reach beyond the not so small world of Arcuri Enterprises and help people— *really* help people who desperately needed it. And for that…? Yes, for that she would go into battle with her boss if needed.

But as her hands had hovered over the blue and pink cloth gift bags Greenfeld's voice had projected her own words back to her, and she'd cursed the man for not being moved, for the barrier between his words and the emotions she felt in her chest. The man was simply not good enough at his job.

Still, Emma chided herself, she couldn't do *everything*. Tonight she should really be checking on how Antonio was getting on in his search.

Although she was pleased with the fiancée options she'd miraculously pulled from the gala at the last minute, she had noticed Natasha's departure from her conversation with Antonio with something horribly like relief. She liked Natasha. The bright, intelligent woman had been at several of the foundation's functions, but hadn't been able to help the awful sting of jealousy curling in her chest as she had seen them talk.

Antonio might be an unconscionable playboy, and she might have had to smooth the emotional waters for his ex-lovers, but she'd never had to see it personally. Through the hackneyed words of the international press that followed him almost constantly, she'd been able to see simply an incredibly attractive man who enjoyed beautiful women with good grace and no false promises.

And if she was foolish to wonder what it would be like to be one of those beautiful women, then that was her own look-out.

She had long given up on fantasies of being a beautiful blushing woman on the arm of a dashingly handsome man. Her experience with cancer had seen to that. It may have stolen her breasts—which she had been prepared for. But somehow it had been the prospect of nipple reconstruction that had truly defined its effect on her sense of self. Unwilling and emotionally unable to face yet another surgery, Emma had instead opted for medical tattoos. The tattooist had been kind and had worked wonders. The tattoos meant that she didn't look in the mirror and immediately see something missing. The implants she could handle, and the scars she could deal with, but that last thing had been the hardest.

And, beyond the fight she'd won against cancer, it wasn't just flesh and time that it had taken from her. It had stolen her parents' marriage, and it had stolen her sense of femininity. At seventeen she'd been a child, and now, at twenty-three, she had yet to feel like a woman. She was unable and unwilling to put herself out there and find someone she might trust her delicate sense of self to—trust, should the worst happen, that they'd be there for her on the other side.

Her eyes were drawn to Antonio's presence across the room. Standing almost a foot above most of the guests, he was never hard to find. And as she saw him laughing with fiancée option number four—one of the last-minute additions she had added just in case—she gave herself a little mental slap.

Putting her feelings back into a box, she went to check on the preparations for the gala meal.

Had anything ever been as annoying to him as this woman's laugh? *Ever?*

Antonio couldn't help but think not, as she pealed out another reel of hysteria at an inane observation that had fallen flat on his own ears.

He couldn't hold it against Emma. Amber—he couldn't keep thinking of her as option four—was fine. On paper. Two degrees…a board member at her mother's make-up company…daughter of an international diplomat. Tick, tick, tick. But in person…? She was a car crash. She was loud, there was that awful laugh, and then there was her appearance. Clearly she was a stunning woman, but as she nearly fell out of her tightly constricting dress he couldn't bring himself to feel anything other than distaste.

'So, you're into horseflesh? I love to have a flutter on the ponies occasionally. You're going to be in Buenos Aires for the first leg of the Hanley Cup next week?'

His noncommittal 'mmm' wasn't enough to put her off. But it did remind him of the need to check in with John—the trainer he had secured for the Winners' Circle from the staff his family had been forced to let go.

It had been both a gift and a curse to work with the gruff northern Englishman. Antonio was still unable to relinquish fully the stranglehold the past had on him even now, in the present. He wondered if Mason McAulty was still furiously adhering to the strict schedule she had set herself…

But his train of thought was interrupted as Amber placed a long-nailed hand on his forearm, and Antonio resisted the urge to flinch.

'Is it true that you have a *female* jockey riding your horse? How simply thrilling!'

Cue more laughter. Laughter that made him wonder what dry response Emma would have come up with.

Damn it.

Emma—the woman he had worked with for eighteen months and never known about her medical history. He wasn't so uncouth as to require one for members of his staff, and neither was he such an ass that he would have treated her any differently. But as his eyes raked over Amber and her figure-hugging outfit he suddenly realised what it was about Emma's figure that had always niggled at the back of his subconscious.

Breast implants. He hadn't initially noticed them—in fact had only just realised that they *were* implants. They weren't obvious—in reality they were incredibly subtle—and the disguising of them was clearly intended by her choice of wardrobe.

In an act of what could only be described as self-preservation, any time he had come near to considering his PA's *assets*, he had swerved sharply away. So, even as a man who considered himself a connoisseur of beautiful forms, perhaps he could be forgiven.

Assimilating this new information about Emma didn't make him think any less of her—only more. It added yet another layer of complexity to a woman who was beginning to take up far too much of his thoughts for a member of his staff.

'And that was when—'

'I'm sorry,' Antonio said insincerely, 'I've just seen someone I need to speak to.'

He left the blonde woman practically stamping her foot in his wake and went to find... Anything would be better than that.

Until he walked smack-bang into Marcus Greenfeld.

'Mr Arcuri,' he proclaimed, before Antonio could extricate himself from the situation. The man took off his greasy glasses and began rubbing them with his tie. 'Kind of you to come. Didn't have to, of course,' he said apologetically. 'I hope you don't mind the...the extravagance. But then, of course, it was your suggestion so, yes... Thank you. I—'

'You have done an amazing job.' The lie was giving the man far more credit than he was clearly due, but it was necessary to ensure that Emma's inspired intervention was fully felt. 'This evening's gala has garnered a huge amount of positivity,' he said, loudly enough for Emma to hear as she made her way over to the two of them.

Did he notice a slight blush on her cheeks?

'Mr Greenfeld... Mr Arcuri—the meal will be served shortly,' Emma informed them.

Antonio's hawk-like gaze raked over her—*all* of her. Even dressed in the clothes he now saw that she wore like armour, she outshone Amber like the north star.

'I was just telling Marcus how much I'm enjoying the gala. A truly wonderful event. And with that in mind I have decided to double the donations raised this evening. Marcus,' he said, turning back to the man, 'please be so good as to announce that before the meal starts. Let's see if it greases some wheels.' He tried not to look at the man's glasses as he spoke.

His statement signalled the end of the conversation, but Marcus Greenfeld still took an awkward moment to realise it was his cue to leave.

Emma was looking at him with huge round eyes. The same eyes that had first caught his attention in London. He needed to get his own eyes off his PA and on to the next fiancée option. He needed to keep his mind on track. He wasn't here for the charity—he was here to help secure the Bartlett deal.

'That's...that's wonderful, Antonio. Thank you so much.'

'You don't have to thank me. It's my charity, after all. Besides... It's good publicity.'

'I don't believe that,' she said, levelling him with a stare that saw far too much, and speaking in a voice that held too much optimism. 'I think you're doing it out of the kindness of your heart.'

'Don't paint any illusions about me, Emma. Trust me—there's very little good left in me.'

'Well, then. I'll just have to nurture that last little bit of goodness.'

As she slipped away into the throng of guests his errant mind wondered what else she might nurture and he cursed himself to hell and back.

When the guests started to make their way in a somewhat chaotic line through to where the meal was being served, he saw Dimitri peel off from a group of attractive women.

'Enjoying yourself?' Antonio asked as they stood back and watched the guests pile in for the meal.

'Absolutely. I wouldn't have missed this for the world,' Dimitri replied, full of laughter.

'I'm glad you find humour in this.'

'And in your purpose,' Dimitri responded, clinking his glass of champagne against Antonio's. 'So, anyone caught your eye yet?'

As Antonio scanned the guests at the gala, all decked in the kind of finery that suited their opulent surroundings, his eyes snagged on Emma once again.

'Emma shared the list of suitable candidates with me, and I must say, apart from that girl Amber, she's chosen wisely. Though if you're not overly taken with option one I'd be happy to take her off your hands.'

'*Che palle*, Dimitri.' Antonio cast Dimitri a dark look, but his friend only shrugged.

'*Ti?*' Dimitri queried in Greek.

'Natasha Eddings—"option one"—is not up for grabs. This isn't a cattle market, Dimitri. This is important. If Bartlett is even going to meet with me, then I need a fiancée to resolve any detrimental effects of my previous…assignations.'

'Is that what the kids are calling it these days?'

'Don't joke. This is a serious matter.'

'I know,' Dimitri said, his eyes shining with understanding. 'But, Antonio, you can't just stumble across a woman you've never met before, make her an offer to be your fake fiancée, expect her to have little or no ulterior expectations, and present her to Bartlett wrapped in a bow.'

Antonio bit back a curse. Dimitri was right. Urgency and necessity had made his usually quick and clever mind sluggish and slow. He saw the many flaws in his plan immediately.

What had he been thinking? He needed the deal, he needed to bring Steele to his knees, and he needed a fiancée who would understand and support him in it.

His eyes caught Emma, laughing with a member of the hotel's staff before stepping away through the glass doors to the balcony that wrapped around the outside of the hotel. She had done so much. He was impressed with how she'd multi-tasked, clearly making an unprecedented success of the event whilst never missing a beat in her day-to-day role. She was conscientious, bright and articulate. And above all she was professional. In short, she was perfect.

'Mum, it's…' Emma paused, pulling her mobile briefly away from her ear to check the screen for the time '…one a.m. in London. What are you doing up?'

'Oh, I got stuck into a painting and the next thing I knew it was midnight.'

As Emma looked out onto the famous New York skyline she imagined her mother in the brightly lit, airy loft of her home in Hampstead Heath. When her parents had divorced her father had been the one to leave, moving into a flat nearer to the school where he worked, but only round the corner from the home they had all once shared.

The divorce had signalled the end of the nightly fights that had become a regular feature of Emma's life—desperate and painful arguments her parents had thought she hadn't heard. The heart-wrenching accusations, the arguments over how differently to handle their sick daughter, and her father's confusion as to why Louise Guilham had changed beyond his recognition.

Emma had initially felt relief when they'd separated, and then guilt, knowing that her father still desperately loved her mother. His painful bewilderment at the transformation in his wife and child had cut Emma deeply, and prompted the awful thought that had it not been for her illness her mother might have somehow stayed with her husband, and she might have somehow found a way to keep them all together.

'Where's Mark?'

Emma liked her mum's partner. He made her happy, and he also gave her the space she needed to be creative at unsociable times. Emma knew better than most that when her mum 'got stuck into a painting' she could be gone for days. She loved her mum's paintings—her favourite one hung on the wall of her little Brooklyn flat—and still felt bad that her mother's work had been put on hold during her illness at a critical time in her mother's career.

'Asleep. I just wanted to know how the gala went.'

'It's still going, but it's going well. Antonio has offered to double the event's donations.'

'That's wonderful, darling.'

But even through her mother's happiness for her Emma could sense her distraction. She was probably staring at the painting critically right at that very moment.

Emma was about to ask when they might come over to visit her. Her mother and Mark hadn't made it out there yet, but that was okay, because she'd hardly had a spare moment since working for Antonio. But as if the very thought of him had conjured him from thin air, she felt rather than heard his presence behind her.

'Love you lots, but I'd better go.'

Emma hung up the call and put her mobile back in her purse. She gathered herself, knowing that her emotions were a little too close to the surface for her to face her boss just yet.

Adjusting her mind's eye back from her home in Hampstead to the beautiful night-time vista of famous skyscrapers silhouetted against the stars, she felt a cool breeze pass over her skin—and that was why she had goosebumps, Emma assured herself. Not because Antonio had come out here to find her.

He should be with the other guests sitting down for the meal. Perhaps he'd come to tell her that he'd found his perfect fiancée, she thought, uncharacteristically bitter.

She needed to pull herself together. Surely she could handle Antonio Arcuri's fiancée as well as she could handle him. But the thought of *handling* her boss gave rise to some very explicit images, and she had to push them aside as firmly as she placed a smile on her face and finally turned to see him.

He stood half in shadow, peering at her through bitter-chocolate-coloured eyes. There was something about the way he held himself. As if his body was restraining some kind of pressing energy. Energy she felt all the way on the other side of the balcony.

'Who was that?'

'What?'

'Who was on the phone that you love?' he asked, his Italian accent thick on the words.

Emma frowned at the personal nature of this conversation. She and Antonio didn't do personal. It was one of the things she liked and respected about him, and in her deepest heart she was thankful for it.

'My mother.'

'So there's no one at home waiting up for you? No boyfriend or otherwise?'

'No,' she replied, still confused.

'Then, Emma, I can see only one option before me. In order to secure the Bartlett deal I need *you*... *You* will be my fiancée.'

CHAPTER THREE

Huh… So *that* was what it was like to be proposed to.

It wasn't exactly how Emma had imagined it happening. Not even in her wildest imaginings. Though, if she was honest, Antonio Arcuri might have featured in some of her more fevered dreams—but never with such shocking words.

'In order to secure the Bartlett deal…'

'You will be my fiancée.'

While she might not have foreseen marriage in her future, if it *had* been to happen she would at least have hoped to be *asked*.

But why had he chosen her? Especially when he had a whole room full of perfectly suitable potential fiancées who were probably now picking the carbohydrates out of an exquisite three-course meal prepared by one of the finest chefs in New York.

She looked at him through the night gloom and saw something in his eyes. Something she had to look away from before it was transformed into pity.

'Who told you?'

'Who told me what?'

'Don't play games with me, Antonio. I'm not stupid.'

Anger ripped through her at an impossible speed. She'd wanted to start over. Start afresh in New York—

where people didn't know, didn't look at her as if she was an unexploded bomb waiting to go off. Yes, her work with the charity had naturally led to some astute observations by a colleague or two. But not Antonio. Because he hadn't known about her work with the charity.

'Is this because you feel sorry for me?'

'No!' he growled.

'I won't be used as some PR stunt to get what you want, Antonio. Playing on the sympathies of Bartlett with my "miraculous survival".'

'*Dio*, what kind of man do you take me for?' he demanded, clearly offended by the implication.

'The kind of man who would go to extreme lengths to acquire the perfect fake fiancée in order to pin down a business deal.'

'Well, I can hardly refute that claim. But my decision has nothing to do with your health and everything to do with the fact that you are a highly accomplished, educated woman who can move within my circles both with and without notice when necessary,' he stated, ticking her qualities off on each of his long, lean fingers. 'And, most importantly, you know that this will be solely a business arrangement. You will have no illusions of emotional investment that other women may mistake my offer to contain.'

'No, I don't have any illusions about the emotional investment behind your *"offer"*,' Emma replied, refusing to remove the sting from her tone.

Struggling to sort through the barrage of contrasting opinions he had bombarded her with, and against the wave of impatience he was sending her way, she turned out to the balcony.

He wanted *her* as his fiancée?

'I'm satisfied that you will not develop feelings for me and I will not develop feelings for you.'

A small sliver of hope curled in on itself deep within her. She should be pleased to hear that. She should want their relationship to be completely devoid of any possible emotional attachment, but somehow it still hurt.

'Why is this so important to you, Antonio?' she asked, hurt driving her to question her boss in a way she had never done before. 'You don't need the financial security of making the Bartlett investment, and you've never once cared about your...colourful reputation before. And surely if you want this deal badly enough you'll find a way to win against this other potential investor. What's really going on?'

He stared at her and said nothing for a moment. But then he spoke, as if realising that her agreement relied on full disclosure—or even part disclosure—and his next words shocked her.

'As I said before, it is not Bartlett that's important. It is the other man who might make investment in his company. Michael Steele is an evil man who cannot be allowed to succeed.'

Emma recognised the name, and knew that he had been the motivation behind some of Antonio's business dealings before.

'Why is Steele so important? Why go to such extreme lengths for a man who...?' She trailed off, not quite knowing who he was.

'A man who destroyed my mother and my sister's happiness—who changed their lives irrevocably and cruelly. This is Steele's last and final chance to gain financial security for himself. If he fails to win the Bartlett investment deal, he will lose his business. And I am determined to make that happen to the man...' He stopped, reluctance and anger warring for supremacy in his features. 'The man who is my father.'

Shock rippled across her skin and shivered through her body. Michael Steele was Antonio's father?

Antonio never talked about his family—had always valued his privacy above all else. She'd once heard him mention his father—whose name he clearly no longer bore. But the darkness in his eyes and tone held so much anger and fury it crashed against her, pulled and pushed her away from Antonio like a tide.

It was unquestionable. And she couldn't help but wonder just how much his hatred of his father—something she simply couldn't comprehend—had driven him to this point.

'I will do anything to secure that investment, Emma. Anything. So if you have a price, name it. I will give it to you on a silver platter should you require it.'

Antonio would find himself a fiancée—whether it was her or someone else. But perhaps she could do something good with his offer. The thought raised hopes in her—some that she had discovered recently and some that she had long forgotten.

'What I want is for you to get rid of Marcus Greenfeld,' she practically growled. 'The man is incompetent and the foundation could be doing so much more. *You* could be doing so much more.'

'Is that it?' he demanded, his sensual mouth forming in a grim line of determination.

'Well, while we're at it, you can give each of my parents an all-inclusive holiday to wherever they want.'

'Done and done,' Antonio said, discarding her outrageous request as if it were nothing. 'You should know that as my fiancée you will be coming to Argentina for the Hanley Cup, once my meeting with Bartlett has been arranged.'

A rush of excitement swept across her skin. She'd always wanted to see the world. It was why she'd come to New York eighteen months ago.

'There will be a need to keep up this façade for a short while after the deal. Six months should be enough. So naturally you will accompany me on my visit to Hong Kong as well.'

As she thought through the future, to the trip to Buenos Aires and the trip to Hong Kong, the reality of what she was agreeing to dawned on her.

'And what about after Hong Kong? After six months when I'm no longer needed as your…your fake fiancée?'

'You'll be taken care of,' he announced.

She was sure he meant that. There was clearly no way she would be able to continue as his assistant once their 'engagement' was broken. She knew that he would provide her with a glowing reference and help secure her a future position, because he was that kind of boss. But she also knew—more than most—that the only person who could take care of her was herself.

No, she had never seen marriage or relationships in her future, but that didn't matter. Antonio wasn't offering her either. But there was something that scared her a little about being cut loose from her role as his assistant. And that, Emma realised, was the true price of what he was asking—her job. She had always meant to use this position as a stepping stone to other things. And maybe this was the not so gentle nudge that she needed.

Perhaps she could find work in Hong Kong? For a man she didn't find so frustratingly attractive. The trip to Argentina would be exciting too, and posing as his fiancée would be a way to help give her parents something too. Marcus Greenfeld would be removed and someone infinitely better, would replace him.

So, yes. Emma was prepared to cut her ties to Antonio once this was done.

'All I want is an appropriate reference.'

'Naturally,' he stated, as if they hadn't just bartered over the rules of their engagement.

Perhaps as his fiancée she would be able to tick off a few more things from her Living List. But she couldn't bring herself to ask for anything specifically for herself. After what she had faced, everything was a bonus. She didn't need anything more. Not really. The only thing she had ever wanted—could ever want—was for her body to feel like hers again. But not even the all-powerful Antonio Arcuri could do that.

'You have yourself a fiancée, Mr Arcuri.'

Finally, for the first time since Antonio had discovered that his father was after an investment in Bartlett's business, he felt the first taste of success on his tongue. Now all he had to do was get Bartlett to agree to a sit-down in Argentina.

His quick mind had already calculated the steps needed to accomplish that. But first he needed to reveal his new fiancée to the world.

He would, he realised, have to find a new PA. And, of course, ensure that Emma would have her pick when it came to choosing her next position. It was a thought that registered merely as an irritation alongside the satisfaction that Emma would be his. No, not *his*, he hastily affirmed. His pretend fiancée. For a business deal. Nothing more. He wouldn't risk *anything* interfering with his ultimate goal.

Another cool breeze brushed past them on the balcony and Emma shivered. He shrugged out of his jacket and placed it around her delicate shoulders. She accepted it without a word, clearly focused on her sudden and surprising 'promotion'.

Knowing they had to return to the gala, Antonio guided her through the balcony doors to the reception room. Even the dim event lighting was harsh on his eyes as they adjusted from the dark starlit night.

At the end of the room the doors were open and the gala guests were beginning to wander back through to the bar to continue with the night's agenda, hopefully having lined their stomachs in order to allow them to further enjoy themselves.

He judged that nearly thirty people were now filling the bar area, and decided that it would be enough.

'We should get ready to leave,' he said to Emma.

'The gala isn't set to finish for another two hours yet. I—'

'You can let the foundation's staff handle the rest. From what I've heard you've handled quite enough already. Besides, I have a feeling you're going to want to make a quick exit.'

'Why?'

He didn't give her time to think about it. He didn't give himself time to think about it. He had already decided his course of action should she say yes out on the balcony. He was about to ensure that the world knew about his new fiancée—in the quickest, most expedient way.

Antonio pulled her towards him, slipping his arms through the space between his jacket and her body. His hands met the curves he'd imagined to be there—the dip of her small waist, the arch of her back. They had a mind of their own as they swept across the silken material of her dress, sparking little bursts of electricity across his skin from the gentle friction. And his lips...

Emma felt the swift, determined crush of Antonio's mouth against hers. The shock of his hands against her waist, her back, startled a gasp from her. His tongue made swift work of the opportunity and plunged between her slightly parted lips.

Fire. Everything he did, every move he made, conjured up only that one word and that one sensation. It felt as if flames were licking across her skin, burning her from the outside in. For a shocking moment she thought her knees might buckle, and thrust out her hands to clutch the material of his shirt in her fists, anchoring them together even further.

As his tongue plunged more deeply into her mouth she felt as if her skin was a barrier—to him, to it, to what she wanted...

And then she heard the whistles. The cheers and the shouts grew louder, until she pulled back from Antonio's embrace and discovered they had a rather interested audience.

If Antonio had still been wearing his jacket she would have tried to hide in its lapels. She wanted the ground to swallow her up.

Until she realised that this public display was exactly what Antonio had wanted.

The stinging blush of embarrassment and shame painting her cheeks prickled and hurt. Of course he hadn't got carried away in the moment like she had. He had intended this. Was experienced in this. Antonio needed this and he needed her to play the part of doting fiancée—not naïve, out-of-her-depth PA.

She saw Dimitri come to the front of the crowd and

watched as a brief look of surprise was replaced with a surprisingly boyish grin.

'Permit me to be the first to congratulate you on your *now public* engagement,' Dimitri announced loudly, encouraging the already jubilant crowd into more cries of excitement and congratulation.

Within seconds mobile phone flashes were dusting them as if in strobe lighting. Antonio anchored her in place, pressed against his chest, smiling for all the world as if he were a newly engaged happy man, and Emma did her best to follow his lead.

After a minute Dimitri stepped forward to shake hands with Antonio, whispering that he hoped they both knew what they were doing through a fixed smile.

'Antonio is a very lucky man, Emma. But he is also a handful. So if you find yourself in need, you just call me.'

Dimitri pressed a kiss to Emma's cheek, and she couldn't help but smile back.

'Thank you, Mr Kyriakou.'

'Dimitri. Please,' he said, dipping his head low and studying her intently.

He didn't look at her in the way other men had once, but in a way that conveyed sincerity. And something slightly darker than his apparent good humour.

'I mean it, Emma. Anything. Just call.'

'Okay—that's enough. I don't need you putting off my fiancée at the very first step, thank you,' Antonio interrupted, with the kind of patience and affection only borne out of a long friendship.

'So,' Dimitri said, stepping back and rubbing his hands together. 'Would you like an impromptu engagement party? Or a highly skilful distraction so you can make a quick getaway?'

'A distraction, please, Dimitri. But nothing—'

'Nothing scandalous. Yeah, I got the memo,' he said with an eye-roll, disappearing into the crowd, calling for champagne and a dance with the most beautiful woman present in the room—aside from Emma, of course!

Antonio guided his assistant to the elevators, hoping that the kiss hadn't dulled her unflappable nature in the same way it had his. *Dio*, had he known that beneath that buttoned-up conservatively dressed professional there was a siren waiting to be unleashed, he might have given a second thought to making Emma his. His *fake fiancée*, an internal voice shouted in his mind.

He would have to keep such displays of public affection to a minimum if he were going to have a hope in hell of containing this situation. So he clung to the next step. Clung to what he knew needed to happen.

'Your passport. Is it still in the office?'

For a moment he thought she might not have heard, but then understanding dawned across her features.

'Yes.'

'And the change of clothes you usually keep there?'

'Yes,' she said, and her efficient swift nod did nothing to dislodge her perfectly placed hair, pinned at the base of her neck. His fingers wanted to reach out and pull that hair apart, feel it against his skin.

He forced himself to focus. 'Given the likely content of tomorrow's newspapers, and the public reaction to our announcement, it might be better if you do not return home this evening.'

Emma frowned, thinking through the suggestion. 'You think they know where I live? But I'm no one. How would they—?'

'You are not *no one*, Emma. You are now the soon-to-be Mrs Arcuri, and I don't think I need to remind you of the interest my considerable wealth brings.'

'And you wouldn't want a camp of reporters outside a tiny one-bed apartment in the deepest depths of Brooklyn?' she asked, with a trace of that British wry humour dancing across her words.

'I am not a snob, Emma.' He swung round to look at her, shocked that she might even think so until he saw the smile painting her pretty features as she turned her head up to his.

'Not going for the Prince and the Pauper angle?'

'I couldn't if I wanted to, Emma. I'm no prince, and I pay you considerably more than what a pauper has.'

Emma let out a huff of laughter as the lift doors opened onto the exquisite chequered foyer of The Langsford. She followed in Antonio's wake as they approached the reception desk. The words *penthouse suite* and *charge to my personal account* drifted through her mind as she watched the interaction, feeling oddly displaced.

It took her a moment to realise that he was organising for her to stay here, in this hotel. She was his assistant, the booking of hotels was usually her domain, and yet it felt… She couldn't find a word for what it felt like to see Antonio in action, catering to *her* needs.

As he led her away from the hustle of the concierge's desk towards a private elevator and presented her with a gold key card, he asked if there was anything she might need from her apartment. Anything that couldn't be purchased for her between now and Buenos Aires. There was no way he would let her go back to her apartment and deal with the gang of wolves that would be sure to be camped out on her doorstep, waiting for an interview.

Assuring him that there wasn't anything, Emma

stepped into the elevator and stopped. Antonio was staying in the foyer. He would either be going home or back to the office, she realised. She felt that she should say something, that there should be some conclusion to the events that had just happened, but oddly she couldn't.

'I'll need you in the office tomorrow morning, to pick up your laptop and passport and amend our travel details before we fly to Argentina.'

She agreed just before the elevator doors closed and she was taken upwards through the building. The smooth, swift motion seeming to increase the swirling in her stomach. What on earth had she just agreed to?

ARCURI OFF THE MARKET FOR GOOD?
BY ROANNA KING

Shock engagement of international
tycoon breaks hearts!

Female socialites around the world woke to breaking hearts this morning at the news that international investment tycoon Antonio Arcuri of Arcuri Enterprises is officially off the market.

The notorious and now presumably ex-playboy, often seen wining and dining a bevy of beauties from models to heiresses, has been stolen from our clutches by...his secretary!

Little is known of the Englishwoman Emma Guilham, other than that she has been in his employ for eighteen months and that she has been unavailable for comment.

Such a surprising turn of events must surely form a suspicion that there will be another shock announcement in just nine months' time. But, whatever the future holds for the happy couple, this intrepid reporter is very much looking forward to what is sure to be the future Mrs Arcuri's grand unveiling in Buenos Aires!

Antonio had known the press fall-out would be big, but Roanna King and her regular exposés on the private lives of the rich and famous had made his engagement sound torrid. That she had put the word *secretary* in italics was bad enough, but the presumption that Emma might be pregnant?

Antonio threw the newspaper across the small table before him in disgust.

He checked his watch. His private jet had taken off from a New York airport less than forty-five minutes ago. Glancing across the narrow cabin now, he observed Emma taking in the lavish decor of the Arcuri jet, and hoped that it hadn't turned her head. She needed to be ready for the call with Bartlett.

A thought which reminded him of the last phone call he'd received on his almost constantly vibrating mobile since the news of his engagement had broken.

No, he'd assured his mother, his PA was *not* pregnant. *Yes*, he was sorry that he hadn't called to tell her himself. *Dio*, he cursed himself, he hadn't even thought to warn her, to tell her. He'd been so focused on Bartlett and his father that he hadn't realised how his engagement would look to his mother and sister.

As to his mother's question about when she might meet her future daughter-in-law, he'd only been able to put her off. *Would* they meet? he asked himself. He had no doubt that the two women would get along fine. More than fine, if he thought about it. His mother would appreciate the smooth efficiency and dry humour of the small brunette. But it sat awkwardly with him, and he couldn't stop the words that Emma had said earlier that day about her own parents from ringing in his mind. *"I won't lie to them."*

She had been forced by the newspapers to contact her mother and father and explain the situation. He didn't like it—he didn't want anything jeopardising this deal—but he hadn't been able to refuse her request.

His own mother was a sentimental woman, who believed that love and happiness were a vital part of life and should be a vital part of her son's life. But he couldn't bring himself tell her that he had no room for such things. So, he'd lied to his mother and ignored the clenching in his gut. It was a sacrifice worth making, he assured himself, as finally Benjamin Bartlett had agreed to a phone call.

He had twenty minutes. Twenty minutes to convince Bartlett to come for a sit-down in Buenos Aires. Or all this would have been for nothing. Rather than allowing doubts to enter his mind, he should be using that driving force to push him forward. He would succeed. He had to.

Emma could feel impatience and expectation pouring from Antonio in waves. She tried to block it out and instead focus on the very strange and really quite wonderful experience of travelling in the company's private jet.

The limousine had taken them to the airport where, instead of queueing to get through Customs and Security, they had simply been looked over and then led up a set of stairs beside the plane.

Emma feared she might have been spoiled for ever.

She had ignored the way that the air stewardess had cast a disparaging look her way, seeming to take in her appearance and discard it as beneath her notice. It wasn't exactly Emma's fault that she was wearing yesterday's office clothes, having been unable to get back to her apartment and not yet having had the opportunity to buy new ones.

Still, she'd accepted the glass of chilled Prosecco the unnervingly beautiful woman had placed on the table in front of her.

The stewardess was clearly reserving her blood-red lipstick smiles for Antonio. Perhaps it was because of the article. She could hardly have missed the headline screaming about Emma and Antonio's shocking engagement on the newspaper beside the man in question. Not that it seemed to prevent the woman's bright gaze lingering on him as if she would like to consume him whole. Nor had it prevented the way her hand rested on his shoulder just a little bit too long to be appropriate.

Emma cursed the way her stomach dropped as she wondered whether they had perhaps enjoyed each other's company before. Jealousy wasn't part of their bargain and she wouldn't let it dim the fizz of excitement that was building as she adjusted to the realisation that they were actually going to Argentina.

Her Living List might be full of hopes and dreams, but they had been practically based on her income, on her finances. This deal with Antonio took her possibilities to a whole new level. As his PA she had only ever borrowed a taste of that elegance, but now she could experience it for herself. Perhaps for these six months she could enjoy all that Antonio had to offer. Well. Almost all. She knew she wouldn't have the one thing that her body refused to realise she *couldn't* have.

Antonio's phone started to vibrate noisily.

'I'm going to put it on speaker,' he said, leaving the

phone to jerk around on the table between them, as if this wasn't the one phone call he'd been waiting a week to receive. 'I'd like your opinion on Bartlett, given your research.'

She nodded, and he finally accepted the call.

'Mr Arcuri?' Bartlett's assistant was on the line.

'Yes.'

'Mr Bartlett for you. Hold, please.'

The line went silent for a moment.

'Arcuri! I hear congratulations are in order...'

Antonio froze at the American's cultured tones; for a second they had sounded so much like his father's. He muted the call momentarily, cleared his throat and then resumed the call, cursing at the fact that Emma had witnessed this errant chink in his defences.

'Thank you, Mr Bartlett, your congratulations are very welcome.'

'Am I to presume that your insistence to speak to me is down to the fact that you have uncovered the news that I am looking for investment?'

'Yes.'

'Then I would love to know your source. I was under the impression that it was a highly guarded secret.'

'A gentleman does not kiss and tell, Mr Bartlett.'

'I would hope that you have been kissing no one other than your fiancée, Mr Arcuri.'

'I assure you that is most definitely the case,' he said, trying to ignore the way Emma was watching him. 'As to how this information was uncovered—I assure you that it was not from any party related to *your* business.'

Antonio knew there was enough weight in his tone to indicate that the leak had come from the only other person involved in the negotiations. His father. It was exactly as Antonio had intended.

'I must say I am surprised,' Bartlett pressed, refusing to rise to the bait, 'that a man such as yourself—a man with a reputation for ruthlessness—would want to invest in *my* business.'

'You have a quite remarkable heritage brand, Mr Bartlett, one that any investor would be lucky to be involved with. And ever since I began my relationship with Emma I have been motivated to make more…holistic business decisions.'

'Your relationship is quite recent?'

'Emma has been with me for eighteen months, and during that time I have come to realise what a wonderful woman she is,' he said, this time unable *not* to look at the woman in question—unable to take his eyes from the faint blush that rose to her cheeks. 'She is kind, caring and compassionate, Mr Bartlett, and I am sure you will discover that yourself, should you choose to meet in Buenos Aires and discuss things further.'

There was a pause on the line.

'As you are aware that I am looking for investment, I am sure you are also aware that your father is the only other petitioner in the matter?'

'Surely whether I am aware or not is incidental? Having two people determined to win investment into your company can only be a good thing for you.'

'I appreciate that, Mr Arcuri, but I refuse to allow this to turn into a circus. I have my reasons for wanting to keep this investment opportunity quiet, and if I am to meet with you in Buenos Aires then I want your assurance that it will remain the case.'

'I promise you, Mr Bartlett, that no one will hear about this matter from me, or anyone connected with me.'

'Good. Then I look forward to meeting both you and

Ms Guilham in Argentina. But I warn you, Antonio, your father's offer is good. You'll have to do something pretty spectacular to rival it.'

Antonio let Bartlett's warning settle in his mind as he finished the call. He gathered his thoughts, and was curious as to what Emma had taken away from the conversation.

'So…?'

'I think you are going to have to work hard to win his approval,' she replied grimly.

Bartlett's warning was irrelevant, he told himself. Antonio had waited sixteen years for this. Sixteen years to take his father down for destroying his home and his family.

He would do *whatever* it took to ensure it.

CHAPTER FOUR

EMMA WAS ROUSED from her sleep as the limousine pulled up to The Excelsus hotel in Buenos Aires and she wished she had managed to stay awake. The view from the plane as it had descended into Argentina had promised a stunning and wonderful place that she'd only ever had an internet connection to. Having booked Antonio's travel itinerary there a number of times, Emma had been eager to see it for herself.

She'd been captivated by the tall, gleaming structures that reached into the sky, surrounded by a harbour of sand and sea, with twinkling with promise and excitement in the morning light, and she was sad that she had slept through the journey the waiting limousine had taken once they had made their way through the sleek airport hallways.

As she got out of the car, surprising both the driver and Antonio—clearly she had been expected to wait for the door to be opened for her—she was hit by an almost cold wind, the kind that she had come to expect from an English autumn. Remembering that Argentina's coldest winter months took place during June and August, the slight chill in the air made Emma nostalgic for home.

When Antonio failed to emerge from the car, she turned back to catch his gaze through the open door.

'I'm going on to the stables. You can go on in and rest up in our rooms if you like.'

But Emma didn't want to go to the hotel. She wanted to see Buenos Aires—wanted to see the grand entrance to the race course and the small lakes she had only seen in internet pictures.

'I'd like to see the stables,' she said, but the slight delay in the careless shrug of his response made her realise that she was imposing. That he might want this time to himself.

'By all means,' he said, gesturing her to return to the car.

She got back into the warm interior, thankful for the heat that softened the surprising chill still stinging her arms. The fresh air had wiped away the jetlag she hadn't so far been aware of. Having stayed awake during most of the flight, she had effectively worked through the night and arrived in Argentina late morning, with only two hours' time difference.

She settled back into the plush leather seat, desperately trying to ignore the proximity to her boss that shouldn't be affecting her the way it did.

Antonio's fierce gaze was locked on the scene outside the window, as if he was actively trying to ignore her presence. But he had agreed that she could accompany him to the stables, and Antonio was not a man who would have agreed had he really not wanted her there, she assured herself.

The car took a sweeping loop away from The Excelsus, and Emma was slightly disappointed to find that it pulled up again only a short while later. The stables were housed directly beside the hotel, and she vaguely remembered that being the reason Antonio preferred to stay there.

This time she waited for the driver to open her door, and a half relieved, half satisfied look crossed the man's features. She thanked him and then stood up to take in the incredible view as he went to open Antonio's door.

The grounds of the racetrack were long and rectangular, flat and surrounded by thin fencing. Off to the left the impressive stretch of the hotel building loomed over the edges of the race course, with thin lines of aqua-blue hinting at the infinity pools that were boasted by the hotel. In her mind she filled in the hundreds and thousands of people who would cover the stands and the balconies on race day, and the incredible noise they must make.

She heard the slam of the car door behind her, and turned to see Antonio stalking off towards a group of large white buildings with terracotta coloured roofs that reminded her oddly of the American stables she had seen amongst the Winners' Circle holdings. She followed him through the fenced-off area, where there were more signs of life, people and horses emerging from corners and shadows as if they had previously been hidden from view.

She was two steps behind Antonio as he went deeper and deeper into the large central building.

To call it a barn would be wrong. The sheer size of it could have enveloped the whole apartment block she lived in back in Brooklyn. This structure had sleek lines, all glistening steel and chrome, and the expansive concrete floor was spotless and wet from where a young teenager further down was cleaning it. The smell of horse sweat and manure was barely discernible, and the only sound she could make out aside from Antonio's leather-soled footsteps was a hushed conversation coming from one of the stalls.

* * *

Antonio was so conscious of Emma's presence he almost missed the broad sound of John's northern English accent coming from the stalls where Veranchetti was currently housed. At sixteen and a half hands, the horse was glorious. Its black coat gleamed in the shafts of sunlight filtering through the window at the back of the stall.

As he neared, the voices became more distinct, and the feminine lilt of an Australian accent came to a halt.

'Antonio?' John's voice called out from inside. 'That you? Reckoned you'd have swung by before now.'

Only John could make the reproach sound like a greeting. Antonio caught Mason's eye as she made her way out of the stall. A brief nod was all she threw at him before heading off out of the building.

'How are you?' John asked, coming out from the stable.

'Good, John. I'm good.'

'I'll say,' John observed, watching as Emma stayed just behind Antonio. 'I take it this is the lass, then?'

Antonio felt himself on unsteady ground as he suddenly realised that he had failed to take into account yet another person he now had to add to his list of deception. John was the only member of his father's staff he'd stayed in contact with after he, his mother and sister had been forced to return to Italy.

It was a contact that he and the other members of the Winners' Circle syndicate had very much used to their advantage.

'Must say, I would've thought I'd not have to hear about it on Twitter.'

'Since when are *you* on Twitter?' Antonio asked, a smile playing at the edges of his mouth. 'John—allow

me to introduce you to Emma Guilham, my fiancée.'
The word felt strange on his tongue.

Emma came forward, having hesitated only slightly
when he'd said *fiancée*. 'Nice to meet you, John,' she
said warmly, reaching out to shake his hand.

'Oh, no, lass, I'm all mucky,' he said, wiping straw
and mud onto his already dirty jeans.

'Don't be silly. I'd hardly be a match for Antonio Arcuri if I was worried about a little dirt.'

John let out a bark of laughter, shook Emma's hand
and turned to Antonio, his eyes approving. 'I'm going
to like her. First one I've met of yours—and the last,
by all accounts.'

Something like guilt threatened to spark in Antonio's
gut, but Antonio pushed it aside. *Dio*, he couldn't let
her anywhere near his sister Cici. His sister would be
broken-hearted when it all came to nothing.

'How's V?' he asked, swiftly changing the focus of
the conversation.

'Veranchetti,' replied John, 'is doing fine. Survived
the trip over and has been acclimatising for a good
while now.'

'And McAulty?' Antonio asked.

From what he'd heard in the last eighteen months
she'd been doing everything she'd said she would—living and breathing the horses from the Winners' Circle
stable. John had been giving him, Dimitri and Danyl
weekly reports, and had voiced his positive opinion
and utter confidence in her on more than one occasion.

'She'll do.'

It was about as high a seal of approval as John would
ever give. And, from the way he was looking at Emma,
it seemed to be covering both of the women who had unexpectedly entered Antonio's life in very different ways.

Antonio had felt the calm of being inside a stable settle over him from the moment he'd come out of the wintry sun and moved into the shadows. But it was an odd calm. It always had been. The kind of calm that happened before a storm was about to hit and change everything.

He wondered if it was like Pavlov's dog—if in some way he'd always feel like this in a stable. It was the one place where he'd repeatedly sought refuge when things at home had got too much. When he'd wanted to take the first horse he saw and ride like hell away from his home, his father and all that entailed. It was the kind of calm that anticipated adrenalin…anticipated action and adventure.

It was the kind of calm he hadn't felt since being forced away from his home, his horses, and his once possible career as an international polo player.

As if John sensed the dark memories taking hold of Antonio, he led them from the quiet peace of the stable back out into the sunlight.

'Were the overnighters okay?' Antonio asked. It would have taken them a long time to get from America to Argentina, with several stops along the way.

'Yep—paperwork was all in place, and everything went well. You might want to check in with the folks from the Hanley Cup. They've got some things for you to sign.' John indicated over his shoulder to where there was a small office hidden amongst the larger buildings.

Antonio nodded his head, willingly taking the proffered escape from the stables and the threatening memories of his past.

Emma didn't know what she'd expected from the stables, but it hadn't been John. In the eighteen months she'd worked for Antonio she'd never had anything to do with the Winners' Circle. He'd handled all that himself. Oh, she'd been curious — but never enough to intrude on Antonio's personal endeavours.

John had watched Antonio walk off towards the office and now turned his attention back to her.

'I've known that one for a long time, Emma.'

'Is this the bit where you warn me off?' she said, half joking and half afraid of what he might say.

'No, lass. Reckon you know what you're getting yourself into. But that boy...he's just like a natural-born mustang. Wild and ready to bolt at any moment.'

Emma wanted John to stop. She was struggling enough to maintain the image of Antonio as her boss and now her fiancée. She wasn't sure she was ready to see him as the boy he'd once been.

'His da,' John continued, 'he were a hard man—no doubt. And he all but broke that boy. You've got him this far, Emma. Hold on to him. Even if he tries to bolt. He's worth it, lass.'

She didn't know what to say. She couldn't tell him the truth. That this engagement of—what?—less than twenty-four hours?—was just for show. Just for a business deal. The sincerity ringing from John's voice was irrefutable.

She smiled, knowing that she couldn't do anything but keep up the façade and not break an old man's heart. 'I'll do that, John. Or I'll try,' she said on a laugh, to lighten the tone.

To change the subject, she nodded back towards the stable.

'Is Veranchetti the horse Mason's going to ride in the Hanley Cup? I'm afraid I don't know much about it,' she said ruefully.

'Yup. They've got good a chance, I reckon.'

'It's an odd name—though I suppose they all have odd names.'

'Cici—his sister—named him after the hero of one of her favourite romance novels. Antonio didn't have the heart to say no,' he said, squinting in the sunlight, looking out at the course.

'Does Cici ride?'

'No, she was never that interested in the horses. But you don't want me raking up old ghosts, Ms Guilham.'

Whether John had purposely shied away from the past, or whether he'd noticed Antonio's return, she couldn't tell. Either way, his presence clearly sounded the end of their conversation.

'John's been telling me that Veranchetti's chances are good. I might even have to place my first ever bet!' she said brightly.

Antonio's dark glance told her that he didn't believe her, and as he said his goodbyes and ushered her back towards the limousine Emma felt horribly as if she'd been treading where she shouldn't have been...

The foyer of The Excelsus gleamed in the sunlight through the glass-fronted entrance. She resisted the temptation to shiver, which was more from the incredible luxury surrounding her than the temperature. Her low heels clicked on the marble flooring as they made their way towards the reception desk.

'Mr Arcuri!' A perfectly suited manager greeted Antonio and then turned his attention to Emma. 'And Ms Guilham. Welcome to The Excelsus.'

Momentarily startled that the manager had greeted her by name, Emma was wrong-footed.

The man pressed a sleek black folder and two black-coloured room cards across the desk towards her. 'Your belongings have been taken up to the suite. Would you like me to show me to your rooms, Mr Arcuri?'

'No, thank you, I am sure that everything will be in order,' Antonio responded, pausing only to pick up the folder and key cards before marching towards a discreet lift hidden behind steel panelling in the opposite direction from the more public elevators in the centre of the foyer.

Emma was left trailing behind, feeling once again unsettled in this environment. The excitement she had felt back in New York when she'd stayed at The Langsford was beginning to rise again. This was a glimpse of a lifestyle, experiences, that she couldn't have imagined putting on her Living List, and she was eager to see her room.

As she came to a halt beside Antonio the question she'd felt niggling at the back of her mind had clearly become apparent.

'Yes?' Antonio demanded, with a return of the autocratic boss she knew he could be, who for just a moment had been absent at the stables.

'How did he...?'

'Know your name? I would think that, just like John, *many* people now know your name. After all, to all intents and purposes, you are the future Mrs Arcuri.'

Emma remembered the press articles speculating on who she was, how she had managed to capture the notorious playboy, whether she might be carrying his child. She was thankful that she had managed to get hold of both her parents to let them know what was about to happen, but hated to think of them reading all the gossip and conjecture.

The discreet lift doors opened and Antonio entered,

waiting for Emma to do the same—but she couldn't. He was in there, taking up the whole space, dominating it. Some kind of self-preservation instinct kicked in, preventing her from joining him. Until Antonio reached out a hand, caught her by the wrist and pulled her right into hell with him.

The move had startled her so much she had fallen against him, found herself pressed against the hard planes of his chest, and the physical contact drew an almost instantaneous reaction from Emma, who had been trying desperately to forget the shocking kiss that had announced their engagement to the world.

He was looking down at her, his dark hawk-like eyes watchful, almost waiting...

'Capable of standing on your own two feet?'

Embarrassment painted her cheeks red as she disengaged her body from his. The lift was ascending with barely a jolt, and she put the flip of her stomach down to the ascent of nearly twenty floors in just seconds.

Coming to a halt, the lift opened onto a hallway with only two doors at opposite ends, and Emma slapped down her active imagination that had been expecting to walk straight out into a penthouse suite.

Not waiting for her, Antonio exited and made his way towards the door to her left. She followed, and as he swiped the key card and pressed his way forward into the suite she hovered by the door.

'Emma?'

'Yes? Oh, sorry. Now that you're safely settled in, I'll take my key and find my room,' she said, trying to look anywhere but at where her new fiancé was standing.

His silence drew her gaze like nothing else could have. He stood there, barely a hair out of place despite the flight and the visit to the stables, his head cocked to one side, and looked at her with something in his eyes she didn't want to name.

'This is your room, Emma.'

Shock kept her in place, hovering outside the door to the suite. She was pretty sure her jaw had dropped.

'That's not going to work, Antonio.'

'Of course it is. You're my fiancée—where else would you be staying?'

'Who's to say that I'm not the kind of fiancée who believes in…in waiting for the wedding night?'

Words like *sex* were dangerous at the best of times, but with him…? She cursed internally. She wasn't going to be able to do this.

'No one—and I mean *no one*—would believe that I would allow my fiancée to have her own set of rooms. We're on this path, Emma, and I will not let anything or anyone question that. This is going to have to be believable, so get used to it.'

He was standing in front of her now, so close, and strangely even more dominating than he had been in the lift.

Before she could take a breath, he continued, 'You have your company credit card?'

Her mind was spinning enough that she was not able to understand why that would matter, but she nodded.

'Good—perhaps if you look the part it will help you act the doting fiancée.'

She looked down in dismay at the sensible, albeit rumpled clothes she had worn on the plane. He was right. Not only did she need a whole wardrobe of clothes—those she hadn't been able to retrieve from her apartment before coming here—but she needed a particular style of clothing.

She scowled at him. *'No one,'* she said, echoing his earlier words, 'would believe you would settle for *doting.'*

The concierge at The Excelsus had arranged for a car to take her to the most exclusive mall in Buenos Aires, with the assurance that it had a wide selection of fashion stores from which she would be able to get everything that she needed.

In the years since her breast reconstruction Emma had taken to shopping for clothes online, enjoying the fact that she didn't need to expose her insecurities to anyone but the four walls of her bedroom. This, however, was daunting. But she knew Antonio was right. The level of sheer extravagance in even the daywear of the women in the hotel had been enough to convince Emma that if she needed to be Antonio's fiancée, on his arm at evening events and at the racetrack, she would need thick and very expensive armour to succeed.

Besides, millions of women around the world who'd had reconstructive surgery did this every day. So could she.

But now, standing in the fourth store she'd entered, she felt the drive and determination that had brought her there beginning to fade. It wasn't just a dress or two that she needed—it was an entire wardrobe. She knew that there were women who would kill to be left free in one of Argentina's hottest fashion districts holding a credit card without a limit, but right now it was all just a little too much.

Some of the shocking and outlandish creations she had seen on display were so far outside her comfort zone, and the sheer sensuality of the Argentinian designs were both tempting and frightening in contrast to the office-style respectability of the clothing she was used to wearing in New York. But this was getting silly. She had spent so long hiding her figure behind loose clothes and dark colours. Perhaps this was a chance to make the most of this opportunity—even if she did feel slightly out of her depth.

She took her courage in both hands and approached a saleswoman who had been eying her suspiciously. Briefly, in a no-nonsense way, Emma explained the situation.

Rather than cloying mawkish sympathy she had prepared herself for, she was surprised and oddly touched when instead the woman beamed, informing her that she would be utterly delighted to help.

Antonio had just exited a shop, with a present each for his sister and mother safely in transit to his hotel, when he'd caught a glimpse of Emma slipping into a store. He'd held back a moment, losing her briefly as she moved amongst the mannequins and rows of designer clothes. Then, curious to see how she was getting on, he hadn't been able to help himself as he followed her in, telling himself that he only meant to make sure that she chose clothing suitable for her new role.

He'd felt the vulnerability coming off her in waves when he'd discussed her need for a wardrobe, and had had an urge to reach out and comfort, to protect. The only other women in his life he'd ever felt like that about were his sister and his mother, and from them he understood only too well how important it was for a woman to feel beautiful in what she wore.

As he neared the back of the shop he was surprised by a high-pitched *coo* falling from the lips of a shop assistant. He turned just in time to see Emma twisting around to catch a glimpse of herself in the floor-to-ceiling mirror by the changing rooms.

Need and desire consumed him fiercely and unexpectedly the moment his eyes snared her. There she stood, in a strapless dress that hugged her perfect breasts and stomach, leaving her arms and shoulders bare while layers and layers of blood-red silk cascaded from her slim waist, looking almost as shocked as he felt.

He watched as she took in her own appearance, her eyes drawing upwards from where the dress fell at her bare feet all the way to the top, where she met his eyes in the reflection of the mirror.

In a second the shock in her gaze was shuttered. Her eyes narrowed and she spun round, looking at him accusingly. 'How did you find me?'

Affronted by the way the fire in her voice matched the temperament of the dress, he couldn't help the retort that fell from his lips. 'I don't have a tracker on your phone, if that's what you're implying.'

She scowled, and oddly Antonio felt—and resisted—the urge to laugh.

'I'm here by mere coincidence,' he concluded.

'You don't believe in coincidence.'

'No,' he said, feeling exasperation rise within him.

He really didn't, and in that moment he wondered what kind of game the gods responsible for their lives were playing. Because that was exactly how he felt right now. *Played*.

As her hands clutched instinctively at the skirts of the dress he remembered just for a moment the feeling of her skin beneath his palms, and he forced himself to turn away before he embarrassed them both. The almost painful shock of arousal had hit him hard, and he knew it had nothing to do with how much time had passed since he'd last been in bed with a woman.

He could almost *taste* desire as he made his way over to the seat beside the dressing room. He was some kind of masochist to stay, but he didn't have the will-power to leave.

A glass of champagne was left discreetly on the table beside the chair, and when he took a sip the bubbles scraped against his raw throat.

'It's not right,' Emma said, looking at him, and for a moment he forgot that she was speaking about the dress.

He felt his eyes narrow instinctively, and everything male in him roared that she was wrong.

Before sanity prevailed.

'Perhaps not. Try something else.'

It was a command. Uttered in a harsh tone. One that did not befit the dressing room, and Emma felt it down to her very soul.

Yet she didn't think that they agreed for the same reason. She had never chosen clothes to accentuate her breasts before. At least not since the surgery. Before that she had been seventeen and happy with her body. Had never suffered from the kinds of insecurities she'd seen in her friends as they judged themselves against each other, against impossible to achieve celebrity figures.

But afterwards? Yes. She had let her insecurities run her wardrobe.

The selection of clothes given to her by the lovely sales assistant here was impeccable. Some of them were rather more extreme than others, but she had begun to view it as a kind of shock therapy. The more extreme made the less outrageous palatable, when once she would have baulked at the whole lot.

Emma had known women—powerful, strong, inspiring women—who had embraced their bodies and their lives with vigour after chemotherapy. She had longed to find that sense of self, and now she was beginning to realise that the courage that had seen her battle fiercely with the chemo was still needed to battle her future.

Stepping back into the changing room, she fought the instinctive urge to run. Run from Antonio's assessing gaze…run from the desire. She wasn't foolish enough to try and hide from what it was that had sprung forth between them.

She undid the zip hidden in the side seam of the dress and it pooled around her feet. She stepped out of the delicate red silk and her body felt the lick as if of flames across her body. There was only a thin curtain of material separating her from Antonio. She knew it and so did he.

Her exposed skin feeling overly sensitive, she reached for the last dress the assistant had procured for her.

Having already chosen some incredible day clothes, she only had evening functions to cater for, and she cursed herself for leaving the best for last. It was her favourite dress of the selection, and she'd wanted to have this moment for herself. But outside sat Antonio, glass in hand, as if he were waiting for a show. Except rather than taking her clothes off she was putting them on.

Suddenly she wanted him thrown off balance as much as she was. She wanted him to be feeling just an ounce of what he was doing to *her*.

Standing in a thong and nothing else, she reached for the dress and stepped into the skirt. The fabric of the dress's blue silk was covered in a subtle lace flower pattern detail, with a figure-hugging bodice. It rubbed against her sensitive skin at the same time as the cool silk soothed. The sleeves were sheer, with the same lace detail covering her arms but leaving her décolletage bare. It covered even whilst it revealed and she silently thanked the shop assistant's perfect eye.

Before she stepped out into the dressing area she looked at herself in the mirror, feeling that same sense of shock she had experienced when she'd seen herself in the red dress moments ago.

Was that really her? Whilst her hair and minimal make-up were almost ordinary, the dress had called forth something within her. Something powerful and feminine... Things she'd always wanted to be but had never seemed to achieve. There was a blush to her cheeks, making more of her cheekbones than she was used to, and the glitter in her eyes shone like diamonds.

She pulled aside the curtain that separated her from Antonio and everything else faded away—the assistant, the shop...it all disappeared and only he came into focus.

And her lungs stopped working.

Because Antonio Arcuri, destroyer and saviour of global companies, was looking at her as if she were the only thing in the world and she nearly came undone.

CHAPTER FIVE

THREE DAYS OF trying to ignore the woman living and breathing in the same suite was driving Antonio insane. He was now thoroughly regretting the impulse he'd had to stay and see Emma's last outfit at the shop. Ever since that moment he'd been imagining what it would be like to peel her out of the silky dress and enjoy every delight her stunning figure had to offer.

But he couldn't. Emma was nothing like the women who graced his bed. The women who lived and played in his world—the women who had the hard edge needed to take his emotion-free entanglements. Emma didn't know how to play that game, and although she might hide it well she would break in his arena.

Besides—as he reminded himself for the hundredth time—there was far too much at stake.

He had done everything needed to ensure the meeting with Bartlett would be a success. He had orchestrated an irresistible deal the man would be insane to refuse. But he didn't like the silence from his father. Didn't trust it. The man must be up to something.

For the first time Antonio found himself wondering just how far he would go to get his revenge.

And the only answer in his heart was, *However far it took...*

It was gone eleven, and Emma had retired to her room almost an hour ago. In that time he'd pulled out all the files on Bartlett they had collated in the last week and turned the sumptuous living room into a practical office. The meeting with Bartlett was set for tomorrow evening—and the day of races that would commence the first leg of the Hanley Cup would start the following morning. Everything was lining up nicely... But he couldn't shake the feeling of an approaching storm.

As if he had summoned demons for Emma too, he heard sounds of distress coming from her room. Worried, he got up from the sofa and was halfway towards her door when he heard her scream. He rushed into her room, barely noticing as the door slammed back against the wall, probably leaving a dent, and took three strides to her bed.

She was tossing and turning, caught up in the cotton sheets, kicking out desperately. He could see the trails of tears on her cheeks. *Dio*, it must be some nightmare.

Remembering how his sister had suffered so badly from them in the year following their departure from the States, he sat down on the bed beside Emma's restless form and gently took hold of her arm.

'Emma...' he whispered. 'Emma, it's just a dream.'

She thrashed against his gentle hold and let out a whimper that struck his heart.

'Emma, come on. It's just a dream. You need to wake up.'

Her eyes sprang open, searching for focus. A shudder racked her body, and she gasped on an inhalation of much needed breath.

'You're okay. It was just a dream.'

But the hurt in her eyes told him he was wrong.

She looked so vulnerable, so in need of comfort, that

it took everything in him not to take her in his arms, to replace the fear in her eyes with want, with arousal. He wanted her to feel the same need, the same desire that burst into life against his skin when it met hers... something he knew could only be satiated by a touch, by a caress.

He cursed himself to hell and back. He couldn't take advantage of her. Not now...not like this. *Not ever*, he warned himself.

Emma took in Antonio's presence. The light filtering through from the living room cast his face in night-time shadows, so much more welcome than her awful dream. For a moment—just a moment—she thought he might reach for her. Might kiss her as she so desperately wanted to be kissed. But seconds passed and he didn't. He held himself back.

She nodded. Resting her hand on his where it held her arm. 'I'm okay. It's okay. I'll be through in a minute. I just need...a minute.'

As Antonio left her room she willed the fierce beating of her heart to slow. Her fingers brushed away the traces of the nightmare from her eyes and she realised that the tears she had thought contained by the dream had escaped.

She moved to the en suite bathroom, passing the wardrobe full of the clothes they had bought two days ago with an accusatory glance, as if they could be held responsible for causing old fears to surface. The fear that the cancer would come for her again, just when she was beginning to hope that she could reclaim her sense of self, reclaim the sense of her body.

She splashed water on her hot cheeks, finally shaking off the hold of her terror. Wide awake, and not ready even to consider going back to bed, she pulled on the hotel's silk robe and padded into the living area of the suite on bare feet.

She took in the devastation caused by Antonio's preparation for the meeting with Bartlett with a rueful smile.

'I am very glad you don't usually work like this. I'd have the cleaners quitting on me each and every day if you did.'

He looked up from the papers he held in his hands, his hawk-like gaze refusing to be distracted by her attempt at small talk.

'Nightmare?'

'Yes. Clearly,' she replied.

She was surprised to see his chiselled features soften.

'My sister used to get them regularly. Would you like some tea?'

'Because I'm English?' Emma asked, holding on to the warm offer like a lifeline.

'Yes. Clearly.'

She smiled as he gave her words back to her.

'What would you have given your sister?'

'Well…' he said, as if searching his memory. But she knew that the answer would immediately be on his lips. 'She was thirteen at the time, but a little limoncello didn't hurt her one bit. Not that this hotel has limoncello stocked in the suite's bar. But there is whisky?'

'I'll take the whisky. Thank you.'

As she watched him step behind the corner bar that edged one side of the suite she took in his powerful appearance. Even three days of solid work, constantly sorting through all the figures and research data that they'd been able to put together, hadn't put a dark hair out of place. Dressed in his suit trousers and a shirt, sleeves rolled back on strong tanned forearms, he was mouth-wateringly handsome.

The brief glimmer of concern in his eyes as he had woken her from her nightmare had been devastatingly tempting, and not for the first time Emma wondered what it would be like to rely on that power, that compassion. A compassion he was yet to show, however, in any of his business dealings.

She turned away from the temptation of his presence and stepped towards the windows that looked out over the stands of the race course. In just a few days they would be full of spectators, sound and chaos. But at that moment they seemed peaceful and quiet. She pressed her hand against the glass and allowed it to leach away some of the fevered heat she reluctantly attributed to the man behind her.

As he approached, a glass of whisky in each hand, she became horribly conscious that she was only wearing a silk negligée and the robe. The cool, delicate touch of the fabric did nothing to ease the prickles of heat racing across her skin at the mere sight of his reflection. Her mind, torn between the horror of her nightmare and the ecstasy of Antonio's proximity, warred between her hurt and her heart…

Her heart should know better. But it didn't. Her heart wanted him to put those damn glasses down and take her in his arms.

Schooling her features, calming the erratic beating of her pulse, she watched as he waited for her to turn, clearly knowing that she had seen him in the reflection in the window.

'My sister never really wanted to talk about her fears, but in the end she saw that it helped.'

Desperate to hold on to any thread that took her away

from her desires, and also curious, given how little she knew about his past and his family, she turned and accepted the glass he offered her.

He moved back to the beautiful sofa and cleared some of the paper from it, making room for her on the opposite end, a safe distance away from his presence.

'How long did she have nightmares for?'

For a brief moment Emma wondered if Antonio would choose to ignore her question, but after a small sigh he started to talk.

'They carried on for a year after my parents' divorce.'

His eyes turned dark, consuming the golden flecks she sometimes saw there.

'It was public and very messy. In order to reduce the settlement, my father paraded my mother's affair through the courts and the international press. He had the divorce granted in Italy, where people are still notoriously moralistic about such things. Had we been in North America, it might have been different. But whatever continent he might have chosen, it didn't seem to affect the press interest.'

He shrugged—such an Italian gesture of dismissiveness for clearly such a painful thing. Emma could only guess at the depths of the emotions he was struggling with.

'How old were you?'

'I was sixteen, but Cici was only thirteen. Without Michael's financial support my mother couldn't stay in America. Her father offered to help, but only if we came back to Italy. So we left.'

'That must have been hard.'

Emma knew what it was like to have her entire world change at such a young age. It had dripped onto her experiences like rain falling through leaves. Each tear-shaped drop hitting another aspect of her life. It could not have been much different for Antonio, his sister and his mother.

'It was. Everything we knew—friends, school, staff. That's where John worked. In my father's stable.'

'You had a *stable*?'

Emma had known that he must have had money growing up—he had some mannerisms that only financial security could give—but the idea of having a stable was almost inconceivable for a girl who'd had a struggling artist mother and a state school teacher father.

Antonio smiled ruefully. 'The full American package. Stables, private education, piano recitals—for Cici, not me. I was on track to be a member of the American polo team. But... I left that behind too.'

She let the silence fall, not wanting to interrupt the hold of his memories. Her heart reached out to the boy who had lost his dream.

'Cici struggled with it more. Losing her friends. And, even though he's an evil bastard, she suffered from the loss of her father too.'

Emma couldn't help but notice how he referred to his sister's pain, but not his own. *Her* father, not his. As if Antonio had cut him out of his vocabulary as determinedly as his father had cut them from his life.

She took a sip of her whisky. His was neat, but he'd added ice to hers which she was thankful for. The ice-cool liquid took the edge off the warmth of the rich Irish blend.

'Cici needed stability in that year, and I worked very hard to give it to her.'

'What about your mother?'

A small smile graced his lips. 'She was—*is*—a beautiful Italian socialite with little education and less work experience. Her father was rich, but bad financial investments had stolen much of his wealth by the time we returned to Italy. He gave us what he could, but I wanted Cici to stay in private education. In order to do that I needed to work after school.'

'And what about you?'

'I,' he said with mock sincerity, 'am an academic genius.'

And she wished he hadn't said it. The playful mask he wore was just as alluring as the truth behind it.

'I didn't need private education. I got my scholarship to NYU...met Dimitri and Danyl. They became my family, each of us having experienced our own hardships. There we were, foreign students, not unaccustomed to America, but perhaps our differences forged our friendship as much as our similarities. We worked hard and played harder. It was at university where we first conceived the Winners' Circle syndicate. My interest in horses had never faded and it was matched by Dimitri's and Danyl's. It was they, along with a small investment from my grandfather, who helped me start Arcuri Enterprises. Within two years I had paid them all back with interest, and bought my mother and sister a house—a *home*—in Italy. Dimitri and Danyl helped me ensure that they would be okay.'

'You protected them. Your sister and mother.'

She cursed her foolish heart for unfurling beneath the warmth of his words as he spoke of his friends, his family. And finally she began to understand Antonio's determination to secure the Bartlett deal. He wanted revenge—that much was clear. He wanted to hurt his father in the only way that he knew how.

But Emma couldn't help the feeling growing within

her that he might not like what he found once he'd achieved it.

'Yes,' he said simply, in relation to her earlier statement, as if it was the only way it could have been.

'It must have been a hard responsibility to bear,' Emma observed.

'I would do it again and again.'

'Where are they now?'

This time his smile broadened fully and her heart nearly stopped at the sight. It illuminated his dark features with light and pleasure, and in that moment she was thankful that he wasn't like this all the time. It would be...devastating.

'A beautiful estate in Sorrento, on the Amalfi coast, with olive trees and lemon groves.'

His simple words conjured a million images in her mind, and she could almost smell a hint of citrus in the air about them.

'And your sister?'

'No more nightmares.'

'Nothing more to fear,' Emma said, her own nerves beginning to twist at the way the conversation was going.

'No.'

'And what is *your* fear, Antonio?'

Emma didn't know what gave her the courage to ask. Perhaps it was the darkness outside, or the intimacy created by the only light in the living room dusting them with a warm, gentle golden glow.

But even in that soft lighting she saw his features grow dark. Something bitter entered the air, and the determination that had hung around Antonio since he'd come back to the New York office and asked her to research Benjamin Bartlett returned.

'That my father will never pay for what he did to my mother and sister.'

And for what he did to you, Emma added silently as the ripple of his words sent icy shivers through her body.

She took another sip of the cool whisky, trying to forestall the question she knew was next on Antonio's lips.

'And what is yours, Emma?'

Antonio watched Emma pull the thin silk robe around her shoulders, covering and protecting herself from the memory of her nightmare. He wished for a moment that she hadn't. The way the soft material had opened just slightly at the V of her chest, the smooth creamy skin thinly veiled, had been his only anchor—his only tie in the storm of emotions that had surfaced beneath his stark words as he'd recounted his past.

He heard the chink of ice in her glass, drawing him back to the present as she rested it between her palms as she might hold a hot drink.

'Well, I suppose the nightmare started in pretty much the usual way—I was being attacked by zombie cats.'

He couldn't help but laugh. 'Zombie cats is usual?'

'Well, hyper real, at least. They were attacking me, and I was managing to escape, but they were keeping me from something. And then I realised that they were keeping me from getting to a doctor's appointment. I was waiting for new test results.' She took a shaky breath. 'The cancer had come back.'

Shivers covered his forearms. He couldn't even begin to imagine that kind of fear. 'What was it like?'

'Horrible,' she said simply, without malice or anger, or any of the kind of emotions he would have projected onto the situation.

He wasn't sure about continuing to ask, but he felt that she needed to talk about it, and he trusted her enough to tell him to stop if he caused too much pain.

'How old were you when you got ill?'

'Seventeen.'

Antonio cursed. It fell from his mouth without thought or he would have held it back, but Emma only smiled her gentle small smile.

'What surprised me was how utterly practical it all was. The diagnosis was shocking, terrible, but there was a chain of events to follow—things to be done and so much to organise. After a few days the diagnosis became a fact. Just a fact. A hurdle—a thing to overcome. All the stress and worry about A levels, about boys, about who was better friends with who…the things that had seemed so important in my day-to-day life…suddenly just seemed so small in comparison.'

'Weren't you angry?' he asked.

'Yes…and no. There wasn't really time to be angry. There was the operation, and then the chemo. And through it all I just felt that I couldn't let the anger take hold. I felt that my anger would feed the cancer, some- how. It's so very different for each person it happens to. Some people are able to use anger to fight it, to give them energy. But I didn't want anything else eating away at me. If I clung to being positive, if I held to the determination that I would beat it, then I knew I would win. I would take back my life.'

She took a breath and he marvelled at her strength.

'I had to put my A levels on hold during the treat- ment. I had a double mastectomy, then chemotherapy followed by breast reconstruction. Some women choose to have the reconstruction immediately following a mas- tectomy, but after speaking to my doctors I wanted to make sure that the cancer was completely gone before moving forward. And at that point I really didn't want another operation.'

Antonio saw the fierceness in her gaze as she spoke. The fire he had only seen glimpses of before was there now, shining in her eyes, burning in flushed cheeks, and it was glorious. He relished her strength and determination, allowed it to feed him too.

'It took about a year, all in all. And by that time, although supportive, my friends had moved on…found relationships, started university, gone travelling around the world. None of which I begrudged for a second. But I felt out of step. Just a little behind. Like this thing had happened to me and no one else. But that wasn't quite true.'

'What do you mean?' he asked.

'One of the hardest things was telling other people. I felt as if I had to manage their emotions, their reactions. I'd find myself reassuring *them* that I would be okay. That it would all be fine. More often than not it was just—' she shrugged '—awkward.'

She took another sip of her drink and a little shiver rippled across her skin as she swallowed the oaky alcohol.

'I had a boyfriend at the time,' she revealed, swirling the ice cubes around her empty glass. 'He was a…a sweet boy. But I think telling him was the hardest. Because the look in his eyes…' She shook her head against the memory. 'It was fear, guilt, anger… Fear of what might happen, guilt that he didn't want this, that it wasn't what he'd signed up for, and anger that this had happened to him. Yes, clearly it was happening to me, but it was something that he might have to deal with.'

'He left you?' Antonio asked, hearing the growl vibrating in his own words. The sheer anger and fury swept up in him by her simple words shocked him.

'No. We'd only been dating—if you could even call it that—for a few months. It wasn't serious, and it probably wouldn't have lasted much longer. So I let him go. He argued with me. I could see that he wanted to do the right thing. But I needed to focus on me, on my fight, not on ensuring that he was okay.

'I was determined to ensure that the cancer cells didn't multiply and spread—didn't affect things outside of my body. It's so hard not to let cancer become everything around you. Everything you see. Family.... Friends. Cancer is a thief if you let it be. It doesn't just take lives, it takes body parts, time, experiences, relationships...

'My parents' marriage broke down soon after my treatment,' she confided. 'They're much happier now, and that's great. But nothing was the same after the cancer. My home, my parents...my body. Everything had changed.'

'I'm sorry.' Even as he said it, he knew the words to be inefficient, wrong...too little.

'Don't be sorry,' she said, a flash of anger sparking in her eyes. 'Don't apologise. Because cancer shouldn't be excused. It's not a thing to pardon or to forgive. It is not a thing to be normalised. You don't get to apologise for cancer. You can help fight it. Help beat it. Help those who *do* fight against it. But *never* apologise for it. There's funding for research and new technologies... that's why charity foundations are so important. That's why *yours* could be so much more.'

Antonio held the weight of her gaze, held the weight of her accusation. He knew she was right.

She seemed to gather herself before him. 'I'm sorry,' she said.

'Don't be. You're right. I should have been more involved. I should have made the time to attend the yearly galas. And you're absolutely right about getting rid of Greenfeld. I've already put motions in place that will remove him from his position. After the success of the gala—which was mainly down to you—the board supports my decision and we're already considering other options. Once this deal is done, I promise you it's the first thing on my list when we return to New York.'

Emma smiled—almost as if she had a secret.

'What?' he asked, suddenly incurably curious about her—everything and anything about her. He wanted to know it all.

'I have a list too.'

Emma couldn't believe that she was telling him about her list. During chemo she had heard people talk about their bucket lists, and had felt overwhelmingly sad that the supposition was at the end there would be death, not life.

'It's my Living List. My mum helped me to make it,' she said, smiling at the memory of being in her parents' sitting room, pen and paper in her hands, as her mother and father encouraged her to write down everything she wanted to do when it was all over.

'What's on the list?' he asked, drawing her from her memory.

She looked at him and realised how their bodies had shifted position on the sofa. Somehow during their conversation she had turned towards him, her back against the armrest, her legs stretched out. If she moved an inch her feet would be in his lap. And Antonio had turned towards her, mirroring her position, one leg bent, anchored over the other.

It was beguiling, having Antonio Arcuri's full attention. The low light from the small lamp on the table beside him shaded half his features, highlighting the cut of his cheekbones, the hollows of his throat…a throat she wanted to run her fingers over, her tongue…

But it was the look in his eyes as he asked the question. Curiosity and something else. Something almost pleasurable.

She felt heat swirl in her stomach and, desperate to dampen this quickening attraction for her boss, she focused on his question.

'A whole lot of things—big and small.'

'What's the biggest?'

'Only a man would ask that first,' she joked, and appreciated the humour that was returned to her in his eyes. 'Okay—I think the biggest would be that I want to see the sun rise over a desert and set over the Mediterranean.'

'In one day?' Antonio asked, his surprise almost funny.

'Not necessarily. I'm not fussy. Just a sunrise. Just a sunset. But, yes, deserts, sea views… I want to see the world. I'm really looking forward to Hong Kong,' she confided.

'I know the perfect place to take you.'

'Where?'

'It's a surprise. But you'll like it,' he assured her, and that thrill of excitement began to unwind throughout her body and across her skin. 'The smallest?' he pressed.

'Ah. The smallest I *have* achieved. I wanted to eat a stack of American pancakes with crispy bacon and maple syrup. It was *divine*.'

He laughed as she groaned with remembered pleasure. 'What else?'

And once again Emma's thoughts went to the one thing that she hadn't been able to write on the list in front of her parents. She was sure that her mother would have understood, but writing *losing my virginity* had just seemed more than a little uncomfortable.

But it was about so much more than simply having sex. At the time, Emma had been approaching her reconstructive surgery with the same practicality that had pushed her through the other areas of treatment.

Now, when she looked in the mirror she just saw shapes. The shapes that had been taken away and then put back on her body. It was hard for her to see her breasts, her body, as her own. To own them, to glory in them. She had a good figure—she knew that. But somehow she had never felt able to exalt in it. To see it as her *own*.

'You didn't ask me to help you achieve anything on your list,' Antonio stated when she didn't answer his question.

'When?'

'When I offered you whatever you wanted.'

'No,' she said. She hadn't. 'These are things *I* want to achieve Antonio. *I* want to make them happen. Asking you to do them for me…kind of feels like cheating.'

He let that lie between them, and the silence was consumed whole by the tension and crackle of attraction on the air between them.

Antonio's declaration to dedicate more time and energy to the charity had been almost fierce. And Emma found herself wondering what it would be like to have that dedication and power directed at her. As a woman. As someone or something beautiful.

She couldn't help but study him once again in the half-light of the room, seeing the way it illuminated his masculine beauty. She could lie to herself and pretend to think that it was her wayward thoughts about her virginity that had conjured her attraction to him by association—not the curve of his almost cruelly sensual lips, the feel of his eyes on her body. She could blame it on the new and surprising intimacy that had been created between them in these last few hours and not on the way his direct gaze, eagle-eyed and intense, seemed to reach into her and kick up her pulse.

But she wouldn't.

She had always found Antonio powerfully attractive. Had always felt prickles of awareness when he was nearby. He was as tempting as the devil.

Those gold flecks had returned to his eyes, surfing the waves of molten chocolate that seemed to radiate…heat. And desire. It became a tangible thing, and she could almost taste it on the air. She felt every single inch of her skin where the silk robe rested against it, felt the smooth material of the sofa beneath her calf muscle. She felt the space between them that seemed at once so small, yet almost insurmountable.

She willed her breath to become silent, knowing that she couldn't give in to the temptation burning between them, reluctant to let sound or action break this strange hold.

But sanity prevailed. Yes, she'd seen more to her handsome boss than she could have imagined. The grief and pain of his childhood had called to something within her. But she couldn't get involved with him. Because for all his promises she couldn't rely on anyone if the worst was to happen. Because it never lasted. Not really. People left, people changed, people wanted other things... And in the end the only person Emma could rely upon was herself.

She looked about the room, finally severing the connection that had formed between them. And then, lifting up a stack of papers, she asked him about Bartlett—a line of questioning that Antonio seemed equally relieved to take up.

'Bartlett's company is a fourth generation, family-owned heritage business and—'

'No, I didn't mean his company. Who is *he*? What makes him tick?'

Antonio paused for a moment, as if he honestly hadn't given it much consideration. He picked up the files and she shook her head, a gentle laugh falling from her lips.

'Antonio...' She couldn't help chuckling as she gently reprimanded him. 'He is the father of two children, Mandy and James, both are at university, both studying business. Mandy, by the way, certainly seems to be enjoying it thoroughly from her Instagram account—'

'You follow her Instagram account?'

'Yes, you asked me to research Bartlett, so I did.'

He nodded, as if slightly surprised. 'How did you get all this?'

'Bartlett's PA—Anna—used to work for someone who does a lot of business with the boss of your London office. We know each other quite well. She helped with some of the information, but she wouldn't cross any lines. Perhaps you should take a look at the notes in the blue folder. They're a bit more personal than business facts.'

But the word *personal* brought back memories of the earlier moment they had shared.

Realising that she had lost his concentration, Emma

felt a wave of tiredness sweep over her, and as Antonio took up several of the documents in the blue folder she decided to leave him to it and return to her room. This time hoping not to avoid her nightmares but dreams of her handsome boss.

CHAPTER SIX

THE NEXT DAY, by the time Antonio returned to the suite, he was physically exhausted. He'd been down to the stables to see John and V, but John had practically thrown him out because his 'state of mind' was affecting the horses. So he'd spent two hours in the gym, pushing himself hard.

Anything to force his shockingly one-track mind away from Emma Guilham and back to the meeting they had with Bartlett in a little over an hour. He had tried to pretend that the intimacy they'd shared the night before didn't mean anything. He'd tried to ignore the strands of desire that had woven between them before she had shifted the subject away from the personal and back on to Bartlett. But he hadn't quite managed to achieve it.

John was right. Antonio had to get his mind in order—had to shelve these thoughts and put them back in the box he never opened. He needed to get Bartlett to choose him, because if he didn't his father would go unchecked. Michael Steele would live his life without ever feeling what his mother felt…his sister felt. The painful sting of humiliation, the acute devastation when everything changed beyond recognition…the realisation that the very fabric of life could not be trusted.

And Antonio needed that—needed Michael to feel that.

He walked into his room and pulled his sweat-soaked T-shirt over his head, discarding it as he crossed into the bathroom. Turning on the scalding hot spray of water, he pushed the rest of his clothes from his body and tried very hard not to imagine Emma doing the same. Before she covered that irresistible body in the dress he'd bought for her that morning.

He hadn't been able to help himself. The clothing she'd purchased on their first day in Buenos Aires was perfectly adequate. But he didn't want 'adequate' for her. After last night, he wanted to see her in colours. Because that was what he had seen when she had talked about her experience with cancer.

He didn't want her to hide her figure behind the blacks and whites she usually wore. He could only guess that she hadn't quite come to accept her body. She hadn't said as much, but he had read between the lines. And he knew exactly how damaging that could be to a woman. To anyone.

And it was a crime—because Emma was simply stunning. So that morning, when he'd been out buying the last thing that would make this 'engagement' seem real, he'd passed a shop window and stopped in his tracks, realising at once that the dress on the mannequin was perfect.

The moment he'd seen it Antonio had wondered what Emma's curves would look like beneath the material— what the silk would reveal or conceal, what sound would it make running across her satin-smooth skin. How the colour would look against the pale cream tones of her bare arms...

The rush of his thoughts sent his body's blood south, shockingly fast, and Antonio gritted his teeth in an effort to keep himself under control and switched the shower from hot to icy cold.

And he knew—*knew* with one hundred per cent clarity—that he could not treat Emma with the same detachment that he used to handle the other women in his life. She wasn't like the women he usually took to bed. The ones who knew that he wouldn't offer them anything more.

He could no longer fool himself that it was because he was putting off anything deeper until after he had brought his father to his knees. He was self-aware enough to know that he didn't trust something as dangerous as love. It was a tool used by those more powerful, wielded to hurt, to harm.

It was as if Emma's honesty had lifted the lid on his ability to lie to himself. He knew that he had avoided anything emotional because of the power it had to be used against him. And he would never be victim to it again. But somehow Emma had managed to sneak beneath the armour he wore around his heart. To bring forth truths from his lips that he'd never shared with anyone other than Dimitri and Danyl.

And whilst everything in him wanted to run, to push her away, to save her from the darkness that threatened to consume him as he went further down his path of revenge, he knew that he wouldn't. That what he was about to do would only bind them together further.

He shut off the shower, dried himself and dressed quickly. He caught his reflection in the mirror. The perfectly tailored suit of dark blue cashmere wool matched his mood. On the bedside table was the small box that he had obtained before going to the gym.

He had thought he would simply go to the shop, make the purchase and leave. But, surprising himself, he had pored over the selection, discarding the more traditional cuts and colours and focusing instead on finding something that was unique and utterly... *Emma*. Not the PA he had spent eighteen months working with, but the woman who had hidden fire within her—the one who in fits and bursts had shown herself to be empowered... incredible, even.

He grabbed the box in his fist, then forced himself to relax his grip, hating what that said about him and his hopes for her reaction as he stalked through the suite. The tight leash on his emotions stretched taut, he called out to Emma, but didn't hear a reply.

He knocked on the door to her room, forcing himself to make it gentle and not pound on it as his heart was pounding within his chest. When there was still no answer he pushed gently on the door, ignoring the voice in his head that told him to turn back.

Smaller than his, though not by much, the room stretched out before him in rich, bold contemporary colours of black, grey and red. Emma had pushed back the curtains, revealing the night-time sky that trespassed over the race course as dusk beat a hasty retreat. Or perhaps it was Antonio who was trespassing...

He turned towards the bathroom, where he could hear the clicking of her heels on marble flooring. He was about to turn around and leave when the bathroom door opened and in walked Emma...

And his breath caught in his lungs.

She was incredible. So beautiful, so strong and powerful.

And he hated the thought that she didn't realise it.

From her feet, the deep, rich burnt orange silk bled upwards into lighter tones of amber and yellow, no less bold, but bright and eye-catching. The dress lay over her chest in a deep V, revealing the valley between her breasts. It clung to a waist that couldn't be broader than the span of his hand. It flared out from there and hung all the way to the floor.

But it wasn't until she stepped further into the room, when the high split revealed perfectly toned legs that went on for miles, that the breath that had been balled up in his chest finally escaped on an inaudible *whoosh*.

The moment she had seen the dress that had been delivered to the suite a few hours earlier her heart had almost stopped. She'd been surprised that her first reaction hadn't been instant refusal, hadn't been the thought that she could never wear such a revealing creation, but instead she was struck by how it reminded her of one of her mother's paintings. It had the same colours of the first piece her mother had produced after Emma had returned home from her last hospital stay.

There was no way that Antonio could have known about the painting, let alone the impact of the dress. But as she'd lifted the delicate material from the white box it had arrived in, and seen the way the rich golden colours shimmered in the light, she had known that she couldn't *not* wear it.

So she had put it on, and stared at herself in the mirror. Simply stared. Bold and bright, the smooth silk hugged curves she had never put on display before. For all her words the night before about being positive, about embracing the future and all it had to offer, she realised that perhaps she had left *this* behind. Allowed it to be swallowed up. That when she had thought her battle with cancer over in fact she had to continue to fight each day, to take back the things she had lost.

More than her breasts and her parents' marriage, her sensuality, her sense of self as a woman.

But now Antonio was looking at her in a way she couldn't decipher.

'How do I look?'

'Amazing,' he said without pause. 'But there's something missing.'

He reached into his trouser pocket and produced a small blue velvet box.

With trembling hands she took it from his palm, trying to avoid the zip and zing of electricity that passed between them. She laughed a little as she struggled with the little metal clasp on the box. But the moment her gaze caught the ring inside she stopped. Everything stopped.

It was a beautiful green sapphire, encased in rose gold. The precious stone was surrounded by tiny diamonds which continued the whole way around the band. It stole her breath—and in some part the walls around her heart.

'It's perfect,' she whispered as she slipped it onto her finger. She couldn't let him do it for her, it would mean too much.

'I'm pleased,' he said, holding her eyes with the same sincerity she had felt from him the night before. 'No matter what happens, I want you to keep it.'

'I...' She was speechless. 'I can't, Antonio. I don't deserve it.'

'It's not about deserve, or need. I want you to have it.'

Emma didn't know what to say. And if, somewhere deep down, there was a single tendril of sadness that this wasn't real, then that was her own fault. She'd known what she was getting into when she'd agreed to this deal. And just because she was emotional about it, it didn't change a thing.

Oh, but she wished she could.

By the time that they left the suite Emma was thankful for the reminder that their relationship was purely a business arrangement.

By the time they got to the lobby Emma had put away the childish hurt and pulled her armour back into place.

By the time the limousine arrived at the restaurant where they were to meet Bartlett, Emma was ready to do battle and slay dragons to help Antonio secure investment in Bartlett's company.

She had felt the hurt emanating from Antonio the night before as he'd told her of his childhood. She could see how important it was to him and wanted to gift him something of what he'd given her... The ability to reach for what it was that she wanted.

The lounge area of the famous Amore por la Comida restaurant spread out before them, coloured in rich amethyst hues set off perfectly by the golden twinkling stars piercing the night sky that could be seen from the windows surrounding all sides of the bar and seating areas.

The impeccably mannered head waiter was about to show them to the table when Emma felt Antonio stiffen beside her. A shiver rippled through his body like a shock wave, and she looked about them to see what might have caused it.

Coming towards them was a tall suited man she had never met before. There was something vaguely familiar about him, but she was forced to turn away from the frigid glare in his crystal blue eyes.

Instinctively she knew that this was Michael Steele, Antonio's father, and she couldn't help the way her hand slipped into the crook of Antonio's arm, as if trying to hold on to him, support him, give him something to warm the air that had suddenly cooled about them.

Antonio should have known. And perhaps deep down he had. Because his father's appearance didn't surprise him as much as it should have. He felt the drive of renewed determination fuel him. Indignation was but a second thought.

'Antonio,' Michael said as he drew close to them. 'I'd say that it's good to see you, but we both know that would be a lie.'

The charming, almost warm, smooth voice sharpened the harshness of his words.

'Why are you here?'

Antonio knew from bitter experience that the less he said to his father the better. He wondered whether Michael would have the gall to admit that he was here, at this exact place and time, because of his meeting with Bartlett. Clearly Michael had his informants, just as Antonio had his.

A cold smile graced lips that should be as familiar to Antonio as his own. In the three years since he'd last seen his father Michael Steele had grown in his mind to monstrous proportions. Instead, all he saw was an old man before him. But Antonio knew that appearances were deceiving and his whole body was on guard.

'Well, I heard rumours about the notorious Winners' Circle syndicate trying to win the hat-trick at the Hanley Cup. Surely that's a feat worth watching? If it succeeds. It would be such a shame if you were to fall at the first hurdle, so to speak. And, of course, it's a chance to catch up with old friends.'

Antonio bit back a curse. The man had absolutely no

interest in the Winners' Circle, and his allusion to 'old friends' could only mean Bartlett.

'I'm surprised you have any friends left, Michael.'

Anger had made him weak and he hadn't been able to prevent the snide comment falling from his lips.

'Come, now. There's no need to resort to childish swipes at your father.' Michael Steele barely allowed time for the reproach to strike before picking up yet another thread of venom. 'And this must be your *convenient* fiancée.'

The dismissive gesture of Michael's hands irritated him less than the fact that his father didn't even bother looking at Emma, let alone acknowledging her in any other way than by reference. Fury scoured him inside out, coursed through his veins. Antonio had long since stopped caring about the painful barbs Michael might throw in his direction, but he would not countenance any rudeness towards Emma.

'Her name is Emma. And you'll afford her the respect she deserves.'

'Respect? For a PA who miraculously becomes your fiancée when you so desperately need your reputation intact? How much did she charge you? I bet she's worth every penny of that green sapphire on her finger.'

His father's ice-cool eyes turned white-hot in a second and Antonio wanted to reach out and grab the man by the throat. But that was exactly what his father wanted. To cause a scene. To create a scandal that would make *him* look like the victim. Just the way he had done with his mother during the divorce.

Antonio had spent years studying his father's playbook, and he would not allow himself to rise to the taunt.

'Priceless,' he replied to his father's taunt.

'What?' he heard his father ask in confusion.

'Emma,' he stated, turning to her, locking his gaze with hers as if it were the only thread he could tie himself to amongst the seething emotions that were threatening to drown him.

She didn't show shock, fear or resentment—just curiosity, as if she too wanted to know what he meant.

'She is priceless. She is everything I didn't realise I needed.'

He watched as her eyes widened in surprise at his words, and hated it that he'd said them for his father—hated that he'd somehow tainted the sentiment.

'And I will not let you diminish her or hurt her. Take swipes at me, old man, or my company, but stay the hell away from her,' he growled.

For a second he saw shock in his father's eyes, but he rallied quickly.

'You think you can go up against me and win?' he snarled.

That was the voice he remembered from his childhood. The one that had haunted his sister's dreams and fuelled his own need for revenge.

'You have been nothing more than a pest, sniffing around my cast-offs. Once I win this investment with Bartlett, be assured the next business I'm coming after, *son*, is yours.'

'That's where you're wrong, *Father*. You won't win this deal with Bartlett. You've overplayed your hand and you're desperate. I can see it. And soon so will everyone else.'

Antonio unclenched his white-knuckled fist and forced himself to relax. He placed his hand on the small of Emma's back and guided her before him. He was thankful when she began to pick her way through the tables towards the head waiter, whose face betrayed no indication of hearing the conversation he must have heard.

Electricity crackled where his hand touched the almost indecently low back of her dress, but that wasn't what disturbed him. He realised that she was trembling—just slightly, not visibly—but he could feel it ripple over the soft, smooth acres of skin beneath his fingertips and he couldn't help himself.

He needed it—he needed *her*. He needed to wipe away that horrible encounter with his father. For her. For himself. He pulled her back, spinning her into him, and reached for what he so desperately wanted.

As his lips crashed down on hers he took advantage of the surprise she clearly felt, once again. How, after only one kiss, the taste and feel of her could be so familiar to him, he couldn't grasp. But his hand flew out to her cheek, holding her for his kiss, feeling her skin cool beneath the warmth of his fingers. He felt the wild flutter of her pulse beneath his palm, and satisfaction thrummed through him as it kept time with his own frantic heartbeat.

His tongue delved deeply into her mouth, relishing the way hers met and matched its every move. He didn't care that they were in a restaurant—didn't care that his father might still be watching. This wasn't for anyone else but them.

Starbursts of arousal and need crept up his spine, flaring and burning away the bitter taste of anger and resentment. And the moment her hand came up to his neck, pulling him to her as strongly as he wanted to pull her to him, he felt satisfaction, ownership, possession. A silent, primal roar sounded in his mind. *Mine*, it cried.

The realisation was startling, and enough for him to break the sensual hold that forged them together.

He drew back from their embrace, staring into eyes that were wide and dark with a desire that matched his own. Emma was breathing quickly, her cheeks flushed, and through the knowledge and the feeling of pleasure that he had done that to her, that he had caused her to feel that way, was a question ringing loudly in his mind.

Just what the hell had she done to him?

The head waiter cleared his throat discreetly and resumed his pathway towards the table where Benjamin Bartlett stood, waiting for them.

If she had known what Antonio had planned to do she would have stopped him. But, whether he'd noticed or not, the encounter with his father had unnerved her. Despite what Antonio had told her the previous night, his description of his father's cruel, ruthless behaviour, Emma had wondered if there was some reason, some explanation for his father's actions. She had thought he'd spoken with the hurt of an abandoned son, and now Emma felt terrible—as if that belief had somehow betrayed Antonio.

Because what she had seen in Michael Steele's eyes, heard in his voice, had convinced her that he was a horrible man, with no conscience nor regard for others. She understood, now, Antonio's need for revenge. Could feel it barely restrained beneath the surface of his skin. The power of it was dark, and she wished so much that he would turn away from it—even though she knew he wouldn't.

But that kiss had momentarily short-circuited her brain. Words of reassurance and support had fled beneath the sensual onslaught of his lips, and the wicked way they had demanded arousal and pleasure from her body had made her quiver with need. A need that went unsatisfied now he'd pulled away from her, leaving her wanting and shaking with desires she had never experienced before.

Realising that he had done that in public, in the middle of the restaurant full of nearly one hundred people, frustrated and angered her. But she needed to put aside that anger, because Benjamin Bartlett was there, standing at their table, waiting for them and looking decidedly uncomfortable.

And Emma was there to help Antonio win him over. Not because of the deal, and not because she was his convenient fiancée, but because she wanted to help *him*. Help him put his past to rest the way he was beginning to do for her.

She forced a smile to her lips, joy to her eyes, and took the hand Bartlett extended to her.

'Ms Guilham. It's lovely to meet you,' he said, his American accent more cultured than she had remembered from the call on the plane to Buenos Aires.

Unlike Michael Steele, Benjamin Bartlett seemed softer somehow, despite his height and lean stature. In some ways he was more like Antonio than Michael. Even though, at that precise moment in time, she could hardly say that there was anything soft about Antonio at all. In fact he seemed almost reluctant, as if still locked into an unconscious battle with his father.

'Likewise, Mr Bartlett. I hope we haven't kept you long?'

'Not at all.'

He waved them away, as if they hadn't just stood there in the middle of the restaurant kissing and instead had merely been a little delayed. And she realised then that what had made Bartlett awkward hadn't been the kiss, but the fact that he had clearly witnessed the interaction between Antonio and his father.

'I meant to ask,' Emma said as they took their seats, reaching for a conversation that she hoped would start them on potentially neutral ground, 'how is Anna's grandson? He wasn't very well the last time we spoke.'

A smile painted Bartlett's features. 'He's doing well, thank you for asking.'

Bartlett turned to Antonio, who hadn't been able to conceal his momentary confusion.

'My PA's grandson had appendicitis, and she had to stay home to care for him last week.' Turning back to Emma, he continued, 'She wanted me to pass on her congratulations. And I'd like to add mine to that,' he said, gesturing to Emma's hand.

The heavy weight of the beautiful green sapphire suddenly felt tight around her finger.

'I must admit I did wonder who it would take to make this reckless playboy settle down,' he said, but a smile took some of the sting out of his words. 'I don't believe he could have done any better.'

Emma forced some heat into her smile as guilt nibbled at her stomach. *Lying.* She was uncomfortable with lying.

'Thank you, Mr Bartlett.'

'Benjamin—please call me Benjamin,' he said, taking his seat and gesturing to them both to do the same. 'I hope you'll forgive us for talking business over our meal?'

'Of course. Antonio's very passionate about your company and I can't help but be intrigued.'

'Oh, really?' Bartlett asked.

'I have a great deal of respect for what you have

achieved,' Antonio stated, finally picking up the thread
of the pitch he'd worked on non-stop for almost a week.

Phrases that Emma had heard him muttering to himself over the last few days ebbed and flowed in the conversation. They ordered drinks and food, and between
the starters and the end of dessert Emma marvelled at
how Antonio used his carefully constructed words to
weave a spell that she was sure Benjamin Bartlett was
falling under.

Each line of his pitch was carefully orchestrated,
bent and moulded to the positive, outlining how Arcuri Enterprises could support, aid, help the company
to grow, rather than muscle in and take over. It was skilful, almost surgical in its precision.

The warmth of Bartlett's interaction with her was
very different from the careful assessment he was giving Antonio. Whilst Bartlett might be congenial, he
was still a fierce businessman who was choosing his
investor wisely.

'You clearly know a lot about my business, Antonio.'

'I use my research well.'

'And what does your research say about me?' Bartlett
asked—and the query not one made out of vanity.

'That you are a traditional businessman who believes in keeping things the way they are. You don't
like change, and you fight vehemently for your company, your brand and its continued success. You don't
believe that a business deal should be done until the
second bottle of whisky has been opened, and as we're
in a restaurant, not a bar, and you have refused a drink
with your coffee, I can tell that you haven't yet made up
your mind about who is best to support you financially
through the next successful stage of your business.'

Bartlett gave a surprised chuckle. 'And how did you know about the whisky?'

Antonio looked to Emma, who leaned in and said conspiratorially, 'Us PAs have our secrets, Mr Bartlett. Do allow us to keep them.'

'Ah... Of course. That is as it should be,' he replied with another warm smile.

Emma laid her fork down, defeated after less than half of the exquisite chocolate dessert she had ordered. In truth, she had neither eaten nor tasted much of the meal they had shared. Her nerves had been wound tight for Antonio. *Because* of him.

'Arcuri, it has certainly been an interesting evening. I thank you for the work you have clearly put into making this pitch, and I hope you will understand if I take this under consideration until next week. I have shareholders—many of whom see your father as a very good option.'

It was a phrase Antonio had expected, but one that was none the less unwelcome. Whether Bartlett had said it to garner a better deal from him, or whether it was the truth didn't really matter.

Yes, he'd seen desperation in his father's words and actions, but it was Dimitri's phrase that ran through his mind as he left the restaurant with Emma. That desperation made people dangerous. And he knew in that moment that he would go to any length, any extreme, to bring his father to his knees.

CHAPTER SEVEN

BY THE TIME they entered the reception area of their hotel, Antonio's thoughts were no longer on Bartlett *or* his father. Something which, at one point he'd thought almost unimaginable. But that had been before they'd come to Argentina—before Emma had worn the dress he'd chosen for her, and before he'd kissed her in a crowded restaurant and wanted the whole world to burn with him.

So instead of planning his next step he was still tasting her on his tongue. Instead of feeling the black plastic key card in his fingers he was feeling her skin beneath the palm of his hand. And there was nothing he could do to relieve the ache in his chest.

Not just because Emma wasn't like the women he usually spent his nights with—women who agreed to his unemotional demands. He saw in her all the goodness, all the soft, delicate parts of her life that had come together like a silk tapestry—one that he should admire and leave untouched. She deserved someone better than him. Someone who wasn't focused on a path straight to hell...someone who wouldn't drag her there with him.

He slid the key card into the slot beside the door and walked into the suite. When he'd left earlier that night, with Emma wearing his ring, on his way to meet Bartlett, he'd imagined that when he returned he'd feel...different. That he'd feel the thrill of satisfaction at ensuring his father's destruction. That somehow meeting Bartlett would have eased the adrenaline he'd felt rushing through him for over a week—would have settled the raging beast within him.

But he didn't and it hadn't.

Instead a different kind of heat burned within him— one that made him feel just as restless and just as dangerous. He stalked over to the bar area, poured two whiskies—one over ice for Emma—and after a second thought added two ice cubes to his own, hoping to cool the fervour of his libido. In his heart, he hoped that she would refuse the drink, that she would bid him goodnight and leave him alone with his new demons.

But she didn't.

Emma closed the door behind her, turning her back momentarily on the man who had come to mean so much to her. She was buying herself time. She knew it. Had known it since before their meal with Bartlett—since the moment Antonio's lips had crashed down onto hers. Perhaps even since the previous night.

It was as if her skin was feeding off the strange tension that had been summoned by their bodies' wants and desires in the car journey back from the restaurant. The silence that had fallen between them only seemed to place a spotlight on it, illuminating what she wasn't naïve enough to dismiss.

But was she brave enough to ask—demand for herself what her body wanted?

Looking at Antonio now, standing before the large windows, his broad shoulders and lean hips accentuated by the smooth planes of his suit, staring out at the stars, she knew that it had always been going to come to this.

He had coaxed from her body things she had never imagined. He had made her feel sexy, wanted and desirable. And Emma didn't want to let go of it—didn't want to sever the strange thread that bound them together.

Her cancer had struck at a time when she had been inexperienced, and nothing and no one had tempted her since.

Until now.

And if some part of her warned that this wasn't just about claiming her body, that it was much more to do with her heart, then she ruthlessly forced that thought aside. She wanted to strike through that invisible wish on her Living List. The one that she'd never had the courage to write down, but now had the courage to ask for.

'Antonio—'

'No.'

'I haven't—'

'You don't have to say it, Emma. You *shouldn't* say it. Shouldn't ask it of me. You should go to bed.'

His tone was dark and heavy—rough like bitter coffee and as tempting as sin.

'You don't know what I'm going to ask,' she assured him…assured herself.

He turned, then. Pinned her with his hawk-like gaze. She knew it was meant to intimidate, but instead it served only to enflame.

'Really? I am a man very well versed in feminine desire, Emma. A woman does not…*you* do not need to put into words what I see in your eyes. What your body is crying out for.'

Embarrassment stung her cheeks. She had thought

that he might be as surprised as she was to find herself asking for such a thing. But he had known. Had seen it in her. Had everyone else?

But she refused to be ashamed of it. She held his gaze, used it to empower her. She felt herself stand tall against the onslaught of his presence.

'You asked me what I wanted, Antonio. Back at the gala. And yesterday you said that I had not asked anything for myself. So now I'm asking. I want *you*. This night. Just one night,' she said, leaving the rest of her thoughts unspoken.

She wanted to feel cherished...wanted to love her body. Wanted *him* to love her body.

'Do you know what you're asking, Emma?'

'Yes.'

'Do you really? A no-strings affair? Just sex? You are too innocent to know the consequences of your request.'

'I'm not going to lie and tell you that I'm experienced, because I'm not,' she said, taking a step towards his forbidding frame. 'I'm not going to lie and tell you that I'm not terrified, because I am. But I know what I want. And now I'm asking you for it. Just one night, Antonio.'

She was only asking for one night because she knew instinctively that she couldn't risk anything more. Yes, she might be inexperienced, but she knew that much.

'Emma—'

It was a plea from his lips. One that she couldn't allow herself to listen to.

She took the final step towards him, closing the distance between them. Looking up at him, standing chest to chest, she saw his lips hovering so close to her own. It was intoxicating. She'd never tasted need, actually *tasted* it on her tongue, but she knew that it would be nothing like the taste of him, his true self. Without the masks, the fakery of performance.

Her chest rose, trying to contain the beating of her heart, pushing against the silk that cleaved in a V to her breasts, as if inviting his gaze, begging for his touch. She had never felt like this. Had never felt the power of desire rushing over her skin, making her bold, making her needy.

'You said I could have anything I wanted. Please... please don't make me—' The word *beg* stuck in her throat.

She reached up, her hand cold against the hot skin of his clenched jaw. He hadn't moved a muscle, but she felt emotion swirling within him with the force of a storm. He was almost vibrating with it.

Their breathing was harsh and it echoed within the silence of the suite. Antonio's eyes were a molten mixture of fury and desire, matching her own. She allowed the heat from his body to lap against hers like a tide, threatening to overtake her and knock her down. Her mouth was inches away from his. But she wanted him to make that last move. She wanted it, needed it—needed him to prove that it wasn't just *her* in this. That he was as weak as she in this moment.

And suddenly his lips were on hers, almost punishingly. His arm snaked around her back, holding her against the onslaught of passion that was so much stronger than a tide. For a moment she basked in that power, in the feel of him encompassing her completely. She allowed it to happen to her, to shock her as his tongue demanded entrance and his body commanded surrender. Then she came to life under the sheer level of need that was binding them together.

She pushed back against the kiss, opened herself to

him. Tongue clashed against tongue, teeth nipped at lips. Her hands unclasped from his shoulders and ran down the shirt covering his chest. She pushed with one and pulled with the other, desperate to feel *more*. His hands wound their way into her hair, and she thought she might have heard a groan as he sank his hands into the sleek knot and sent the pins flying, leaving her dark auburn hair to cascade down her back.

He started to walk her backwards and she felt his strong thighs against hers in an almost erotic slide. The slit of the silk skirt parted, allowing her bare legs access to the rich material of his trousers, making her feel naked against him.

As if he, too, was thinking the same thing, one of his hands left her hair, trailed over the naked V left by the silk around her chest, down to her waist. His hand flared to span it for just a moment, before lowering even further down, skating over her hip before his fingertips traced their way to the cut in the skirt and slipped through to the bare skin of her thigh.

Emma gasped as his hand wrapped around her bottom, bringing her thigh up, allowing him to step fully between her legs, and gasped again as she felt the hard ridge of his arousal at her core. It was a promise. It was a threat.

He pulled back from their kiss, gazing down on her as if warning her that this was the point of no return, failing to realise that she'd crossed that bridge a long time back. As if her body was completely his now, her hips pressed forward against his, desperate to feel him deeper, *needing* to feel him deeper.

They came up against the arm of the sofa and he guided her back, perching her there.

'Had you asked any other man, Emma, he would

have taken you to a bed covered with roses,' he ground out against her lips, unaware that that she wouldn't have wanted that. Simply because it wouldn't have been *him*. 'Had you asked any other man, he would have showered you with gifts and seduced you with words,' he continued, unaware that he had given her the greatest of gifts, offering her words of truth instead of lies, and that it meant so much more.

'I am not that man,' he said, as if answering her thoughts. 'But,' he said, with a fierce sincerity that pinned her heart, 'I will stop at any point. Know that. You are in control here, Emma. This is your decision. If you want me to—'

She cut off his words with a kiss of her own—just as powerful, just as impassioned as any of those he had given her.

As if the last barrier had been broken, a flood of need passed between them in that kiss. His hands ran the length of her chest and breasts, down once again to the silky slit in the dress. She nearly cried out as his hands caressed the soft skin of her thighs, as his hands found the thin piece of material holding her thong together and pulled, tearing the string as if it were nothing and tossing it aside. He brought his hands down around her bottom and lifted her up against him, the material of his trousers pressed against her core, shocking her and setting a fire within her.

He stepped back, and the loss of heat from where his body had pressed against hers allowed the cool air of the room to raise goosebumps on her arms. At least that was what she told herself as she shivered against his touch. His fingers found the slick wet heat of her core, at first gently running over her clitoris, bringing an unbidden cry from her mouth.

She thought she heard him curse, but she couldn't tell. The sensations he was wringing from her body were overwhelming. She might not know what to do, but her body moved instinctively, her legs opening to his hand as his fingers mirrored his tongue as he kissed her, pushing into her, delving further and deeper. Her body arched back over his powerful arm of its own volition, pulling her away from his kiss.

Need rose deep within her, yearning, demanding something that she couldn't fathom. Her breath became gasps, and she felt unable to contain all the emotions, all the sensations within her. She cried out, his wicked sensuality bringing forth even more want, and found herself begging, pleading for something she couldn't quite name.

She barely noticed him settle between her legs, but the moment his tongue pressed against her core, wet heat against wet heat, a wildness was wrenched from her and she came apart in an explosion of white fire-bursts. Stars dusted the back of her eyelids and she fell into an abyss.

Antonio watched as Emma's orgasm spilled waves of shivers across her skin, flushing her cheeks with pleasure, and he was speechless. He had never seen anything so beautiful, tasted anything so sweet, experienced anything so humbling as this moment.

But as she opened her eyes, and he saw wonder and awe painted in them, he knew it wasn't enough for him to know these things. She must too.

'Do you trust me?' he asked.

'Yes,' she said simply.

He gently reached for the shoulder straps of her dress. Emma stiffened.

He knew that she was scared, embarrassed...he couldn't even begin to imagine what else she might be feeling. But he wanted to help give her back her body. He wanted her to appreciate it as it should be appreciated.

He moved slowly and gently, allowing her to get used to the idea. He pushed aside the thin straps of silk and bared her to him. He could see that she was struggling, but all he saw was perfection. Beautiful and powerful. Her breasts bore faint scars from the surgeon's knife, and as he pressed open-mouthed kisses to her skin he marvelled at the tattoos that had skilfully created nipples and areolas.

He brought his hands round to cup her breasts and nearly groaned out loud at their rightness. They felt heavy as they spilled into his hands. His thumb ran gently over her skin, and her answering shudder as it did so almost brought a smile to his lips as he bent forward and took one breast into his mouth. He laved her breasts with his tongue, first one, then the other. Emma hung her head back, pressing them further into his mouth, and he returned the favour as he pressed his groin into hers, bringing her back to him with a piercing need that nailed them both.

The sensations Emma felt were foreign and strange. She wanted his touch so much, and frustration, resentment and sadness warred in her chest. She hated it that her nipples were no longer there. This was the bit in her treasured romance books that she always skipped over. How the hero would touch, kiss and tease the heroine's nipples until they became taut and tight. She missed that feeling with an ache so deep. She hated it that her body would never be able to do that.

She had feared so much that this would hurt even
more in practice than in thought. But she had been
wrong. Antonio had caressed and kissed her breasts,
rather than avoiding them, had touched her so much
that she wasn't sure she could take it any more.

Her hands went to the silk straps of the dress. She
wanted to turn away.

'Don't hide from me, Emma. You're so brave and so
very strong,' he said between each kiss and caress of
her breasts. 'You said that what you wanted most was
this…but this isn't about me.'

She wanted to tell him that he was wrong, but in the
deepest part of her she knew that he was right.

'This is about you. You've had the courage to ask
for what you want…it's time to *take* what you want.
It's time to stop hiding in the shadows and step into the
light. You're beautiful. So beautiful, Emma…'

She hated it that his words stirred her heart, felt tears
forming at the edges of her eyes, betraying her.

'I want you to say it,' he told her.

She turned her head away from him. The words were
locked in a throat tight with emotion. She didn't want
to say it, but Antonio asked again. Not angry, not frustrated, but with understanding and compassion shining from his eyes.

'I'm beautiful…' she whispered.

'Again, Emma,' he commanded.

'I'm beautiful,' she said, this time with a little more
strength. 'I *am* beautiful,' she said, finally allowing belief to make the words strong.

Antonio scooped her up from where she was perched
on the arm of the sofa and carried her through to the
bedroom. And when her head rested on his chest he

shook away the thought that it felt as if it had always been there.

He gently laid her on the bed, watching her eyes slowly focus on him where he stood over her, still dazed from her own empowerment and her orgasm. And even though he was so ready to take her, so ready to find his own release, he wanted her to be with him, wanted her to feel everything that he felt.

If this was his one stolen moment, then he would make it count.

Antonio's hands left her chest to pull at the edges of his shirt. Impatient to feel her skin against his, he ripped the shirt apart, sending buttons flying across the room, watching as Emma's eyes widened in both shock and arousal.

As his hands went to the waistband of his trousers, hers found the zip at the side of her dress.

'Stop,' he commanded. Her eyes found his, her cheeks painted red with desire and perhaps just a trace of embarrassment. He leaned forward. 'That's for me to do, Emma. That's *my* pleasure.'

He leaned back and brought down the zip on his trousers, relishing every second as she watched him slowly push them off his legs. He watched her restless legs, sliding up and down against each other as if the friction might get close to the pleasure he could administer.

He smiled knowingly, stepping forward, pressing her thighs apart and bringing the palm of his hand to rest at her centre.

Emma jerked her hips against the contact of his hot palm between her legs. There was nothing but the autumnal silk of the dress between his skin and hers, slick and ready.

He sat on the bed next to her, reaching around to her side and slowly, ever so slowly, releasing the dress's zip from its casing, drawing it down to where it ended at the top of her hip. His hands swept under the material, feeling their way across her stomach and up to her breasts. He moved one hand down in between her legs and parted her there with his fingers.

As her hips rose off the bed to meet his hand he swept the burnt orange silk from beneath her, moved it up above her waist with his other hand. He brought her breast to his mouth and whipped the material over her head as he savoured her breasts, relishing each cry that fell from Emma's lips.

He gathered the dress in his fist and threw the crumpled silk onto the floor, then leaned back and took her small dainty feet in his hands. He stroked the insides of her feet and placed them apart, moving in between her legs. As his hands caressed their way up her calves, over her knees and up her thighs, Emma sighed, watching his hands work their way up over her hips towards her breasts, her spine arching off the bed, pressing them into his palms.

For what seemed like hours he stayed there, caressing, licking, tasting all that she had to offer. Watching her both lose herself and find herself in the passion they were creating together.

Reluctant to leave the soft satin of her skin, he leaned towards the bedside table and took protection, tearing off the foil and positioning the latex over himself. Her small hands came over his as he rolled the condom over his length, her fingers wrapping around his erection, smoothing down to the base.

Before she could chip any more away from the last

shreds of his will power he picked up one of her hands, whilst positioning himself at her slick core.

He looked at her, silently begging her... For refusal or acceptance, he didn't know any more. Her hands slid around him, clasping his hips and gently pulling him towards her, sealing their fate.

As he slowly pushed himself between her thighs he kissed the inside of her palm and entered her so carefully it was almost torture. But it wasn't torture at all. It was bliss. She was so wet, so ready for him, and he sank deep into the tight, wet heat of her, allowing her body to shift and make room for him entirely.

Never before had he felt so deeply connected, so deeply *with* someone. And something inside him shifted. Something he couldn't allow to take hold.

He inched forward just a little more, and Emma's eyes widened and locked on to his.

He waited for her to acclimatise to him, and when he saw that she had he withdrew and plunged back into her, deep and hard. Her cries of pleasure rang out in the room, urging him on, into her again and again. An incredible sensation was stretching throughout his body, taking a firm hold on his chest and what lay hidden there beneath his ribs, and he knew—*knew* that this wasn't just sex.

His cries soon joined hers and he grasped her wrists, holding them above her head, staring down into her eyes. He couldn't hold back any more—he couldn't hold *anything* back any more.

Sensing that she was on the brink of her second orgasm, feeling the tightening of her muscles around him, hearing that special, perfect pitch of her voice, he thrust into her one last time, and they fell together even more deeply over the edge than ever before.

* * *

Antonio woke in a panic. His heart pounded in his chest, a cold sweat gathered on his brow, and his head was filled with thoughts of his father cruelly ripping him from Emma's sleep-fuelled embrace.

It took him a moment to place himself. A thing that had never happened to Antonio before in his life. Not when he, his mother and sister had been wrenched from America and sent back to Italy…not in any of the numerous hotel rooms where he had spent countless nights for his business.

But the fear didn't recede. Unaccountably, Antonio couldn't shake the feeling that something awful was on the horizon—waiting to crash down and blow everything to smithereens.

Emma turned beside him, the smooth sleek line of her spine exposed where he had pulled the sheets back from their stranglehold around his chest. He needed to move, needed to leave the safe haven of her bed, was reluctant to somehow infect her with his thoughts.

He grabbed his trousers from where he'd thrown them off only hours before and padded his way through to the living room, gently closing the door on the passion and emotion of earlier hours.

He forced his legs into the trousers and fastened the zip and the button around his waist. Signs of their lovemaking were everywhere. Discarded clothes, rumpled paper and documents from the Bartlett deal neither of them had seen in the urgency of their need.

He paced the room. Back and forth. And still couldn't shake the feeling of impending doom. His father had something. Something that Antonio didn't. Something on Bartlett, he decided. He was too self-assured for a man on the brink of destruction. That was what had bothered him most about his father. Yes, he'd seen desperation—but he'd also seen triumph.

And then he did something he'd never thought himself capable of.

He found his mobile phone amongst the chaos of the room and pulled up the number of Arcuri Enterprises' private investigator.

Not caring what time it would be in America, he spoke quietly and efficiently, outlining his need for the man to dig up anything and everything he might be able to find on Bartlett, or his family. Only days ago Emma had pointed out that Bartlett's daughter was something of a party girl. She might be on to something.

If Antonio felt any guilt then he forced such a feeling aside, bringing to mind instead that horrible confrontation with his father. The only way to fight a monster was to become one himself. His father would pay for what he'd done. And if that meant reducing himself to his father's level, ruining his soul, Antonio was willing to do so.

CHAPTER EIGHT

CLASH OF THE TYCOON TITANS!
BY ROANNA KING

Arcuri vs Steele, son against father,
who will win?

It would seem that Antonio Arcuri's shock engagement was just the beginning. The business world is holding its breath as father and son pitch for the same deal! Sources close to the tycoons have suggested a last-ditch battle of wills.

For years Arcuri has nipped at the edges of Steele's business dealings, and is now pulling out all the stops to slash and burn with his legendary ruthlessness—his father, no less.

And while women around the world are still mourning the loss of this international bachelor, men are salivating, placing bets on who will draw first—and last—blood.

With so much on the line for these two men, it will certainly be a clash of the tycoon titans!

DIMITRI'S GREEK-ACCENTED VOICE rose above the hum of the crowds as he read the article out loud, clearly just for the hell of it.

'At least they didn't mention Bartlett by name,' he noted.

'I doubt very much that it was by mistake or from some inherent sense of propriety. This has the stink of my father all over it,' Antonio growled.

'He must be desperate if he's willing to risk such exposure, given how notoriously private Bartlett is,' Danyl reflected, looking out at the race course from the balcony of the hospitality suite set aside for the Winners' Circle.

Discreet servers had placed trays of delicate food there, none of which was appealing to Antonio at that moment. He shifted his sunglasses back over his eyes.

Danyl turned in his seat beside him, pinning him with a powerful gaze. 'You have something to hide?'

'No,' came Antonio's terse reply.

Danyl gave a spectacularly *un*-regal grunt in response, and placed a Bloody Mary on the table in front of him. 'Hair of the horse that bit you, so to speak.'

Antonio ignored them both and took a mouthful of the thick, spicy tomato juice.

'Virgin?' queried Dimitri as Danyl rolled his eyes.

The sting of tabasco sauce caught Antonio in the back of the throat and he forced himself to swallow the drink through a throat thick with convulsions.

'For God's sake, Dimitri.'

The sounds of the crowd and the announcements over the Tannoy drifted up from the race course below.

'Did anyone see Mason this morning?' Antonio asked, when in truth his mind had been searching for Emma. Emma whom he'd left sleeping in the hotel room while he'd sneaked out like a thief.

'John was guarding her like a dog. He wouldn't let anyone near her this morning. Said something about not letting us "psych her out".'

'Us or you, Danyl?' Dimitri asked. 'You still haven't said how you know her.'

'I still haven't said that I *do* know her.'

Antonio let the sounds of his friend's light-hearted squabble fall over him as he tried to block out the memory of Emma's sighs of pleasure that still, even now, thickened his blood.

He clenched a fist, trying to regain control of his errant body. He couldn't believe what madness had overtaken them last night. He'd promised her only one night, but now he wondered if he could keep that promise. It wouldn't last—it couldn't. He would only end up hurting her, letting her down, drawing her deeper into his own need for revenge.

'You might want to put that glass down, Antonio,' Dimitri said, his words cutting through the emotional fog that was surrounding him.

'Mmm?'

'The glass. If you carry on, it might just crack.'

Antonio looked down to see white knuckles encasing thin glass and put the drink back on the table. Danyl was looking at him with a raised eyebrow, wry curiosity painting his features.

'Dare I ask how the Bartlett deal is going?'

'Actually, our meeting went very well. Even after my father made his surprise guest appearance.'

Concerned silence met his statement. Danyl and Dimitri were watching and waiting for the explanation they knew he would give them. They alone knew the depths of his hatred for his father, the true extent of which he hadn't been able to confess to Emma.

They greeted his account with an anger and fury that matched his own. And Michael Steele's treatment of Emma was high on their list of his crimes.

'Are you sure you want to go that way?' Dimitri asked when Antonio confessed the action he had directed his PI to.

'If there's anything to find you can be sure that Michael will have already discovered it, and he will plan to use it to his advantage.'

'And are you willing to do the same? To use blackmail to get what it is that you want?'

A commotion at the paddock drew their attention and prevented Antonio from needing to answer Dimitri's question. As Antonio recognised Mason's colours and Veranchetti's proud stance he forced all other thoughts from his mind.

Emma wove her way through the throng of people in the stands towards the stairs to the hospitality suite, where she knew Antonio and his friends—the Winners' Circle syndicate—would be. The day was beautiful, despite the bad weather forecasted for later. It was strange to think that there could be anything like rain on the horizon when the air, despite being stirred up by the spectators, was calm and the sun was strong.

She felt a laugh rise within her chest and stifled it. Here she was, in a sea of people, and no one was looking at her because of what she lacked. She was invisible. And yet she felt as if she knew a secret that no one else did.

Throughout the night she had reached for Antonio, had felt him reach for her, and they had teased and taunted each other to completion more times than she could believe. Those precious hours were a montage of sensation and feeling, always with the heat of Antonio beside her, over her, behind her. It was as if her body had craved that warmth, needed it to come alive again.

She felt re-made—re-worked in a way she couldn't have expected. It was as if an old ache around her heart had lessened and she felt lighter than she had done in years.

She had woken alone and hadn't been surprised, re-alising that on some level she must have heard him leave. A web of nerves had tightened around her stomach. How would they be the next time they encountered each other?

No, she thought now, pressing a hand against her belly to quell the butterflies. She wouldn't be embarrassed about last night. They were adults. And what they had shared was incredible. Antonio had made her see herself in a way she had never done before and that was something more precious than she ever could have realised.

She felt strong and, yes, even a little giddy. Last night she had seen him, Antonio Arcuri, as needy and as aroused as her. She had met him as an equal and nothing would take that away. And to be his equal—not his PA, and not his fake fiancée? It thrilled her.

Was this what love was? *Desire*, she hastily corrected herself. A high that made her feel powerful, strong? She relished that feeling and all of a sudden her chest was fit to burst. Excitement swept through her as she began to climb the steps towards the balconies bordering the race course.

Her heart pulsed within her chest and she wondered how anyone could live like this, in this constant state of awareness and excitement. Would it go away? Would it dim over time? Did she want it to?

For so long, so many years, she had wanted to feel this way. Wanted to own herself, to feel cherished and desired. Somehow, despite her optimism and determination to experience all that life had to offer, she had let herself hide from the one thing that she had truly wanted.

Here she was, on the brink of having it all, and suddenly she felt the fear that it could all be taken away. And that was when she knew just how much she had sacrificed—just how much she had pushed deep down within her, ignoring the wants and desires that she craved.

This man—hell-bent on revenge, but capable of the tenderness of last night—had stolen her heart. The goodness in him that she could see made those feelings even more powerful. She wanted him to win the Bartlett deal against his father. Not because of the hatred that Antonio felt for him, but to put an end to it so that Antonio could move on.

Even from this high up Antonio could imagine—could remember—the feeling of sitting on top of a powerful horse pawing at the ground with shod hoofs, the flex of the animal's muscles beneath the saddle, the creaking of leather, the way a horse would lift and shift beneath him. The thrilling rush of adrenaline that would pound through both him and the horse together, as one. That moment just before the horse would pull back, ready to launch itself forward, ready to catapult into a gallop and leave just about everything behind.

At one point in his life riding had meant freedom— escape from a father who had made his and his mother's and sister's lives a misery. In the end, he realised, he'd not escaped anything.

As the noise picked up around the grounds, mixing with incoherent announcements from the Tannoy, Antonio battled with the past and the present. Somehow he knew that it was all rooted in the events of the night

before. Bartlett, his father, Emma, business, passion…
All of it was making him feel as if he were on some
precipice, and he couldn't tell whether he was about to
be saved or doomed.

The shrill of the bell signalling the start of the race
cut through the stands as the barriers on the starting
gate opened and the horses leapt forward.

For just a moment the breath caught in his lungs.

But it wasn't because of the race.

He felt her presence behind him, as she stepped out
on to the balcony that jutted out over the course below.
He teased himself, holding himself back from the moment when he would turn and look at Emma. A test of
sorts. One that he failed.

She was dressed in a white sleeveless top with dark
blue flowing trousers. Her thick dark hair swirled
around her. She raised her hand to catch at the strands,
sweeping them back from her face as she looked down
at the horses, rather than at him.

His heart thumped painfully in his chest as tension
ran through the crowd on a ripple that reached all the
way to the balcony. Urgency filled the air, and the noise
created by the people reached higher towards a cre-
scendo that, just for a moment, he thought might never
find its peak.

And still he could not take his eyes from the woman
who had come to stand beside him. He felt her on his
skin, through the layers of his clothes, over the hours
since they had shared a bed. The bed he wanted to take
her back to and never leave.

Suddenly her body sprang into action. Both arms
were raised and she was punching into the air, her cry
of surprise matched only by the furious yells of the two
men beside him. A fist thumped on his back—Dimitri,

lost in his excitement. And Danyl was staring deep into the winner's gate, as if not really sure he had seen Mason McAulty lead Veranchetti to victory.

Antonio hadn't. All he'd seen was Emma. And he shuddered as a cold bead of sweat trickled down his spine.

He watched with an unwarranted anger unfurling in his stomach, seeing Danyl and Dimitri sweep Emma up into swift, joyous embraces. The small balcony suddenly seemed overly full as waiters descended with bottles of champagne and hands reached over the balcony walls to offer congratulations and cheers of success.

A possessive streak he hadn't realised he owned coursed through his body. If he'd noticed the flash of the cameras, he couldn't say. If he'd told himself it was for appearances' sake, rather than the desperate need to feel her lips against his, it would have been a lie.

He pulled her to him—a move that was becoming increasingly familiar and ever more welcome—until he was an inch…a breath…away from a kiss that he already knew would enflame the burning furnaces of his desire. Something that would have the power to take away the painfully fierce anger boiling in his chest as he thought of his father, as he thought of his own actions.

He teased them both, watching the hazel flecks of her eyes dissolve into sea-green depths. Over the din, the shouts and cries of the crowd around them, he heard her gasp, saw the moment surprise sizzled into expectation and want, and pushed the moment further. To when nothing else could be seen, heard or felt—when it was just the two of them.

When he could make her realise that this wasn't for the press, for Bartlett, for anyone else other than him and her.

And then he took what he so desperately wanted.

* * *

Emma felt her hand creep up towards Antonio's neck, pulling him deeper, forging them together with tongue and teeth. She laved his tongue with her own, brought the thumb of her other hand to the corner of his mouth, relishing the sensual power she wielded now, daring him to taste her. Taste more of her.

She gave no thought to anyone around them, no feeling for the concern as to where this might lead, and it thrilled as much as terrified her. She matched his almost desperate movements with her own, taking everything he had to give and offering her all in return.

He had turned her into a wanton woman and she shamelessly claimed him for the world to see. She wanted to imprint herself on him, wanted to eradicate the memory of all who had come before her. Wanted to be the only thing he needed.

'That's enough, you two,' Dimitri called out, bringing Emma crashing back to the present.

She slowly pulled back, satisfaction stretching through her to see Antonio Arcuri as dazed and shocked as she felt.

'No,' she whispered, for his ears only. 'It's not enough,' she said with a gentle shake of her head—before she turned a beaming smile on Antonio's friend and relinquished her hold on Antonio to accept a glass of champagne .

'Gentlemen. Congratulations,' she said, in a surprisingly steady voice.

Three hours later and the promised storm had bruised the sky a deep purple, but for all its bluster it had still failed to break. The wind was whipping up the leaves around the trees that lined the streets below, reminding

Antonio of the crowds of people surrounding the winner's gate earlier. The press had burst upon them in a hail of flashbulbs, firing questions about the next two races, to be carefully deflected by three men who knew better than to engage with the paparazzi.

Mason McAulty, the female jockey whose name was now on everyone's lips, had been discreetly spirited away by John, moved on to prepare for the next race in Ireland almost before her feet had left Veranchetti's stirrups.

Danyl, who had watched her go with the same frantic energy of the storm, had barely commented on the win—as if both relieved and concerned by it—and had simply stalked through the halls of The Excelsus towards the private function room that had been prepared for the closing event of the Hanley Cup's first leg.

It was a glamorous affair, attended by royal dignitaries, international syndicates, horse breeders and owners. Models hung from arms like accessories, but none took Antonio's notice. A waiter passed by with a tray full of the finest champagne, but even the promise of cool nutty flavours and frothy light bubbles wasn't enough to disguise the taste of Emma still on Antonio's tongue.

It was addictive. He wanted more. And he *never* wanted more.

He made his way over to the bar, looking for a drink that would succeed in refocusing his tastebuds. Bartlett would be there to celebrate the Winners' Circle's success, although he was still to confirm whether he would choose his father or him. But Antonio knew. He would be chosen in the end. He was now sure of it.

Dimitri was at the bar, his brooding presence enough to create a wide berth around him, clear of people. Danyl was still looking out over the race course through the windows as the first drops of promised rain slung themselves against the glass. In contrast to the gloss and sheen of revelry that dusted the other guests, the members of the Winners' Circle seemed consumed by their own demons.

Dimitri reached behind the bar, ignoring the frown from the barman busy with another customer, grabbed a glass and poured Antonio a drink from the bottle of obscenely expensive whisky beside him. Dimitri threw an impressive stack of pesos onto the bar, which mollified the barman.

'Why does this feel like a wake rather than a victory?' Dimitri demanded. 'Come on—we're celebrating!'

Antonio cast a glance in Dimitri's direction. There was a light in his eyes that Antonio hadn't seen for far too long. 'What is it?'

Dimitri's gaze was fierce. 'They got him! The SEC have finally brought civil charges against Manos,' he said, spitting out the name of his half-brother, 'and my name is finally and completely cleared.'

'Now, *that* I can drink to,' Danyl said, and he leaned over and poured himself a large helping of whisky.

'It's been a long time coming,' Antonio added, 'but well worth the wait.' He savoured the burn of the alcohol in his throat.

'I'm sorry that I can't stay for longer,' said Danyl. 'I have to fly home. My mother has been talking about brides and babies again.'

Dimitri choked on his drink. 'Nothing, and I mean *nothing*, would tempt me into taking a bride, let alone having a baby,' he said, slamming his glass down on the bar. 'But it seems that the same cannot be said for Antonio.'

He felt the weight of both men's gazes on him. 'It's

just for show. Bartlett needed reassurance to get him
to the table—Emma offered that.'

He saw Dimitri's eyes lock onto something over his
shoulder. 'I don't think that's the only kind of entice-
ment she's offering,' Dimitri replied.

Antonio's stomach clenched even before he had seen
her—awaiting, expecting, the punch to the gut he had
begun to experience each time he caught sight of her.
The hair on his neck prickled as he forced himself not
to immediately turn towards the entrance to the bar.
Holding off the moment for as long as possible…both
punishment and penance.

'You bloody fool,' Danyl said.

'What?' Antonio asked.

'You've slept with her,' Dimitri accused.

Finally lifting the leash on his body, Antonio turned
to watch her enter the room. She was wearing the mid-
night-blue lace dress he'd seen her try on in the dressing room the other day. It wrapped around her skin as
if it had been painted on, and yet there was nothing in-
decent about it. Only the reaction it had caused in him.

Because although he was an experienced man, and
he'd had his fair share of women, nothing he'd seen until
that moment had made him want to back a woman into
the nearest room, throw out any people in the near vicinity and rip the clothing from her body.

And Antonio had the unnerving suspicion that she
knew it too. She was taunting him in that dress, making him want to take back his promise from only hours
before…the promise that they could only ever have one
night. Because right then he wanted to live that night
over and over and over again.

He watched her walk over to Bartlett, rather than
avoiding the man as he himself had done so far. He

nearly flinched when she laid her hand on his arm, offering him a smile that was both familiar and pleased. When she whispered something in his ear, eliciting a fond reaction from Bartlett, Antonio nearly broke a wisdom tooth because his jaw was clenched so hard.

'She's making some powerful friends, Arcuri,' Dimitri warned. 'You'd better watch out.'

Antonio couldn't take his eyes off her as she turned in their direction and wove through the tables dotted between them. And she held his gaze for all she was worth, right until she stopped barely a foot away from him. Then she turned her amazing smile on his companions.

'Gentlemen,' Emma said by way of introduction, 'how far into the celebrations are we? Starting gate or halfway?'

'A little bit of both. Emma, I must say, you look ravishing!'

'Why, thank you, Dimitri. As always, you look devastatingly handsome.'

'Careful—if you carry on being so charming I might have to steal you away from Antonio myself.'

She laughed, and laughed even more when she heard Antonio's answering growl. If she'd ever wondered what it might feel like to be the centre of his world... Well... She was beginning to feel it now.

'What's your poison, Emma?' Dimitri asked, and for all the outward brooding she had seen in him from across the bar when she'd first entered, there was something almost kind in his eyes.

She took in their glasses, and the outrageously expensive bottle of whisky, but decided against the heady amber liquid she now associated with dark nights and deep secrets.

'Prosecco, please.'

The barman nodded, and placed a full flute on the bar.

She turned to Danyl. 'Your Highness,' she said, with a small bow of her head, knowing from experience that anything more overt would rankle. For someone who held such a public position, the Sheikh of Terhren was a deeply private man.

'My assistant wishes to pass on his congratulations and his immense relief,' said Danyl. 'He is very much looking forward to a time when he no longer has to do battle with you. You have knocked his considerable confidence in his own abilities.'

She knew it was flattery, gentle and teasing, and it felt so good to be amongst Antonio's friends. It wasn't often that she saw this side of her fiancé—her *boss*— she hastily corrected herself. Though she couldn't really say that he was her boss any more. Last night had put an end to that and replaced stern reminders of her place with delicate strands of hope. Hope that this could be so much more.

She turned to greet Antonio and the words stuck in her throat. He looked so sexy, so powerful. He hadn't changed, as she had, and was still dressed in the same dark trousers and shirt open at the collar that he had been wearing earlier that day. But where before there had only been traces of stubble, now a dark shadow covered the planes of his cheeks and strong jawline and her fingers itched to reach out, to touch the deliciously rough edges.

She didn't have to wonder what he thought of the dress. It was all there in his eyes. It was the same struggle she'd had when she'd looked in the mirror before coming to the bar. Was this the right thing to do? Was she brave enough to take what she wanted and damn the consequences?

Looking at Antonio in that moment, she felt a smile pull at the edge of her lips. One that found a quick answer.

He leaned in and bent his mouth to her ear. The warmth of his breath threw cold shivers down her back as his words reached her.

'You're going to pay for wearing this dress later,' he warned darkly.

'Is that a promise?' she enquired innocently, while the devil in her danced.

'Oh, so much more than a promise, Emma,' he said, before returning to the circle of his friends.

Something like relief spread through her chest. It was all going to be okay. Dimitri pressed her glass into her hand and drew back to make room for her at the bar. No, she decided, it was going to be more than okay.

Antonio watched Emma chat happily with two of the world's most powerful men and wondered how she could ever have doubted herself. The promise he'd made to her, warning her that it would only ever be one night, was turning to ash, leaving only the taste of anticipation on his tongue. He wanted her. He would have her. Tonight.

And suddenly it seemed that it was all possible. That he'd get the Bartlett deal, that he would wreak his revenge on his father, that he might even get to keep Emma for a while. He could certainly make her happy—perhaps help her tick off some more of the things on her Living List.

Pleasure uncoiled in his chest—a different kind from what he was used to. This wasn't the thrill of the chase, or the knowledge that he had won some kind of challenge. It was the kind of pleasure he'd experienced only a few times as a child at being given something… Something precious…a gift without strings. And he wanted to unwrap that present. Right now.

Some hours later Emma was making her way back to the bar from the bathroom when the concierge found her.

'Ms Guilham, there is a package for Mr Arcuri at reception. We didn't want to interrupt him.'

Emma looked in Antonio's direction, and seeing him surrounded by his friends, laughing with a lightness she hadn't seen from him for quite some time, she understood the concierge's quandary.

'Are you happy for me to sign for it?' she asked, and when he agreed she followed him out of the bar and through the much quieter halls to Reception.

The sudden silence of the corridor made her feelings of happiness seem so much bigger, so much harder to contain. She had enjoyed talking to his friends, the feeling of being amongst them. The bond they shared was so clear and so strong it was a wonder to her. And she questioned for the first time whether perhaps it was *she* who had caused the distance between her and her friends from school, that perhaps *she* had kept that distance.

Emma decided that enough was enough. No more hiding when there was so much joy, so much of this indescribable feeling to experience.

The concierge reached behind the desk and produced a thin manila envelope, along with an electronic pad for her to sign on receipt.

She gently pulled the envelope open and, seeing the name 'Bartlett' on the cover sheet of the papers in neat handwritten capitals, didn't think anything of it. Not for a moment did she consider that it was something she shouldn't see.

But as she pulled out the documents inside the folder she realised just how wrong she had been.

CHAPTER NINE

ANTONIO HAD STARTED to wonder where Emma had got to about an hour ago. Danyl had left—he was returning to Terhren—and Dimitri had turned his attentions to a rather beautiful Iranian woman.

Antonio had no intention of blocking his pursuit. Ever since Dimitri's imprisonment a cloud had hung about him. And the news of his half-brother's involvement in his imprisonment had not done as much as he'd thought to lighten it.

Unease started to nibble at the edges of the excitement he'd felt earlier in the evening. It wasn't like Emma simply to disappear. He knew he hadn't missed her amongst the glittering, bejewelled guests at the Hanley Cup's closing party. He had lost that sense of her. That he could feel her presence should have been warning enough. But the fact that he couldn't...

He made his way back to the suite, his heart pounding, aware that something must be terribly wrong. Which was perhaps why he was not surprised to find the rooms shrouded in darkness when he entered.

Emma stood in front of the huge windows, illuminated by the bursts of lightning that fired through the night sky. The storm that had been promised was finally breaking.

His gaze caught a glimpse of the private investigator's dossier on the side table—open. And that was the
moment he knew that everything he thought he might
have had, everything that had made him feel so much
hope, was about to slip through his fingers. Not just the
Bartlett deal, but Emma too.

In the time it took for another burst of lightning to
burn through the night-time sky he realised suddenly
just how much she had come to mean to him—how
much he wanted her to be his. And not just until after
the deal…after Hong Kong. He wanted to show her the
world. He wanted to help her achieve everything on her
Living List. He wanted to make her his for ever.

But then he saw her bags, packed and waiting by the
door to her room, and knew he'd been foolish to allow
himself to think such thoughts. He could never have
her—not whilst seeking his father's punishment. He
could never have her and still do the things that needed
to be done—to become a monster to catch a monster.
But it didn't stop him from wanting to try.

'What is this?'

Her voice cut through the silence. The question
echoed in the burst of thunder that rolled across the
race course outside.

'Emma—'

'What *is* it?' she demanded, her voice suddenly more
powerful and commanding than the elements raging
beyond the windows.

'It's a file I requested to be compiled on Bartlett.'

'Do you not think that you offered the best deal to
Bartlett?' she asked.

'Yes.'

'Do you not think that you deserve to win this con-
tract on your own merit?'

'Yes,' he growled, his anger, his fear, all working to meet her tone.

'Then explain to me what *that* is.'

'It's insurance.'

'Insurance?' she spat.

He had never heard her tone so dark, so angry, and he hated that he had made it so. Hated that he had tainted her in any way because of his need for revenge.

'That isn't insurance. That is the complete and abject desecration of a person, Antonio. Your PI has dug up dirt on Mandy Bartlett and—what? You were going to use it to blackmail Bartlett into letting you invest in his company?'

He met her accusations with silence. There were no shields to protect him from the truth of her words.

'Is this because of what I said the other night? Because I followed her on social media and saw that she was young and foolish?'

The heartbreak in Emma's voice was too much for him to bear. But he simply couldn't tell her that she was wrong.

'Did it give you a lead to where your PI should look?'

'Yes,' he said, the word drawn from the very depths of his soul.

She turned her back to him and finally he glanced at the open folder—pictures of a young student spilled from it. Snapshots of a small blonde partying with her friends. And while one or two showed a happy, fun-loving girl, a few he could see peeking out beneath showed that she had started to experiment with drugs, that images of her scantily clad, showed her in poses that were highly salacious.

The thought of sharing them with the girl's father turned his stomach.

But the accusation, the pressure of the weight in Emma's eyes made him angry. Angry that his father had forced him to this—angry at himself. So he turned that anger and used it against Emma.

'It's hypocrisy. That *I* needed *you* to make me seem more palatable to Bartlett when his daughter is—'

'Stop,' Emma commanded, her hand coming up between them to accentuate her words unconsciously. 'Stop right there. It's *not* hypocritical to hold to a moralistic lifestyle while another human being chooses not to. This is a young girl taking a bad path. Those frozen snapshots aren't the whole picture of who she is and what she will be. Though they will be the *only* picture if you give them to her father.'

She was almost out of breath. She desperately wanted him to see what he was doing, to see where he was going. It was a path she wasn't sure he was going to come back from.

'Mandy Bartlett is a young girl making mistakes and hopefully she will learn from them. What she is *not*, Antonio, is a pawn to be used in a sick game between you and your father.'

'It is not a sick game, Emma. My father deserves to burn in hell for what he did.'

'Because he left you? Antonio, I realise that it must have—'

'No!' he roared. 'This isn't about him leaving, nor blackening my mother's name, nor forcing us to leave our home. *Dio*, we could have handled that. But Cici... She had more than just nightmares after the divorce,' he said, his voice hoarse with the emotion he had bottled up for years.

* * *

As if it were yesterday he remembered his mother's frantic phone call from Italy, just six months into his time in New York, begging him to come home immediately. She had been incoherent, and the only thing he'd managed to gather was that Cici was in hospital.

Nothing—*nothing*—had ever made him feel so terrified as those seven hours on the private jet Danyl had secured for him.

Until he'd seen the sight of his sister's small, impossibly emaciated frame. The doctors had explained that she must have been hiding it for years.

Antonio had known *exactly* how long she'd been hiding her eating disorder from them. At sixteen she'd weighed less than she had at thirteen, when Michael had changed their lives for ever.

And he'd not known. He'd not seen it.

His mother had been as truly shocked as he, and together they'd spent the next two weeks not leaving her side. The sounds of his sister's sobs had cut him deeply. He just hadn't been able to comprehend the negative sense of self coming from his once fun-loving, happy sister.

She had taken all the hurt and all the pain of her father's rejection, of being cut off from her friends and the life she had once known, and turned it in on herself. And he'd felt…angry and furious. He had known exactly who was to blame and had vowed to have his revenge.

Antonio hadn't realised that he'd been speaking—saying the words of his mind out loud to Emma in the suite—until he felt the rawness in his throat, saw the gathering tears framing her eyes.

She crossed the distance between them in quick

strides and wrapped her arms around him. Her body gave warmth and life to his that had turned so cold. She pressed kisses to his neck, pulling his mouth to hers, and he greedily consumed what she had to offer.

This kiss was so different from those that had passed between them before. Not one borne of a selfish need for satisfaction, of the infernal heat of their desires, but one of warmth, of comfort, of support and the one thing he could not bring himself to name.

He sought out the areas of her skin not concealed by the lace fabric of the dress. He needed to feel her beneath him, to take every comfort she was offering and more. In their kiss he tasted the salty sweetness of her tears, evidence of her grief for him and perhaps even of his own.

'I'm sorry,' she whispered against his lips. 'So sorry that you and Cici had to go through that.'

And he felt it down in the darkest part of his heart—her words beginning to shine a soft light on a place he'd thought unreachable. The place he'd thought irrevocably damaged by his father, by shock and fear for his sister.

Emma's heart had wrenched open at the sight of Antonio in such pain. He was on a precipice—one foot on land and one hovering above an abyss. Her only thought at that very moment was to comfort, to love the man she knew he could be—the man torn apart by a sense of injustice, the man who was devastated by the consequences of the careless actions of his father.

Her hands traced the lines of his strong jaw. His skin was cold to her touch, as if his memories had leached the warmth from his body. She imbued her kisses with every emotion she felt for him, desperate to show him that love had the power to heal. Not with words. Antonio wasn't ready for words. But with actions, deeds.

For just a moment he seemed simply unable to accept what she had to offer, and she wondered if she might not be able to reach him. Then, on a deep shudder, as if a barrier had fallen down and crumbled through his body, she felt his hands on her body. Touching, caressing, pulling her towards him.

Soft warmth turned to molten heat and threatened to consume them both whole.

Pulling him gently within her embrace, she walked them backwards towards her room, sidestepping the bags she'd placed there only an hour before. She drew him further, feeding him with need and desire and the love she felt for him.

Her hand went to her hair, releasing the pins that held it in place, allowing it to tumble down around her shoulders and arms. She found the discreet zip hidden at her side and pulled it down, peeling the lacy fabric from her skin.

His gaze seared her as she stood before him but she bore it, stood tall and proud beneath it. Wearing only panties and her heels, she felt no sense of the self-consciousness she had experienced the first time they had come together. There wasn't even a thought to her breasts or her femininity. There was only her need for him, her love for him, and it felt more powerful than anything she had experienced before. She revelled in the way his gaze ravaged her body—not just one part, not just *that* part, but all of her. As if he were seeing her for the very first time.

But he seemed struck still by the storm of emotion she read in his eyes. Not unsure, but unmoving. So she crossed to him, her hands going to the buttons of his shirt, undoing them so that she could feel the warmth and heat of his powerful chest. She marvelled at the light but rough dusting of hair beneath her fingers, at the way his heart raged beneath her hand. She followed the hollowed dips to the waistband of his trousers and unbuckled their fastening.

Throughout all of it he had yet to move, as if he were simply incapable of it. But tension and energy pulsed beneath his skin, begging for release, demanding it.

She left the trousers open and returned to his chest, pushing the shirt from his body, relishing the way he shivered beneath her touch, warmed beneath her kisses. But still he held himself back from her in a vice-like grip of control.

He was so glorious. Standing shirtless in her room. Her fingers traced the span of his upper arms, the de-fined muscles of his torso, the tense muscle offering such power and protection. She wanted to feel his arms about her, wanted to be in his embrace.

And suddenly, as if he'd heard her need, her desire, Antonio swept his arms around her, holding her to him as his open-mouthed kisses plunged the hollows of her neck. Electric currents matched only by the lightning crashing outside the windows licked up her spine and across her exposed skin.

In the space of a heartbeat he had taken control—or lost it. Emma couldn't really be sure. He devoured her with his touch, fed on her as a starving man would his first meal. He walked her back to the bed and came down on it with her, not once breaking the contact of his lips.

His hands and mouth worshipped her body, explor-ing every inch of her. She kicked off her shoes, leaving only the small thong covering her modesty. His hands gently pressed her thighs apart and he pressed hot wet kisses against the material. Her own answering wetness was no longer an embarrassment, simply a declaration of her desires and needs. He teased her through the fabric, making her desperate to remove this last barrier between them.

She groaned—or he did. Their united need was no longer distinguishable. Her hips bucked off the mattress, her body making its own demands while her mind and heart simply loved.

With swift movements he removed his clothing and shoes and leaned over her, his arms coming to rest either side of her face, holding her, cherishing her there. He pressed the length of his body over hers, the weight comforting, enticing, and elicited a restlessness from her body that was almost fevered.

His erection pressed against her abdomen and she sneaked a hand between them, taking hold of the length of him, exploring him with her fingers. His skin was smooth and hot, his arousal powerful, as she stroked teasing shudders of pleasure from him.

His gaze found hers in the darkness of the room and no words were necessary. He removed her thong—not quickly, or urgently, but slowly, pulling the lace slowly down each thigh, his hands sweeping it further, over her ankles, taking his time. Not to allow her fears to be allayed, but her desires to be inflamed.

He came back over her, gold flecks shining in the hot molten lava churning in his eyes. It seemed for a moment as if he wanted to say something, as if the words had somehow caught in his throat. But she didn't need words.

She reached for him then, her hands coming to his back, urging him to her, urging him into her, and as he entered her she felt him fill all the empty spaces she hadn't realised she had until she'd met him. Until she'd seen the man beneath the outer layer he wore about him like armour. Until she'd seen the man he could be.

He pressed deeper, further into her, filling her from the inside out as if they were no longer two people but one. And then there was no room for thought, only sensation. The slick slide of him within her was teasing dizzying need and arousal from her. Pushing her closer and closer to the edge of that same precipice she had sensed him upon.

Lost. He was lost. Antonio was drowning in a sea of emotion and sensation. Emma had cast a spell over him, soothing long-held hurts and filling the spaces with *her*. She was all he could see, all he could feel.

He plunged into her, wringing a cry from her lips, answering the one made by his soul, no longer wanting to think, no longer wanting to hurt. He took her mouth with his, exalting in the sweetness of her, his tongue mirroring his body's actions. He consumed the breath she exhaled, not wanting even that to escape his reach.

Sensation and need became overwhelming as he drove them again and again towards the edge of their release and pulled back. Desperate to stay in this state of bliss, desperate to hold back from the moment it would all come crashing down.

He teased and taunted, wringing pleasure from them both in equal measure. Sweat slicked his brow and hers. The room was filled with the gasps and sighs of exquisite arousal as time suspended its march as if just for them, giving them the simple gift of each other.

But soon need became a palpable thing and he could no longer hold back. He drove them both to the brink, holding them there on the edge. He could taste it on his tongue, in his throat, and hear it in the desperate cries falling from Emma's perfect lips.

With one final thrust he plunged them into the abyss, the joint feeling of their completion sending them into a spin he was sure would never stop.

Antonio woke from the sleep he hadn't realised had fallen over him. He knew before he had even opened his eyes that Emma wasn't with him. It was as if his body had become so attuned to her presence that he no longer needed sight.

And he didn't want to move. Didn't want this moment to happen. Because despite what had just passed between them he knew there was only one outcome— could only ever have been one outcome.

Reluctantly he left the bed, making his way to a bathroom wet with condensation from a shower he hadn't heard Emma take. He couldn't look at himself in the mirror as he stepped beneath the hot spray of water, shutting off the voice that called him a coward in his mind. Whether because of what he would do or couldn't do he didn't know.

Drying himself with a towel, he grabbed his discarded trousers and thrust his legs into them. The fact that only twenty-four hours earlier he had done the same, taken the same action, wasn't lost on him.

The night before he had been about to make a decision that would turn the tide in his battle against his father, no matter the cost. And now he knew instinctively that he would be asked to make the same decision again.

He walked through to the living area of the hotel suite, sidestepping Emma's bags, still packed from hours before. If his heart ached to see them there, he forced it aside.

Emma was sitting on the sofa, illuminated only by the light of dawn breaking over Buenos Aires through the windows. He tried to force a smile to his lips, but couldn't. There wasn't one answering his gaze as she caught sight of his presence.

Antonio was surprised to find that he no longer felt the sting and heat of anger. There was only resignation and sadness for something that was yet to pass. The kind of prescient ache that met inevitability.

'Are you going to use this?' she asked, holding the dossier on Mandy Bartlett.

Emma's heart was torn in two as he stood there, bisected by the shadows of the sunrise. Half in shade, half in light. She wondered which side he would choose. She had asked him the one question she wasn't sure she was ready for him to answer, but knew that she needed hear it.

'If I have to,' he said, and his words made her want to weep.

'Really? You'd destroy this man's family, just like your father did, to get what you want?'

'He deserves it, Emma.'

'Michael might—but does Benjamin Bartlett? Does Mandy?'

She hoped that she could make him see. Before he did something that would change him for ever.

'I will do *whatever* it takes. You already know that.'

She was surprised to hear softness in his voice—not anger, not fury, but gentleness, as if he were preparing her for news she didn't want to hear.

But she wasn't done fighting yet.

'No, I know you, Antonio. I have seen the person beyond the bitter hatred of your father, beyond the fear of the damage done to your sister. I've seen the love you have for her and your mother, the love you have for Dimitri and Danyl. I have seen the man you think you are not, and he is amazing. But if you do this,' she said, hoping against all hope, 'if you use this dossier you will destroy the goodness in you.'

She hated it that she was almost pleading now.

'You don't need to stoop to this level, Antonio. You're better than that. You could win the deal without it. I know it... I know it because I love you.'

Antonio's hand flew up between them, as if warding off her words.

'Don't say that, Emma.'

'Why not? It's the truth. I love you. I can see the man that you are beneath this path of revenge you're on.' She just hated it that he couldn't see it for himself.

'Emma, please—'

'No. You've shown me that all this time I've been hiding. You told me as much last night, when we were together. But it wasn't just my body that I was hiding. And you know that. You knew it then and you know it now. I was hiding from reaching for what I really wanted.'

No longer could Emma hold back the words and thoughts that had been forming, slowly shaping in her mind and heart.

'All this time, all these years, despite my Living List, despite the things I wanted to achieve—events and experiences that are almost meaningless in themselves— what I was really hiding from was love. And now that I *am* reaching for it, asking for it—asking to be loved by you and asking you to be worthy of that—you refuse?' she demanded.

She knew that he felt something for her—possibly even met her love with his own. Whether he would choose that instead of his need for revenge she really wasn't sure. But she knew that their love wouldn't survive if he chose wrong.

'I told you when we first made this deal, Emma, that emotions weren't going to be involved. They *can't* be involved.'

'But emotions are the one thing that's been driving you this whole time!' she cried.

'I can't afford to let my father get away with it. He is a villain, Emma.'

'But are you willing to *become* him to get what you want? Are you willing to become a villain yourself?'

'Emma, if *I* found this, then I guarantee you that my father will have.'

For the first time Emma heard something like desperation enter his voice.

'Then help Bartlett find a way through it,' she said, hoping that Antonio would find a way through his need for revenge. 'Show him the kindness that your father never showed to your mother or you or your sister.'

'I just can't take that risk. I *need* to do this.'

The despair in his voice nearly broke her. Nearly sent her running to this man who had stolen her heart like a thief. But she couldn't—no, she *wouldn't*.

'Then you do it without me.'

She made her way towards the cases by the door, but his words stopped her mid stride.

'It wouldn't have really mattered, though, would it?' he said, his words icy cold and ruthlessly quiet.

'What are you talking about?' she asked, turning towards him, confused at the change in his tone.

'Whether you had discovered this or not. You wouldn't have trusted me—trusted *this*—so you're leaving before you find out.'

'I—'

He didn't let her finish. 'Just like you did to that scared seventeen-year-old boy who might have battled through his fears for you. It's just another excuse to stop yourself from taking a chance.'

Emma felt the blood drain from her face, sucked into the vortex of ice running through her core. *Fear.* She felt fear.

'What is it, Emma? You think we're all going to leave? That we're not strong enough to stick it out with you?'

Antonio's words cut her, chipped away at the frigid centre of her. She hated him then. Hated it that his words were unearthing her deepest fears. The fears she barely allowed herself to admit to owning. The fears that held a mirror up to herself while she threw her accusations at him.

Of course she was scared! She was terrified. Terrified of him using the information in the dossier and even more scared of what it would mean if he *didn't*.

Because then she'd have to stay—really invest—wouldn't she? Not just some giddy, excited fantasy feeling such as she'd been enjoying these last few hours. But the harder stuff—the things that would make her or break her. In that moment she was on the precipice. The edge of a giant cliff-face. One that meant she would have to finally place her trust in someone not to hurt her. Not to leave.

Had she done that? Had she really let her seventeen-year-old boyfriend go without giving him a chance? Was she doing the same again with Antonio?

Her head ached and her mind swam, and in that moment she clung to the only thing she had in front of her.

'You want me to give *what* a chance? Your deal? The

role of fake fiancée? Or could we actually be more than that, Antonio?' she demanded.

It was as if they had become prize fighters, each taking the most painful chunk out of the other.

'There's just six days until the final meeting.'

It seemed neither was willing to admit just how far they'd come, just how much they meant to each other.

She shook her head, her heart breaking into a thousand pieces, the hurt magnified by each fracture, as if punctured by the shards of itself.

'If you can come up with this,' she said, gesturing to the documents that had torn them apart, 'then you can come up with an excuse as to where I am for Bartlett. But, Antonio,' she said—her last warning, her last hope, 'I'm telling you. There's no coming back from this. If you do this you'll be worse than your father. Because you *know* what you're doing, what you're risking, and just how many people you're hurting.'

Antonio didn't move while she retrieved her bags from the doorway to her bedroom. He didn't react to the kiss she placed on his cold cheek and he didn't say a word as she closed the door to the suite behind her.

Emma knew that it was the last time she would see Antonio. Oh, she was sure she would see pictures of him—might even happen upon him in person. But that person wouldn't be the man she had fallen in love with. If he did this—if he used that folder—she would never see that man again.

CHAPTER TEN

ANTONIO HEARD THE pounding on his New York penthouse apartment door and honestly couldn't tell if it was
real or the manifestation of his hangover. Each strike
followed the words that had been turning over and over
in his mind since he last saw Emma.

You'll be worse than your father.

They had become a mantra, a taunt, a final threat
hovering over him. One that he couldn't escape. Because he couldn't help feeling that Emma might be right.
That in seeking his revenge he would actually be *worse*
than his father.

The thought scoured him from the inside out, carved
away at the deep ache in his chest.

Reluctant to open his eyes, he turned over and
promptly fell onto the floor. The sofa. He'd been on
the sofa.

He heard the door swing open and a pair of expensive black leather shoes came to stand very, *very* close
to his head. He heard a string of Greek swearing, fit to
turn the air blue, and the shoes disappeared. Antonio
groaned, knowing that he'd sunk pretty low this time.

He'd been back in New York for two days since returning from Argentina, and in that time he'd answered
none of the phone calls from his office, despite the ris-

ing panic in his CFO's tone. Instead he'd done nothing but drink and stare at the dossier on a woman he'd never met, might never meet, but who had come to represent the final blow to his relationship with Emma.

Antonio mustered the energy to roll onto his back, every muscle and brain cell protesting. Apart from his heart. His heart relished it, clearly deeming him worthy of such extreme levels of—

Ice-cold water crashed down on his head, the shock making him inhale quickly and deeply, taking half of the liquid into his lungs. He lurched up and bent over, choking and ready to kill Dimitri, holding a now empty jug.

'I've seen you in some pretty bad states, but this is just pitiful.'

'Get out.'

'No.' Dimitri held out a hand and hauled Antonio off the floor.

'Coffee,' was all about Antonio could manage to get out of his mouth.

'Shower,' Dimitri commanded.

It took a moment, but Antonio finally got himself off the floor and made his way through to the kitchen of his apartment, to find Dimitri manhandling a miniature saucepan on the stove.

'Did I fall through the rabbit hole?'

'It's called a *briki*. For an Italian, your coffee equipment is woefully lacking. It's a disgrace.'

'And you just *happened* to have this in your pocket?' Antonio asked, even the image of his friend with a *briki* in his pocket failing to raise a smile to his lips.

Dimitri looked affronted. 'Last year—Christmas. I didn't know what to get you. Emma suggested something that would make you more human in the mornings. It was in the back of your cupboard.'

'And the coffee? It doesn't look like it takes ground beans.'

'That I *did* bring with me.'

Antonio leant back on the kitchen counter that he rarely used and waited as Dimitri poured thick dark liquid into two small coffee cups.

'What are you doing here?' Antonio demanded, thankful that Dimitri ignored the hostility in his tone.

'You didn't answer your phone.'

'What's happened? Is everything okay?'

Panic rose in his chest, filling up the spaces and making it impossible to breathe. Had things got so bad that he had turned his back on his friends? Had something happened to Emma? For just a moment he felt the sliver of guilt as sharp as a chef's knife.

'Well, Danyl's trade negotiations are hanging by a thread, but he'll fix that. My father's company is on the brink, but *I'll* fix that. What are *you* going to do?'

Antonio cursed.

'You really messed this one up,' Dimitri said, casting an angry glance in his direction. 'And Emma is too good a person to mess with. So get in the shower. You smell like self-pity and alcohol and I don't like it. Be quick.'

Antonio forced himself under the hot water jets of his powerful shower. But it did nothing to remove the taint of dark grime he felt on his skin—had felt ever since seeing the photos of Mandy Bartlett his PI had dug up...ever since Emma had walked away from him.

Antonio decided to leave his hair wet. Although he was feeling much better, rubbing his head didn't seem that appealing. He entered his kitchen to find Dimitri poring over the images in the folder on Mandy Bartlett, and felt oddly furious that yet another person had seen them.

'Damaging stuff.'

'Yes,' Antonio practically growled, feeling oddly proprietorial over the contents of the folder...over Mandy's downward descent.

'Girl needs some sense knocked into her.'

'She needs help, Dimitri.'

'Yeah. Not sure her father will give it to her if he gets hold of these, though,' Dimitri mused. 'So Emma's gone, then?'

'Yes.'

'A shame. I like her.'

Antonio felt himself bristle.

'Don't be stupid—not in *that* way. So you can put the caveman back in the box.'

Antonio took a sip of the rich, peaty coffee, almost scalding his tongue in the process. He wasn't sure whether he was ready to hear what Dimitri had to say, but he knew Dimitri would say it anyway.

'Look, I know how much this deal means to you. I know your need for revenge, Antonio—trust me,' said Dimitri. 'I really do. And I will support whatever decision you make. Because you're my brother. You're my family. I don't believe those people who say you can't pick your family because I can and I have. You and Danyl—you're it. Whatever you choose to do with Bartlett is your own matter. I'm not here about the deal. I'm here about *her*.'

And finally all the resistance, all the avoidance that he'd practised since Emma had left him in the hotel suite in Argentina, dropped away.

'She held a mirror up to me, Dimitri. And I didn't like what I saw,' he admitted finally. The ache in his chest was opening up into a river of pain. 'The horror in her face...the betrayal... I don't think I can come back from that.'

'We all have to face the darkest parts of ourselves at some point, Antonio.'

There was no judgement in Dimitri's eyes, but in a way it only served to enrich the last memories he had of Emma and all the emotion he had seen in *her* eyes.

'Do you love her?'

'Yes. I do,' he replied—without thought, without pause.

He'd known it when he'd gone to the hotel suite that last night in Buenos Aires—known it as he'd allowed her to walk away from him. Had known it because it had hurt more than any other single thing in his life.

She had offered him everything. Love, acceptance, a way forward—a way other than the path of his revenge—and he had refused it all. He had refused *her*.

'Then you do what it takes, Antonio.'

'Even if that means letting go of the feud I have with my father?'

Emma pulled the cotton robe around her shoulders as she sank into her mother's sofa in the small house in Hampstead Heath. She had flown back into London four days ago and had slept for practically all of them, as if her body's learned response to trauma—emotional or physical—was rest.

So much had changed since she'd last left this house. Not only for her, but for her mother. Her old bedroom was now the spill-over storage area for Mark's hobby—his cars. Spare bits of machinery, cases of tools, several worn, torn and oil-stained clothes hung over the corners of barely held together boxes.

She was surprised to find that it didn't upset her. She was glad that her mother had found Mark—a kind man who loved her deeply. How could she begrudge her mother the very thing she wanted for herself? But every time she thought of Antonio her heart ached a little more. She knew that she was feeling grief—grief for him, for herself. But even through that pain, the exhaustion and the upset, she knew that she should get up every day and fight for the future she had once closed herself off from.

The sitting room was still just how she'd remembered it. Books lining two sides of the room, paintings framing the windows on the front wall, and covering the back wall completely, as if they were puzzle pieces, separated by only the thinnest of gaps of wall. It felt familiar—but not as soothing as it had once been.

Her mother entered the room, her jeans and loose shirt covered in mismatched blotches of cast-off paint, thin lines from where she had cleaned the pallet knife she used against her thighs.

Louise Guilham was beautiful. Emma had inherited her mother's thick dark hair and slender form. But it wasn't her physical appearance that made her beautiful. It was her happiness in following her dream of painting, in her love for Mark. It glowed from her skin and Emma felt sallow and shadowed in comparison.

She mustered a smile as her mother looked momentarily confused to find Emma curled up on the sofa at five in the afternoon, a robe wrapped around clothes she had slept in, not having had the energy to change. That was her mother's way when she was locked into a painting. The world could descend into Armageddon and she'd still be considering which colour to put where.

'Would you like a cup of tea?' Louise asked.

'I don't suppose you have any whisky?' Emma replied, memories of a conversation with Antonio so very close to the surface of her thoughts.

Her mother raised an eyebrow, but disappeared into the kitchen, returning with two glasses full of ice and amber.

'Do you want to talk about it?' she asked Emma, pressing the glass into her hands and taking a seat beside her on the old, battered but comfortable sofa.

Emma turned, resting her back against the sofa's arm, stretching out her legs. Her mother took Emma's feet in her hands and put them on her lap, passing soothing strokes over her bare skin as she had once done so many times when Emma had been ill.

Over the last four days, between hours of sleep, Emma had unfolded the story of her and Antonio, opening her heart and her mind to the mother she wouldn't hide a thing from—ever. But now Emma felt the stirrings of the question she had always wanted to ask and never had the courage to.

Until now.

'Not about Antonio, no. But I want to talk to you about Dad.'

'Oh? Okay.'

Mark hovered in the doorway. He must have heard Emma's question, and now he sent them both a gentle smile. He announced that he was '*just going to pop to the pub*', and left them alone, free to talk openly.

Yet another thing for which she was grateful to Mark.

'Mum, was it my fault that you and Dad split up? Was it because I got ill?'

'Oh, Em,' her mother said. 'How long have you thought that?'

'Since it happened,' Emma admitted guiltily.

'Oh, my love. No. No, it wasn't your fault at all— and neither was it because of the cancer,' she said, both sincerity and sadness in her voice.

Her mother's attention drifted to the window and she sighed.

'Your father and I met and married when we were very young. We loved each other greatly. And when you came along we loved you even more. But unlike some couples who are able to grow together, grow *up* together, we just...*didn't*,' she said, with a small shrug of her shoulders.

'So you stayed together because I got sick? That's even worse,' Emma said, guilt piercing her already fractured heart.

'No, sweetheart, we stayed together because we loved *you*,' her mother said, her voice and tone adamant and powerful. 'And that love was a strong, beautiful amazing thing that saw us all through the darkest of times. Neither me nor your father would change a day of it.'

Emma felt a huge weight lift from her chest as the fear that had been holding her back for so long left and was replaced with the truth in her mother's words.

Looking back, it was as if the memories that she had always shied away from had been freshly painted over, dusted in fine golden light, showing her different images. Where once she had felt guilt and sadness, she now felt strength and light. Seeing the way that they had stayed together as a gift.

And in that moment she realised that Antonio had been right. She *had* been running away from him. Consumed by her own fears, she had run away from her feelings. She had not stayed with Antonio when he had most needed her. Worse, she had done the very thing she had always been scared that someone would do to her.

'Oh, Mum...' Emma couldn't help the cry falling

from her lips. 'I left him…' she said, tears trembling at the edges of her eyes.

Her mother laid a reassuring hand on her legs. 'From what you told me, Emma, he had a decision to make and he had to make it by himself.'

'Mum, I love you. So, so very much. But I have to go.'

Antonio resisted the urge to place a finger between his collar and his neck in an attempt to loosen the feeling of a noose tightening around him. He could not—*would* not—show any sign of weakness in front of his father *or* Bartlett.

They were in the boardroom at Bartlett's sleek offices, just a few blocks over from Antonio's own office. That he was being forced to breathe the same air as his father angered him. But he had to let that anger go. Bartlett had promised a decision today, after final pitches from himself and Michael Steele, in a move that was both highly unusual and had taken on the air of a courtroom with closing arguments.

His father had blustered through his determined statements—more of the same kind of financial arguments that had been printed in the world's international press over the last week. About how Michael's age and experience gave more weight to his investment and the promise that he could best his son financially.

Which he couldn't.

But apparently the more he said it, the more Michael thought Bartlett would believe it. Michael had also made asinine suggestions as to Antonio's scandalous reputation and the damage it would do to Bartlett's company—in spite of his recent, perhaps even *conve-*

nient engagement—and once again Antonio's anger that his father should involve Emma in this had been swift.

But just as swift was the recrimination that he had brought Emma into it himself.

Antonio took a moment, after his father had finished, and Bartlett turned his attention to him. He checked his feelings, checked his decision and felt at peace. Possibly for the first time in years.

'So much has been said about the strength, might and determination that got my father here,' Antonio began. 'About how he's the right man to invest in your company and see it into the future. But I disagree. And not just because I don't believe him for a second.'

He pushed the threads of anger aside, holding on to the purpose of his intention for the meeting. Holding on to the memory, the realisation of what Emma had shown him.

'It's not very often that business deals come down to right and wrong. You're a man of strong morals, Mr Bartlett,' he said, holding the older man's gaze, needing him to see the truth of the words he was about to say. 'And if I'm honest—*truly* honest—I can't say the same of myself.'

He saw the shock on Bartlett's face, heard the small gasp that spoke of his confusion at a man appearing to sabotage his own pitch.

'I came after this deal not because I want to invest in your company, Mr Bartlett, but because I want my father not to.'

He didn't have to look at his father to know that he was practically vibrating with glee—he could feel it in the air, the drop in temperature from Bartlett's end of the room matching the raised heat from his father's.

'And in order to do that I betrayed and treated badly

a woman of such high integrity that she would put us all to shame. She certainly put *me* to shame,' he admitted, feeling the words ring true in his heart. 'She showed me that I was reaching only for revenge when what I should have been reaching for was to be *better* than him—better than my father. A better man for myself and the woman I love. I did and still do want to invest in your company, Mr Bartlett. But not at the price of my morals or my heart. And I should warn you that if you choose my father, you'll be selling your soul to the devil. Make your decision, Benjamin. And once you have—whatever it is—there is a matter I'd like to discuss with you. One that I'd like to help with, if you'll let me.'

With that, Antonio got up from his chair and turned—expecting to leave, expecting to walk out into the sunshine of a New York summer, expecting to track down Emma wherever she might be and beg her forgiveness.

But it seemed she had other ideas.

Emma was standing in the doorway of the boardroom, and his first thought was how truly amazing she looked.

Her eyes shone, and her hair was loose around her shoulders—it was the first time he'd seen it so during the day, outside of the nights of passion they had shared. She was dressed in a brightly coloured dress that hugged her chest and waist, flared about her legs, and a simply outrageous and uncharacteristically Emma pair of high heels encased her feet.

But it was exactly how he'd always imagined her. Bright, feminine, sensual and powerful.

'How much did you hear?' he asked, walking towards her, hoping that she wasn't a figment of his fevered imagination.

'Everything,' she said, allowing him to guide her away from the office.

He couldn't take his eyes from her—couldn't bring himself to say another word until they were free from the office, the deal, his father. He wanted to leave it all behind him.

Well, not *all*. He had meant what he'd said to Bartlett. Once the deal was made—whether Bartlett chose him or not—Antonio wanted to speak to the man about his daughter. He either knew and wasn't sure how to proceed, or he didn't know and would need help and support to get through to her. But Antonio wouldn't allow the situation with Mandy Bartlett to go unchecked.

They emerged from the office onto the sidewalk and, still without a word, he took her hand and led her as quickly as her heels would allow across the road, towards the lower entrance of Central Park. He wanted life, greenery and peace to be the background of their next conversation. Not the high-rise hustle and bustle of Manhattan.

Walking away from the summer crowds of tourists gathering around the ice-cream sellers and busking musicians, Antonio drew them towards the quieter pathways, dappled with leafy shade and cool breeze. But when he got where he'd wanted to be he suddenly found himself unsure. What if she didn't want him? What if his decision hadn't made any difference to her feelings?

In the end it seemed that Emma found her courage before he did. She stopped, gently pulling on his arm, turning her towards him.

'Antonio, I'm so sorry that I left you,' she said. 'I never—'

'Don't be sorry,' he interrupted, hating it that she felt an ounce of sadness or regret about the actions that had forced him to confront his feelings in a way that nothing else had. 'I needed to see the true depths of the darkness I was about to fall into before I could reach for you, before I could reach for the light.'

He paused, hoping that she understood his words, took them into her as deeply as he meant them.

'I want to be worthy of you, Emma. I want to be better than him. I am now and will continue to be. Whether you'll do me the honour of becoming my wife or not. I know you will—'

'Wait,' she said, throwing up a hand between them. 'What?' she asked.

He cursed, realising that he'd blundered over the most important thing he'd ever asked in his life. The first time they had done this it had been for the deal. This time he wanted it to be a moment that she cherished, that she remembered, might even tell their children about one day.

'Emma, I love you. So very much,' he said, digging into his pocket for the small box he'd arranged to have sent over from the shop in Buenos Aires. 'I know you heard what I said in the room with Bartlett and my father—but I want you to hear it now. Here, without them present, not for show or for a deal, but for *you*. For years I've shied away from love, from meaningful relationships, because I thought that love was a destructive, harmful thing. Something my father used against my mother—something that left my sister destroyed when it was withdrawn from her. And something that left me with my own scars. But that wasn't true. You showed me, that last night in Argentina and in so many ways preceding it, that love is a healing, powerful, amazing thing. I know now that what my father did wasn't borne of love. And no matter what happens—whether you say yes or not—I want you to know that I love you, and I will love you every single day for the rest of my life if you will let me.'

He got down on one knee, drawing the curious gazes of some of the few people passing by. And it was then that Emma truly knew the power of their love as it washed over them both from his words, his eyes, his heart.

'Emma Guilham,' he said, taking her hand in his, 'would you do me the incredible honour of being my wife?' he asked, sending her heart soaring higher than she had ever felt.

She couldn't help the laugh that escaped her lips, but she too had words she wanted to share. Things she wanted him to understand so that they could move ahead with all the love and security she knew they would both feel.

She gently tugged at him, attempting to pull him up from where he knelt. And she laughed again when he shook his head and refused, drawing even more attention from the people passing.

'If you won't stand then I shall have to come down to you,' she taunted.

'So be it. I will not move until I've had your answer,' he said, a stubborn determination filling his words in a blissful promise that she wouldn't have thought him capable of when she'd first met him.

So she did as she had said and took to her knees, facing him, holding her gaze with his and, just like Antonio, not caring of the attention they were drawing.

'For so long I thought myself strong, capable—no,' she said as he tried to interrupt her, knowing that he would contradict her words, but knowing too that she needed to say them. 'I was, am and will continue to be a survivor. But for all the promise and hope put into that list I made as a seventeen-year-old, I never had the courage to ask for the things that I truly wanted. Self-acceptance, self-love and ultimately true love itself. Antonio, you showed me that my scars are beautiful, you taught me to reach for the things I was too scared and too unwilling to admit to myself that I wanted, and you proved to me that doing so, whether successful or not, was the real gift. You showed me that it was okay— more than that, *vital* for me to put my whole self out into the world. And I love you for it, and I will love you for it until my last breath. So, yes, Antonio Arcuri, I *will* marry you.'

The moment the words had left her mouth Antonio pulled Emma to him in a kiss that she would never forget. It was full of the taste of love, passion and everything in between. It was full of light, laughter and finally, the knowledge that they would live happily ever after.

EPILOGUE

One year later...

ARCURI WELCOMES THE
BIRTH OF HIS SON!
BY ROANNA KING

International tycoon announces the
birth of a beautiful baby boy!

Hearts across the world might have burned with envy at the pictures of Antonio Arcuri's wedding only four months ago. The shocking speed not only of his engagement to Emma Guilham—his one-time PA—but his subsequent marriage raised more than a few eyebrows amongst our hallowed readership.

One could argue that the reason for this was the soon-to-follow birth of their son, little Luca Arcuri. But that would be an argument from a harder heart than mine.

Because it's clear to see the love shining in the eyes of this proud papa, and I can only wish them luck in their future endeavours.

So let me be the first to congratulate you, Mr Arcuri, on the wonderful birth of your son.

EMMA ENTERED THE large open-plan living room of their house in Sorrento, with her gorgeous son Luca cradled in her arms, to find Antonio talking to himself.

'*"Harder heart than mine..."*' he muttered angrily. '*"Let me be the first..."*' Really, how dare she?'

Antonio threw yet another one of Roanna King's articles into the bin.

Emma laughed—something she did so very much these days—and crossed the room to pull him into a kiss that wasn't nearly as deep as she'd like, but perfectly respectable given there were three of them squashed into each other's arms.

'How dare who?'

'Mmm?' he asked, as he took in the sight of his wife and child. 'I've forgotten—not important.'

And he meant it. All he had ever wanted was here in this room.

So much had changed in the year since he had discovered Bartlett wanted investment in his company— since he'd demanded that Emma find him a fiancée. At the time he'd thought that what he'd wanted was revenge, to destroy his father. But things hadn't quite turned out that way.

Soon after his *second* proposal to Emma, Benjamin Bartlett had got in touch. Apparently Michael Steele had tried to use the information about his daughter against him, but instead of buckling to the demands he'd made Bartlett had stuck to his instincts, turned to Antonio instead, and together they had worked to help Mandy Bartlett weather the storm that Michael Steele had launched upon the poor girl.

Sometimes Antonio very much wished that he'd found a way to avoid that for Bartlett and his family, but Antonio was beginning to realise that accepting the consequences of one's actions was an important part of the healing process.

Bartlett's shares had wobbled for a few days under the negative press, but with Antonio's investment they'd soon recovered. With Antonio, Emma and her father's support, Mandy Bartlett had gone into rehab and ended up finishing her degree and passing with high honours, and the Bartletts were now a firm fixture in their social calendar.

And as for Michael Steele—it hadn't taken long for the press to turn against the man. Once they'd discovered that it had been *he* who had leaked the dossier about Mandy's troubles, and there had been the suggestion—though unproved and unsupported—that it had been in retaliation for a rejected business venture, it had sickened the international press.

Hounded and stalked by their fury that he could abuse such an innocent young girl, Michael had found his existing business associates driving as far from him as possible. The man had become a financial and social pariah—though Antonio had been surprised to discover that it hadn't felt as good as he'd thought. It had been a period that had been difficult for Antonio, when he'd realised just how far he had nearly sunk himself. But Emma had helped him through with patient love, sweet comfort and reassurance.

Shortly after Antonio had made good on his first promise to Emma, and the Bartletts had been present, alongside Dimitri and Danyl, to toast Emma's new role as head of the Arcuri Foundation—celebrations that had gone on long into the night, full of joy, laughter and hope for the future.

Despite their busy schedule, they had already ticked off several of the things on Emma's Living List. Even now, standing in their home in Sorrento, he remembered the exquisite joy in Emma's eyes as they'd shared a sunrise over the Terhren desert, and the happiness shining just as bright when they'd seen the sun set over the Mediterranean, surrounded by their closest friends, Danyl and Dimitri, and their respective families.

'Where are you?' Emma asked, and smiled as she passed his son to him.

'Right here, where I should be,' replied Antonio, drawing his thoughts away from the past and holding their precious son to his chest.

He watched Emma, stepping over the changing mat and the stacks of muslins, nappies and other little things he'd never thought to find such joy in, as she went to the mirror that covered almost the entire length of one wall. He watched her as she checked her hair and her brightly coloured dress. He never tired of seeing her in autumn colours, and he was sure that he hadn't seen her wear black since Buenos Aires.

He gently put his sleeping son in the small bassinette beside the sofa, already missing the soft, gentle comfort of having him in his arms, and walked to his wife, unable to resist the urge to hold her, touch her. He wondered if he ever would.

He pressed a starburst of kisses along the beautiful length of her neck, knowing Emma would understand the gesture and the silent, sensual request behind it.

Emma playfully slapped his arms away from her. 'You know we don't have time, Antonio. Danyl and Dimitri will be here with their families in little over two hours, and Danyl's protection services always make such a drama about the whole thing—they'll be at the door in twenty minutes.'

'Having a sheikh as a friend has both its perks and its curses,' Antonio growled.

That each of the Winners' Circle had found happiness and love within the space of such a short time was still a marvel to all three men. But those were stories for another time. For now, Antonio's only thought was of his wife, and just what he could do with twenty little minutes.

A wicked smile crept across his face, and Emma soon discovered that twenty minutes could be just as pleasurable as a lifetime.

* * * * *

MILLS & BOON

Coming next month

CONSEQUENCE OF
THE GREEK'S REVENGE
Trish Morey

'Going somewhere, Athena?'

Breath hitched in her lungs as every nerve receptor in her body screeched in alarm. Alexios!

How did he know she was here?

She wouldn't turn around. She wouldn't look back, forcing herself to keep moving forwards, her hand reaching for the door handle and escape, when his hand locked on her arm, a five fingered manacle, and once again she tasted bile in her throat, reminding her of the day she'd thrown up outside his offices. The bitter taste of it incensed her, spinning her around.

'Let me go!' She tried to stay calm, to keep the rising panic from her voice. Because if he knew she was here, he must surely know why, and she was suddenly, terribly, afraid. His jaw was set, his eyes were unrepentant, and they scanned her now, as if looking for evidence, taking inventory of any changes. There weren't any, not that anyone else might notice, though she'd felt her jeans grow more snug just lately, the beginnings of a baby bump.

'We need to talk.'

'No!' She twisted her arm, breaking free. 'I've got nothing to say to you,' she said, rubbing the place where his hand had been, still scorchingly hot like he had used a searing brand against her skin, rather than just his fingers.

'No?' His eyes flicked up to the brass plate on near the door, to the name of the doctor in obstetrics. 'You didn't think I might be interested to hear that you're pregnant with my child?'

Continue reading
CONSEQUENCE OF
THE GREEK'S REVENGE
Trish Morey

Available next month
www.millsandboon.co.uk

COMING SOON!

We really hope you enjoyed reading this book. If you're looking for more romance, be sure to head to the shops when new books are available on

Thursday
4th October

To see which titles are coming soon, please visit
millsandboon.co.uk

LET'S TALK
Romance

For exclusive extracts, competitions
and special offers, find us online:

 facebook.com/millsandboon

⬡ @millsandboonuk

🐦 @millsandboon

Or get in touch on 0844 844 1351*

For all the latest titles coming soon, visit
millsandboon.co.uk/nextmonth